UNDER THE COLORADO SKY

A. ROUCHER

OTHER WORKS BY A. ROUCHER

A CROWN OF ASH AND FLAME: ELDARA SERIES

THE IRONBOUND WAR: ELDARA SERIES

DELIVER US FROM EVIL

DELIVER US FROM EVIL - THE BROKEN COVENANT

THE RANGER'S OATH- YA

THE IRON RIDGE- YA

THE LAST SUMMER- YA

OPERATION: CHRISTMAS MORNING- YA

PROPERTY OF

UNDER THE COLORADO SKY

Copyright © 2026 by A. Roucher

All rights reserved. No part of this book may be reproduced or transmitted in any form or by any means, electronic or mechanical, including photocopying, recording, or by any information storage and retrieval system, without written permission from the publisher, except in the case of brief quotations used in reviews or articles.

To my wife: you gave me time when it was scarce, grace when I missed the mark, and love without limits.

CONTENTS

Chapter One
Leaving the City

By the time the newsroom clock ticked past eight, the overhead lights had taken on that particular humming weariness Emma Hall knew too well. The place was still awake, still buzzing, but it was a tired kind of buzz, like a beehive that had been shaken one too many times.

Phones rang in fits and starts, police scanners crackled, keyboards clattered in frantic bursts. The air smelled like burned coffee, printer toner, and the faint, lingering tang of someone's reheated fish from hours ago. Big city journalism, she'd once thought, would smell like ink and history. Mostly it smelled like exhaustion and bad takeout.

"Hall, you got the quote from the councilman yet?" her editor shouted across the bullpen.

Emma pinched the bridge of her nose before turning in her chair. "Just came in. He said, 'We're evaluating all options and remain committed to transparency.'"

A laugh rippled up from nearby desks. Someone mimed gagging.

"Ah yes, transparency," called one of the copy editors. "My favorite synonym for 'you'll never know what we actually did.'"

Her editor, Mike, leaned around his monitor, his tie loosened and his shirt sleeves rolled to his elbows. He'd been in newspapers long enough that ink seemed permanent on his fingers and at the edges of his nails. "You know the drill, Emma. Make him sound like he's saying something without letting him say anything. I need that piece in twenty."

"You got it," she said, automatic.

She turned back to her computer screen. Her fingers found the keys like muscle memory, but something in her chest balked. Another quote, another non-answer, another story that barely skimmed the surface of anything that actually mattered to her.

To her left, the city skyline pressed against the floor-to-ceiling windows, glass and steel catching the last smear of sunset. For the last hour she'd watched the oranges fade to purple, then to the flat, dull black of a Denver summer night. Somewhere below, sirens whooped and faded. Traffic crawled. Rooftop bars flicked their fairy lights on, like the city was telling itself a bedtime story it no longer believed.

She typed anyway.

Councilman Reyes, responding to allegations of improper spending, said the city was "evaluating all options" and "remained committed to transparency" as the investigation continued…

Words, words, words. She could assemble them in her sleep. Lately, she felt like she was.

"Shots at O'Malley's after this?" a voice piped up behind her.

Emma twisted in her chair. Kelsey, her friend from features, balanced a stack of proofs on one hip and a reusable water bottle in her hand. Her lipstick was perfect, her hair still glossy despite the long day. Kelsey thrived on the newsroom chaos the way some people thrived on fresh mountain air.

"Sam says he can meet us around nine," Kelsey added. "He knows the bartender now, so we can skip the line."

"Sam knows every bartender," Emma said. "I'm pretty sure it's in his DNA at this point."

"Exactly my point. So, you in?" Kelsey bumped her shoulder lightly against Emma's. "You look like you need a drink. Or three."

Emma's cursor blinked at the edge of the sentence, insistent. Councilman Reyes… remained committed to transparency.

"I've still got to file this," Emma said. "And I'm wiped. Rain check?"

Kelsey's smile faltered, then rallied. "You always say that lately."

"I know." Emma tried for light. "One of these days I'll actually mean 'rain check' and not 'permanent hibernation.'"

Kelsey studied her for a moment, the newsroom noise dimming for both of them. "You okay, Em?"

Close enough, she thought. Still breathing. Still showing up. That counted for something.

"Just tired," she lied. "The city council and I are in a toxic relationship. It'll be better when we finally break up."

"You're too good at this to break up with it," Kelsey said automatically. That was what everyone said. You're good at this. You're lucky. People would kill for your job.

Emma smiled anyway. "Go. If you see Sam, tell him I said to stop texting me pictures of his drinks like they're ransom notes."

"Will do." Kelsey squeezed her arm, then melted back into the traffic of bodies and voices.

Emma turned back to her screen. The words blurred. She finished the story by habit, polishing the sentences, slipping in a detail from an earlier interview that made the whole thing sound vaguely more informed than it really was. When she hit send, the rush she'd once felt, satisfaction, adrenaline, a sense of impact, was notably absent.

She closed the file. The moment the document vanished, another file slid into place in her mind, like a program booting up in the background.

Her novel.

The word felt ridiculous for something that existed mostly as scraps and false starts. But she'd called it that once, and the name had stuck somewhere inside her, stubborn as a burr.

She toggled windows and opened the project, the one she kept tucked at the edge of her screen like a guilty secret. Scrivener sprang to life, all its neat little folders and organizational tools faithfully waiting. On the left, a list of chapter titles, some with a few hundred words, most with exactly zero. On the right, the main document.

A blank page. Cursor blinking. She could hear its impatience.

"Okay," she murmured under her breath. "Let's try this again."

She set her fingers on the keys. Nothing came.

Her brain, so quick with councilman quotes and city gossip, went perfectly still. Not the good kind of still, the kind that preceded a revelation. The heavy kind. The kind that felt like standing in front of a locked door and knowing you'd already lost the key.

She clicked into one of the older files instead. Draft_Chapter1_v3. The opening paragraph stared back at her.

In the city that never gave you a moment's peace, Claire Adler had learned to carve out quiet in the spaces between deadlines,

She grimaced. Too on the nose. Too close to home. She'd tried disguising herself under different names, different cities, an entire cast of invented people. Somehow the same thing always crept back in: a woman who was very good at writing about other people's lives and very bad at actually living her own.

She skimmed two more false starts. One was a mystery, one a romance, one some kind of literary hybrid she'd never had the nerve to show anyone. All of them petered out around page twenty.

The cursor on the blank document kept blinking. Blink. Blink. Blink.

She stared until the newsroom around her dissolved into a smear of motion and sound. Phones, keys, low laughter, the sports guys arguing over someone's batting average. The glow of screens on tired faces. The constant, grinding hum of urgency.

Her chest ached, sharp and surprising. She pressed her palm against the center of it, smoothing the fabric of her blouse as if she could iron out the feeling.

It wasn't just tiredness. It hadn't been just tiredness for a while.

Emma saved her work, closed the novel document, and shut the laptop with more force than necessary. The little thump drew a glance from Mike, who was on his way past with a marked-up printout.

"You, okay?" he asked.

There it was again. The question that was starting to feel like background noise.

"Yeah. Filed the Reyes piece," she said. "Anything else you need tonight?"

He checked his watch, then the mostly-emptying newsroom. "You've been pulling doubles this week. Go home. If something breaks, I'll call you."

She hesitated. "Mike?"

He paused, eyebrows up.

"You know how you keep threatening to make us take our vacation days so we don't lose them at the end of the year?"

"That's not a threat, that's HR policy," he said dryly. Then his face shifted, curiosity slipping in. "You thinking of actually listening to me for once?"

The word formed in her throat before she could overthink it.

"Yeah. Maybe more than a few days." She swallowed. "What would it look like if I took… I don't know. The summer."

His brows climbed higher. "The whole summer."

"I've got the time banked," she said quickly. "I checked. I could do unpaid for what I don't have. You always talk about sabbaticals like they're a thing. I know we're not academia, but,"

"Whoa, whoa." He lifted a hand, newspaper pages rustling. "Slow down, Hall. What's going on?"

She opened her mouth to give one of the easy answers, burned out, need to recharge, want to travel, then closed it again. This man had watched her chase down crime scenes and council scandals for the past six years. He'd seen her cry once, in the bathroom, after a particularly bad apartment fire. He deserved more than a line.

"I'm stuck," she said finally. "Not with the job, exactly. I can still do the job. But everything I write for myself…" She gestured vaguely toward her closed laptop. "It's like the words won't come unless it's a deadline and somebody else's problem."

His gaze softened with something that looked suspiciously like understanding. "You want to write that book you keep pretending you're not working on."

She blinked. "How do you know about that book I keep pretending I'm not working on?"

"You think you're the first reporter to sneak fiction onto a work machine?" He snorted. "You all get the same look on your faces when you think nobody's watching. Like you're cheating on your beat."

Heat crawled up her neck. "I'm not trying to quit journalism."

"Didn't say you were." He rapped the stack of papers against his palm, thinking. "Okay. We're short-staffed, but when are we not. Summer's dead-ish. I can swing an unpaid sabbatical with HR if we couch it right. You know how to write a compelling argument."

Her heart thudded faster. "You'd really sign off on that?"

"I'd rather give you three months now than lose you for good when you finally hit the wall." He shrugged. "Besides, maybe you'll come back with a bestseller and I can say I knew you when you were chasing traffic counts."

A laugh bubbled out of her, thin but real. "So that's a, yes?"

He eyed her. "You sure you know what you're asking for? This isn't a vacation, Hall. You're not great at doing nothing. You'll climb the walls in a week."

"I'm not planning on doing nothing." She thought of the blank document, the blinking cursor. The way the city air felt lately, thick, hard to breathe. "I just… need somewhere quieter. Somewhere that doesn't talk back."

Mike studied her for a long moment, then nodded once. "Email HR tonight. Copy me. Put 'sabbatical' in the subject line and make it sound like you're going to come back a better asset than ever. I'll back you up."

Relief hit so hard she had to grip the edge of the desk. "Thank you."

"Don't thank me yet. I might be a fool." He started to move on, then paused. "You got someplace in mind?"

The question loitered in the air. She hadn't, not really, not until two nights ago when, after another failed attempt at a first chapter, she'd wound up scrolling through vacation rentals at three in the morning. Beach condos, mountain cabins, city lofts in other cities. All of them felt like different versions of the same noise.

Then she'd seen the listing. A small, unassuming cabin with a sloping porch and a view of open fields, tagged: "Writer's Retreat Cabin on Working Ranch, High Meadow Ranch, near Cottonwood Ridge, CO."

The photos had been simple. A weathered wood fence. A barn in the middle distance. Green pastures rolling toward blue shadowed mountains. A little table and chair on the front porch, facing west where the sun dipped behind the peaks. She'd felt something in her chest unclench, just a fraction, at the sight of it.

"Yeah," she said softly, more to herself than to Mike. "I think I do."

He nodded once. "Then go find it. Just make sure your phone still works in case the world ends."

"Understood."

He walked away, already barking instructions at someone else. The newsroom swallowed him; the rhythm of keys and voices picked up again.

Emma sat for a moment longer in her swivel chair, hands folded around the closed laptop. Her heart drummed against her ribs, half exhilaration, half fear. Three months. An entire summer. What if she wasted it? What if she came back with nothing but a sunburn and a half-finished manuscript of the same non-story she'd been writing in circles?

What if she didn't come back at all?

The thought startled her, sharp and clear. She shoved it aside for later.

For tonight, there were more practical things to do.

By 10 p.m., she was in her one-bedroom apartment, stripping the city uniform from her skin, blouse, slacks, flats kicked into the corner. The place was small and neat, the way apartments tended to be when home was mostly a place to sleep between shifts. A bookshelf sagged with old paperbacks and journalism trophies. Her desk in the corner was a smaller version of her newsroom workspace: laptop, notebooks, pens, sticky notes with half-formed ideas scribbled across them.

She dropped her bag, flopped into the chair, and woke up the laptop again. The listing was still open in a browser tab, its thumbnail photo like a portal.

High Meadow Ranch Cabin – Cottonwood Ridge, Colorado.

Cozy one-bedroom writer's cabin on edge of working cattle ranch. Porch with mountain views. Peaceful, quiet. Wi-Fi available, but spotty, best for those looking to unplug.

There were a few reviews, all glowing. Best sleep I've had in years. Perfect for my art retreat. Loved watching the sunset over the pastures.

Her mouse hovered over the "Book Now" button. Her bank account balance flickered in the back of her mind, student loans, car payment, the modest emergency fund she'd been carefully not touching.

"You can't do this," whispered the practical voice. "It's irresponsible. Stay home. Take a staycation. You can write in this apartment the same as anywhere else."

Except she knew she couldn't. She'd tried. The hum of traffic, the glow beneath the blinds, the constant awareness of neighbors on the other side of the wall, it all crept into her sentences, jittery and restless.

She clicked "Book Now" before she could talk herself out of it.

Dates: June 1 – August 31. Three full months. The computer did its math, spit out a number. It was not small. It was also not impossible. Between savings and some careful budgeting, she could make it work. Just barely.

She entered her card information with fingers that trembled. When the confirmation screen appeared, Reservation confirmed! the tremor moved up her arms and into her chest. Too late to back out now.

"Okay," she whispered to the empty room. "You did it."

The apartment didn't answer. The city outside murmured, honked and sirened like always, oblivious to her little rebellion.

She spent the next hour pulling out a suitcase and making lists. What did you take to a ranch? She had hiking boots and a reasonably sturdy pair of jeans, but most of her wardrobe announced I spend my life in climate-controlled buildings.

She scribbled: jeans, T-shirts, flannel, sweater, notebook, laptop, power cords, favorite mug, the blanket her grandmother had knitted years ago, a soft, mossy green thing that always smelled faintly of lavender no matter how many times she washed it. She paused over the last item, then added: courage.

It looked ridiculous on the page. She left it there.

By midnight, the suitcase lay open on the bed, half-packed. Clothes were folded in tentative stacks. Her little bookshelf had a new gap where she'd pulled her most beloved paperbacks, books that had reminded her why she'd wanted to write in the first place. A scratchy mix of classic novels and unabashed romances, of stories where people chose love over fear.

She sat cross-legged on the bed, the city lights leaking in at the edges of the blinds. Her phone buzzed with messages from Kelsey and Sam.

Kelsey: You missed a good one. Some guy tried to sing a country song with a beer in each hand. Disaster.

Sam: You would've had a field day live-tweeting this. Seriously though, you, okay?

Emma typed and deleted three responses before settling on:

Emma: I'm okay. Big changes coming. Will explain tomorrow.

Sam responded with a string of wide-eyed emojis and a GIF of someone clutching pearls. Kelsey just sent a heart.

She set the phone on the nightstand, clicked off the lamp, and lay back. The ceiling above her was an anonymous white, unblemished, indifferent. It would be different at the cabin, she imagined. Maybe there'd be wooden beams. Maybe she'd fall asleep to the sounds of crickets instead of sirens, wake to birds instead of car horns. Maybe the sky would feel close enough to touch.

Hope and terror tangled together in her stomach. Out there, she wouldn't have deadlines to hide behind. No editor to blame for what she did or didn't write. It would just be her, the quiet, and the blank page.

Sleep came eventually, not deep but enough. When her alarm went off the next morning, the decision was still there, solid as the suitcase on the floor.

Two days later, she turned in her last story of the week, hugged Kelsey awkwardly in the parking garage, and let Sam clap her on the shoulder while declaring she was "going to come back a famous author, don't forget us little people."

She turned in her ID badge at HR with a temporary visitor pass issued in its place, a symbol of how nothing was really permanent. She signed the sabbatical paperwork with shaking hands and went back to her apartment for the last time in a long while.

The morning, she left, Denver was already warming up, a bright, glaring blue sky stretched over concrete. Emma loaded her car with the careful urgency of someone trying not to wake a sleeping giant. Suitcase. Box of books. Laptop bag. Grocery sack of snacks. The green blanket, folded and tucked on the passenger seat like a quiet co-pilot.

She took one last look at her building, the narrow brick facade, the third-floor window that had been hers, and felt... not sadness, exactly. More like stepping away from a party that had gone on too long.

The drive out of the city felt like shedding skin. High-rises gave way to shorter buildings, then to warehouses, then to open stretches where the highway ran straight as a ruler toward the hazy line of the Rockies. Traffic thinned. Her shoulders sank an inch, then another, as the miles unspooled beneath her tires.

She turned the radio on, then off again. The chatter of morning shows grated. Music felt wrong too, every song either too bright or too mournful. Eventually she settled for the low growl of the engine and the wind whipping around the car.

Her heart, restless in her chest since the moment she'd clicked "Book Now," began to settle into a new rhythm. She passed small towns with names she'd never heard of, their main streets a blur of diners, gas stations, and feed stores. The highway narrowed to two lanes, then curved and bent with the contours of the land. Yellow caution signs warned of elk and sharp turns. She saw more pickup trucks than sedans, more hats than briefcases at the gas station where she stopped for coffee.

After a couple of hours, a green sign appeared on the roadside: Cottonwood Ridge – 12 miles.

Her fingers tightened on the steering wheel. This was it. The name she'd typed into the reservation form, the one that had felt as fictional as any of her characters. Cottonwood Ridge. It sounded made up. It sounded like somewhere you could start over.

The turnoff came sooner than she expected, a simple exit ramp that emptied onto a two-lane road flanked by fields and clusters of trees. The town itself announced its presence with a weathered wooden sign: Welcome to Cottonwood Ridge, Elevation 7,200. Population: whoever stuck around.

She smiled despite herself.

The main drag was modest, brick storefronts, a hardware store, a diner with a faded mural of mountains on its side, a coffee shop with a chalkboard sign promising "The Best Pie Above Sea Level." People moved at a different speed here. Slower, unhurried. A woman in a sundress carried a box out of the florists. Two older men sat on a bench outside the diner, coffee mugs in hand, watching the world in no particular rush.

The GPS on her dashboard chimed, instructing her to take a left at the far end of town. She obeyed, following a narrower road that climbed out of Cottonwood Ridge and into the open, the town falling away behind her like a dropped coin.

Fields unfurled on either side, some green and well-watered, others still brown and scrubby from winter. Cattle dotted the slopes, dark shapes against the grass. A fence line ran alongside the road, weathered posts and strands of barbed wire.

After a few miles, she saw it: a simple wooden gate with a sign hung between the posts. The letters were hand-painted but careful.

High Meadow Ranch.

Her throat tightened, completely out of proportion to the piece of wood in front of her. She pulled over to the shoulder and sat for a moment, engine idling.

This was it. The place she'd seen in pixelated photos, the one she'd staked her savings and her stubborn little dream on. Somewhere beyond that gate was the cabin, the porch with the view, the sky that seemed so much bigger than the one above Denver's glass towers.

Her heart beat loud in the quiet car. Hope rode shotgun with fear, both of them looking out at the fields and wondering if she'd made the biggest mistake of her life or the best one.

Chapter Two
First Glimpse of the Rancher

The gravel road wound deeper into High Meadow Ranch, narrower and rougher than the pavement she'd left behind. On either side, the land rolled out in generous sweeps of grass and sage, dotted here and there with dark shapes of cattle. Fences ran alongside the road, some sections mended recently, others leaning a little, gray with age.

Emma eased her car over a rut and winced as something in the undercarriage thunked. "Sorry," she muttered to the vehicle, as if it could hear. "City girl, remember? I brought you into this."

She slowed as the ranch road forked. A small hand-painted sign pointed left: HOUSE / BARN. Another arrow, smaller, pointed right: CABIN.

Her pulse stuttered. The cabin was real enough to have a sign. Real enough that her turning that way would make this whole ridiculous plan not just theoretical anymore.

The cabin came into view a minute later, perched on a gentle rise above the road. It was smaller than the listing photos had made it seem, but somehow that made it more inviting. Weathered wood siding, a pitched roof with dark shingles, a little covered porch that wrapped around one side. Two wooden rocking chairs sat near the front window, a small table between them. Someone had put a pot of red geraniums by the door, their petals bright against the muted boards.

Beyond the cabin, the land fell away into a wide pasture. A weathered barn with a metal roof sat down the slope, near a cluster of corrals. Behind everything, mountains shouldered up against the sky, blue-gray and solid, their peaks ghosted with lingering snow.

Emma pulled off the road into the hard-packed dirt apron in front of the cabin and killed the engine. Silence dropped around her, surprisingly thick. No sirens, no honking, no upstairs neighbor stomping; just the ticking of the cooling car, the whisper of wind through dry grass, the faint low of a distant cow complaining about something.

Her heart beat in the empty space. She sat for a moment, hands still on the steering wheel, letting the reality of it soak in.

You did it. You actually drove away.

There was a flicker of panic, little and sharp. What if there'd been a mistake with the reservation? What if she'd misread the dates and showed up to find another family already settled in, kids' bikes strewn on the porch? What if,

A movement down by the barn caught her eye. A pickup truck, old, dark green, rumbled out from behind it and started up the slope toward her, dust puffing under its tires. It crested the rise and rolled to a stop beside her car with a soft crunch. The engine shut off.

The man who climbed out looked like he'd been carved out of the same weathered wood as the cabin and left in the sun to age. He was tall but stooped a little from years of work, his shoulders broad under a faded plaid shirt. His hair, what she could see of it under a sweat-darkened hat, was mostly gray, matched by the scruff along his jaw. Deep lines fanned from the corners of his eyes, the kind etched by squinting into bright light and smiling often.

He took in her car, her, the loaded backseat, in one slow, thoughtful sweep. Then his mouth tugged into a half-smile.

"You Emma Hall?" he called, voice rough like gravel but not unkind.

She scrambled out of the car, brushing road dust off her jeans. "Yes. Hi. That's me." She waved, immediately regretted how awkward that felt, and turned it into a gesture toward the cabin. "Is this…? I mean, I hope I didn't drive up to someone else's house."

He chuckled, the sound low and warm. "If you did, they've been stayin' there rent-free for a good long while now. This is the place." He jerked his chin toward the cabin. "Writer's retreat cabin, that's what the listing calls it, right?"

"That's what it said." Emma felt heat creep up her neck. Writer. The word always felt like borrowed clothing. "I, uh, write. Or try to."

He walked around to the back of her car with the patient, steady gait of a man whose knees had opinions but who wasn't about to give in to them. "Name's Hank Lawson. I help out around here. Caleb asked me to meet you; make sure you found the place without gettin' stuck in a ditch."

"Hank." She smiled, the name fitting him somehow. "Nice to meet you. And thank you. I only almost got lost twice."

"Only twice?" He opened the trunk before she could reach for it. "You're ahead of the curve. Last lady who came out here ended up down by the creek, swearin' her GPS told her to drive into the water. City folk put too much faith in that little voice."

"I would never," Emma said solemnly, then ruined it with a grin. "I mostly trust coffee."

"Then you'll do just fine." He hauled her suitcase out like it weighed nothing. The old joints might protest, but the muscles remembered their work. "You travel light for three months."

"Oh, there's more," she said, opening the back door. "This is just the clothes. The real weight is books and existential dread."

He gave her a look that suggested he wasn't entirely sure she was joking, but he smiled anyway. "We'll see if the fresh air can't scare some of that off. I'll grab the suitcase and your boxes. You want to get the door?"

She fumbled through her bag; found the key the owner had mailed her, a plain brass thing on a tag that read CABIN in cramped letters, and led the way up the porch steps. The boards creaked a little under her feet, a friendly noise. She unlocked the door and pushed it open.

Cool shadows and the faint scent of wood and lemon oil greeted her. The main room was open and simple: a small living area with a worn but clean couch, a coffee table, a bookshelf with a scattering of paperbacks and old National Geographics. A compact kitchen occupied one corner, white cabinets, a little stove, a fridge, a tiny table pushed under a window. To the right, a doorway led to a short hall. She could see the edge of a bed, a dresser, a door that presumably led to the bathroom.

It wasn't fancy. It was also spotless, and something in her shoulders that had been braced since Denver finally let go.

"It's perfect," she said, more to herself than to Hank.

He stepped in behind her with the suitcase and placed it just inside the bedroom doorway. "We try to keep it comfortable. My wife, God rest her, picked most of this out years back when we first started rentin' the place. Said if we were gonna have strangers on the ranch, we might as well give them a decent couch to sit on."

Emma ran her fingers along the back of that very couch, feeling the faint smoothness where countless hands had done the same. "She had good taste."

"She usually did." His voice softened briefly, the way it did when old memories rose. Then he shook it off and turned back for the car. "You got boxes?"

"Two in the backseat," Emma said, trailing after him. "And a plant."

He peered into the car. "That little thing?"

"My last surviving houseplant." She lifted the pot, a droopy spider plant in a chipped blue container. "If it dies, I'll know for sure city life killed my soul."

"Then we'll keep it alive," Hank said. "This place is hard on quitters, but it's kind to things that try."

He carried the boxes while she ferried the plant and her laptop bag. On one trip, she paused on the porch, letting her gaze slide past the cabin to the open fields beyond.

In the mid-afternoon light, the pasture grass moved like water in the wind. The barn down the hill leaned slightly, but its roof looked solid. A couple of horses grazed near the fence line, tails swishing lazily. Beyond them, the land dipped into a shallow valley, then rose again toward the mountains, which loomed larger here than they had on the highway. Their shoulders were massive, their peaks still tipped in snow, as if winter hadn't entirely let go up there.

Emma's city-trained brain tried to assign words to the view, vast, quiet, overwhelming, and gave up. The silence wasn't empty. It hummed, somehow, with the distant low of cattle, the occasional clink of metal from down near the barn, the steady whisper of wind in dry grass.

Hank came up the steps beside her, one of the boxes tucked against his hip. He followed her gaze, his own expression turning… not proud, exactly. Something steadier than that. Familiar affection.

"Not a bad backyard," he said.

"It's…" She shook her head, searching. "Big."

He chuckled. "Big'll do for a start."

They set the last box inside. Emma hovered in the middle of the small living room, the way one does in a hotel room before deciding where to put their things, aware that once she unpacked, she'd be staking some sort of claim.

"I can show you how the heater works, where the breaker box is, all that in a minute," Hank said. "But first I should probably do the official welcome speech."

"There's an official speech?" she asked.

"There is now." He hooked his thumbs into his belt loops, rocking back on his heels. "This here cabin sits on the north edge of High Meadow Ranch, which covers a good stretch of that valley you saw and some of the hills beyond. Belongs to Caleb Walker, he's the one you've been emailing about the rental. I run around and do whatever needs doin' that he can't get to fast enough."

"Walker," Emma repeated, filing the name away with the rest. "So, this is… his family ranch?"

"Has been for a few generations," Hank said. "His granddad carved it out. His daddy built it up. Caleb's, keepin' it goin' by sheer stubbornness and caffeine." A corner of his mouth quirked. "Ranch life looks romantic on calendars, but between you and me, the real romance is not losin' the place to taxes and feed bills."

"So, the Airbnb helps," she said.

"It does." He didn't sound apologetic about it, just factual. "Caleb wasn't too keen on the idea at first. Doesn't love the thought of strangers wanderin' around. But the cabin was sittin' empty since my wife passed, and the county don't take sentiment instead of money. He came around when he realized folks like you were lookin' for some quiet and not expectin' a dude ranch with mints on pillows."

"No mints?" she said. "I'm getting ripped off."

Hank's laugh rumbled through the little room. "We can probably rustle some up at the diner if it comes to that."

He tipped his hat back a little and sobered. "Point is, you're welcome here. Cabin's yours for the summer. There's a little trail down the hill to the barn if you ever need help, and a property map in that kitchen drawer there so you don't wander into the neighbors' land and get yourself yelled at. Long as you shut the gates behind you and don't try to pet the bulls, you and Caleb'll get along just fine."

The casual mention of bulls made her glance sharply out the window. "There are bulls?"

"There are always bulls." He seemed amused by her alarm. "Don't worry, they won't come knockin' on your door. Just give the big boys space and use the gates, not the fences. If you've got questions, ask. Better a silly question than a broken leg."

"I'll make a note," she said faintly.

He nodded toward her laptop bag. "You said you're writin' a book?"

"That's the plan." The admission tasted both exciting and embarrassing. "We'll see if the book cooperates."

"Cabin's had good luck with that," Hank said. "Had a painter out here once, quiet fellow, stayed a month. Left with a truckload of canvases. A lady last fall said she finished her dissertation. Cried when she left, poor thing. Place has a way of givin' you back pieces you didn't know went missin'."

The words landed somewhere deep in her chest, in the hollow spot she tried not to examine too closely. She cleared her throat.

"I'm hoping for that," she said. "The pieces' part. I don't know if I'll cry when I leave. I'll get back to you on that."

"I'll take that as a good sign if you do." Hank slapped his hands together lightly, dust floating in the late afternoon light. "Now, before I start soundin' any more mystical, you want the tour?"

She did. He walked her through the cabin with easy efficiency, pointing out the light switches, the water heater closet, the extra blankets folded in the bedroom chest. The bathroom was small but clean, with white tile and a claw-foot tub that made her inappropriately happy. The bed was a full-size, covered in a faded quilt whose pattern suggested someone had poured love and patience into hundreds of tiny stitches.

"Wi-Fi password's written on that card by the router," Hank said in the kitchen, tapping the counter. "It'll work most of the time. If the wind's blowin' wrong, you might lose it. Not the worst thing in the world."

"Depends on how many angry emails my editor sends," Emma said.

"You on sabbatical, he can yell at the air if he wants." Hank opened a cabinet. "We stocked the basics. Coffee, sugar, some canned stuff. There's a little store in town for the rest. Diners' decent, too, if you don't feel like cookin'."

"I can cook," she said, then amended, "I can follow directions on a box."

"That's ninety percent of it." He closed the cabinet, then seemed to remember something. "Almost forgot, you'll want to know about the well. Waters from a pump. Perfectly good, but if you hear it kick on in the middle of the night, that's just someone flushin' a toilet somewhere. Don't panic."

"I'll try not to," she said, though she suspected she'd jump out of her skin the first few times anyway.

He walked her back to the door, then paused on the threshold.

"If you need anything, you can holler down at the barn, or there's a landline on the wall you can call the house with." He nodded toward a cream-colored phone hanging by the kitchen. "Cell service is patchy, but it's decent near the porch. Mountains like to play favorites."

"Got it." She followed him out onto the porch. The sun had shifted lower, the light deepening to a richer gold. Long shadows stretched from the fence posts, from the cabin eaves, from her car still dust-coated from the drive.

"I'll leave you to settle in," Hank said. "Caleb'll be up this way in a bit when he's done checkin' the herd. He'll want to say hello; make sure you don't have plans to knock down any fences or turn the cabin into a nightclub."

"I left my disco ball at home," Emma said. "So, he's probably safe."

Hank smiled, eyes crinkling. "Don't worry about him if he seems quiet. He's got more words than he lets on. Just takes time gettin' 'em out, is all."

He tipped his hat in a small, old-fashioned gesture that felt oddly formal and genuine all at once, then headed down the steps toward his truck. She watched him drive off around the curve of the hill toward the barn, the dust trail catching the light.

When the truck disappeared, she found herself alone again with the cabin and the wide sky.

She took a breath. The air was different here, not just in smell and temperature but in texture. It felt like something she could actually fill her lungs with instead of something she had to fight through.

Rubbing the back of her neck, she went back inside and started unpacking. Clothes found their way into the dresser drawers. Her few framed pictures, her parents on a beach years ago, a candid of her and Kelsey laughing at a Christmas party, a snapshot her mom had taken of Emma at age eight with ink-stained fingers and a notebook, went on top of the dresser and the little kitchen shelf. Her books lined up on the low shelf by the couch, a small army of stories that had carried her through various seasons of life.

She set her laptop on the table by the window, facing the pasture. For a long moment she just stood there, fingers resting on the closed lid, imagining herself sitting in that chair in the blue-gray light of early morning, writing something that didn't evaporate after page twenty.

"Okay," she murmured finally. "You and me, laptop. No excuses now."

It didn't answer, naturally. She left it there to scowl at her later and went about making the place feel less like a stranger's cabin and more like somewhere she could stay. The plant, poor drooping thing, took up residence on the windowsill, where the filtered light might revive it.

By the time she'd finished, the sun was slanting lower and her stomach reminded her it had been a long time since the last gas-station granola bar. She found the coffee tin, the filters, the simple drip pot. The routine was familiar, comforting. Measure, pour, wait. The smell of brewing coffee folded into the already-present scent of wood and dust and lemon oil.

Mug in hand, she stepped back out onto the porch.

The sky had started its slide toward evening glory. Clouds high up had gone soft and streaky, catching the light in blushes of pink and orange. The mountains darkened, their details flattening into layered silhouettes. The pasture glowed; every blade of grass tipped with gold.

Down near the barn, movement caught her eye again. This time it wasn't Hank's truck. It was a horse. The animal came into view at an easy sprint, moving along a fence line she hadn't noticed before. Its coat was the color of old pennies, mane and tail black as ink. On its back, a rider sat straight and easy, hat low against the light. The horse carried both of them up the gentle slope as if it had done so a thousand times.

Emma found herself stepping to the edge of the porch, mug forgotten in her hand. The horse slowed to a walk as it neared the cabin, the rider guiding it with minimal movement. The man, Caleb, she realized with a small jolt, checked the cabin with a quick, assessing scan, taking in the car parked out front.

Up close, he looked younger than she'd briefly imagined from Hank's stories, and older at the same time. Late thirties, maybe, though it was hard to tell in the angled light. His hair was dark beneath the brim of his hat, his jaw rough with the kind of stubble that could go rugged or careless, depending on the man. He wore a denim shirt, sleeves rolled to his forearms, and jeans dusted with the same powdery earth that coated his boots. His shoulders were broad, his arms strong under the fabric, but nothing about his posture was showy. He sat the saddle like he'd been born there, weight balanced, easy, a natural extension of the horse.

What caught her most, though, was the way he carried his stillness. There was no fidgeting, no wasted motion. Even as the horse shifted its weight, he adjusted almost imperceptibly to keep balance. It was the same quiet coiled energy she'd seen in certain people in the city, the cops who'd seen too many scenes, the veterans who came back to tell their stories. People who'd learned that movement had consequences.

He reined the horse in a few yards from the porch. The animal snorted, tossing its head once before settling, as if recognizing home.

"Afternoon," he said.

His voice wasn't as rough as Hank's, but it had the same gravel in it, softened by something deeper. It was the kind of voice you wanted to lean in a little to catch, not because it was weak, but because he wasn't going to waste extra volume on words that didn't need it.

Emma set her mug on the railing carefully, suddenly aware of the way her travel-wrinkled T-shirt clung to her, the messy state of her ponytail. "Hi. Emma Hall." She wiped her palm discreetly on her jeans before offering it. "Thank you for… letting me stay here."

He shifted in the saddle and reached down, taking her hand briefly. His grip was firm but not crushing, warm and callused in a way that made an unreasonable part of her brain think, Of course, he works with his hands all day. His gaze met hers only for a moment, dark and steady, then flicked away to take in the rest of the situation.

"Caleb Walker," he said. "Heard you made it up the road without incident."

"Only a few minor incidents," she said. "I hit a pothole that might've been the size of a small swimming pool, but we survived."

One corner of his mouth twitched, there and gone. "Road's due for a grading. Been on the list." He glanced toward the open cabin door again. "Hank, get you settled?"

"Mostly. He gave me the full tour. I know where the extra blankets and the existential wisdom are stored."

That ghost of a smile flickered again, stronger this time. "Yeah, he's good for both of those." His gaze came back to her, searching but not invasive. "You drive in straight from Denver?"

"Yeah. Left this morning," she said. "I think my spine is still somewhere around mile marker 93."

"It'll catch up eventually." He shifted the reins in one hand, the other resting loose on his thigh. "Road back to towns about fifteen minutes if you need anything. Diners decent. Grocery store's small, but you won't starve. If you do, Hank'll take it personally."

"I'll try not to cause any nutritional crises," she said.

"Appreciated." There was a beat of silence, not quite awkward, just... careful. "You work at the paper, right? In Denver?"

Her mouth tilted wryly. "Word travels fast in small places, huh."

"Hank likes to know who he's lettin' on the ranch," Caleb said. "He said you write."

"Journalism mostly." She gestured vaguely toward the cabin, toward the laptop inside. "And supposedly a book. That's what this," she indicated the porch, the view, "is about. Trying to figure out if the book is real or just something I say I'm going to do one day."

He considered that, his eyes tracking the line of the mountains for a moment. "Quiet helps with that." He nodded toward the open space. "Harder to pretend you don't want something when there ain't noise drownin' it out."

The observation landed with more weight than she expected. She wondered if he was talking about her or himself. Maybe both.

"I'm hoping so," she said. "The quiet, I mean. Denver's... loud."

He gave a small, acknowledging grunt. "It is." From the way he said it, she believed he knew, personally. "You'll get some noise here, too. Cows, coyotes, Hank cussin' at machinery. But it's different."

She smiled. "Different sounds good."

Another small silence fell. Emma didn't rush to fill it for once. The air between them wasn't exactly charged, but it hummed with something like cautious curiosity.

Caleb cleared his throat, businesslike. "Couple of things while I'm up here." He nodded toward the fields. "You're welcome to walk the property around the cabin. There's a trail down to the creek behind it. If you go past the posted signs, you're on the neighbors' land. They're decent folks, but their bull's got less charm than they do, so best not to test fences."

"Duly noted," she said.

"Gates you find closed, leave 'em closed. Ones you find open, leave 'em open. That's kinda the rule of thumb." His gaze flicked down to her shoes, old running shoes, already dust-streaked from trips back and forth to the car. "And if you're walkin' out in the grass, keep an eye out for snakes. They usually don't want anything to do with you, but don't give 'em a reason to change their minds."

Emma resisted the impulse to yank her feet up. "Bulls and snakes," she said weakly. "You're really selling the place."

"Figure honesty saves us both trouble later." His tone wasn't unkind. "You'll be fine. Just watch where you put your hands and feet. And don't try to pet any calves you see. Their mamas take offense."

"I'll stick to petting the coffee maker," she said. "It seems safe."

"That's Hank's machine. Ask him first." The corner of his mouth tugged again, and she realized this was him teasing. Dry, understated, but there. "If you're plannin' on drivin' into town after dark, watch for deer on the road. They like to pretend they're invincible."

"So do some Denver drivers," she said. "At least the deer have the excuse of being deer."

He let out a small breath that might have been a laugh. It was hard to tell. Emma found herself wanting to see what a full laugh looked like on him, how it might change the hard lines of his face.

Behind him, down by the barn, Hank's truck emerged again, heading for another part of the property. The older man glanced up toward the cabin as he passed.

Caleb followed the truck's path with his eyes for a second, then brought his attention back to her.

"If you need anything, first stop is Hank," he said. "He's closer and he likes feelin' useful. If somethin's wrong with the cabin, plumbing, heater, roof leak, you tell us right away. Don't sit on it bein' polite. These old buildings appreciate a little fussin' before things get bad."

"I can do that," she said.

He nodded once, satisfied. "All right. I'll let you get settled, then. Long drive."

"Yeah." Suddenly she was aware of the ache in her shoulders, the slight fuzziness in her head that came from too much highway and too much adrenaline. "Thank you for... all this. For letting people stay here."

"Cabin would've fallen in on itself by now if we didn't." He shifted the reins, the horse flicking an ear back in response. "Plus, Hank likes the company. Says the place feels less lonely with a light up on this hill."

"What about you?" The question slipped out before she could stop it.

He stilled minutely, the way an animal might when hearing something unexpected. "I'm down there," he said after a beat, nodding toward the cluster of house and barn. "Keeps me busy enough. Loneliness is kind of a luxury these days."

Her reporter's instinct pricked, questions about what had once filled the days before "these days," about who he'd shared this place with, but she bit them back. That wasn't why she was here. She'd told herself she was leaving the habit of turning everyone into a story behind, at least for a while.

"Well," she said instead, "for what it's worth, I think the light up here will be on a lot. I'm hoping to keep it burning late while I remember how words work."

He studied her for a long second, something softer flickering behind his eyes. "Then I hope the place gives 'em back to you," he said quietly.

The simple sincerity of it surprised her. "Me too."

He touched the brim of his hat in a small, almost old-fashioned gesture. "Welcome to High Meadow, Ms. Hall."

"Emma," she corrected gently.

"Emma, then." The name seemed to sit comfortably in his mouth.

He turned the horse with a barely visible shift of his weight. The animal moved down the slope, hooves thudding softly on the packed earth. As they descended, the sun caught Caleb's profile, the stark line of his nose, the set of his jaw, the faint hollow at his temple. There was something in the shape of his back as he rode, straight, controlled, but not relaxed, that spoke of a man who'd spent a long-time expecting thing to go wrong and forcing them back into order when they did.

Emma watched until horse and rider reached the barn. He dismounted in one easy motion, hand on the saddle horn, boots hitting the dirt with a muted thud. A dog she hadn't noticed before came loping out from behind the building, tail whipping, circling his legs. Caleb bent to scrub its head once before leading the horse inside.

Only when the barn doors closed behind them did she realize she'd been holding her breath.

She let it out slowly, the tension trickling away. The wind stirred the hair at her temples, bringing with it the smell of dust and hay and something sharper, pine, maybe, from the line of trees at the far edge of the property.

"He doesn't show much," she murmured, echoing Hank's earlier warning. But under the reserve, she'd caught glimpses. A careful kindness. A deep, bone-level tiredness. A low glow of something like stubborn hope, the kind you only carried if you'd seen enough loss to understand the cost.

Her fingers found the mug on the railing again. The coffee had gone lukewarm, but she sipped it anyway.

Behind her, in the cabin, the laptop waited on the table by the window, blank page ready. High Meadow Ranch settled into the long exhale of evening, sky stretching wide above them all, and the summer she'd come looking for quietly began.

Chapter Three
New Routine, Old Wounds

The first morning at High Meadow Ranch began with light. Not the weak, filtered kind that crept reluctantly through city blinds, cut into slats by neighboring buildings. This light came in whole, unbroken, flooding the cabin through the eastern window as soon as the sun cleared the ridge. It slid across the floorboards, climbed the wall, and landed squarely on Emma's face where she lay tangled in her grandmother's green blanket.

She woke with a start, disoriented. For a heartbeat she thought the noise she heard, a distant lowing sound, was the city rumbling past her window. Then the smell of the place reached her, wood and dust and the faint lemon cleaner Hank favored, and she remembered.

Not Denver. Cabin. Ranch. Mountains.

She lay still for a moment, listening. The world out here had its own sounds: the airy rustle of wind against the cabin boards, the distant complaint of a cow, the muffled clank of metal from somewhere down near the barn. No sirens. No upstairs neighbor dropping something heavy. No early-morning buses braking outside.

Her phone, face-down on the nightstand, vibrated against the wood with a tinny buzz, like it resented the quiet and was trying to claw noise back into the room.

Emma groaned and rolled onto her side. The screen lit her face in blue when she picked it up. Notifications marched across the top: three emails, one from her editor, another from HR confirming her sabbatical details, a third from an unknown PR list that had ignored the fact she'd unsubscribed months ago. Two texts from Kelsey. One news alert about a fire somewhere off Colfax.

She thumbed through them sleepily.

HR's email was boilerplate: We have received your request for unpaid leave for the period of June 1–August 31; your benefits will remain active; please contact us if you have questions. Mike's forwarded note below it was shorter, handwritten before the signature block: Go write your damn book, Hall. Don't make me regret this.

Her chest squeezed, a complicated mix of guilt and gratitude and the familiar pulse of obligation. She could almost hear the newsroom buzzing without her.

Kelsey's texts were more direct.

KELSEY: Did you survive the drive?

KELSEY: Send pics. I want to live vicariously through your rustic writer life while I drown in city council meetings.

Emma smiled despite the sleep grit in her eyes and typed back with one thumb.

EMMA: Alive. No bulls have charged me yet. Cabin is cute. Views are… a lot. Will send pics after coffee.

She hesitated, then added:

EMMA: Tell Mike thanks again. And if he guilt-trips you about me, remind him HR signed off.

A few dots appeared, then disappeared, then reappeared. Emma could picture Kelsey, hair pinned up, coffee balanced on a stack of files, tapping on her own phone between layout deadlines.

KELSEY: He's walking around saying things like "she better come back with a Pulitzer draft." You broke the man.

KELSEY: Seriously though, we already miss you. Now go be brilliant. Or at least go be not here. That's step one.

Emma snorted softly and set the phone down, screen darkening again. For a moment she let herself drift on the temptation to scroll, social media, news, other people's words filling the space where her own might go if she gave them half a chance.

She knew that pattern too well. Five minutes "just checking in" became forty-five lost to endless, frictionless consumption. Headlines about crises she could do nothing about from here. Photos of friends' nights out at places she no longer wanted to be. A hundred small invitations to compare her life to everyone else's best moments.

No.

Emma sat up, throwing the blanket back. The air in the bedroom carried a morning chill that seeped pleasantly through her T-shirt. She walked barefoot to the little window and peered out.

The pasture behind the cabin glowed in early light. Dew, or whatever passed for dew in this climate, caught on the grass, making the slope shimmer. A lone horse grazed near the fence line, tail flicking slowly. Farther down, near the barn, she spotted movement, two figures, one tall and straight, one just a little bent, moving through a group of cattle.

Caleb and Hank. Day already underway while she was still thinking about coffee.

She tugged on jeans and a sweatshirt, the hem of it brushing the top of her thighs. In the tiny bathroom, she splashed cold water on her face, scrubbed her teeth, dragged a brush through her hair until the curls tamed themselves into something that could be bullied into a ponytail. No makeup. She'd brought some, but the idea of mascara and foundation felt faintly ridiculous out here, like wearing heels to a hiking trail.

In the kitchen, the ritual of making coffee grounded her. Filter, grounds, water, the slow drip into the pot. While it brewed, she opened the cabin door and propped it with a small rock, letting in the cool air and the sounds of the ranch.

Out in the pasture, a calf bawled, high and insistent. A dog barked once, sharp and authoritative, then again, herding something back into place. A man's voice, Caleb's, carried faintly up the hill, a low murmur too distant for words but edged with command. Hank's answer came back lighter; a drawl stretched across years. They formed a kind of rhythm.

Emma poured coffee into her chipped blue mug, added a splash of milk, then carried it to the small table by the window. Her laptop waited where she'd left it the night before. She flipped the lid open and watched the screen wake up, the familiar desktop background, an old photo she'd taken of a mountain lake on a rare weekend trip, fading into place.

The Scrivener icon blinked at her like an accusation. She clicked it anyway.

The interface blossomed: the binder with its list of chapters on the left, the main pane in the middle, blank and vast. Yesterday's mental bravado shrank a little at the sight. It was one thing to drive hours to a cabin and announce to HR that you were "taking a sabbatical to work on your novel." It was another thing entirely to stare at an empty document while the cursor blinked, patient and unimpressed.

Outside, she saw movement through the window, Caleb and Hank walking along a fence, flanked by a small group of cows, a couple of calves with sticks for legs stumbling after their mothers. Caleb moved with the same contained efficiency she'd noticed the evening before. Even at a distance, she could see how he carried his weight: balanced, centered, ready.

She looked away quickly, ashamed of how easy it was to let her attention drift outward. That was another old habit, the reporter's urge to watch, observe, listen, record. Other people's stories were always easier than her own.

Emma set her fingers on the keyboard.

New document. Chapter One.

The blank title box waited. She typed:

The city was a mouth that never stopped talking,

Too dramatic.

She deleted that too and leaned back, rubbing her forehead with her thumb.

The urge to check her phone rose like a tide. Just a quick scroll, a tiny hit of validation from somewhere else, a text, a like, a news alert. Proof that the world still existed beyond this cabin and this blank page.

No.

She pushed her chair back, stood, and crossed to the counter where she'd left the phone. The screen lit under her hand, the gallery of apps glowing like small, hungry mouths.

Emma tapped open the settings instead.

Airplane Mode: On.

Wi-Fi: Off.

The little icons dimmed. The world outside receded. A hush fell in her head, different from the physical quiet around her. Scary, in its way. Liberating, in another.

She set the phone face-down on the kitchen shelf and returned to the table. This time, when she sat and faced the screen, there was nothing jumping at the edge of her vision, nothing asking for her to react.

Still the words didn't come easily. Her brain scrabbled at excuses, coffee was too hot, chair was slightly uncomfortable, she should really finish unpacking first, maybe go into town and buy a different notebook because obviously the right notebook was the key to everything.

She took a deep breath and told herself she could write badly. No one was watching. No one was waiting for this to hit a midnight deadline. It didn't matter if the first page was terrible. It only mattered that it existed.

Hands hovering over the keys, she tried again.

The city had a way of getting inside your skin.

The line wasn't perfect. It wasn't even particularly good. But it sat there, black on white, stubborn and real.

She kept going.

By the time the sun cleared the ridge fully and spilled through the window in a bright rectangle across her table, Emma had written three pages. Some sentences were clunky. Some wandered. A few surprised her, moments of clarity she hadn't seen coming.

She lost herself for a little while, following the line of the story instead of worrying whether it would hold.

Outside, Caleb and Hank moved through their own routines.

Down in the corral, a small dust storm rose as they eased a group of cows through a gate. The morning air carried the musky smell of animals, the sharp tang of manure, the clean, sweet scent of hay. A dog, a spotted blue heeler named Gus, darted along the edges of the herd, nipping at heels, flanking stray calves back into line with quick, decisive movements.

"Easy," Caleb murmured to the cattle, his voice as much for them as for himself. "Easy, easy. That's it."

He stood at the gate, one gloved hand on the metal, the other raised in a loose, relaxed posture that belied the focus coiled in his body. Years of this had taught him the small signals, the flick of an ear, the tension in a neck, that meant an animal might bolt. His eyes moved constantly, assessing, counting without quite counting.

Hank stood a few yards away, leaning on a fence post, providing backup in the way of men who'd done this so many times their presence alone steadied the whole affair.

"You know," Hank drawled, as the last cow shuffled through, "you ever decide to get out of this line of work, you'd make a hell of a traffic cop."

Caleb swung the gate closed and latched it. "Pretty sure I'd get fired on day one," he said. "I'd try to move the cars with a dog and a stick."

"Most folks in Denver could use that kind of direction," Hank said. "Saw a video the other day," he caught himself, lips quirking at the idea of 'the other day' being months ago; time out here didn't track with the internets. "Anyway. Cows make more sense than people, most days."

"Cows don't try to sue you when they get themselves stuck in a ditch," Caleb said.

"That you know of." Hank clicked his tongue. "Come on, let's get a look at 17. He sounded off this mornin'."

They moved along the fence line, boots scuffing in the dirt. Gus trotted at Caleb's heel now that the work of moving cattle was done, tongue lolling happily from his mouth.

In Caleb's head, a different sort of map unfurled. A mental ledger. Fences that needed mending before the next storm. A section of irrigation pipe he'd been meaning to replace. The barn roof would hold another winter if he got up there and patched the weak spots before the first heavy snow. The tractor had been making a noise yesterday that didn't bode well; he'd have to call the mechanic in town and beg another favor or set up another trade.

And money, always the undercurrent. The feed bill due at the end of the month. The vet's invoice. Property taxes looming like the peaks on the horizon.

Over all of it, his father's voice floated, not nagging, exactly. Just present. A tone that mixed pride and worry and the kind of love that had never quite found all the words it needed.

"Keep this place alive, son."

He could still see his father's hands in that hospital room, big, work-worn, the knuckles swollen from arthritis and old injuries, the skin gone thin and bruised. Those hands had done everything on this land. Raised fences, delivered calves, fixed engines that should've died three breakdowns ago. They'd picked up Caleb when he'd fallen as a kid, cuffed the back of his head when he'd mouthed off as a teenager, clapped his shoulder when he'd come home from basic training.

In the end, they'd been light on the sheets, reaching for nothing but his son's wrist and a promise.

"Don't let it go," his dad had rasped, breath rattling. "Your granddad bled for this place. I did too. Don't… don't let it be for nothin'."

Caleb had swallowed hard around the lump in his throat, a thirty-year-old man suddenly feeling ten again. "I won't, Dad. I'll take care of it."

"Of you," his father had corrected, eyes fierce even in the dim. "It'll take care of you too, if you let it."

He hadn't known then how heavy that promise would feel later, when the reality of bills and drought and a broken engagement piled on top of the grief. He'd made it anyway, because what else could he have done? Let his father die thinking it was all going to fall apart? That he, Caleb, would walk away and leave High Meadow to be carved up into vacation homes and weekend hobby farms?

No. Even now, years later, his jaw tightened at the thought.

"Hey," Hank said beside him, breaking into the old memory. "You with me, or did you fall asleep on your feet?"

Caleb realized he'd stopped at the gate without opening it, hand resting on the chain but not moving. Gus sat at his heel, looking up expectantly.

"I'm with you," Caleb said. He blew out a breath and unhooked the chain. "Just thinkin' through the week."

"Thought I smelled smoke." Hank's eyes crinkled. "Come on. 17's not gonna diagnose himself."

They stepped into the pen. The cow in question, a rangy black steer with a white blaze on his face, stood off to the side, shifting his weight from one hoof to another in a way that wasn't quite right.

Caleb approached slowly, voice low and soothing. "Easy, boy. Let's take a look."

They worked him into a smaller enclosure, Hank swinging gates with practiced timing. Up close, Caleb could see the swelling around the animal's ankle, the tender way he set the hoof down.

"Twisted it on a rock, maybe," Caleb said. He crouched, looking for any puncture that would suggest something worse. "We'll have to keep him out of the rough pasture a few days. I'll call Dr. Morales, see if she can swing by tomorrow, but I don't think it's broken."

Hank nodded. "You handle the animal doc. I'll handle reworkin' the grazing plan. I know how you get when the spreadsheet doesn't match reality."

"The spreadsheet never matches reality," Caleb muttered. He straightened, dusting his hands on his jeans. "Reality doesn't care about my tables."

"Maybe that's your problem right there," Hank said. "You keep expecting it to."

They got 17 settled with easier access to water and hay. The rest of the morning unfolded in a pattern of physical tasks: checking water troughs, walking fence lines, repairing a section where a deadfall tree had toppled the top wire. Caleb's back ached by midday, and sweat plastered his shirt to his spine, but the familiar strain calmed something in him. Work he understood. Problems he could see and touch.

It was the ones he couldn't, numbers in a bank account, the thinness of their margins, the uncertainty of weather, that gnawed on him later, when the day got quiet.

As the sun climbed, he caught, in a break between chores, a glimpse of the cabin on the hill.

The porch had looked empty when he rode past earlier. Now, in the heat-hazy distance, he could just make out a figure moving from table to kitchen, mug in hand. Emma. Her hair was pulled back, dark against the pale of her T-shirt. She moved with an energy that suggested she wasn't entirely awake yet, but trying.

The knowledge of her presence at the edge of the property was… strange. Not unwelcome, exactly. Just new.

He'd resisted the whole cabin rental idea at first. The notion of strangers on the ranch, especially near the north pasture where things got rough, sat wrong in his gut. This land had always been a family thing, passed down through calloused hands and stubborn hearts. Opening even a sliver of it to outsiders felt like giving up something he couldn't get back.

But Hank had made good points. The cabin had been sitting empty since his wife died, gathering dust and mice and memories. The county tax bill had not been sitting empty. And the few people they'd had stay so far had mostly wanted what the ad promised: quiet, some space, a view.

"Besides," Hank had said, "might do you good, havin' some new faces around that aren't cattle."

Caleb had grumbled and pretended not to care, but he'd drawn a firm line: no vacationers who wanted to "play cowboy." No groups. No parties. No bachelor weekends with beer cans left in the creek.

Apparently, God, or the rental site algorithm, had a sense of humor. Instead of any of that, they'd gotten a journalist with tired eyes and ink in her bones.

He wasn't sure yet if that was better or worse.

By the time the sun tipped downward again, the day's heat eased. Caleb and Hank wrapped up the most pressing tasks, leaving a dozen smaller to-dos to crowd tomorrow's mental list instead.

"You go on up and get supper started," Hank said, leaning against the fence post, breath misting just faintly in the cooling air. "I'll run the tractor back to the shed."

"I can do that," Caleb said, wiping sweat from his forehead with the back of his wrist. Dust streaked the motion.

"You can, but I got a radio show comin' on in the truck I like more than that tractor." Hank's grin flashed, quick and sly. "Besides, you move that beast around more than I do. You're liable to start hearin' its feelings if you don't let it rest."

"Tractors don't have feelings," Caleb said.

"Neither do you, according to certain people, but I know better." Hank clapped him lightly on the shoulder. "Go on. I'll be along."

Caleb shook his head, but he didn't argue. Truth was, the idea of a cool shower and a break from the sun tugged at him.

From the cabin porch, Emma watched him go, mug cradled in her hands.

Her writing session had sputtered. After the initial burst this morning, the words had slowed, then stalled entirely. She'd pushed through two more pages, but the last one had hurt. The story wanted to veer into territory she wasn't sure she was ready to walk through, even on paper.

When the words slowed to a crawl, she'd given herself permission to stop. She'd made a promise in the city that she'd show up every morning and give the book her best hours. She hadn't promised herself she'd write from dawn till midnight on day one.

Now, standing in the late afternoon light, she stretched her back until it popped. Her legs wanted movement. Her eyes wanted something farther away to focus on than the edge of her computer screen.

Her gaze drifted down the hill, following the line of the lane past the cabin, the fences, the barn. Watching the men work had become a kind of unintentional background to her morning, figures moving against the bright green, the occasional shout rising faintly when a cow proved uncooperative. It was a world she didn't understand yet, but it felt... solid. Concrete.

She saw Hank now, a small figure near the tractor, and Caleb walking with the dog toward the house. From this vantage point, they were all pieces in a landscape painting. It felt intrusive to stare, so she didn't. Not for long.

Instead, she walked around the side of the cabin to the back, where Hank had told her a little trail led down to a creek. The path was narrow but clear, the dirt tamped down by the passage of boots and paws. Grass brushed her calves, leaving a faint tickle. The sun filtered through a thin line of cottonwoods ahead, their leaves trembling in the easy wind.

The creek, when she reached it, was smaller than she'd imagined, more a wide stream than a river. Water whispered over smooth stones, sunlight making shards of light on the surface. Someone had set a weathered log along one bank as a seat. She lowered herself onto it, the cool shade wrapping around her like a different world.

For a few minutes she just sat and listened, letting the sounds of moving water and bird calls unknot the muscles at the back of her neck. The urge to reach for her phone returned, absent now of any practical purpose and more about habit. She resisted it, fingers clenching lightly on her mug instead.

Time stretched. Long enough that she lost track of the minutes, which was, she realized, partly the point of being here.

When the air began to cool and the shadows lengthened, she made her way back up the hill.

Down at the main house, the evening settled in with its own rituals.

The ranch house sat not far from the barn, a two-story structure with white-painted siding and a deep front porch lined with chairs. Inside, the floors creaked in familiar places. A ceiling fan hummed in the kitchen, pushing the day's heat around more than it actually moved it out.

Caleb stood at the sink, washing his hands, watching the dirt and sweat swirl off in the steady stream of water. His knuckles were scraped in a couple of places. He flexed his fingers, checking for the stiffness that sometimes followed a hard day. Not too bad today. He'd had worse.

He caught his reflection in the small window over the sink, a smudge of a man behind streaked glass, dark hair flattened by his hat, stubble shading his jaw, lines he swore hadn't been there ten years ago carved around his mouth and eyes. His father's nose. His mother's cheekbones. A face that belonged to this kitchen, this house, the way the old table and the mismatched chairs did.

Hank's boots thudded on the porch, then the hallway. The older man appeared in the doorway, wiping his hands on a towel.

"Tractor's tucked in for the night," Hank said. "Didn't even whine about it."

"That's because you didn't drive it long enough for it to start complainin'," Caleb said.

"Perhaps" Hank said with a grin.

"Hungry?" Caleb said, reaching for the pan of roasted potatoes he'd put in the oven earlier. He set it on the stove top and grabbed a rag, flipping the chicken breasts in the cast-iron skillet. He cooked simply out of necessity, nothing fancy but enough to keep body and day moving.

Hank sniffed appreciatively. "Smells good. You could teach half the men in town a thing or two about fendin' for themselves."

"Half the men in town have wives or mothers who'd take offense at that," Caleb said. "I had both, once. They're the reason I know how to cook in the first place."

"Your mama'd be proud you remembered." Hank's voice softened briefly as he set the plates on the worn table. "She'd be less proud about how often you let work make supper late."

"Ranch doesn't punch a clock," Caleb said, but he knew Hank was right. The man's late wife had drilled into both of them the value of sitting down to a meal before midnight whenever possible.

They ate at the scarred oak table that had seen three generations of Walkers and Lawson drift through. Quiet reigned for the first few minutes as hunger did its work. The ticking clock on the wall, the old one with the brass pendulum and the slightly off chime, filled the space between clinks of fork against plate.

Hank broke the silence first.

"Saw your cabin guest out on the porch some today," he said.

Caleb kept his eyes on his plate. "Yeah?"

"Mm." Hank chewed, swallowed, washed it down with a sip of iced tea. "She's got that look about her."

He didn't have to ask what look. He'd been seeing it in the mirror more often than he cared to admit. Tired around the edges. Hungry in the middle, but not for food. For something else.

"City got its hooks in her?" Caleb asked.

"Looks like the city chewed on her a while and spit her out here to recover," Hank said. "She been writin' all mornin'. Could see her through the window hunched over that fancy laptop. Took a walk down to the creek later. Didn't fall in, far as I could tell. That's a good sign."

Caleb's fork paused halfway to his mouth before he resumed the motion. He'd noticed the walk too, from a distance, the small figure following the path, the way she'd stopped at the water and sat very still.

"I told her you're the one to holler for if she needs anything," Hank added. "But she strikes me as the kind who'll try not to. Doesn't wanna be a bother."

"That'd be nice," Caleb said. "Be a change from half the folks we used to get when your cousin ran that bed and breakfast in town. Remember those?"

Hank chuckled, a wheezy sound. "Oh, I remember. City folks demandin' organic pancakes at six a.m. and complainin' 'bout the rooster crowin'. It's a farm, lady, not a spa."

"This one's at least seen farm animals before," Caleb said, remembering the way Emma had watched the cattle, curious rather than alarmed. "More than some of 'em."

"More than some of us, once upon a time," Hank said, giving him a pointed look. "You forget you went off to be a soldier before you came back to be a rancher. Took you a while to remember which end of the cow was which after that."

Caleb snorted. "I never forgot that."

"You forgot plenty," Hank said, but there was affection there. "You remembered fast enough when your daddy got sick, though."

The reminder settled between them, not unwelcome, not exactly comfortable either.

Caleb poked at a potato, his appetite briefly dimmed. "You were here," he said. "You saw how it was."

"I did." Hank leaned back in his chair, letting it creak under his weight. "You came back when he called. Took over when he couldn't. A lot of men would've said they 'couldn't get away from work' or 'had obligations elsewhere.'"

"I had obligations elsewhere," Caleb said quietly. "There were people depending on me there too."

"I know," Hank said. "And you still came. No one's sayin' it was easy."

The Army felt like another lifetime sometimes, and like yesterday on others. Sand and heat and the metallic tang of adrenaline sat under his skin in layers that didn't care how many years had passed.

He'd been good at that job. Good at reading a situation, moving people, making decisions quickly. The skills translated to ranching more than he'd expected, triage here, too, just with cows and fences instead of wounded men and broken vehicles.

The ghosts came home with him all the same.

Some nights in the small hours, lying in the dark of his childhood bedroom after his father had fallen asleep down the hall, he'd wake with his heart hammering against his ribs, convinced he'd heard the dull thump of mortars. It was just the old house settling, or wind against the siding. His body hadn't yet gotten the memo that it was allowed to stand down.

His father's cough down the hall had been another kind of alarm, one he couldn't answer with patrol reports and supply requests. He'd answered it by trading one uniform for another, fatigues for work shirts, boots for boots, just with different dirt under them.

"Anyhow," Hank said, apparently determined not to let the mood sink too deep, "what I was sayin' is, that girl up in the cabin? She's here for a reason. Might be nice if she figures out, you're not a complete ogre before August."

"I'm not an ogre at all," Caleb said, too quickly.

"Mm-hm. Tell that to your face." Hank forked another piece of chicken. "All I'm sayin' is, you could do worse than smile at her once in a while and make sure she doesn't get ate by a mountain lion."

"There aren't mountain lions right up here," Caleb said. "Not close. They stay higher."

"Mostly." Hank raised his brows. "And if one of 'em decides it wants an adventure?"

"I told her about snakes and bulls," Caleb said. "I'm not givin' her nightmares on day one."

"Fair enough." Hank chewed thoughtfully. "You know, your daddy always said this house felt too quiet after your mama passed. Said the rooms echoed different."

Caleb's jaw tightened around his bite. "He said that to you?"

"He said all kinds of things to me he didn't say to you," Hank said, gentle but honest. "He wanted to protect you from some of it. You know how he was."

Caleb did. His father had always been more comfortable with effort than emotion, with fixing the pump than naming the fear that the pump might fail. The softer words came sideways, in the middle of other tasks. Or not at all, left for Hank to hear instead in evenings on the porch once Caleb had gone inside.

"He told me more than once," Hank went on, "that he was glad you'd built a life somewhere else for a while. That he didn't want this place to be the only thing you ever knew."

Caleb looked up sharply. That wasn't a version of the story he'd kept in his head. His had always been the opposite: his dad, proud of the ranch, wanting his boy to carry it, worried he'd go off and never come back.

"Why didn't you tell me that?" he asked, not accusing, just tired.

"Would it have changed anything?" Hank countered. "You still had sand in your boots and duty on your shoulders when you came back. You still loved this land. You still promised him you'd keep it alive. Some things you had to figure out without feelin' like you were lettin' him down for wantin' somethin' different."

Caleb's fingers curled loosely around his fork. The thought, his dad being glad he'd left once, sat uncomfortably in his chest and then, slowly, loosened something that had been knotted there a long time.

"I'm not leavin'," he said, as much to himself as to Hank. "Not now."

"I know," Hank said. "But you don't have to make this place your whole world to honor what he built. Your daddy knew that, even if he didn't know how to say it. Maybe you can be the one to do better about sayin' things."

"Sayin' what?" Caleb asked, wary.

"Whatever needs sayin'," Hank said simply. His eyes twinkled. "Start small. 'Good mornin' is nice. 'How's the writin' goin' is also a fine choice."

"There it is," Caleb muttered. "I was waitin' for you to circle back around."

"You knew I'd get there." Hank's grin was shameless. "Look, I'm not tryin' to marry you off to every woman who sets foot on this ranch. But you got a woman on your land right now who understands work and words. Seems like the least we can do is not scare her off."

"I didn't scare her," Caleb said. "I said hello. Gave her the safety speech. That's neighborly."

"It's a start," Hank allowed. "Tomorrow, maybe you manage 'how was your drive.' Baby steps."

"I already asked her that," Caleb pointed out.

"So, you're ahead of schedule." Hank tossed his napkin onto his empty plate. "Keep it up and you might even get to the part where you two talk about somethin' other than bulls and gates before summer's over."

Caleb pushed his potatoes around the plate, not quite meeting Hank's gaze. The image of Emma on the porch, mug in hand, the way she'd looked at the land and at him with equal parts curiosity and wariness, flickered in his mind.

"We'll see," he said quietly.

Hank watched him for a long moment, reading more than Caleb said, as he always did. Then he stood, chair scraping on the worn wood floor. "I'm gonna go catch the end of that show about old country songs before I forget what music is. You clean up in here, and then maybe think about what your daddy would say if he saw you hidin' from your cabin guest like she's a tax collector."

"She might be worse," Caleb said. "She's a journalist."

"That's just a fancy word for someone who asks questions," Hank said over his shoulder. "You've dealt with worse."

He left the kitchen humming under his breath; some tune from decades ago. The house settled around his absence.

Caleb gathered plates and carried them to the sink. Warm water, dish soap, the squeak of sponge on ceramic, it all gave his hands something to do while his mind wandered again.

He didn't intend to hide from the woman up on the hill. He had work. She had her book. Their paths would cross when they needed to. He'd make sure she had what she needed to be safe, and that would be that.

Probably.

Still, when he stepped out onto the back porch later, mug of his own coffee in hand, the impulse to glance up toward the cabin was too strong to ignore.

The porch light burned there, a small, steady glow against the oncoming dark. Behind the window, he could make out the outline of someone moving, Emma, most likely, clearing away her own dinner dishes, or pacing with the restless energy of someone whose mind wouldn't shut off.

He watched for only a second, long enough to see her pause at the glass and look out. From this distance, he couldn't see her expression. He doubted she could see his. Two figures in two houses, both thinking more than they said.

Gus pushed his head under Caleb's hand, demanding attention. Caleb obliged, fingers threading through fur.

"Long summer ahead, boy," he murmured.

The dog sighed in agreement and settled at his feet.

Above them, the sky deepened into a rich indigo scattered with stars. High Meadow Ranch exhaled under it, the routines of work and the weight of old promises folding into the new rhythm of a cabin light on the hill and a city girl trying to remember how to write a story.

Chapter Four
Fence at Sunset

By the time the sun slid low enough to set the tops of the cottonwoods on fire, Emma's brain had all the consistency of overcooked pasta.

She'd done her duty that day: put in her hours at the little table by the window, written until the words stopped making sense, taken a break down by the creek, come back and written some more.

Emma, for her part, had a mug full of cold coffee and a neck that protested every time she turned her head.

The cabin was warm from the afternoon, breathable but still holding the day's heat. She stood in the middle of the living room, stretching her arms overhead until her spine popped, then rolled her shoulders slowly. The muscles along her shoulder blades, unused to this much sitting without the distraction of breaking news, complained.

"Okay," she told the room. "Enough for today."

Her gaze slid toward the open door. Outside, the light had gone thick and rich, that magic hour photographers loved. The thought of sitting under it instead of watching it through glass tugged at her.

She grabbed her small spiral-bound notebook and a pen from the table, leaving the laptop to sulk in peace, and stepped out onto the porch.

The evening air kissed the sweat at her temples, cooling it. The sky over the pasture was a long gradient from gold near the horizon to a deeper, gentler blue higher up. The mountains wore a softer set of shadows now, their hard midday edges blurred. The grass on the slopes below the cabin had gone from green to something more complicated, green shot through with copper and amber where the light struck.

She sank onto the wide porch rail, one foot hooked around a support post for balance, notebook propped on her knee. From here she could see most of the near pasture and, if she turned her head, a stretch of fence line that ran along the boundary between the cabin's little patch and the wider ranch.

It was that direction she noticed movement.

About fifty yards away, where the fence dipped slightly between two posts, a man stood with his back to her, shoulders bent slightly as he worked. Even at this distance, she recognized the easy, contained way his body moved. Caleb.

He'd shed his hat, leaving his dark hair flattened in a careless arc. His denim shirt was darkened at the spine and under the arms, clinging to the planes of his back. The setting sun painted his profile in sharp lines when he straightened, wire cutters in one hand, a loop of fencing wire in the other.

He was, objectively, a compelling figure: the kind artists put on book covers and calendars, all purposeful angles and quiet competence. That was not why she watched. That's what she told herself, anyway.

She told herself she was watching because she was supposed to be learning this place, learning the work that went into the scenery she'd been so eager to claim as inspiration. Fences didn't just appear, neatly dividing pasture from pasture. Someone had to stretch the wire, sink the posts, mend the breaks where weather and animals and time had done their inevitable damage.

She opened the notebook and scribbled:

Evening light pouring itself over the land like honey. Fence lines like scars and stitches, holding it all together.

She frowned at the line. Too metaphorical. Too much. She scratched it out and wrote beneath it:

Fence = literal. Stop trying to turn everything into a symbol.

Her pen hovered. Below that, she added, almost despite herself:

But maybe some things are both.

A short bark of laughter escaped her. If anyone ever bothered to dig through her notebooks after she was gone, they'd find a battlefield of false starts and arguments with herself.

Down the hill, metal clinked. She glanced up again.

Caleb had bent to inspect a section of wire. Up close, she imagined, the wire would be rusted in spots, shiny in others where fresh repairs had been made. His gloved fingers tested the tension, then he set the cutters to a frayed section and squeezed. The wire snapped with a muffled twang.

The movement was efficient, practiced. He didn't waste gestures. Each one had a purpose: cut, twist, hook, pull. He worked the broken section free, coiling it neatly instead of letting it drop where some calf or deer could find it later.

She found herself watching the way the muscles in his forearms bunched under his rolled sleeves, the way his shoulders shifted when he braced a boot against the bottom wire and leaned his weight into it to help it stretch. He made the work look easy. She knew, intellectually, that it wasn't.

The pen in her hand hovered again. She wrote, without thinking too hard about it:

Man at the fence. No wasted motion. Like he's learned the cost of doing anything twice.

Her cheeks warmed at the line. It felt too intimate somehow, too perceptive for how little she actually knew him.

As if sensing her gaze, Caleb straightened and looked toward the cabin.

Caught, Emma did the least subtle thing possible: she pretended she'd just noticed him at that exact moment. She lifted a hand in an awkward half-wave, notebook still resting across her knees.

He hesitated a beat, long enough for her to second-guess the wave, then lifted his own gloved hand, fingers curling in something that was more acknowledgment than greeting. After a moment, he bent back to the fence.

She watched him for another second, then forced her eyes back to the page. She'd come out here to write, not to stare at the rancher like some kind of creep.

The dragonfly that landed on the porch rail beside her was easier to look at. Its wings were delicate, iridescent in the slant of sun, its body a thin line of electric blue. It cleaned its front legs with the meticulousness of a cat, then took off again, catching the light like glass.

Emma jotted down a description, letting small details anchor her back into the habit of noticing. That was something she trusted, the muscle she'd built as a reporter. Observe, record, make sense later.

The sound of wire scraping against wood pulled her attention back outward.

Caleb had moved a little farther along the fence, toward the corner where the property line turned. The distance didn't feel as far now. The evening did that, collapsed space, softened edges. The world felt closer together and farther apart in the same breath.

She watched him hitch a length of new wire to the post, threading it around an insulator, then pull it taut with a metal tool that creaked under the strain. His jaw worked slightly as he put his weight into it. A thin line of sweat darkened the back of his neck, catching there before disappearing under his collar.

Her water bottle sat sweating on the little table by the door. She glanced back at it, then at him.

He'd probably brought his own, she told herself. Ranchers knew better than to wander into fields without water. It wasn't her business if he wanted to be stubborn. He might not even appreciate her interrupting his work.

Another creak of that tool. Another set of pulled muscles in his arms. The sun slipped a little lower, flooding the fence line in light.

She capped her pen, shoved the notebook under one arm, and stood. "Okay," she muttered. "We're doing this. Neighborly, not weird."

She grabbed the water bottle on her way past the door and made her way down the steps into the yard, gravel crunching under her sneakers.

The path to the fence wasn't a path so much as a series of trodden-down spots between clumps of grass. She picked her way carefully, remembering his warnings about snakes and being absurdly grateful every time the ground ahead proved to be just dirt and rocks.

Caleb heard her before she reached him. Years of needing to know who was coming up behind him, in very different landscapes, had trained his body to react to changes in sound and rhythm.

He straightened from the post and looked over his shoulder.

Emma slowed, suddenly aware of every inch of dust on her jeans, every flyaway hair escaping her ponytail. The notebook felt silly under her arm, the water bottle heavy in her hand.

"Hey," she said, pitching her voice a little louder than normal so it would carry without her having to shout. "Thought I'd come inspect your fence work."

One of his brows ticked up, just barely. "You qualified for that?"

"Absolutely not." She stopped on the safe side of the wires, careful not to get too close. Up close, the fence felt more imposing, four strands of wire stretched between posts, glinting faintly. "But I brought you a bribe anyway." She held out the water bottle.

His gaze flicked from her face to the bottle and back again. For a second she worried she'd miscalculated, that he'd refuse it with offended self-sufficiency. Instead, he shifted the tool to one hand and stepped closer, reaching over the top wire to take it.

"Thanks," he said. "I was just thinkin' about goin' back for one."

He unscrewed the cap and took a long drink. Seeing his throat work as he swallowed did things to her attention she chose not to analyze.

"Figured I owed you for the snakes-and-bulls lecture," she said lightly. "Consider this hazard pay."

"Lectures are free," he said, wiping his mouth with the back of his wrist before handing the bottle back. "It's the hospital visits that get expensive."

"Still, I appreciate knowing what not to pet," she said. "I'll adjust my life goals accordingly."

He huffed something that was almost a laugh. The sound warmed the air between them.

Up close, she could see the fine dust on his shirt, the way it clung to the fabric where sweat had dried into salt patterns. His hands, still gloved, were lined with dirt where the leather folded. His forearms were tanned darker than the rest of his skin, a farmer's tan that told the story of someone who spent most days outdoors, sleeves rolled up to expose the same strips of skin to the sun.

Her notebook slipped slightly under her arm. He noticed it.

"You get some writin' done today?" he asked, nodding toward it.

"Some," she said. "About three pages of pure genius and five of complete crap. Which I think averages out to mediocre. So, you know. Progress."

His mouth twitched, that almost smile playing at the corner. "Three pages of genius in one day sounds like a good haul to me."

"You haven't read them," she pointed out.

"Don't need to." He moved back to the post he'd been working on, setting the tensioner tool into place around the wire. "I've strung enough fence to know the first stretch always feels like crap. You look back later and realize it's what's holdin' the rest up."

She blinked. That was possibly the most comforting and infuriating metaphor anyone had offered her in months.

"Did you just… compare my messy first draft to barbed wire?" she asked.

"Barbed wire's over there." He jerked his chin toward a different section of fence. "This is smooth wire. Less likely to rip you open if you mess with it wrong."

"Wow. You really know how to flatter a girl's artistic process."

"Didn't say you were the wire," he said. "Said the first part has a job even if it ain't pretty."

He leaned into the tool, arms flexing. The wire creaked, then tightened, gaining a new, purposeful line. He hooked it off and checked the tension with a pluck of his fingers. The wire gave back a low, humming note.

"Feels solid," he murmured.

"You do this a lot?" she asked, grateful for the excuse to keep him talking while she watched the work.

"Too much." He wiped his brow with his forearm, glancing along the fence line. "Winter's hard on posts. Cattle are harder. Wind does its best to help 'em out."

"Is this the cabin side?" She nodded to the area behind her. "Or does it all kind of blend together?"

"This line marks where we decided to keep the guest area separate from the main pasture," he said. "Figure folks renting don't always want to wake up with a cow in their front yard."

She pictured that, some vacationing couple opening the cabin door to find a large cow chewing thoughtfully on the geraniums. "That feels… fair."

"You ever want to walk beyond this line, you can," he added. "Just let one of us know first so we don't lose track of you out there. Harder to guess where someone is when there's more ground under 'em."

"I'll try not to wander too far," she said. "I got lost in a Target parking lot last month. I don't think I'm ready for the open range."

"That why you came out here?" he asked, like he wasn't entirely joking. "Done with gettin' lost in parking lots?"

She hesitated.

The easy answer sat on her tongue: I just needed a change. Wanted a break. Thought it'd be pretty. Something light, deflective.

Instead, maybe because of the light, or the work, or the fact that he'd just compared her draft to fence wire in a way that made weird sense, she let a little more truth slip out.

"I couldn't hear myself think in the city anymore," she said. "There's always something shouting in your face. Sirens, traffic, people, notifications. Even when it's quiet, it's… not really quiet. It's just noise at a lower volume." She gestured toward the valley, the sky. "I figured if I was going to write anything real, I needed to go somewhere that would actually shut up."

He straightened and rested his forearms on the top wire, gloves dangling from one hand now. The stance made him look more approachable, like a neighbor leaning over the fence for a chat, even if his shoulders still held that built-in tension.

"Does it feel quieter here?" he asked.

"Out there?" She tipped her head toward the open land. "Yes. In here?" She tapped her temple with the end of her pen. "Questionable."

He nodded, understanding flickering across his face. "Noise doesn't always turn off just 'cause everything else does."

"No." She looked down at the notebook in her hand, at the smudged ink on her thumb from where she'd brushed a note too soon. "But at least here I only have to deal with my own thoughts."

"You say that like it's the easy part," he said, something like wry humor in his tone.

She huffed out a breath that might've been a laugh. "I didn't say it was easy. Just... honest."

He watched her for a moment. There was something steady in his gaze now, something that made it feel less like he was sizing up a stranger and more like he was trying to make sense of this person who'd suddenly appeared in his orbit.

"The land's loud in its own way," he said finally. "Different kind of loud. Weather, animals, little problems that turn into big ones if you ignore 'em. I thought comin' back here would be the quiet version of what I was doin' before. Turns out it's just... a different sort of busy."

"Before," she repeated. "The Army?"

He nodded once, looking out over the pasture instead of at her. "Spent most of my twenties in places where quiet meant bad things. Too quiet, and you started waitin' for somethin' to blow up. Literally." His jaw flexed. "Took a while after I got home to stop listenin' for explosions every time there was a pause."

Emma's pen stilled against the notebook. She'd interviewed veterans before, sat across from men and women with haunted eyes as they told her about sand and heat and loss. She'd asked questions, recorded quotes, tried to do their stories justice in columns that ran alongside ads for grocery sales.

This was different. There was no recorder on the table between them, no notebook open to trap his words. Just a fence, a sunset, and a man talking because he'd decided to, not because she'd asked him to for a story.

"Does this place help with that?" she asked quietly. "Not listening for explosions?"

He was quiet for a long moment. Long enough that she wondered if she'd overstepped.

Then he nodded. "Yeah," he said. "Mostly. Took a bit. At first, every sound I heard, I tried to peg to somethin' I recognized from over there." He jerked his chin in a vague easterly direction, even though the places he meant were much farther than that. "Helicopters, engines, distant booms. Took time to relearn how to hear cows bellerin' and wind in trees and not think it was coverin' somethin' else up."

He glanced at her, just once. "Didn't help that this place got a different kind of quiet right after my dad died. House didn't sound the same without him coughin' in the next room."

She thought of her own small apartment in Denver, the thin walls, the neighbors whose arguments had become an accidental soundtrack to her insomnia. She couldn't quite imagine silence feeling wrong. But she could imagine the shape of someone not being there where they always had been, and how that absence might hum.

"I'm sorry," she said. The words felt small, but they were all she had.

He shrugged, but it wasn't dismissive. More an acknowledgment that grief didn't need commentary. "It's been a few years."

"Still," she said. "I'm sorry."

He didn't say thank you, exactly. But he dipped his head once, a small concession.

The breeze picked up, carrying the scent of dry grass and distant manure up the hill. Somewhere farther down, one of the cows lowed, a drawn-out complaint about some thing or another. Gus barked once, sharp, then again from near the barn.

Emma tucked a strand of hair behind her ear and shifted her weight on the gentler slope of ground, the toes of her sneakers digging into dust. The notebook under her arm felt heavier now, full not just of her own lines but of everything she wasn't writing down.

"How long have you been back?" she asked, trying to keep her tone light enough that he could ignore it if he wanted.

"From the Army?" He rubbed his thumb along a nick in the wood of the fence post, the gesture more about having something to do with his hands than actually studying the damage. "Been… what, Hank'd say six years now? Give or take. Came home after my second deployment when my dad's cancer started gettin' bad. Stayed." His mouth twitched. "Place has a way of makin' it hard to leave again once it gets hold of you."

"Like kudzu," she said.

He gave her a questioning look.

"Climbing vine," she explained. "From the South. It takes over everything if you're not careful. I did a story on invasive species once."

"Sounds about right." A sliver of humor returned. "Land'll grow on you like that if you let it. It'll choke you too, if you don't learn how to say no to it once in a while."

"Have you learned to say no?" she asked.

His gaze drifted out over the pasture. The silence that followed that question was a different kind than before, not empty, but filled with thoughts he wasn't handing her just yet.

"Work in progress," he said at last.

She smiled, recognizing the phrase. "Same."

They fell quiet for a moment, both looking out over the field as if they'd coordinated it. The cows closer to the barn were silhouettes now, black shapes against the brightening orange near the horizon. The sky had dragged its colors up higher, blues deepening, the first faint star daring to appear before the rest.

From this angle, the mountains were less jagged, more like the backs of sleeping animals. She wondered how many times he'd watched sunsets from this exact spot, how many fence posts here had been set by his father's hands, his grandfather's.

"You ever think about doing something else?" she asked quietly. "Other than… this?" She swirled her pen to encompass the fence, the fields, the chore list she imagined lived behind his eyes.

He didn't answer right away. His hand went to the top wire again, fingers testing the tension like he couldn't help himself.

"Used to," he said. "When I was in high school, thought about goin' to school for mechanical engineering. I liked takin' things apart, figurin' out how they fit together." His mouth curved faintly. "Didn't love the 'sittin' in one place' part of that plan, though."

"And then you went into the Army instead," she said.

"Seemed like the thing to do," he said. "Needed to get off the ranch, see somethin' beyond this valley. My dad understood, even if he didn't say so plain. Figured I'd do my time, come back if it made sense. Or not."

"But you came back," she said.

"I came back," he echoed. "Place needed me. He needed me. And once you've spent enough time in places that don't care if you live or die, land that does starts to look pretty good."

She studied his profile as he spoke, the way his eyes moved over the hills as if he were reading something written there that she couldn't see.

"What about you?" he asked, shifting the attention. "You always know you wanted to write?"

"Pretty much." She let out a breath. "I was the kid who stayed in from recess to finish her story about the heroic hamster. My parents thought it was a phase. Then high school newspaper happened, and suddenly I was staying late to lay out pages and pick headlines. College paper. Internships. Then I blinked, and I'd been at the Denver paper for six years."

"You're good at it," he said. It wasn't a question.

"Yeah." The word came out flatter than she meant. "I mean, I'm good at the job. Deadlines, sources, fact-checking. I can make a story sound important even when it's really about zoning laws."

"Zoning laws can ruin a man's day," he said, dry.

She smiled. "Spoken like someone who's had a run-in with the county board."

"Couple times," he said. "They like their rules. I like my land. We have… discussions."

She could imagine those discussions: him in a button-down shirt that still didn't quite hide the calluses on his hands, sitting at some ugly laminate table under fluorescent lights, the disconnect between his world and theirs humming like faulty wiring.

"Anyway," she said, dragging herself back to her own train of thought, "I kept telling myself I'd write the Big Book Someday. Capital B, capital B. But there was always something. One more story. One more special project. One more breaking-news situation that made fiction feel frivolous."

He made a quiet sound that acknowledged both the excuse and the truth in it.

"And then," she went on, "I realized I was thirty-one and my entire identity was wrapped up in being 'good at the thing that's slowly draining me.' So, I asked for the summer off." She gestured toward the cabin. "And here we are."

"Here we are," he agreed.

The wind shifted, carrying a cooler edge now that the sun was sliding toward the jagged line of peaks. Emma shivered, goosebumps rising along the bare skin of her forearms.

He noticed. "You need a jacket," he said. It came out more like an observation than an order, but there was a note of concern under it.

"I'm fine," she said automatically.

He gave her a look that clearly said he'd heard that line before from other people in other contexts. "You'll be fine with a jacket," he said. "Mountains cool off fast once the sun dips. Last thing you need is a summer cold because you were tryin' to prove something to nobody."

Her instinct to bristle softened when she realized there was no judgment in it, just practical experience. She glanced down at her T-shirt, then back at the cabin.

"I'll… go grab one in a minute," she conceded.

He nodded, satisfied, and turned back to the fence, checking another section with a quick, practiced motion.

The familiarity in the exchange surprised them both. For a beat, it felt like the kind of conversation people had after weeks of knowing each other, not two days. There was an ease there, small but unmistakable, that hadn't quite been earned yet and so made both of them warier than they might admit.

Emma shifted her notebook from one arm to the other. "Do you ever get tired of fixing the same things?" she asked. "Fences, troughs, engines. The work that's never really done?"

He thought about that.

"Yeah," he said finally. "Sometimes. You fix one thing and two more break. Or you put in a day on somethin' and a storm rips it apart in ten minutes." He gave the wire a final pluck. "But there's somethin' about seein' the result with your hands. You tighten a fence; you can lean on it and feel it hold. You mend a pipe, water flows again. You don't always get that kind of clear cause and effect elsewhere."

"Like in a war zone," she said quietly.

"Like in a war zone." His voice was flat for a moment. Then he shrugged. "Or in a city hall. Or a newspaper. Lotta words flyin' around, not always much you can point to and say, 'I did that, and it made this difference.'"

She thought of countless articles she'd written that had landed with a splash and then vanished under the next wave of outrage or apathy. It had all mattered, on some level, she believed that. But the tangible impact had been harder to see than a mended fence.

"Sometimes I think that's what I'm jealous of," she admitted. "You get to see what your effort does. I get to see a spike in page views and maybe an email from someone who's mad I misquoted their favorite restaurant's hours."

He considered her, his expression unreadable for a beat.

"Page views don't keep cows in," he said. "But words stick in people's heads longer than fences stay up, if you're doin' it right."

"Not sure if that's comforting or terrifying," she said.

"Depends on what you're puttin' in there," he said. "With any luck, three pages of genius and five of crap averages out to worthwhile."

She smiled, genuinely. He had a knack for cutting through her spirals with plain language.

The sun kissed the peaks now, a thin line of blazing orange along their edges. The sky above them deepened into a richer blue, the first true stars appearing, bolder than the earlier tentative one. Shadows lengthened along the fence, the wires now dark lines against the warm glow.

Emma hugged the notebook closer to her chest, more for warmth than modesty, though both felt relevant suddenly. The air had that sharp edge that warned of how fast the temperature could drop once the sun disappeared entirely.

"You should get that jacket," Caleb said, more gently this time.

She nodded. "I will. Before your bulls decide I'm a popsicle."

"Bulls are down in the lower pasture," he said. "But there's coyotes who'll complain if they hear you chattering your teeth all night."

"Wouldn't want to upset the wildlife," she said.

He wiped his hands on his jeans, then slid the gloves back on. "I'm gonna finish this stretch while there's still light. If you're walkin' back up, watch your step. Ground's uneven right there by that mesquite." He pointed with his chin at a small shrub she hadn't even registered as separate from the rest.

She looked where he indicated and realized the dip in the ground beside it would indeed be an excellent ankle-twisting trap in dimmer light.

"Thanks," she said. "I'd hate to go back to Denver and tell everyone I broke my leg on day two of my grand adventure."

"You'd have a hell of an icebreaker at parties," he said.

"Assuming I ever go to parties again," she said.

He didn't respond to that, but something in his eyes suggested he understood the sentiment more than he'd say.

She took a step back from the fence, then another, giving him space to return to his work. The pull to linger a few minutes longer, just to watch him move, to listen to the soft sounds of metal and leather and evening, was there, undeniable and new.

She ignored it. Slow burn, not wildfire, she reminded herself. She hadn't come here for a man. She'd come here for herself. Anything else, if it happened, would complicate a plan that was wobbly enough as it was.

"Good luck with the fence," she said, retreating toward the cabin.

"Good luck with the book," he answered.

The words, simple as they were, chased her up the hill.

On the porch, she turned once, just before stepping inside.

Down below, Caleb was bent over the wire again, silhouette outlined against the last flare of sun. He looked like part of the land, like one of the fence posts set deep into the earth, holding a line that might otherwise give way.

She went inside and closed the door softly, more to keep the chill out than to cut off the view.

Behind her, the cabin exhaled its own kind of quiet. The table by the window waited, the laptop lid closed, the pages she'd written that day safe in their digital folder. The notebook in her hand, held scribbled metaphors and half-formed thoughts, the edges of something that hadn't yet decided what shape it wanted to be.

She set the notebook down, pulled a sweatshirt over her head, and stood at the sink, washing her mug. Through the small window, she could see the fence line still, a darker stripe against the slope. A man who'd spent his twenties in loud, dangerous places was out there mending a barrier that would keep his cattle in and, perhaps, his own history in check.

Up here, a woman who'd spent her twenties chasing other people's stories sat down to try, again, to write her own.

The moment between them at the fence, that brief, unexpected chill and warmth all at once, hung in the air like the last smear of gold on the horizon. Both of them had felt the tug of it. Both of them, for now, stepped back.

Outside, the sun slipped fully behind the mountains. The sky turned to deep cobalt, then ink. Stars punched through. High Meadow Ranch shifted into night, fences holding, hearts holding their own lines for a little while longer.

Chapter Five
The Mentor, the Past

By the third morning, Emma realized she'd fallen into a kind of orbit.

Wake up with the sun bleeding around the curtain edges. Make coffee. Open the laptop. Wrestle words until her brain felt like chewed gum. Walk to the creek when the sentences got too sticky. Come back, write a little more. Watch, from a distance, as Caleb and Hank moved through the day in arcs that made more sense than anything she was putting on the page.

High Meadow had its own gravity. She could feel it tugging on her, rearranging the map of what mattered and what didn't.

By late morning that day, the tug took the shape of a thought: You should probably learn where you can walk without getting lost or accidentally trespassing.

Hank had mentioned a map in the kitchen drawer. She'd glanced at it, but lines and labels on paper weren't the same as putting boots on dirt and finding the turns for herself. Besides, she'd been telling herself for two days that she should go say thank you for the groceries they'd stocked in the cabin.

And, if she was being honest, part of her wanted to see the ranch up close, not just from the hill. The barn, the house, the little world that had built the man fixing fences at sunset.

She shut her laptop, slipped her feet into her sneakers, grabbed a light jacket against the lingering morning chill, and headed down the hill.

The path toward the main house followed the curve of the slope, skirting a smaller paddock where two horses grazed. One lifted its head as she passed, studying her with liquid dark eyes. She slowed, holding out a hand automatically.

"Hi," she murmured. "You're beautiful. And I have absolutely no idea what I'm doing."

The horse snuffed, then returned to pulling mouthfuls of grass, apparently unimpressed.

The closer she got to the heart of the ranch, the more details unfolded. The barn was bigger than it looked from the cabin, its red paint faded, the roof patched in a couple of places with sheets of newer metal that shone dull silver. A line of smaller outbuildings marched away from it, tool sheds, feed storage, a chicken coop that clucked faintly. Fences radiated in a pattern that had grown organically over years, more like tree rings than any strict grid.

The house sat a little apart from all of it, as if someone had once thought, Let's give ourselves ten yards before the work reaches the front step. White siding, a deep porch with a swing at one end and two rocking chairs at the other. The screen door stood half-open, propped by a rock, letting in air and sound.

For a second, standing at the foot of the steps, Emma hesitated. This was more than the porch of a rental cabin. This was someone's home, had been someone's home for decades. It held stories she had no automatic right to.

Then the screen door creaked wider and Hank stepped out, wiping his hands on a dish towel.

"Thought I heard city footsteps," he said. "Y'all walk different, you know that?"

She blinked. "We do?"

"Mm." He squinted at her shoes. "More… careful, like you're always expectin' a skateboard or an open manhole to jump out at you. Country folks are too tired to be that cautious all the time."

She laughed, the sound easing some of the tightness in her chest. "I'll try to develop a more confident stomp."

"Don't rush it. We'll ease you in." He nodded toward the porch. "Come on up. You lost, or just sightseein'?"

"A little of both," she admitted, climbing the steps. "I wanted to ask about hiking trails. And also, to bug you for more of whatever coffee you stocked in the cabin, because it's saving my life."

"Ah, priorities." Hank's eyes crinkled. "We take caffeine seriously around here. Come on in. I was about to put on a fresh pot anyway."

Inside, the house smelled like coffee, old wood, something savory that had soaked into the walls from a hundred dinners. The kitchen was the kind that hadn't been remodeled in a long time, not because no one cared, but because everything worked well enough that replacing it seemed frivolous. Oak cabinets scarred in places, countertops that bore the faint ring-shaped ghosts of innumerable mugs. A round table sat in the center, covered in a vinyl cloth printed with fading blue checks.

Hank moved around the space like he'd been born to it. Coffee tin, filter, water. The clink and whoosh and drip of the machine were as much background music here as scanners and ringing phones had been in Emma's newsroom.

She perched on a chair, fingers tracing the pattern on the tablecloth.

"Caleb's out?" she asked, hearing, and hating, the casual tone in her own voice.

"Down checkin' the south pasture," Hank said. "He'll be back in an hour or so, dependin' on how contrary the herd's feelin'. They get ideas as the day goes on." He glanced at her. "You need him for somethin' particular?"

"No," she said too quickly, then softened it. "Just curious how far it is to town on foot, in case my car decides to explode."

"Town's a ways to walk unless you're real dedicated," Hank said, amused. "Seven, eight miles depending how you go. Fine for a day-long hike, not so fine if you're carryin' groceries. We got better options than you hoofin' it with milk and eggs."

"Okay, no hero hikes to the grocery store," she said. "I was mostly thinking of shorter trails. Somewhere I could go without falling off a cliff or trespassing into someone's yard."

"There's plenty of land you can wander without gettin' shot at," Hank said dryly. "We ain't that kind of country."

He fished a folded sheet of paper out of a drawer and spread it on the table. It was a hand-drawn map of the ranch and its immediate surroundings. The lines weren't perfectly straight, but they were confident, this hill here, that creek there, a little X where the cabin sat.

"Your place is up here," he said, tapping the X. "House and barn down here. This line here's the creek trail. You've found that already from the tracks on the bank."

Emma flushed, absurdly pleased that he'd noticed. "Yeah. It's my new thinking spot. Or non-thinking spot."

"Good spot for both." His finger traveled farther. "This way here, you follow the creek down until it feeds into Cottonwood Run. That's a longer walk. If you cross here," he indicated a bridge marked by two short lines, "you'll hit a trail that loops back around toward town if you keep goin' long enough. That's for days when you've got time and cell service enough to call if you twist an ankle."

"Got it," she said, leaning in. "And the ones I should absolutely not take unless I have a guide dog and a helicopter?"

"That'd be this ridge here." He traced a line up into the drawn mountains. "Beautiful, but the trail's rougher. Drop-offs, loose rock. I don't recommend it until you've got your mountain feet under you. And even then, I'd feel better if you took someone who knows where the ground disappears."

"Noted," she said. "I'll save the dramatic vistas for book two."

He chuckled, then poured coffee into two chipped mugs and set one in front of her. The liquid was dark and smelled like it had been roasted by people who believed caffeine was a moral imperative.

"So, you really plannin' on walkin' all over my map there?" he asked, settling into the chair opposite her.

"Some of it," she said. "Depends how much time I can carve out without feeling like I'm cheating on my own schedule. I promised myself mornings for writing. Afternoons for… not staring at a cursor until my brain melts."

"That's a good promise," Hank said. "Gotta let your mind stretch its legs as much as your body. Else they both cramp up on you."

She sipped the coffee, grateful for the heat and the steadying bitterness. Her gaze drifted back to the map, then up to the window over the sink, where a slice of the pasture and fence line was visible.

"How long have you been here, Hank?" she asked. "On this ranch, I mean."

He wrapped his hands around his own mug, considering.

"Long time," he said. "Walker place was one of the first I hired on to after I got outta my own dumb youth. Your age, as a matter of fact." His eyes twinkled. "Thought I knew everything back then. Turned out I didn't know the difference between a sick cow and a tired one. Cal's daddy set me straight on that real quick."

"Caleb's dad," she said. "What was he like?"

Hank's expression shifted, the humor softening into something more reflective.

"Tom Walker was a good man," he said. "Hard, when he needed to be. Stubborn as a fence post in frozen ground. He and this land were tied up in each other so tight, sometimes I wondered which one was keepin' which alive."

Emma could see it, a little: a younger version of Caleb's build, maybe, back straight, hands callused from the same work.

"He grew up here too?" she asked.

"Born in that back bedroom," Hank said, nodding toward the hallway. "So was Caleb. Three generations of Walkers under this roof." He smiled faintly. "Tom used to say you could hear the land in the floorboards if you listened right. I thought he was full of it until I'd been here a few years."

Omniscient memory slid over the present like a second layer.

A boy, small and solemn, trailing after a larger man across a frosted pasture. The boy's legs work hard to keep up, his breath puffing in quick clouds. The man slows his stride without making a show of it, letting the distance shrink.

"Hands out of your pockets, Cal," Tom calls back over his shoulder. "You trip with your hands stuffed in there, you're gonna eat ground face-first, and your mama'll tan both our hides."

The boy dutifully pulls his hands free, fingers reddened by cold. He reaches out to run them along the rough top of a fence post as they pass. The wood bites into his palm, grounding and solid. He likes that feeling. Likes the way his father's footsteps leave prints in the thin layer of snow and how his own smaller ones slot into them.

Later, there's the smell of coffee and bacon in the kitchen, the radio playing some old country song, his mother humming off-key as she flips pancakes. Tom sits at the table, ledger open, brows furrowed as he compares numbers, making the same kind of mental list his son will one day make without even realizing the habit started here.

The house is full, in those days, of voices and clatter. Of worry, sure, the ranch has never been easy, but also of laughter, arguments over nothing, plates set down with affection and frustration in equal measure.

"He loved that boy more than he knew how to say," Hank murmured, drawing Emma back. "Tom wasn't much for fancy talk. He'd show you more than he'd tell you."

"Caleb said he understood when he left for the Army," Emma said. "Even if he didn't say it plain."

"He did," Hank said. "Tom came sittin' out on this very porch the day the recruiter dropped Caleb off from the little station in town. Watched that boy drive away to go be a soldier." Hank's gaze went distant, to a spot somewhere beyond the wall. "Didn't say much. Just… sat. Tilted his chair back like he always did when he was thinkin' hard. Then he said, 'Well. There he goes.'"

"Just like that?" she asked.

"Just like that," Hank said. "But his knuckles were white on the armrests. I thought he was gonna break the wood. Later, when we were out fixin' a trough, he said more. Said he was proud the boy wanted somethin' for himself besides the ranch. Said he'd always worried he'd pinned too much hope on his only kid stayin' put." He paused for a beat. "Said he'd rather have a son who left and lived his own life than one who stayed and resented him for it."

Emma turned that over. It didn't quite match the narrative she'd been building unconsciously, that Caleb had come home to please a father who expected it. Maybe the reality was more complicated. Most things were.

"Caleb said his dad asked him to keep the ranch going," she said.

"He did," Hank agreed. "Toward the end. When the doc finally gave it a name they couldn't fix. That's a different kind of conversation, though."

He stood to refill their mugs, giving himself something to do while the air thickened with old memory.

Omniscient memory unspooled again.

Hospital light is a strange thing. Too bright and too flat all at once. It turns everyone the same shade of pale.

Tom lies in a bed that looks wrong for him, his broad frame too big for the rails, the gown gaping along his collarbones. The man who used to hoist bales one-handed now has to catch his breath after shifting an inch. The oxygen cannula looks like an insult.

Caleb sits in the visitor's chair, elbows on his knees, hands wrapped around each other so tightly his knuckles creak. He's still got the Army cut then, hair shorter on the sides. There's sand in the seams of his duffel bag, dust from another continent still clinging to his boots. He came straight from one kind of war into another without enough time to switch gears.

"Should've left things in better shape for you," Tom rasps, voice frayed.

"They're fine," Caleb says automatically. "Everything's... we're okay."

Tom gives him a look that says he knows a comforting lie when he hears one. "The roof leaks. South fence is a mess. Price of feed's gone up twice this year. Don't blow smoke at me, son."

Caleb's throat works. He can call indirect fire on a radio, he can shout orders over gunfire, but he doesn't know how to do this. There's no drill for watching your father's body betray him.

"I'll fix it," he says finally. The words come out rough. "I'll fix what I can."

Tom's hand, big, veined, too slender now, reaches for his wrist. His grip is still surprisingly strong. "Don't you break yourself tryin' to fix everything," he says. "Keep the place alive. That's all I'm askin'. Don't let 'em carve it up. Don't let it die easy."

He closes his eyes then, breath whistling. It's Hank who's in the doorway, watching, who sees the way Caleb ducks his head, just once, like the weight of that promise has settled on his shoulders physically.

Back in the kitchen, Hank set the coffee pot down with a small clink.

"Your daddy ever ask you to promise somethin' when you weren't sure you could keep it?" he asked.

Emma thought of her own father, certain lectures that had felt like prophecies. Be careful. Don't waste your gifts. Don't settle.

"Not like that," she said softly.

"Tom did," Hank said. "He meant well. He wanted Caleb to feel trusted. Wanted him to know the place was his if he wanted it." He sat again, his old joints making a faint protest. "Didn't mean to lay the whole weight of three generations on that boy's chest, but that's what it felt like."

"How old was Caleb?" she asked.

"Thirty," Hank said. "Young enough to still figure himself out. Old enough to know what losing a parent really means."

Emma wrapped her hands around the mug, letting the heat soak into her palms. "And he stayed."

"And he stayed," Hank echoed. "Came back early from that last deployment. Packed up his life in a couple of days. Moved back into his old room like he'd never left, only now he was the one takin' care of the man who'd taken care of him."

Another memory, from above and within.

Night again. The house is quieter now that hospital equipment has taken over what should have been living room space. Hank sleeps on the couch some nights, so he can help with lifting, with turning Tom so he doesn't get sores.

In the kitchen light, Caleb stands at the sink, rinsing out a basin. There's a damp towel over his shoulder; the front of his T-shirt smudged with something he doesn't want to identify. He moves with the careful, self-conscious efficiency of someone who's trained to put on tourniquets but never to tuck a pillow under a neck gently.

His father dozes in the other room, the TV on low. Some game show blinks colors across the wall.

"You're doin' fine," Hank says quietly from the doorway.

"Feels like I'm fumblin' everything," Caleb mutters. He sets the basin down harder than necessary. Water sloshes. "Out there, if I screw up, there's a manual. A chain of command. Someone else to blame. Here, it's just…" He doesn't finish.

"Here, it's just love," Hank says, not unkindly. "Messy, sloppy, no-instructions love. You're allowed to fumble that. Your daddy knows you're tryin'."

Caleb grips the edge of the sink. His shoulders shake once, just once. It could be a shiver. It could be a sob. He straightens before it can become more.

"He looks smaller," he says, voice low. "He was never small."

"All men look small in hospital beds," Hank says quietly. "Doesn't mean they are."

The funeral comes on a bright, cold day when the mountains feel too sharp against the sky. The church in town is full, the pews crowded with faces from every chapter of Tom's life, ranchers in clean boots, county officials in pressed suits, the lady from the diner who'd always had his coffee ready.

Caleb stands near the front, hands clasped in front of him, jaw set. He wears a suit that doesn't quite fit in the shoulders, like he's still growing into the space his father used to occupy. People shake his hand, murmur, "He was a good man," over and over until the words blur.

Outside, at the graveside, the wind cuts through his coat. Hank stands beside him, a solid presence, while the pastor says things about dust and life and eternity. Caleb watches the casket lower; his father's name carved into the polished wood.

Keep this place alive.

The words echo louder than the pastor's. Louder than the breeze in the pine trees at the edge of the cemetery.

He doesn't cry until later, alone in the barn. It's an ugly, quiet thing, shoulders hunched, hands braced on a stall door. The horses shift nervously, picking up on grief they don't understand. Gus, still a pup then, noses at his boot, whining.

"It's all right," Caleb tells the dog, voice ragged. "We're all right."

He's half trying to convince himself.

Back in the kitchen, Hank took a slow sip of his coffee, eyes focused on a knot in the table wood.

"First calvin' season after Tom passed damn near broke him," he said. "We'd always had at least two sets of hands, Tom and me, sometimes a hired boy or two. That year it was just me, him, and a dog with more enthusiasm than sense."

"What happened?" Emma asked.

"Same thing that always happens," Hank said. "Cows got themselves in trouble. Weather turned rough at the wrong moment. One heifer had a calf comein' breech in a snow squall. Took us hours to get the little fella out, then longer than that to get him breathin'."

Memory once more.

Snow whipping sideways across the yard, the world reduced to white and gray and the shapes immediately in front of them. The barn is a dim refuge, breath from cows and men steaming in the cold air.

Caleb's arms ache from effort, from reaching in and twisting, following Hank's calm instructions. "Easy now. That's it. Turn him just so. Don't fight the contractions; work with 'em."

The calf finally slides free in a slippery rush. For a terrifying second, the small body lies still, too limp. Then Hank is there with straw, rubbing hard, while Caleb clears the tiny nostrils with rough, practiced motions he learned in a hurry.

"Come on, little man," he mutters. "Come on."

The calf coughs once, then draws a shuddering breath. A weak bleat follows. Relief hits so hard it buckles Caleb's knees. He sits back hard in the straw, mud and birth fluid soaking into his jeans.

Hank chuckles, exhausted. "There you go," he says to both of them. "Told you we could do it."

Later that night, when the barn is quiet and the snow piles up against the doors, Caleb makes another list in his head, not of tasks, but of moments like this that his father used to weather without apparent effort. The realization that he has survived one of them without his dad's presence cracks something open: grief, yes, but also a strange, sharp pride.

He is, against his own fear, capable.

Emma listened, the pictures forming with an ease that surprised her, calves and storms and grief all living alongside each other under the same roof.

"How old was he then?" she asked. "When his dad died."

"As near as I recall, thirty," Hank said. "World still flexible in some ways, not so much in others."

"And you were here the whole time," she said.

"As much as he'd let me be," Hank said. "Boy's got a streak of 'do it himself' so wide you could drive the tractor down it. Got that from his daddy, too."

Emma smiled faintly. She could see that, how Caleb had waved off her thanks for the water with a shrug, how he'd been almost offended at the idea she might walk alone in the cold without a jacket. A man who wanted to take care of things, even when he wasn't sure how.

"Does he ever..." She trailed off, unsure how to frame it without sounding nosy. "Talk about any of this? With you?"

"Sometimes," Hank said. "In his own way. We don't sit around havin' heart-to-hearts like we're on one of those daytime shows. We talk in between fixin' things. That's how men like us are built." He gave her a knowing look. "He's told you somethin' already, hasn't he?"

"Just that the land was the only place that made sense after the Army," she said. "And that quiet meant something different over there."

"That's more than he tells most folks," Hank said. "You must've asked good."

"I wasn't really... asking." She stared into her coffee. "He just... said it."

"Then you were listenin' good," Hank corrected. "People can tell when they're bein' listened to for real."

Her journalist brain filed that away with a tiny sting. How many times had she listened with half her mind thinking about word count and deadlines? How often had she been there with a recorder but not with her whole self?

"Does he mind..." She gestured around the kitchen, up toward the cabin. "Having me here?"

Hank smiled, a corner of his mouth lifting. "If he minded, you wouldn't be. Caleb's not shy about sayin' no when he needs to. He might grumble about the cabin rental idea in general, but he said yes to you. That's somethin'."

"He didn't have much choice," she said. "You'd already listed it."

"Nah," Hank said. "We had a couple inquiries before you. He turned 'em down. Didn't like the looks of 'em. Didn't like the way they talked about 'experiencing the rustic lifestyle' like we're a theme park."

Emma choked on a laugh. "Oh God. I can imagine. 'Do you have any cows I can milk for my Instagram?'"

"Exactly." Hank pointed a finger at her. "You came askin' if you could get some quiet. If the Wi-Fi would be strong enough for you to work but not so strong you couldn't escape it." His eyes softened. "That told him enough."

That he'd chosen her, her request, her words, for this space settled over her with surprising weight. Not romantic, not yet, but personal in a way that made the cabin feel less like an anonymous rental and more like a shared project.

"I don't want to be in the way," she said quietly.

"You're not," Hank said. "You're a light on the hill." He shrugged, almost embarrassed by his own phrasing. "Place feels less lonely with a window lit up, up there in the evenings. Makes it feel like there's more life than just us and the herd."

Emma remembered the first night, seeing the house's porch light from her cabin, how it had reassured her. Funny to think the reverse was true too.

She cupped the mug, fingers tracing a chip near the rim.

"Hank," she said, choosing her words carefully, "I know I'm new. And I don't want you to tell me anything that isn't mine to hear. But I… I'd like to understand him. A little. Not to write about. Just," She groped for the right term. "For context."

"Context," Hank repeated, amused and thoughtful at once. "You can take the girl out of the newsroom…"

She flushed. "Guilty. Occupational hazard. I like to know how things got to where they are."

"Nothing wrong with that," he said. "Long as you remember a man's past is his to share. I can tell you what I've seen from my chair, but that won't tell you everything. Might even tell you the wrong thing, if you squint at it from the wrong angle."

"I understand," she said. And she did. She'd seen enough lives flattened in print to be wary of making that mistake herself.

He studied her for a moment, weighing something only he could see. Finally, he nodded.

"What I'll say is this," he said. "Caleb is not just a grumpy rancher. He's a man who's had more weight set on his shoulders than most fellas carry by his age, and he's still standin' under it. Sometimes he stands a little crooked. Sometimes he forgets he's allowed to set some of it down. But he's not just the scowl you see when the weather report's bad."

A smile tugged at her lips despite the seriousness in his tone. She had seen that scowl once already, when he'd come in muddy and tired the second morning and looked at the sky like it had offended him personally.

"He got his heart broken once," Hank added, more gently. "That'll make a man cautious about showin' what's underneath the work and the fences. Doesn't mean there's nothin' there. Just means it's precious to him."

Emma's pulse stuttered at that, even though it wasn't as if she hadn't guessed.

"High school sweetheart?" she asked, trying for neutral.

"Yeah," Hank said. "They grew up together. Thought they'd build a life on this land, once upon a time. World had other ideas."

"What happened?" The question came out before she could stop it. She winced immediately. "Sorry, that's,"

"Curiosity," Hank said. "Part of who you are. Nothin' wrong with it." He took a sip of coffee, buying himself a second. "Best I can say without strayin' into gossip is, she wanted somethin' else. More road, less fence. More airplane windows, fewer sunrises over the same hill. I don't begrudge her that. World's big, and some people feel smaller if they stay in one place too long."

"And Caleb…" Emma prompted softly.

"He came back from seeing too much of the world," Hank said simply. "Wanted one place that didn't change every five minutes.

Somewhere he could walk a line he knew." His eyes met hers. "Two people wantin' opposite things. Neither of 'em bad, but hard to reconcile."

The way he framed it, no villains, just mismatched needs, settled something in her. It painted a picture of a younger Caleb she could almost see: hopeful, tired, maybe trying to hold onto both duty and love and finding his hands too full.

"He ever talk to you about it?" she asked.

"Bits and pieces," Hank said. "Most of what I know, I saw. You can tell a lot about a man by how he mends what's left after somethin' breaks."

"And how did he mend?" she asked.

"He worked," Hank said. "Harder than he needed to, sometimes. Like if he could just fix every broken hinge and leaky pipe, he'd fix the ache in his chest too." He tilted his head. "He also didn't date much after. Kept to himself. That part worried me more than the extra fence posts."

Emma's fingers tightened on the mug. She imagined that, long days, long nights, no one to share the weight with except an aging ranch hand and a dog.

"He's not shut off from the world," Hank said quickly, as if sensing where her mind went. "He's just... cautious about who, and what, he lets in. You can understand that, I reckon, if you've ever been let down by somethin' you thought was solid."

Emma thought of the newsroom, the way it had once felt like a family and then, slowly, more like a machine. Of the relationships she'd let drift because deadlines had seemed more urgent than dinners. Of the way the city she loved had started to feel like it was squeezing her instead of holding her up.

"Yeah," she said quietly. "I can."

They sat with that for a minute, sharing a silence that wasn't empty.

Somewhere outside, a truck engine turned over, then shut off. Boots thudded on the porch. Caleb's voice, faint through the wall, spoke to Gus, the dog's answering bark enthusiastic.

Hank glanced toward the doorway, then back at her.

"Point is," he said, lowering his voice just a hair, "you're gonna see him in a lot of different lights while you're here. The man who reminds you to wear a jacket, the one who scowls at clouds, the one who can sit on a horse like he was born there, the one who maybe stares off at the hills like he's somewhere else entirely. All of that's him. None of it is the whole him."

"And you're telling me this because…" she prompted, though she thought she knew.

"Because I like you," Hank said bluntly. "And I like him. And I think it'd be a shame if you took one look at his rough edges and decided that was all he was. He doesn't need you to fix him. He's not some broken project for a big-city girl to work on over the summer. But he's worth seein' clear, if you're inclined to look."

Emma's throat tightened. No one had ever put it to her quite that way.

"I'm not here to fix anyone," she said. "God knows I can barely fix my own plot holes."

"I believe you," Hank said. "Just… keep your eyes open. For him, for yourself. This place has a way of showing you things you weren't lookin' for."

Journalist curiosity, the part of her that had always leaned forward when someone said, "You want to know something?", stirred. But the itch was different now. It wasn't about angles or headlines. It was about wanting to know how a man like Caleb Walker came to exist in the particular shape he did, and what it meant to share a summer on his land.

Bootsteps approached the kitchen. Hank straightened, the subtle shift of a man switching gears.

"Speak of the devil," he murmured.

Caleb appeared in the doorway, filling it. His hat was in his hand this time, hair damp with sweat at the temples, shirt darkened down the spine.

He took in the scene with a quick flick of his gaze, Emma at the table, Hank with the coffee pot, the map spread out between them. One brow lifted a fraction, the only sign of surprise.

"Didn't know we were havin' a council meetin'," he said.

"Every good government's got a journalist involved somewhere," Hank said cheerfully. "Emma here was askin' about trails. I was just tellin' her where she can and can't break her neck without supervision."

"Appreciated," Caleb said. His gaze lingered on the map, then on Emma. "You plannin' on runnin' off to the back forty already?"

"Not without a guide," she said. "Just wanted to know where my jurisdiction ends."

"Your jurisdiction," he repeated, a little amused.

"The part where I'm allowed to wander around talking to myself without spooking your cows," she clarified.

He huffed softly. "You talk to yourself; they'll just figure you're one of us. We all do that after a few weeks out here."

Hank stood, patting the table. "I'm gonna go start supper. You two can argue about jurisdiction all you want."

He left them there with the map and the coffee and the soft echo of his stories hanging in the air.

Emma felt the weight of what she'd just heard and what she wasn't going to say about it. It made her look at Caleb differently, not as just the man on the horse, or the one tightening fence wire, but as the kid in boots trying to match his father's stride, the soldier in a suit at a graveside, the son bending under promises and still standing.

"Thanks for the coffee," she said to Hank's retreating back, then looked up at Caleb. "And for the map. I promise not to trespass into any neighboring states."

"Appreciate that," Caleb said, stepping closer to glance at the paper. His finger traced one of the lines Hank had shown her. "If you're lookin' for a good afternoon hike, this loop here's your best bet. Follows the creek most of the way, not too steep. Good views."

"You sound like a brochure," she said.

"I sound like a man who's had to go lookin' for lost calves in all of these spots," he said. "Trust me, I know which ground will roll your ankle and which won't."

Journalist curiosity stirred again, this time directed at him. She wanted to ask, then why do you keep walking the ground that hurts? But that was too much, too soon, and not fair to ask in front of his kitchen table.

Instead, she pointed at the creek loop. "I'll start there. Maybe tomorrow. After I get my pages in."

He nodded, approving. "Mornings for the book, afternoons for not goin' crazy. Good system."

She blinked. "Did Hank tell you that, or are you spying on me from the barn?"

"He told me you were actually writin' in there," he said. "Said he hasn't seen anyone hunch over that table like that since his wife was doin' tax season."

Emma smiled, unexpectedly pleased by the comparison, even to something as mundane as taxes. It meant she looked like someone working. Someone serious.

"Well, I'm trying," she said. "We'll see if the words cooperate."

He looked at her a beat longer, something steady and unexpectedly gentle in his eyes.

"They will," he said.

It wasn't the casual encouragement she was used to; you've got this! You're amazing! the cotton-candy pep talks of friends who meant well but didn't understand the grind. It was a simple statement from a man who knew what it was to keep showing up to hard work with no guaranteed outcome.

She felt it land deep.

"Thanks," she said, the word thicker than usual.

Hank's voice called from the stove, breaking the moment. "Cal, you want to bring in that box of onions from the porch before the coons get ideas?"

"On it," Caleb called back.

He tipped his head toward the door. "You're welcome to stay for supper sometime, if you want a break from cookin' for one. Tonight's nothin' fancy, but there's always too much."

Her heart did something odd at the casual invitation, half flutter, half flinch.

"I don't want to impose," she said.

"Wouldn't have offered if it was an imposition," he said simply. "Hank likes a full table. Says the food tastes better when there's more people complainin' about it."

She laughed. "I'll take you up on it. Maybe not tonight, I should probably figure out how not to burn pasta at altitude first. But... soon."

"Soon," he echoed, with a small nod.

She stepped away from the table, folding the map so she wouldn't crease it wrong. As she reached the doorway, she glanced back once more at him, standing there, hat still in hand, dog nosing at his boot, the kitchen light catching on the lines around his eyes that hadn't been there ten years ago.

Her curiosity burned, yes. But it was more than that now. It was a quiet, growing desire to know the whole of him, not just the edges he showed by default.

Outside, the air hit her cooler, cleaner. She tucked the map under her arm and started up the hill toward the cabin; the stories Hank had given her threading themselves into the landscape as she walked.

The path seemed different now. Each fence post, each patch of grass, each outbuilding had a ghost version overlaying it, Tom's boots on the step, a younger Caleb's laughter in the yard, hospital silence behind thin walls, Hank's steady presence in all of it.

The ranch wasn't just a scenic backdrop anymore. It was a living, breathing thing, built out of generations of effort and sacrifice and small joys.

And up there, in her little cabin at the edge of it all, Emma Hall sat down at her table with her notebook and her laptop and the knowledge that the man who owned this land was not just a quiet shadow moving along fence lines.

He was a story. Not one she'd been assigned, not one she had any right to write without him. But one she was slowly, carefully, starting to read.

Chapter Six
First Real Connection

The car chose late afternoon to die on her.

It had been one of those days where the hours slid by quietly. Emma had kept her promise to herself, wrote all morning, a good solid chunk of words that didn't feel entirely like garbage. After lunch, she'd walked the creek loop Hank had shown her on the map, following the water's lazy curve through cottonwoods and scrub before it funneled into a narrower cut in the land.

By four o'clock, sun still high but the air easing off its midday edge, she decided she should probably do the responsible thing and go into town. She was running low on fresh fruit, the cabin's milk was an optimistically dated half-gallon, and if she didn't check in with Kelsey and her parents soon, someone was going to call the sheriff.

So, she packed reusable bags into the backseat, grabbed her wallet and keys, and headed for the car with the faint, practical satisfaction of an adult who is Doing Life Things.

The sedan sat in its customary patch of dirt beside the cabin, dustier than it had been when she arrived but otherwise unremarkable. She slid into the driver's seat, tossed her bag onto the passenger side, and stuck the key in the ignition.

Turned it.

Nothing.

No thrumming engine, no coughing attempt to start. Just a muted click and a disheartening silence.

She tried again, because that's what you do when machines defy you. Key out, key in. Turn.

Click.

"Come on," she muttered, leaning her forehead briefly against the steering wheel. "Don't do this to me."

She listened. The dash stayed blank. No feeble glow, no error messages. Just dead plastic.

Battery, her brain supplied. Great.

She sat back, exhaled, and looked around as if someone might materialize to hand her jumper cables. The cabin's porch was empty. The slope down to the barn was quiet, though she could hear, faintly, the clank of something metal and Gus's far-off bark.

Emma bit her lip. In the city, she would have called roadside assistance, grumbled about the wait, maybe snagged a latte while the tow truck threaded through traffic. Here, her phone sat on the console showing one sad bar of service that winked out when a cloud drifted in front of the sun.

She tried dialing the number on the rental agreement anyway. The call failed twice before it even connected.

"Of course," she said to the empty car. "Of course this is how we're doing things now."

She checked the time: 4:17. Plenty of daylight left, but she imagined herself hiking into town laden with grocery bags after dark and shuddered.

All right. Different plan.

She took a breath, grabbed her keys and phone, and climbed out. The air hit her cheeks cooler than it had at noon. Down the hill, near the barn, she could see the faint shape of a truck parked half in shadow.

Caleb or Hank would know what to do. Of course they would. Jump-starting a car was probably a basic life skill out here, like knowing how to read the sky for weather or which part of a cow to avoid if you valued your kneecaps.

She just had to go ask.

The walk down felt longer than usual. Not in distance, but in the way, embarrassment stretched it. She'd only been here a few days and she was already showing up needing help. City girl can't manage her own car, news at eleven.

The barn doors were open, the interior lit by a mix of daylight and the dim glow of a single hanging bulb. The smell hit her first, hay, manure, motor oil, a hint of leather. Gus trotted out to greet her, tail wagging, then circled back to hover at her side as if escorting her in.

"Hey, buddy," she murmured, giving the dog a quick rub behind the ears. "Take me to your leader."

The leader in question was near the far end of the barn, half under the hood of an old tractor. Caleb's legs and boots were visible, braced apart. The rest of him was bent over the engine, hands deep in unseen machinery. A radio somewhere hummed low, more static than song.

"Hank?" she called, before she could chicken out.

It was Caleb who straightened, wipe rag in hand. He turned, caught sight of her, and removed the rag from where it had been draped over his shoulder.

"He's run into town," he said. "What's up?"

Up close, he smelled faintly of grease and sweat and something sharper, maybe the solvent he'd been using. His shirt sleeves were rolled above his elbows, the skin of his forearms streaked where he'd wiped them on his jeans instead of the rag. There was a smudge of oil near his temple, just beneath the line where his hair fell.

Emma's brain, traitorously, noticed all of that before it remembered why she'd come.

"My car," she said, then winced at how dramatically that came out. "It. Um. It's not starting."

He frowned, automatically slipping into assessment mode. "You have gas?"

"Yes," she said with dignity. "I stopped on the way up here. It's the… it won't turn over. Just clicks."

"Battery." He said it like a diagnosis. "You leave your headlights on?"

"I don't think so," she said, though now she doubted everything. "I haven't driven it since I got here. Maybe I left a dome light on? Or it's old. Or the car hates me."

He wiped his hands more thoroughly and reached for his hat on a nearby hook. "Let's go take a look."

He moved past her, long strides eating up the path up the hill. She had to hurry to keep pace, her shorter legs working harder.

"These rental cars sit for a while sometimes," he said as they walked. "Batteries go weak. Cold nights don't help."

"It was fine for twenty minutes on the highway," she said. "Now it chooses to die when I want groceries. Very on-brand."

"You try callin' the rental company?" he asked.

"I did. Phone gave up before they did." She held up the device. "Our friend the single bar is not cooperating today."

He grunted, which she interpreted as agreement with her assessment of their fickle overlord, cell service.

When they reached the cabin, he went straight to the car, sliding into the driver's seat without ceremony. He turned the key once, listening. The same disheartening click, the same stubborn silence.

"Yep," he said, stepping out. "Battery's flat."

Because he couldn't help himself, he flicked the headlight switch to Off, making sure, then checked the interior lights. Everything seemed in order.

"Could be it was weak when you got it," he said. "You only drove a few hours. Sometimes that's not enough to make up for sittin' on a lot for weeks."

She felt absurdly vindicated. "So, I didn't kill it?"

"Not all on your own," he said. The near-smile that ghosted over his mouth took the sting out of the words. "We'll jump it. You can go into town, let it run a bit. If it dies again after that, then we'll talk about callin' for a new battery."

"Okay," she said, relief loosening something between her shoulder blades. "What can I do?"

"Stay out of the way of the cables," he said. "Other than that, just… hang tight."

He jogged back down the hill, Gus trotting after him. Emma watched him go, then watched herself in the reflection of the car window, cheeks pink from exertion and embarrassment. She made a face. "You are a competent adult," she told her glass twin. "You just… specialize in different competencies."

She waited on the porch, notebook in hand more out of habit than intention. The sky had started its slow shift toward evening, light angling lower. The air was soft, with that dry crispness that promised a cooler night.

Within minutes, Caleb reappeared in his truck, the old green one she'd seen rumbling around the ranch. He pulled alongside her sedan, noses nearly touching, and cut the engine. Gus hopped out and circled the vehicles, tail wagging, as if supervising.

Caleb hopped down, grabbed a set of heavy jumper cables from behind the seat, and flipped open the truck's hood with a practiced motion. He popped the sedan's hood next, propping it open with the thin metal rod.

"You ever done this before?" he asked, glancing at her.

"Watched a YouTube video once," she said. "Does that count?"

"Not for this," he said dryly. "YouTube's full of folks who'd hook these up backwards and then act surprised when their battery explodes."

He spoke as he worked, clipping red to positive, black to negative, in the correct order, double-checking each connection. His movements were steady, unhurried. Not a performance, just a man doing a thing that needed doing.

"There's a sequence to it," he said. "Clamps on the good battery first, then the dead one. Last thing you wanna do is get these crossed and give yourself a light show."

"I'm all set on fireworks," she said. "Had enough of that covering New Year's Eve three years in a row."

He gave a quiet grunt that might have been a laugh, then stepped back from the tangle of cables.

"Okay," he said. "Stand clear. I'm gonna start the truck, let it run for a minute, then you try yours. Don't turn your key until I say. You don't want a surge when it's not ready."

She obeyed, standing a safe distance away with her hands stuffed into her jacket pockets, feeling vaguely like she was supervising a medical procedure.

The truck rumbled to life easily, engine settling into a low, steady idle. Caleb listened for a second, gauging the sound, then nodded to himself.

"All right," he said, raising his voice a bit over the engine. "Give yours a try."

Emma slid into the driver's seat, heart thumping more than the situation warranted. She wrapped her fingers around the key and turned it, half expecting another lifeless click.

The car coughed, sputtered, then caught, the engine roaring louder than usual before settling.

"Yes," she breathed. "Thank you, automotive gods."

She glanced up and caught Caleb watching through the windshield, his expression more satisfaction than surprise. He held up a hand, wait, then uncoupled the cables in reverse order, moving carefully, making sure the clamps didn't touch.

When everything was safely apart and the hoods were closed, he stepped to her open window.

"Let it run," he said. "At least fifteen, twenty minutes. Better yet, drive into town. Don't shut it off until you're done shoppin'. When you park, find a pull-through space if you can, just in case we gotta deal with it again."

"You speak fluent Car," she said, impressed.

"Just enough to get by," he said. "Like my Spanish."

That piqued her curiosity. "You speak Spanish?"

"Enough to order dinner and get chewed out by Dr. Morales when I don't give her all the details about a cow," he said. "Learned some overseas. Learned more from the vet."

She filed that away, another unexpected facet.

"Thank you," she said, more serious now. "Really. I would've been up here googling 'how to fix a dead battery without tools' until dark."

"You'd have found fifty videos and none of 'em as useful as walkin' down to the barn," he said. "You don't have to solve everything yourself out here."

The words hit a little too close to a lesson she'd been avoiding for years.

"I'm… working on that," she said.

He studied her for a second longer, then stepped back. "Text Hank when you're headed back uphill," he said. "Just so someone knows where you are if the car decides to play dead again."

She nodded, then rolled the window up enough to start backing out. As she turned the car toward the lane, she glanced once at the rearview mirror.

He was standing beside his truck, watching her go, one hand resting lightly on the hood as if feeling the vibrations. Gus sat at his heel, ears pricked.

It wasn't until she'd crested the first small rise and the cabin and barn dropped out of sight that she realized her heart was still beating a touch faster than it should be for such a short sprint.

Town proved an easy drive once she got past the initial anxiety. Cottonwood Ridge was exactly what it had promised from the diner windows the other day: small, practical, quietly charming. She hit the grocery store, grabbed basics, milk, eggs, bread, a handful of vegetables, pasta, a jar of sauce. On impulse, she added a pack of chicken breasts and a bag of rice. She didn't know what she was going to do with them yet, but the idea of cooking something real, not just microwaving a frozen burrito, appealed more out here.

She kept the engine running while she loaded bags into the trunk, then drove a slow loop around the town square before heading back. No warning lights appeared. The car seemed, for the moment, to have forgiven her.

By the time she turned onto the ranch road, the sky had started its drift toward evening again. Long shadows stretched from fence posts and boulders. The mountains glowed in layers, gold at the base, purple-tinged near the peaks.

Her cabin came into view, snug on its rise. The relief that washed over her at the sight of it surprised her with its intensity, like she was coming home rather than returning to a temporary rental.

She parked, this time leaving the hood alone but listening carefully as she turned the ignition off. The engine settled into silence with no ominous clicks.

Groceries made three trips: two for the bags, one for her dignity as she nearly tripped over Gus, who had appeared mid-unloading to sniff everything with enthusiasm.

"Hey," she scolded lightly. "You're not getting the chicken. That's for humans."

"That depends on how she cooks it," a voice drawled from the porch steps.

She looked up, startled; to see Caleb leaning against the rail, arms crossed loosely over his chest. He'd changed his shirt sometime between the barn and now; this one was clean, a soft plaid that had seen better days. His hair was damp, as if he'd showered off the day's grit. The smudge of oil near his temple was gone.

"How long have you been lurking?" she asked, more breathless than the situation warranted.

"Long enough to make sure you made it up the hill," he said. "Hank made me promise not to let you vanish into the canyon if the car died again."

"Car behaved, for once," she said, lifting the last bag. "Small miracles."

He moved forward, taking the bag from her without fanfare. It was the heaviest one, weighed down by milk and fruit.

"You don't have to," she started.

"I'm right here," he said simply. "Might as well use the arms God gave me."

It was so matter-of-fact that arguing felt foolish. She followed him inside, watching as he set the bag on the counter with the same care he'd used on the battery cables.

"You got enough for an army," he observed, glancing at the spread as she unpacked.

"I panicked," she admitted. "My city brain went, 'You're ten miles from the nearest restaurant, buy everything.'"

"You forget we got a diner and a general store," he said.

"I didn't forget," she said. "I just… wanted to see if I could feed myself without takeout boxes."

He leaned a hip against the counter, watching her arrange eggs in the fridge door, stack cans in the cupboard.

"You know how to cook?" he asked.

"I can follow instructions," she said. "And my mom made sure I wouldn't starve alone. I'm not a gourmet, but I can turn raw chicken into something vaguely edible."

"That's a valuable skill out here," he said. His gaze flicked to the clock over the stove. The hands pointed to just after six. "You eaten yet?"

"No." She straightened, closing the fridge. "I was going to throw something together. You?"

"Had lunch." He shrugged. "Been too busy since."

She hesitated, then heard herself say, "I was thinking of making… something. Pasta, maybe. Chicken. There'll be plenty. Do you…" Her voice trailed off as nerves caught up. "I mean, if you have work,"

"I've always got work," he said. "But it'll still be there after supper."

The way he said it made her suspect that was a relatively new philosophy.

"So… that's a, yes?" she asked, heart picking up.

He nodded once. "If, you're sure. Cabin's your space. Don't want to intrude."

"You saved my car," she said. "The least I can do is feed you subpar pasta as thanks."

"Sold," he said.

Cooking for someone else added a new layer of urgency to the process, but it also made it feel less like a chore and more like an event. She filled a pot with water, set it to boil, then sliced chicken breasts on the small cutting board, aware of his presence at the edge of her vision.

He didn't hover, exactly. He moved around the cabin with a kind of contained restlessness, checking the window, rubbing Gus's ears when the dog flopped down in the doorway, scanning the books on her shelf without picking any up.

"Can I help with somethin'?" he asked eventually, watching her wrestle with a stubborn jar lid.

"You can use your farm-boy strength on this jar," she said, handing it over.

He took it, twisted once, and the metal seal popped with a satisfying sound.

"Show-off," she murmured.

"Just years of openin' feed bags and medicine bottles," he said. "Pasta sauce is easy compared to those."

She tossed the chicken pieces into a skillet with a blob of butter and a sprinkle of salt and pepper. The sizzle filled the small kitchen, the smell of browning meat making her stomach growl.

"Don't expect anything fancy," she said. "My capabilities plateaued at 'barely adult' when I started working nights. I used to live on newsroom pizza and bad coffee."

"Newsroom pizza sounds rough," he said. "Smells good in here, though."

"It's the garlic powder," she said. "It tricks your nose into thinking you know what you're doing."

He set out plates without being asked, finding them easily. They settled at the little table by the window once she'd piled their plates with pasta, chicken, and sauce. The sun was lowering, but there was still enough light to see the pasture slope outside, tinted gold. She flicked on the overhead lamp anyway, the warm spill of it cozying up the small space.

"This looks good," he said, picking up his fork.

"Wait until you taste it," she said. "Appearances can be deceiving."

He twirled a forkful, took a bite, and chewed thoughtfully. She watched him, ridiculously anxious for his verdict.

"Not deceivin'," he said after swallowing. "You won't starve."

"High praise," she said, but the relief that loosened her shoulders was real.

They ate in companionable quiet for a few minutes, the clink of silverware and the distant sound of cattle mingling with the low hum of the fridge. Gus sprawled under the table, ever-hopeful.

"So," Caleb said eventually, setting his fork down for a moment, "tell me true. Are you missin' the city yet, or are you still in the honeymoon phase?"

She wiped a bit of sauce from her lip with her thumb, considering.

"I miss the good coffee shop on the corner," she said. "And Thai food. And being anonymous in a crowd sometimes. But…" She glanced out at the land, the way the hills folded into each other. "I don't miss the sirens. Or the traffic. Or the way my phone would light up at three a.m. because something horrible happened and we needed a headline."

"That's your job?" he asked. "Rollin' out of bed to write about bad things?"

"Not always," she said. "But often enough. Fires, accidents, scandals. People doing awful things to each other. Eventually it starts to feel like the world is nothing but that. You know it's not true, logically, but your nervous system doesn't care."

He nodded, eyes dropping to his plate. "I get that."

She traced the rim of her glass with her finger. "We did good work sometimes," she added. "Stories that mattered. Corruption exposed, funds raised, missing people found. But for every one of those there were ten pieces of… filler. And lately, it felt like my life was just an endless loop of other people's crises."

She sighed, the sound carrying more weight than she'd intended. "I got really good at telling everyone else's story. And really bad at noticing I didn't actually have one of my own."

He looked up, studying her face in the lamplight.

"What do you mean?" he asked quietly.

"I mean," she said, searching for words, "I can write a profile that makes you feel like you know someone you've never met. I can pick the right quote, the right detail, to make a reader care. I've spent years amplifying other people's moments. But if you'd asked me six months ago what my moments were, I would've pointed to my bylines like they were enough. And then I realized they weren't."

Her thumb moved back and forth along the glass, catching a bead of condensation.

"There was this night," she went on, surprising herself with the memory. "About a year ago. We had a story break late about a hit-and-run. Whole family in the crosswalk, driver didn't stop. I wrote the piece. Talked to the cops, tracked down a neighbor, found some old photos of the victims online. It was awful and heartbreaking and I did what I always do, I tried to make it human, make people feel something beyond rubbernecking."

She paused. He waited.

"I filed at midnight, grabbed a slice of cold pizza from the newsroom break room, and then I went home to my apartment and watched reruns of some dumb sitcom until I fell asleep on the couch. Next morning I woke up, went back in, and did it all again. And I remember standing at my kitchen counter that morning, staring at the coffee maker, thinking, 'Is this it? Is this my life? Bearing witness to everyone else's worst day and then going home to leftover pizza?'"

The confession hung between them, raw and oddly freeing.

"And now?" he asked.

"Now I'm up a mountain in a cabin on a ranch I do not understand," she said, a wry smile tugging at her mouth. "Trying to write about people who don't exist, who might be more real than I've let myself be. Trying to figure out if I can be good at writing about a life and living one at the same time."

He absorbed that, leaning back slightly, chair creaking.

"I used to think the ranch would give me that balance," he said after a moment. "Work and life all in one place. Didn't realize for a while that it could also swallow everything else up if I let it."

She tilted her head. "Swallow how?"

He gestured vaguely toward the window and beyond, where the land lay in softening light. "There's always somethin' that needs doin' out there. Fence down, calf sick, water line clogged. Sun up to sun down, you can fill your day with tasks that are important and never know who you are outside of 'em."

His eyes dropped briefly to his hands, fingers rough and nicked, resting around his fork. "The ranch is… an anchor," he said. "Keeps me from driftin' off into places I don't need to be. Gives me somethin' solid to push against. But sometimes it feels like a cage too. Like if I step too far away, the whole thing'll collapse and it'll be my fault for lettin' go."

She thought of the promise to his father, the hospital room Hank had described, the weight of Keep this place alive.

"Is that why you don't go into Denver much?" she asked softly.

He huffed out a breath that wasn't quite a laugh. "News travels."

"Hank," she said.

"Hank," he agreed. "Man talks more than he thinks he does."

"He cares," she said. "About you. About this place."

"I know," Caleb said. "He's earned the right to clip his opinions to my ear."

He glanced at her, then back at his plate.

"I don't like cities much anymore," he admitted. "Too many people. Too many things outta my control. Noise that isn't mine. I go when I have to, vet conferences, supply runs if we can't get somethin' shipped, that kind of thing. But I'm counting the minutes until I'm back past the last traffic light."

"How many minutes?" she asked, a hint of teasing in her voice.

He considered. "'Bout thirty, if I'm bein' honest. Last trip I took in, I broke out in a sweat tryin' to find parking."

"Parking will do that to you," she said. "I thought I'd have a panic attack the day I tried to park downtown during a Broncos game."

He smiled, small but more present than the ghosted versions she'd seen before. "I believe it."

She twirled her fork, pushing pasta around more than eating it now.

"It's funny," she said. "You came back here because the world was too much. I came out here because the world felt like not enough, somehow. Too many people, not enough… me, in my own life."

"It can be both," he said. "Too much and not enough. Depends on what you're lookin' for."

"What are you looking for?" she asked before she could stop herself.

He sat with that for a moment, gaze drifting to the window, where the light had gone from gold to a deeper amber.

"Depends on the day," he said finally. "Some days I'm lookin' for nothin' more than a calvin' season without a disaster and enough money in the bank to pay the feed bill. Some days I remember I'm thirty-six and think maybe that shouldn't be the only thing on the list."

He rubbed a thumb along a nick in the table's edge, a gesture she'd seen him use on fence posts, tractor fenders, anything that bore the scars of work.

"I thought I had it figured out once," he said. "Thought I'd have a family here by now. A wife, kids growin' up under the same sky I did. That plan went sideways."

He didn't elaborate, and she didn't push. The shape of the missing fiancée already hovered at the edges of their shared story. Filling in the details without his say-so would have felt like a betrayal.

"But you still want that," she said gently. "Some version of it."

He was quiet long enough that she thought he might dodge the question.

"Yeah," he said finally, voice low. "I do. I won't pretend I don't. But wantin' it and knowin' how to get there from where I'm standin' are different things. Hard to invite somebody into a life that's this… tethered. Harder still to tell where the line is between takin' care of what my dad built and lettin' it own me."

She watched him, the way his mouth flattened, not in anger but in thought.

"I don't think it has to be one or the other," she said quietly. "You or the ranch."

He looked at her, brows slightly furrowed. "And you'd know that how, Miss 'I Only Know How to Write About Other People's Lives'?"

She smiled, rueful. "I don't. Not really. I'm just… extrapolating."

"Big word," he said. "Impressive."

"Thanks, my student loans are thrilled," she said.

The joke loosened something between them. The heaviness of the conversation didn't vanish, but it shifted, the sharpest edges dulled.

They finished the meal in a more comfortable quiet. When they were done, he reached automatically for their plates, stacking them, moving toward the sink.

"You cooked," he said. "I'll rinse."

"You don't have to,"

"Emma." His tone was gentle but firm. "Let a man do the dishes."

Her name in his mouth did something odd to her heartbeat. She surrendered the plates.

They fell into an easy rhythm. He rinsed and stacked in the rack; she dried with a dish towel that had definitely seen better years, cotton thinning at the edges. The cabin felt smaller with both of them moving around in it, not in a claustrophobic way, but in that way, spaces do when they're suddenly full of more than one person's energy.

At one point, they reached for the same glass. Her hand closed over his for a second, warm, callused skin under her fingers.

The contact was brief, but it sent a small, unwelcome jolt up her arm. She sucked in a breath at the same moment he stilled.

He didn't yank his hand back. He didn't make a joke. He just… paused.

For a heartbeat, the world narrowed to the square foot of space where their fingers touched and the faint sound of water dripping from the faucet.

She looked up. He was already looking at her.

The air shifted. The lamplight seemed warmer, her awareness suddenly acute, the curve of his mouth, the darker stubble along his jaw, the flecks of lighter brown in his eyes she hadn't noticed before. The way his shoulders seemed broader at this distance.

There was a beat, a full, suspended second where every story she'd ever consumed about moments like this flared to life in her head. The lean-in, the luminous first kiss, the neat narrative arc of two people moving closer because of shared vulnerability.

Her breath caught. His thumb twitched under hers.

Then, almost imperceptibly, he eased his hand out from under hers, transferring the glass to her grip.

"Careful," he said. His voice was a fraction rougher than before. "It's slippery."

Reality snapped back, a bit too loudly. The faucet dripped again. Gus sighed under the table.

She swallowed. "Right. Wouldn't want to break your only wine glass."

He huffed something that might have been a half-laugh, stepping back, deliberately putting more space between them.

"I should… get goin'," he said after a beat, wiping his hands on the towel. "Got an early start tomorrow. Fence check down by the river before it gets too hot. And Hank'll be wonderin' if I fell into a ditch."

She nodded, fingers tightening around the glass she was now undeniably responsible for.

"Thank you," she said, the words covering more ground than just jumper cables and dishwashing. "For the car. For dinner. For… listening."

He met her gaze briefly, something almost rueful in his eyes.

"Right back at you," he said.

They moved toward the door together. He grabbed his hat from the hook where he'd hung it, settled it on his head with a practiced tilt. On the threshold, he paused, one hand on the frame.

"If that car gives you trouble again," he said, "don't sit up here worryin' about it 'til midnight. Call. Or walk down. I can't fix everything, but I can fix a battery."

"I will," she said. "I promise."

He studied her for a second, as if gauging whether she meant it, then nodded.

"Night, Emma."

"Good night, Caleb."

He stepped off the porch, Gus bounding ahead of him. She watched as he walked down the path, his figure gradually dissolving into the deepening shadows. The last of the sun caught his shoulders, his hat brim, before the dusk took over.

Inside, the cabin felt different in his absence. Not emptier, exactly. Just… aware of the shape he'd left behind.

She finished drying the dishes slowly, replaying the evening in her head, the quiet competence under the hood of the car, the way he'd listened without flinching when she talked about burnout, his admission about the ranch being an anchor and a cage. The almost-moment at the sink, the way her heart had lurched, the way he'd stepped back.

He'd chosen distance. For now. Gone before the impulse to close that space could turn into something neither of them was ready for.

In the house down the hill, Caleb closed the door behind him and leaned against it for a second, eyes shut.

He could still feel the ghost of her fingers over his, the echo of her words in his head. Only good at writing about other people's lives, never living her own. It had hit something in him he didn't have language for.

Gus nudged his leg, whining softly, sensing the odd vibration in his person.

"I know," Caleb muttered, giving the dog's head a rough rub. "Don't look at me like that."

He moved into the kitchen, the familiar clutter a comfort. He rinsed his own solitary mug in the sink, listening to the quiet of the house. The ranch was the same as it had been that morning. The same as yesterday. The same as the day before that.

And yet. A cabin light on the hill, a woman with ink on her fingers and questions in her eyes, had shifted the axis of his little world just enough that he noticed.

Up there, she sat at her table, opening her laptop again, fingers hovering over the keys. A different kind of story waited for her now, not just the one she was writing, but the one she was starting to live.

They had shared a meal, a conversation, a near-mistake and a conscious choice not to make it yet.

Slow burn, the universe seemed to murmur. Slow.

Outside, the Colorado sky deepened into star-pricked navy. High Meadow Ranch settled into night, fences holding, hearts keeping their own uncertain but deliberate distance, for now.

Chapter Seven
Ghost of the Ex

The bell over the diner door jangled the way it always did, too cheerful for a place that saw as many tired ranchers and shift workers as tourists.

Caleb stepped inside, boots thudding lightly on the worn linoleum, and paused just long enough for his eyes to adjust from the hard midday light. The smell wrapped around him familiar as an old jacket: coffee that had been sitting a little too long on the burner, bacon grease embedded in the walls, a hint of bleach from a recent pass with the mop.

Cottonwood Ridge's lone diner hadn't changed much in the years he'd been coming here. Same cracked red vinyl booths, same laminated menus printed with old photos of the town in black and white. Same pie case up front, glass slightly fogged, three uneven slices of something that claimed to be apple waiting on chipped plates.

The lunch rush had ebbed, leaving only the usual handful of locals and a pair of tourists arguing softly over a map at the corner table. The air hummed with low conversation and the occasional clink of silverware.

"Hey there, Walker," called Jenna from behind the counter. She'd been pouring coffee in this diner since he was in high school, her ponytail gone a little thinner over the years but her voice just as bright. "You're late today. I was startin' to worry I'd made too much chilli."

"Truck needed a tire," he said, sliding onto a stool at the counter. "You know how it is."

"Those ruts down near the river'll eat rubber for breakfast," she said, shaking her head. "You want the usual?"

He hesitated. The usual, burger, fries, iced tea, sat heavy on an already long list of afternoon chores. He thought of the fence line he still needed to walk, the pump that had been making a noise he didn't like.

"Just soup and a sandwich," he said. "And coffee."

"Livin' wild," Jenna teased. "You want today's soup or yesterday's?"

"What's yesterday's?" he asked.

"Chili," she said.

"Chili's not soup," he said.

She shrugged. "Around here it's whatever I write on the board. Tomato today. You'll survive."

"Tomato, then," he said.

She topped off his mug while he shrugged his jacket off. The first sip was hot and bitter in a way that woke him up rather than offended him. He let his shoulders drop, just a fraction, as his body recognized the space as something like neutral ground. Not the ranch. Not the house full of memories. Just somewhere in between, where he could be a man at a counter instead of the sum of every obligation.

Back home, the day had started early. He and Hank had been out before sunrise checking the south pasture, eyes adjusted to the gray-not-quite-light that concealed as much as it revealed. A calf had looked off; they'd separated him and called Dr. Morales. The vet had promised to swing by later, casual in tone but precise in her questions. After that, there had been a water line to clear and a meeting with the feed rep who'd driven out in a dusty SUV full of samples and caveats about prices.

A trip into town had been inevitable. Tractor part from McGinn's, a deposit at the bank, mail to pick up at the post office. He'd thrown the diner in as a concession to his own human needs.

Jenna slid a paper placemat in front of him, then set down a bowl of tomato soup that still steamed and a plate bearing a grilled cheese sandwich oozing just enough to promise satisfaction without scalding.

"You hear the news?" she asked, leaning on the counter for a moment.

He lifted his spoon cautiously. "'Bout the county fair?" he guessed. "Saw the flyer."

"Not that," she said. "Though we're always lookin' for contestants for the pie-eatin' contest, if you're interested."

"Pass," he said. "What news?"

She glanced down the counter, then back at him, lowering her voice just enough to signal gossip rather than public announcement.

"Walker girl's back in town," she said.

It took him a beat to realize she didn't mean his family. In that pause, the world kept moving. Someone laughed over by the window. A fork scraped a plate. The tourists folded their map.

Jenna watched his face, probably waiting for the reaction she expected: surprise, curiosity, some shade of interest.

He managed a noncommittal, "Oh?"

"Yep." She nodded, savoring the tidbit. "Saw her mama at the post office this mornin' and she said Abby's home for the summer. 'Visiting family' is the phrase she used. Which I take to mean she's recoupin' from whatever fancy life she's got out there now."

The name landed with a dull thud somewhere under his breastbone. Abby.

For a moment, the diner blurred at the edges.

He hadn't said her name out loud in a long time. Hadn't had to. People in town knew enough not to bring her up around him often. When they did, it was usually carefully, the way you mention a storm that knocked down your barn years ago, you acknowledge it, nod at the damage, then move on.

"That so," he said, managing to keep his voice level.

Jenna, misreading his composure as indifference or inviting, went on. "Her folks are tickled. Said she might be stickin' around a few weeks at least. Get a break from all that traveling." She topped off his coffee again, even though he'd barely taken two sips. "You run into her yet?"

"Nope," he said lightly. "Been out at the ranch, same as always."

"Well, you know this town," she said. "You can't sneeze without someone you know handin' you a tissue. She'll show up here sooner or later. Probably wantin' pancakes." She smiled fondly at some memory. "Girl could eat her weight in pancakes in high school."

He knew. Saturday mornings, back when life had been simpler and the future had been an untested thing, they'd have taken up a whole booth over there by the window. Abby's laughter had bounced off these walls, her boots hooked around his ankles under the table. Jenna had brought extra syrup without being asked.

"Guess folks do come back," Jenna said, more to herself now. "Even the ones who swore they'd never look at another cow again."

Caleb managed a small, noncommittal sound. He didn't trust his tongue with full words yet.

Someone called Jenna's name from the far end of the counter. She glanced that way.

"Anyway," she said, patting the edge of his placemat with a familiarity that was almost maternal. "Eat your sandwich before it gets cold. You look like you missed breakfast."

"I didn't," he said.

"You look like you did," she replied, then moved away to refill someone else's cup.

He sat there, spoon hovering over his soup, as his heartbeat thudded in his ears.

Abby's back.

The information rearranged the room. Suddenly, every shadow might be her. Every laugh might belong to that voice he'd once have picked out of a crowd of a hundred.

He hadn't seen her in… four years? Five? Time blurred around that break in his life the way it did around the years he'd deployed. Before and after. Clean lines. Messy transitions.

The spoon dipped. He brought it to his mouth on autopilot. The soup tasted like it always did, a little too tangy, a little too salty, but he barely registered it.

Memory was a cruelly efficient thing when it wanted to be.

High school hallways that smelled like floor wax and adolescent chaos. He's seventeen, she's sixteen, her hair pulled back with a bright scrunchie that doesn't match her shirt. They lean against lockers between classes, stealing minutes they shouldn't have. Her laugh comes easy; his doesn't yet, but it does around her.

"Promise me you won't get stuck here forever," she says one afternoon, eyes bright as she stares out the window at the football field. "The world's so much bigger than Cottonwood Ridge."

He shrugs; hands stuffed in his pockets. "My whole world's right here."

She swats his arm, though he can see the smile she's trying to suppress. "You know what I mean. Don't you want to see something else?"

He looks at the mountains, the sky, the long sweep of pasture beyond the school. "I do," he admits. "I just... don't hate the idea of comin' back to it, that's all."

Later, it's prom night. He's uncomfortable in a suit, but she looks like every bright dream he's ever had in a dress that shimmers when she moves. They dance in the gym under paper stars that don't catch the light the way her eyes do. At some point, he forgets to be self-conscious about his two left feet.

Then graduation comes and goes. The recruiter's pamphlets on his desk. The ranch ledger on his father's kitchen table. Abby sitting cross-legged on his bed, flipping through a travel magazine.

"Paris," she says, tracing a picture of the Eiffel Tower. "Rome. Tokyo. I want to see all of it. I don't care if I have to backpack or wash dishes or sleep in hostels. I just... I don't want my whole life to be the ten-mile radius around this town."

He lies beside her, shoulder to shoulder, staring at his ceiling. "I could get on board with seein' some of that," he says. "But I still like the idea of comin' back."

"Of course you do, ranch boy," she teases, rolling onto her side to look at him. "You're rooted."

"So are you," he says. "You just don't know it yet."

When he signs his enlistment papers, she's there, quizzing the recruiter more than he does. After boot camp, they grab those diner pancakes every weekend he can get home, savoring the pockets of normal in between stretches of sand and steel.

He proposes under the old cottonwood near the north pasture, the one that still stands, gnarled and stubborn. She laughs and cries and says yes, yes, of course, and they spin in the cold air, breath visible, future a blur of overlapping plans: she'll finish her degree in Fort Collins, he'll get stationed stateside eventually, they'll figure out the geography as they go.

Then deployments come. One, then another. The phone calls get shorter when they can get through at all. The gap between what he's seeing and what she is widens in ways they don't know how to bridge. He comes home on leave older than his years, sleep sanded down, eyes checking exits automatically when they sit in crowded spaces.

She leans into his shoulder in the diner booth, fingers tracing the edge of his sleeve where a tan line marks where his watch usually covers. "I hate who the Army makes you," she admits once, eyes full of conflict. "I hate that it takes you away. I hate that you flinch in your sleep now."

"It won't be forever," he tells her, voice low. "We'll get through it. Then we can pick up where we left off."

She looks at him then with a tenderness that already has farewell in it, though he doesn't see it at the time.

Then his father gets sick. The calls back home take on a different tone. Hank's emails mention doctor appointments and tests and "nothing you need to worry about yet," which of course means exactly the opposite.

By the time he gets permission to come home early, the prognosis is clear in everyone's eyes even if they dance around, it with words.

He's home in his childhood bedroom, duffel bag still smelling of dust and sweat from halfway across the world, when Abby comes by with a casserole dish she didn't make and a face that's been thinking too many thoughts.

They sit on the porch steps while the sun sinks behind the hills, his father's voice faint in the house as he laughs at something on TV with Hank.

She reaches for his hand. "Cal," she says gently, "you know I love you."

He exhales, tension he's been holding since he stepped on the plane home easing a fraction. "I know," he says. "I love you too."

Her grip tightens.

"I don't think I can be your wife right now," she says.

He feels the words before he understands them. Like someone's pulled the gravity out from under his feet.

"What?" he says, eloquent as ever.

"You're... you're here but you're not," she says, eyes filling. "You're halfway over there and halfway at the hospital and halfway at the ranch and there's not much left for you. Or for us. And soon your dad's gonna... and you're gonna be pulled even tighter. Into this place. Into all the things it needs."

"I can manage it," he says, jaw clenching. "People do this. They have families and take care of their parents and farms and everything else. It's not,"

"I don't want to be an 'everything else,'" she says softly. "I don't want to feel like the thing you're failing at, at the end of the day because you just don't have anything left."

He stares at her. "That's not what,"

"And I don't want to stay," she says, the words coming faster, as if ripping off a bandage. "Not forever. Not the way you do. I thought maybe I did, once. But... I want to go. To see things. To be somewhere where my whole self isn't wrapped up in this town and this land and this house." She gestures vaguely at all of it. "I want to belong to myself for a while."

He flinches as if she's struck him. "That's what you think bein' with me would be? Not belongin' to yourself?"

"I think I don't know how to be half-in here and half-out there," she says. "And you, Caleb, you can't be half in on this ranch. You can't. It'll eat you alive if you try. Tom needs you. Hank needs you. This land sure as hell needs you. There's not room in there for… for me. Not the way I need to be."

"You want out," he says flatly. "That's what this is."

Her eyes shine. "I want… something else," she says. "And I don't think it's fair to either of us to pretend I can stay and not resent it. Or that you can leave and not resent me."

He remembers every firefight, every moment he's thought, If I can just get home to her, everything will make sense again.

Now she sits beside him on the porch and says she needs to leave so she can make sense of herself.

He doesn't yell. He doesn't plead. He's too tired for that. His father is sleeping in the next room. The ranch ledger on the table shows numbers that don't add up. His body is in a perpetual state of alert.

"Okay," he hears himself say, as if from a distance.

She blinks. "Cal,"

"If that's what you need, okay," he repeats. His chest feels hollow, like someone's scooped something vital out with a shovel. "You should go find what you need."

Tears spill over; she wipes them away angrily. "I don't want to hurt you."

"You don't get to not," he says quietly. "That's the deal when you leave."

They sit there a while longer, two kids who aren't really kids anymore, watching the sun sink behind the same hills his father has watched his whole life. Eventually she gets up, presses a kiss to his cheek that feels like a goodbye and a thank you and an apology all at once, and walks down the path to her car.

He doesn't watch her drive away. He stares at the cottonwood instead, the one that bore witness to his proposal and now to this. At some point, Hank comes onto the porch and sits beside him, silent, the way real friends do when there's nothing useful to say.

Later, she sends a letter. Then another. He writes back haltingly at first, then less often. The distance grows. Her emails fill with pictures of cities and hostels and new jobs, his with updates on his father's treatments, the weather, the price of hay. They lose track of each other's details.

By the time Tom dies, they haven't spoken in a year.

Back in the diner, Caleb stared at his soup, the surface of it trembling slightly as his hand shook.

"Everything okay, hon?" Jenna asked as she passed, a plate of fries balanced on her arm.

He forced his fingers to relax around the spoon. "Yeah," he said. "Just thinkin' about that tire bill."

"McGinn cut you a deal," she said. "He always does. Man likes his eggs too much to gouge you."

He made a sound that might have passed for agreement.

He finished the meal mechanically, tasting little. When he laid his cash on the counter, Jenna patted his arm, misreading the faint paleness in his face as fatigue.

"You get some sleep sometime this week, you hear?" she said. "Ranch'll still be there if you close your eyes for more than four hours."

"Ranch doesn't agree with you," he said, finding the familiar banter again. "But I'll see what I can do."

As he stepped back out into the bright midday sun, the bell jangling farewell behind him, the world seemed too sharp. Shadows cut harder. Colors glared.

Abby's back.

He walked to his truck on autopilot. The repair shop sat just across the street; the new tire he'd paid for earlier glinted faintly. He climbed in, turned the key, and listened to the engine rumble to life.

For half a second, he imagined seeing her here, now, walking out of one of the shops, her hair shorter or longer, her clothes different, but her presence the same. How would he feel? Anger? Regret? Relief that she looked happy? Or just that hollow scooped-out sensation all over again?

He didn't have an answer, which unsettled him more than any of the options.

Instead of turning left toward the hardware store, he turned right, pointing the truck down the road that led back toward High Meadow.

The drive home felt longer than usual. His hands were steady on the wheel, but his mind was anywhere but on the road. He forced himself to check the rearview, the side mirrors, the speedometer. Muscle memory took care of the rest.

Hank was on the porch when he pulled up to the house, a glass of iced tea sweating on the railing beside him. The older man squinted toward the truck, reading Caleb's mood the way he read weather, by the set of his shoulders, the tightness around his eyes.

"See a ghost in town?" Hank called as Caleb climbed out.

"Something like that," Caleb said, closing the door with a little more force than necessary.

Hank's gaze sharpened. "That bad, huh?"

He almost didn't answer. Then he remembered there weren't many ghosts Hank hadn't already met.

"Jenna says Abby's back," he said. The name sounded strange out loud, like he was testing whether it still fit in his mouth.

Hank's brows lifted a fraction. "Ah," he said. "That ghost."

Caleb snorted. "Apparently I'm the last to know."

"Her folks didn't call and give you a heads up?" Hank asked.

"Why would they?" Caleb said. "She's their daughter, not my responsibility." He rubbed the back of his neck. "Said she's here for the summer. Visitin' family."

"That what Jenna told you?" Hank's tone was neutral, but there was something wary in the set of his jaw.

"That's what she told the whole town," Caleb said. "I just happened to be sittin' at the counter at the time."

Hank took a slow sip of tea, giving him space to blow off steam or retreat. When Caleb didn't offer more, he set the glass down.

"How's that sittin' with you?" he asked.

Caleb shrugged, a sharp, brittle gesture. "Fine," he said. "She's allowed to come home. It's her town too."

"Not what I asked," Hank said.

He scrubbed a hand down his face, the day's stubble rasping against his palm. "I don't know how it's sittin'," he admitted. "Felt like someone kicked a hornet's nest in my chest, if you wanna know the truth. Didn't realize there were still that many in there."

Hank's gaze softened. "Time helps," he said. "Doesn't always clean everything out."

"Thought I'd done a decent job of movin' on," Caleb said, frustration edging his words. "Got my routines. Got the ranch. Got…" He hesitated. "Got a tenant on the hill who can't cook pasta half bad."

Something flickered in Hank's eyes at that, but he didn't pounce on it.

"You have moved on, some," he said. "Not movin' on doesn't always look like pining on the porch, you know. Sometimes it's just little pockets of hurt you forgot to check behind the furniture."

Caleb let out a breath that carried more than just air. "Feels like those pockets just dumped themselves out all over the diner floor."

"Then maybe it's good they got aired out," Hank said. "Better than you stepping in 'em without lookin' later."

He didn't say later when you're standin' in front of some other woman, but the implication hung between them. Caleb heard it anyway.

"I'm not gonna go lookin' for her," he said. "If that's what you're worried about."

"I'm not worried," Hank said. "You two had your path. It forked. That's life. I just don't want you borrowin' trouble if your paths happen to cross at the feed store."

"I can handle a Hello," Caleb said, though he wasn't entirely sure what that would feel like.

Hank studied him, then nodded. "All right," he said. "Just remember: you're not the same man she left. That's gonna count for somethin', whatever happens. Good or bad."

He pushed off the railing, the boards creaking. "You got that part for the tractor?"

"Yeah," Caleb said, glad for something solid to turn his attention to. "Gonna go put it on before it gets too hot."

He headed to the shed, each step grounding him more than the last. By the time he had his hands on metal again, cool, reassuring, needing things like bolts and grease instead of emotional clarity, his breathing had settled.

Work had always been his refuge. When things inside his head got too loud, he turned outward: to the list of tasks, the order of operations, the things he could fix with enough effort.

He threw himself into it now. Changed the tractor part, checked the oil, topped off the diesel, moved bales, repaired a sagging section of fence that he'd noted two days ago and bumped down the priority list. It all moved up now, because anything he could do with his hands was better than sitting still long enough for his thoughts to catch up.

From the hill, unseen, the cabin watched like a small square of light against the sky. At some point during the afternoon, Emma stepped onto her porch, notebook in hand, scanning the fields with a contented, distracted gaze. She saw the truck move past the barn. She saw one of the tractors trundle toward the north pasture. She saw Gus racing after a line of dust.

She did not see the way Caleb's jaw tightened as he worked, or the extra half second, he took to pet the dog's head, grounding himself. She didn't know the name that had been dropped into his day like a stone into still water.

What she noticed was simpler: he hadn't come by the cabin that day.

Not that he owed her that. They'd shared one meal, one strangely intimate set of confessions over pasta. That didn't oblige him to show up at her door with updates like they were tracking some shared schedule.

Still, she'd half-expected to see him at some point, if only in passing. To hear the distant murmur of his voice as he talked to Hank outside the barn, to catch a glimpse of him at the fence line. To share another small encounter, the kind that had started to stitch themselves into a pattern she couldn't quite define.

Instead, the ranch hummed at a slightly different frequency. The work continued, as it always did. But the man at the center of it had drawn in on himself, his orbit tightening.

She wrote that day, more than usual. Words poured out in fits and starts, some of them clearly fueled by something restless she couldn't name. Her protagonist reacted with disproportionate anger to a minor slight in chapter five. Emma caught it, laughed at herself, and dialed it back, but the spike of emotion had come from somewhere.

When her eyes crossed from staring at the screen, she stepped out to the porch with her notebook and scanned the sky, just to give her brain something else to look at.

Caleb was a small figure in the distance, driving fence posts in with methodical force. The repetitive motion, even at this remove, broadcast tension. He didn't look toward the cabin. If he was aware of her, he gave no sign.

She told herself she was imagining it. That he was simply busy. That this was what ranch life looked like, a man working, not a man pointedly avoiding the woman uphill.

Even the omniscient narrator saw only the practical on the surface: a day full of tasks, a man tired at the end of it, a woman whose frustrations found their way onto a page. The deeper truth, that a name from the past had reanimated old hurts, making Caleb wary of letting anyone too close while those ghosts rattled their chains, is not something either of them could see clearly yet.

That evening, as the sky went from blue to bruised purple, Emma walked down to the creek instead of toward the barn. She told herself she needed the sound of water more than she needed conversation. She sat on the log Hank had pointed out and watched the ripples catch the fading light, notebook closed in her lap.

Up at the house, Caleb ate supper with Hank at the oak table, pushing food around his plate more than actually consuming it.

"You gonna tell her?" Hank asked at one point, nodding toward the vague direction of the cabin.

"Tell her what?" Caleb said, feigning ignorance out of stubbornness.

"That the ghost of girlfriends past is haunting about town," Hank said. "That you might be a bear for a few days until you get your head sorted."

"She doesn't need to know my dating history," Caleb said. "She's got her own life to untangle. I'm not droppin' my mess in her lap on week one."

"She's here," Hank pointed out. "On your land. If you start actin' like someone took your favorite wrench away, she's gonna assume it's her fault."

"I'm not," He stopped, realizing how that sounded. He exhaled. "I'll... keep it together."

"Wouldn't hurt to give her a heads up that you got hit with some old news," Hank said. "Doesn't have to be a confessional. Just 'hey, if I seem off, it's not you.' Women appreciate that kind of clarity."

Caleb stabbed a piece of chicken more viciously than it deserved. "I barely know how to do that with you," he muttered. "You want me practicin' on the woman I'm tryin' not to make uncomfortable?"

Hank's brows crept up. "The woman you're tryin' not to make uncomfortable," he repeated slowly. "That's an interestin' way to phrase it."

He ignored the bait. "She's here to write," he said. "Last thing she needs is to get dragged into my ghosts. Abby's back. Fine. She's got her path. I got mine."

"Paths cross even when you don't plan 'em to," Hank said. "Town's not that big."

"Then I'll deal with it when it happens," Caleb said, the finality in his tone more for his own benefit than Hank's.

He kept his word, at least about one part. He didn't go looking for Abby. He didn't alter his routes to avoid places she might be. He simply did what he'd always done when the world inside got messy: he worked.

By the end of the week, fences that had been on the "later" list had been mended. Tools were sharpened. A section of the barn that had needed cleaning for three seasons finally met a broom. The extra effort didn't go unnoticed by Hank, who let it run its course rather than prying the shovel out of his hands.

From Emma's vantage point, none of the details that gave those tasks their emotional weight were visible. She saw only a man who seemed a little more distant than he had over pasta and confessions. A man who, when their paths crossed at the mailbox halfway between cabin and house, tipped his hat and spoke politely, but who didn't linger over small talk the way he had that night over pasta.

"How's the writing?" he asked one afternoon, leaning a forearm casually on the box while she sifted through junk mail and a package with her mother's return address.

"Messy," she said. "But words are happening. I'm calling that a win."

"Words are better than nothin'," he said.

"You, okay?" she blurted, then immediately regretted the directness. "I mean, busy week?"

He hesitated just a fraction too long.

"Yeah," he said. "Just… got some things on my mind. Nothing you need to worry about."

She nodded, accepting the answer because she had no right to do anything else. "Well, if you need someone to complain about sentence structure to, I'm your girl," she said lightly. "If it's anything useful, Hank's probably a better bet."

That got a ghost of a smile. "Duly noted," he said. "Try not to let the adverbs win."

"They're relentless," she said.

He tipped his hat and moved on, boots crunching on gravel.

She watched him go, a small line forming between her brows.

Back in the cabin, she opened her mother's package, cookies, a new notebook, a handwritten note that wove pride and worry in equal measure. She smiled, then sat at the table, pen hovering.

Under the wide Colorado sky, High Meadow Ranch went on with its business. Cows grazed. Water ran in the creek. Fences stood and fell and were mended again. A writer in a cabin and a rancher in a house moved through their days on parallel tracks, each feeling, in their own way, the presence of something unseen pushing at the edges of the life they thought they understood.

Chapter Eight
Chores and Pages

The days began to fall into a shape.

It wasn't the rigid, clock-driven pattern of Emma's life in Denver, no buzzer at six, no sprint for the shower, no train schedule, no editorial calendar pinned to an internal system. High Meadow had its own timetable, one that followed light and weather and the multiple moods of cattle.

She slipped into it gradually, like easing into a river until the current caught her.

Most mornings started the same way now. She woke with the first wash of pale light spilling across the cabin ceiling, the air still cool enough to make her toes curl when they hit the floorboards. She walked into the kitchen, started the coffee, and opened the front door while the machine gurgled and hissed.

The porch had become her office.

She took to sitting there bundled in a sweatshirt, knees drawn up, laptop or notebook balanced on her thighs, a mug steaming on the railing beside her. The sky would still be in the process of deciding what it wanted to be, thin gray at the edges, faint wash of color over the peaks, a hint of pink that might turn into a full blaze or might just fade into blue.

She started writing before her brain had time to object.

She'd discovered, almost by accident, that those first thirty minutes after waking were the quietest her inner critic ever got. Too drowsy to conjure up every reason she was a fraud, too early for emails or texts from the city, her mind felt… looser. Less barricaded.

So, she wrote. Sometimes nonsense, dialogue fragments, image scraps, lines that sounded too poetic when she looked at them later. Sometimes whole scenes arrived in one messy rush.

Her novel had slowly shifted under her fingers. The project she'd outlined in Denver had been another twisty urban thing, crime and secrets and city lights reflecting off wet pavement. Easy to sell. Easy to pitch. Safe, in that predictable way she knew the beats.

Out here, everything she'd planned had stopped making sense.

Her protagonist, who she'd named Zoe when she'd first started scribbling ideas in a coffee shop, refused to stay in the city. Every time Emma tried to place her in a high-rise newsroom with flickering fluorescent lights and a malfunctioning air conditioner, the woman walked out of the scene and onto a porch somewhere, staring at open land.

At first Emma had fought it. It felt too on the nose, too obviously stealing from her own life. But characters, like cattle and perhaps like people in general, had minds of their own. Eventually she stopped trying to drag Zoe back to the city and followed her out where she wanted to be.

The story that started unfolding was quieter than anything she'd written; plot points were less about explosions, literal or metaphorical, and more about choices that changed the shape of a life slowly rather than all at once. Scenes played out in small kitchens, in fields at dusk, in the space between two people doing a job together with their hands.

City Emma would have scoffed, a little, at the lack of "stakes." Porch Emma was starting to understand that living with someone day in and day out, weathering ordinary disasters, loving them anyway, that was a kind of high-stakes she'd rarely given space to in her work.

Between paragraphs, between sips of coffee, her gaze drifted from the screen to the world below.

Most mornings, Caleb and Hank were already moving by the time she stepped out. Tiny figures at first, framed by the barn doors or cutting across the yard. As the light strengthened, she could make out more details: the tilt of a hat, the shift of weight as they lifted something, the puff of breath from the horses in the coldest hours.

Sometimes they drove the cattle up from the lower pasture, Gus flanking the flanks, a slow-moving spill of brown and black that looked almost like a river when she squinted. The low calls they traded with each other carried up the hill faintly, indecipherable but steady. Sometimes they split up, one heading toward the pump house, the other checking fence lines.

It became a kind of moving backdrop to her mornings: cursor blinking, coffee cooling, men and animals and machines tracing the same patterns over and over in the fields below.

After a week, she realized she wasn't just watching. Her brain had begun to count on the choreography.

On the mornings when she didn't see Caleb immediately, if he was working at the far edge of the property, or if Hank had gone into town early, there was a small, stupid flicker of disappointment she refused to examine too closely. On the mornings she caught a glimpse of his truck heading toward the south pasture, that disappointment turned into something else, not quite relief, but a sense that the day was starting the way it was supposed to.

By late morning, the sun higher and her coffee consumption at dangerous levels, she'd close the laptop, stand, and stretch until her spine protested. The work didn't stop, exactly, it just changed shape.

One of the first times she'd wandered down toward the barn after those morning sessions, Hank had looked up from where he was stacking small square bales in the older part of the hay shed and said, "You got legs and hands, don't you?"

"Yes…" she'd said warily.

"Then you're qualified," he'd grinned, gesturing to the stack. "Grab and go. Don't worry, I won't have you liftin' the big ones yet. Gotta build you up to that."

"This is your recruitment speech?" she'd asked, but she stepped forward anyway, hands hooking under the twine of the next bale.

They weren't light. Not compared to the tote bags and laptops she was used to lugging. But they weren't impossible either. Her arms strained a little as she lifted, muscles along her shoulders protesting. Hank guided her on how to turn, how to set the bale on the ever-growing stack without wrenching her back.

"Use your legs more," he'd coached. "Back's for show. Legs are for work."

By the third bale, she'd found a rhythm. Lift, step, twist, set. Lift, step, twist, set. Straw dust floated in the air, caught by the sun in shafts that looked dramatic enough to belong in a movie about noble farmers. Her T-shirt stuck to her back. Sweat collected at the base of her neck.

It felt… good.

By the time they finished that particular stack, her arms shook a little when she held them out, and there was a scratch on her forearm where a stray stalk had caught her. She sat on an upturned bucket, chest heaving, watching Hank tie down the last few bales.

"You didn't drop any," he'd remarked, impressed.

"I was too scared the needles under there would kill me if I did," she'd said, nodding at the hay hooks hanging on the wall.

Hank laughed. "Those've seen their share of clumsy hands. You did fine." He'd squinted at her. "How's your head?"

She'd blinked, thrown. "My… head?"

"Writin'," he'd clarified. "Words. You've been up on that porch for hours every mornin'. Figured your brain might be stew by now."

"Oh." She'd rolled her shoulders, feeling the ache there already settling into something almost pleasant. "Actually…" She'd frowned, thinking. "This… helps."

"Physical work?" he'd guessed.

"Yeah," she'd said slowly, surprised at how sure she was. "Somehow moving my body makes the stuck parts in my head less… stuck." She'd smiled, feeling slightly sheepish. "Who knew manual labor had artistic benefits?"

"Anyone who's ever shoveled a barn and come up with their best ideas halfway through," Hank had said. "You think the good country songs got written at desks?"

So, the pattern formed. Mornings for words. A stretch of time, afterward, for small tasks Hank or Caleb would trust her with.

She didn't ask for the work, exactly. But she stopped avoiding it. When Hank mentioned he needed an extra set of hands for something, she volunteered before her old instinct to demur could kick in. When Caleb needed someone to hold a board steady while he drilled, she found herself saying, "I can do that," instead of, "I'll get out of your way."

It started with small things.

Holding the other end of a tape measure while Caleb calculated the lumber for a repair to the chicken coop. Fetching the toolbox he'd left three feet away when his hands were full under the truck. Closing a gate behind Hank when his arms were full. Each time, a little more of the invisible line between "guest" and "temporary resident" blurred.

One afternoon, she found Hank in the equipment shed trying to wrestle a wheelbarrow full of fence posts over a small lip in the concrete. He grunted as it caught, wheels bumping uselessly.

"Need a push?" she called.

"Need a brain transplant," he said dryly. "Didn't factor in my age versus this incline."

She set her weight behind the handles, bracing her feet. Together they heaved the front end up and over. The load rolled forward into the light.

"See?" he said. "You're already earnin' your keep."

"You're going to spoil me," she said. "Denver never appreciated me this much."

"I doubt Denver had this many manual tasks," he said.

"Depends how you feel about copy-paste," she replied.

Not all her contributions were successful. There was the time she tried to help move a portable panel and nearly took herself out when she misjudged its weight, saved only by Caleb's quick grab on the other side. Or her first misadventure with a wheelbarrow, which she overfilled with manure and then had to gingerly coax up a slight incline while her arms trembled and Hank laughed from a safe distance.

"Bite off what you can chew," he'd called. "Not what'll choke you."

"I'm learning," she'd panted.

"You are," he'd agreed. "That's the important bit."

Caleb watched all this with a mixture of appreciation and wary amusement.

He didn't go out of his way to include her; that wasn't his style. But he didn't stop her when she drifted closer, either. If Hank roped her into a chore, Caleb quietly adjusted the task list so nothing truly dangerous ended up in her path. He let her hold boards while he hammered, but he didn't ask her to operate the post driver. He showed her how to latch a gate so it wouldn't swing open on its own, but he kept her well back from any animal that weighed more than she did.

"You gonna wrap me in bubble wrap too?" she'd joked one day when he cautioned her about where she was standing in relation to a skittish mare's hindquarters.

"Bubble wrap's expensive," he'd said. "I'll settle for you not standin' where a thousand pounds of nerves might decide to put a hoof."

She'd shifted obediently. "My mother thanks you."

"She doesn't even know me, yet" he'd replied.

That unthinking future tense, doesn't know yet, sat between them for a heartbeat after he said it. He'd busied himself with a strap before it could turn into something heavier.

The work did what work always does for bodies unused to it: it hurt, then it made her stronger.

Muscles she'd forgotten she had announced themselves the first week. She'd collapse into bed at night with her shoulders singing and her thighs aching from climbing the hill multiple times. But instead of the jittery, overcaffeinated exhaustion she knew from too many back-to-back deadlines, this tiredness felt… earned. Clean.

Her sleep changed too. In Denver, sleep had often been a reluctant truce, her mind grudgingly shutting down for a few hours only to rocket awake at three a.m. with some headline or sentence fragment nagging at her. Out here, she fell into deeper rest. She still woke up earlier than she would have in the city, but the time between closing her eyes and opening them again felt less like a battle.

That clarity bled back into her writing.

Her trees in the book were no longer vague "green things" framing a scene; they were cottonwoods with leaves that turned pale on their undersides when the wind picked up.

Her editor brain, the one that had been trained to cut anything that smacked of indulgent description, hovered uncertainly over passages like that. Then she let them stand. This book wasn't about car chases and bombshell revelations.

The more she wrote, the more the line between observation and invention blurred. Sometimes, in the middle of a sentence, she'd pause and realize she was smiling.

Caleb, from his vantage point on the ground, noticed changes of his own.

He didn't have language for them at first. Just a series of impressions.

The "city girl" on the hill no longer walked like a weekend tourist when she came down toward the barn. She'd started picking her steps differently, eyes scanning the ground for holes or rocks, body instinctively leaning into the slope rather than fighting it. She still wore sneakers most of the time, but they were dustier now, laces double-knotted.

When she held a board for him to drill into, her arms didn't tremble the way they had the first time. She set her feet shoulder-width apart, braced, the way he'd shown her. When he warned her to watch her fingers, she rolled her eyes instead of going pale.

"Do you think I'm this clumsy?" she'd asked once.

"I think wood doesn't care how careful you are," he'd answered. "It just falls where it falls."

"Cheerful," she'd said. But she'd moved her thumb anyway.

He overheard her humming sometimes. Little scraps of melody as she hauled an empty bucket or checked if the cabin's porch light was working. Not the stressed-out, clipped breaths of someone racing a deadline, but the absentminded tune of a person whose mind was ticking in a different way.

He also noticed that when he or Hank asked how the writing was going, she didn't deflect as quickly.

Instead of, "Oh, you know, I'm failing gloriously," she'd say, "I got a really good scene today," or, "I finally figured out why my main character keeps ignoring her love interest."

Once, she said, almost shyly, "I like this book. I don't know if it'll sell, but I like it."

"That counts," Hank had said, nodding.

"How much?" she'd asked, half-joking.

"A lot more than plenty of other things people do for money," Hank replied.

Caleb had been oiling a gate hinge nearby, listening without meaning to. The quiet conviction in Hank's tone, and the way Emma's shoulders relaxed at his words, stirred something in him.

He was careful, though, about how much space he gave those stirrings.

Since hearing that Abby was back in town, a part of him had tightened in self-defense. He'd kept his distance from main street, timing his trips so he was in and out quickly. He kept his head down at the feed store, exchanged necessary pleasantries, and left. He didn't go into the diner again that week.

On the ranch, the best version of him emerged as always: the man who knew the land, who knew his animals, who could fix what could be fixed and accept what couldn't. That version knew how to look someone in the eye and give them an honest answer about the weather, the hay crop, the odds of a calf pulling through.

The version of him that had been twenty-five and in love and overwhelmed at the hospital was quieter, tucked away behind layers of habit and distance. Still there, but not in control.

Emma, sensing without knowing why that something had shifted, respected the space he seemed to be drawing around himself. She didn't push. She didn't ask why he'd gone from sharing a meal at her table to maintaining a little more distance in their conversations. She matched his level, friendly, steady, present when they worked together, but not prying.

She could feel, though, that he was watching her in a slightly different way.

Not critically. Not in a way that made her skin crawl. More like a man measuring how someone new fit into the existing pattern of his life. Testing, without touching, the idea of making room.

One afternoon, as summer crept forward and the heat pressed down harder in the afternoons, she joined him and Hank in moving cattle from one pasture to another. It was a simple rotation, they explained, give one section of grass a chance to recover while another got grazed.

"You're up for a bit of walkin'?" Hank had asked. "Nothing too fancy. Just help us keep 'em pointed the right direction."

"I'm up for discovering new muscles to hate me tomorrow," she'd replied.

They gave her the safest position, along the side of the herd, far enough back that she wasn't in any danger of getting run over if they spooked, close enough that her presence helped keep the animals flowing along the path instead of deciding to break for the creek.

"Use your arms," Caleb had said, demonstrating. "Big movements. You don't have to get close. Just make yourself a wall they don't wanna cross."

She'd felt ridiculous at first, waving her arms and calling "Hey, hey, keep moving," at animals that outweighed her by several orders of magnitude. But it worked. When one cow looked tempted to drift toward a particularly juicy patch of green, she stepped sideways, arms out, and the animal reconsidered.

"You're a natural," Hank had called.

"Tell that to my city friends," she'd shouted back, laughing, as dust rose around them, catching the light.

By the time they'd gotten the herd into the new pasture and secured the gate, her hair was escaping its ponytail in frizzy curls, her lungs full of dust and exhilaration.

She'd leaned against the fence, catching her breath, watching the cows fan out into the grass.

"Feels like we just moved an ocean," she'd said.

"Slow ocean," Caleb replied, joining her at the rail. He was breathing a little harder himself, sweat darkening the brim of his hat.

"A very loud, opinionated ocean," she added as one of the calves let out a long, dissatisfied bawl.

"Grass is always greener in the place we just kicked them out of," he said.

"Inspirational," she murmured, then, without thinking, added, "I might steal that."

He glanced at her, amused. "That how writers work? You just wander around collectin' things people say?"

"Pretty much," she said. "Consider yourself on the record."

"I didn't sign a waiver," he said.

"You let me feed you pasta," she countered. "That's informed consent."

He shook his head, but the smile that tugged at his mouth was real and not just a fleeting twitch.

The more she wore herself out alongside them, the more she understood the peculiar satisfaction in ending a day filthy and tired and able to point to tangible things: a fence line tightened, a load of hay stacked, a herd in the right pasture.

There were no page view statistics here, no social media metrics. There were cows chewing, a water trough filled, a gate latched. Immediate, concrete feedback. It did something to her brain chemistry that felt, frankly, addictive.

It also did something to her sense of place.

On her third week there, she caught herself, walking back to the cabin with a leftover sandwich from Hank's kitchen, thinking, I'll head home and finish that chapter.

Home.

She stopped on the path, the word echoing oddly.

Denver was still home, technically. Her stuff, her furniture, the errant houseplant she'd begged the neighbor to water, it was all there. Her parents' house, two suburbs over, would always be home in a different way. But the cabin, with its slightly uneven floor and its stubborn front door that needed an extra hip bump to shut properly, had started to stake a claim.

It wasn't about ownership. She knew she was there on borrowed time and borrowed space. It was about belonging. For the first time in a long time, she lived somewhere she could name all the sounds the house made at night. She knew which board creaked when she walked from the bed to the bathroom. She knew the pattern of the wind through the trees outside. She knew that if she flipped the porch light on after dark, someone down at the ranch house would likely notice and mark her mentally as "in for the night."

The land itself had begun to inscribe itself into her personal mythology. The big cottonwood by the creek took on outsize importance in her mind, a landmark in her internal map as much as on the real one. The particular way the ridge to the west cut into the sky at sunset became a reference point when she thought about "day ending."

Late nights found her at the tiny cabin table, pages of printed draft spread out, red pen in hand. Sometimes, when the words blurred, she'd step outside and lean on the porch rail, looking down at the pinprick of light in the ranch house window.

Once, very late, she saw a figure on the house porch, Caleb, hatless, leaning against the railing with his forearms, looking up toward the cabin. She couldn't see his expression; the distance and dark swallowed details. But the way he stood, still, shoulders slightly bent, looked familiar. She'd seen it earlier that day when he'd paused, resting on the fence after moving the herd. A man between tasks, body temporarily idle while his mind kept cataloging.

She lifted a hand before she could think better of it, a small wave that probably didn't even register at that distance. He didn't react, or if he did, it was too subtle for her to see.

She dropped her hand, feeling oddly foolish and strangely comforted at the same time.

Here was a woman who had spent years using her brain as her primary tool, discovering the satisfaction of letting her muscles share the load. She felt the click in her own head as she realized that being tired from hauling hay was different from being tired from scrolling through endless comments. It was a difference she didn't yet have all the words for, but her body understood.

Here was a man who had once wanted the world and then been overwhelmed by it, now watching someone from that other world acclimate to his. He both admired and feared how quickly she was adapting, because it suggested that perhaps the life he'd built, the one he sometimes resented and sometimes clung to, might be more inviting than he'd allowed himself to believe.

In the overlap of their days, those mornings where she wrote while he checked water lines, those afternoons where she held a board while he hammered, those evenings where she ate Hank's stew at the ranch house table and listened to them bicker about feed prices, something tentative and persistent grew.

Not a romance, not yet. That would require declarations neither of them were ready to make and a level of clarity about themselves they had not yet achieved.

But a rhythm. A shared cadence.

In the city, Emma's life had been divided into segments measured by the blinking cursor and the deadlines on her calendar. Here, her days were measured in porch mornings, chores, walks to the creek, and the number of times she looked up without realizing it to see where Caleb was on the land below.

Her book's word count ticked up. The story she was telling on-screen took shape alongside the story she was living, each informing the other in ways she tried not to overanalyze.

"That's what happens," she muttered to herself, "when you fall in love with a place."

She froze at her own words.

With a place. She'd meant with a place.

She closed the laptop gently and walked out onto the porch, where the late afternoon sun painted everything in long, low shadows. Down in the yard, Caleb and Hank were working a length of hose, testing a repaired water line. Gus darted in and out, trying to bite the spray.

Emma leaned on the railing, watching, then picked up her notebook and wrote, almost without thinking:

Sometimes, what changes your life isn't a lightning strike. It's a dozen mornings on the same porch, watching the same man walk the same fence line, and realizing that your heart has started keeping time with his footsteps.

She stopped. Put a line through that last clause. Too much.

But even crossed-out, it glowed faintly on the page.

She looked at the line, and then at the ranch, and then at the small dot of a man below who had no idea he'd accidentally walked into the margins of her notebook.

"Slow down," she told herself under her breath.

The land around her, with its patient cycles of grass and water and work, seemed to nod in agreement.

There was plenty of summer left. Plenty of fences to mend, pages to write, chores to learn, ghosts to face. For now, it was enough that the days had found a rhythm and that, for the first time in a long time, she woke up more curious about what her own life would bring than about anyone else's breaking news.

Chapter Nine
The First Ask for Help

By the time the fourth week rolled around, Emma had started to recognize the particular look Hank got when he was about to "volunteer" her for something.

It wasn't the same as his you're-about-to-step-in-a-cow-pie expression, or his this-story's-gonna-take-a-while expression. It was subtler: a brightening around the eyes, a faint shift in his stance like he'd just thought of something entertaining and useful all at once.

She saw it that morning before he even opened his mouth.

She'd been on the porch since sunrise, laptop open, mug of coffee gone lukewarm by her elbow.

Emma had just written a line she liked enough to underline when boots scuffed on the path. Hank appeared at the bottom of the steps, hat pushed back, one hand resting on his lower back.

"Morning, porch princess," he called.

"Morning, hay tyrant," she called back. "If you're here to recruit me again, I should warn you I'm filing for overtime."

"You're a volunteer," he said. "Volunteers don't get overtime. They get character."

"Pretty sure I've got enough character," she said, closing the laptop and setting it on the small side table.

"We'll see about that." He tipped his head toward the hill behind the cabin. "You busy the next hour?"

She glanced at the screen. The blinking cursor could wait. "Depends what 'busy' gets me out of."

"Gets you out of sittin' in that chair 'til your back fuses," he said. "We're movin' some steers from the north lot down to the catch pen by the road. I got two hands and a truck with a mind of its own. I could use a third thing."

"Is the third thing my brain?" she asked. "Because that's questionable before ten a.m."

"The third thing is someone who can drive in a straight line at two miles an hour," he said. "Caleb's fixin' the gate hinges down there. We need the truck to follow him nice and slow while he leads them in. I'd do it, but I promised Dr. Morales I'd be at the south pasture to hold a cow for her. She prefers the cow; I already know that."

Emma hesitated only long enough to register the flutter in her stomach at the thought of Caleb plus gates plus close quarters. Then she stood.

"I can drive a straight line," she said. "I think. I've driven downtown Denver during a snowstorm. How hard can two miles an hour be?"

"Famous last words," Hank said cheerfully. "Come on. I'll give you the two-minute orientation."

She grabbed her jacket on instinct, mornings up here still carried a bite, then followed him down the path. The truck in question sat in the gravel turnout by the cabin: the older green pickup she'd seen Caleb use for everything from feed runs to fence checks. It bore the scars of its usefulness, dings along the sides, a cracked taillight, a front bumper that had clearly kissed a few rocks, but it looked solid.

"Ever driven a stick?" Hank asked as they approached.

Her stomach dipped. "Uh… define 'driven.'"

"Got in, stalled it three times, cussed, and got out?" he suggested.

"Yes," she said. "I have absolutely done that."

He chuckled. "Well, good news. This old girl's an automatic. We don't put more strain on ourselves than we have to."

She exhaled. "Thank God."

He swung the driver's door open and gestured her in. She climbed up, feeling the unfamiliar height. The bench seat creaked under her as she slid behind the wheel. The steering wheel felt thicker than her sedan's, the dash simple, no touchscreen, just knobs and gauges.

"All right," Hank said, bracing one hand on the open door. "Basic rules. She pulls a little to the right, so don't fight it too hard. You start over-correctin', you'll be zigzaggin' across the pasture like a drunk snake.

You're gonna be in low gear, foot barely on the gas. Think turtle, not rabbit."

"Turtle," she repeated. "Got it."

"Wheels follow wherever you look," he added. "You stare at Caleb's back, you'll run over him. Keep your eyes where you want the truck to go. He'll keep his out of your way."

"Reassuring," she muttered.

"You'll be fine," Hank said. "You get in trouble, take your foot off the gas, don't slam the brakes. Soft foot. Let the ground do some of the work."

He walked around to the passenger side, stuck his head in the open window long enough to point out the gear shift, the four-wheel drive lever, the parking brake.

"When you get down to the catch pen, he'll holler at you to stop," he said. "Trust his hollerin'. He knows when to call it."

She nodded, absorbing as much as she could. "And you're… not coming?"

"I told you, Dr. Morales has a date with a cow," he said. "She scares me more than any vehicle. I'll be watchin' from that ridge there." He pointed to a rise that overlooked the north lot. "I want to see how my two favorite stubborn creatures handle each other."

"Your what?" she asked.

"Truck and Caleb," he said, expression innocent. "What'd you think I meant?"

She rolled her eyes, but her cheeks warmed anyway. "I think you're enjoying this too much."

"Old man's privileges," he said. He slapped the side of the truck twice. "Go on. He's waitin' down at the lot. Just follow the road until it turns to dirt, then through the gate. You can't miss him."

She slid the key into the ignition, started the engine, and listened as it rumbled to life. It sounded different from her car, deeper, louder, vibrating through the seat.

"Easy," she told herself under her breath, shifting into drive.

She eased her foot off the brake and let the truck roll forward. It felt both sluggish and powerful, like steering a small boat with a very big motor.

Hank stepped back, hands on his hips, watching as she navigated the turn onto the ranch road. She resisted the urge to wave; two hands on the wheel felt like the smarter choice.

"That's it," he called. "Just remember, if you break it, you fix it."

"Not helping," she yelled back, but she was smiling.

As she rolled down the hill, dust kicked up behind her, floating in the early light. The road curled along the slope, dipped past the creek, then climbed gently toward the north lot. She kept her speed low, content to let the truck do most of the work.

Ahead, she saw the gate Hank had mentioned, a wide opening in the fence, currently closed. Beyond it, a small herd of steers milled, flicking their tails. Beyond them, the catch pen by the road waited, empty.

Caleb stood by the gate, a coil of rope over one shoulder, hat low against the light. He turned at the sound of the approaching engine, eyes narrowing automatically to read the situation. For a brief second, confusion crossed his face when he saw Emma behind the wheel instead of Hank.

Then he wiped his palm on his jeans, rolled his shoulders, and stepped forward, opening the gate wide.

"Morning," she called, leaning partly out the window.

"Morning," he replied. His gaze flicked over her quickly, taking in her grip on the wheel, the determined set of her jaw. "They sendin' you down here as my chauffeur now?"

"I'm told I'm overqualified," she said. "Apparently the truck and I just need to 'have a conversation.'"

"That sounds like Hank," he said dryly. "All right. Here's how this is gonna go."

He walked closer, one hand settling on the edge of the open window. The proximity made the cab feel smaller, the air thicker.

"I'm gonna get them pointed toward the road," he said, nodding toward the steers. "Once we start movin', I want you just behind, slow and steady. Don't crowd 'em, they'll spook. Don't lag too far, or they'll decide to turn and visit you instead."

"Oh, good," she said. "Being trampled by livestock was definitely on my bucket list."

His mouth twitched. "They're more scared of the truck than you are of them," he said. "Mostly. Keep your speed so I'm in your hood's line of sight. If I wave for you to slow, you ease off the gas. If I wave stop, you stop. No sudden stompin' unless somethin' four-legged is in the way."

"Got it," she said. "You're in charge. I'm just the engine."

"Exactly," he said. "Think you can handle bein' bossed around for half an hour?"

"I work in a newsroom," she said. "This is nothing."

He gave her a long, appraising look that sent a little electric line down her spine. Then he stepped back, slapped the hood twice, and moved to the gate.

He waved to her once more, signaling her to pull through and set up in position. She guided the truck into the pasture, heart thumping a little faster now. The steers shifted, snorted, eyeing the vehicle warily.

Caleb positioned himself ahead of them, a solid, familiar figure. He called out in low, steady tones, moving his arms, guiding their attention. The animals responded, heads bobbing, a tide of bodies turning toward the open side of the field.

"Easy," he called over his shoulder, voice carrying. "Ease up."

She feathered the gas, letting the truck crawl forward. The engine idled strong, the speedometer needle barely above zero. She watched his back primarily, as she'd been warned not to, but she kept half her focus on where she wanted the truck to go, the narrow corridor between steers and fence.

It wasn't elegant. The wheel tugged against her palms, wanting to follow every small rut. Once, she over-corrected and the truck lurched toward a cow's hindquarters.

"Whoa," Caleb called sharply, lifting a hand and sliding sideways to put himself between animal and bumper. "Easy! Take your foot off the gas."

She did, instantly. The truck slowed; the steer flicked its tail and moved away, unimpressed.

"Sorry," she called, cheeks burning. "She likes to wander."

"She's testin' you," he said, tone calm again. "You're doin' fine. Little more left. There you go."

They inched forward like that, man and machine nudging the herd along the worn path toward the catch pen. Dust hung in the air, softening edges, making the morning seem hazy and unreal.

Inside the cab, Emma found a rhythm. Look where you want to go. Light foot. Trust his signals. Her world narrowed to the slow roll of rubber over dirt, the sway of a tail here, a tossed head there, his hand cutting through the air to tell her more, less, now.

He glanced back periodically, checking on her, on the way the truck tracked.

She looked… focused.

From his angle, Caleb could see the way her hands gripped the wheel, not white-knuckled, though they had been at the start, but firm. He could see the line of her brow, knit in concentration, lips pressed together in a half-determined, half-amused line.

He'd expected her to balk when Hank suggested she help with this. Most city folks flinched when asked to do anything that involved large animals and vehicles with opinions. Instead, here she was, muscling the old truck along without panicking, recovering from that near-miss without dissolving.

The first time he'd driven this truck in a pasture, he'd been sixteen and cocky. He'd hit a rut too fast and opened his head on the steering wheel, earning six stitches and a scar his mother had shaken her head over for years. Emma was doing better than he had on his first go.

"Steady," he called as they approached the gate by the road. "Little more. Little more. And… whoa there."

He held up a flat palm. Her brake lights flared, the truck easing to a stop. The steers shuffled past him into the pen, some reluctantly, some as if this were just another tedious part of their routine.

He swung the gate closed once the last tail cleared, looping the chain through automatically. Then he turned back toward the truck, walking up to the driver's side with long, easy strides.

She rolled the window down, pushing hair out of her face with one forearm. Dust streaked her cheek where she'd scratched an itch.

"Well?" she asked, braced for criticism.

He rested a forearm on the window frame again, leaning in a little. From this close, he could see a few strands of hair plastered to her temple with sweat, the faint smear of dirt on her jaw, the bright spark in her eyes that said adrenaline was still humming.

"You didn't kill anybody," he said. "Truck's still in one piece. Cows are where they're supposed to be. I'll call it a win."

"Ringing endorsement," she said, but her shoulders sagged with relief.

He let the corner of his mouth lift. "You did good," he added, softer. "Not everyone picks up on the feel of the ground that quick."

She blinked. "Thanks," she said. "It was weirdly… satisfying? Like slow-motion Mario Kart with higher stakes."

"Can't say I'm familiar with that comparison," he said. "But I'll take your word for it."

She twisted to look back at the pen, watching the animals settle. "They really do just follow if you point them right."

"They'll follow peace," he said. "You get 'em riled, you're in trouble. Keep the pressure steady, give 'em somewhere to go, and they'll take it."

"That sounded metaphorical," she said.

"Don't know about that," he replied, though a part of him filed the thought away. "You can park her up by the barn now. I'll run the gate by the road."

She nodded, shifting the truck into drive again, carefully navigating the narrow strip between fence and ditch. He watched until she cleared it, his eyes tracking the rear wheels almost unconsciously.

Up on the ridge, Hank had indeed found a vantage point. He'd finished with Dr. Morales faster than expected, and curiosity, not to mention a certain fondness for meddling, had pulled him toward the little rise that gave a good view of the north lot.

He stood there, hands resting lightly on his hips, watching tin and dust and two small human figures choreograph the slow migration of steers.

"Well, I'll be," he muttered as Emma recovered from the near-miss with the cow. "She didn't scream. That's somethin'."

He watched the truck move, her corrections gradually smoothing out. He'd seen plenty of young men puff themselves up and take a job like this too fast, too aggressive, turning a simple chore into a circus. Emma, despite her nerves, took direction, adjusted, found the balance between control and letting the machine do its thing.

His gaze slid from the truck to the man walking just ahead of it.

Caleb's shoulders sat a little higher than they had the week before. His stride still carried the underlying weariness of someone with too much to do and too few hands, but there was an energy there Hank hadn't seen in a while, a subtle quickening when he turned to check on the truck, the smallest of grins when he thought no one was looking and saw the city girl handle herself.

"About time that boy had somethin' good walk onto this land," Hank thought, not for the first time, but with more conviction now. Not just a temporary distraction, but something, or someone, with the potential to wedge open the parts of Caleb that had rusted shut since Tom and Abby and the war.

He knew better than to rush anything. Good things that lasted didn't usually arrive with fanfare; they crept in on quiet boots and slowly made themselves indispensable.

Down by the barn, the truck pulled up and parked. Hank watched as Emma climbed out, stretching, patting the hood affectionately as if she'd just completed some kind of bonding exercise with the vehicle.

"See?" she said to the truck, not realizing her voice carried. "We can be friends."

Caleb, closing the gate by the road, shook his head with a small snort even from that distance.

Hank smiled to himself and turned away, letting them have their moment without an audience.

By the time he ambled back down to the yard, they'd moved on to the next small chore.

Emma stood in the shade of the barn, a halter rope in her hands, the other end attached to a bay mare with a suspicious eye and a tendency to dance sideways.

Caleb was adjusting the saddle, checking the cinch. The mare shifted her weight, head tossing.

"Whoa, easy, Sage," he murmured, hand firm on her shoulder. "Stand, girl."

Emma kept two feet planted, one slightly ahead of the other like he'd shown her, hands steady on the rope about a foot below the clip.

"She doesn't like me," Emma observed as Sage tossed her head again, snorting.

"She doesn't like new situations," Caleb said. "You're just part of the new." He glanced at Emma's grip. "You're doin' good. Keep your hands loose but not slack. If she pulls, don't yank. Just… be a post."

"A what?" she asked.

"Post," he repeated. "Plants in the ground, doesn't take it personal when somethin' leans on it."

"Great," she said. "My dream role. Human fence post."

He ducked his head, hiding a smile. "Posts are important," he said. "Whole ranch falls apart without 'em."

The mare sidestepped suddenly, testing. Emma's body rocked with the movement, arms flexing. She instinctively wanted to pull back hard, but she remembered his instruction and simply held firm, letting her weight do the work.

"Hey," she said calmly. "None of that."

Sage stilled, more from Caleb's soothing hand on her neck than Emma's words, but he noticed the way Emma's tone stayed even.

"Good," he said. "You, okay?"

"My biceps are confused," she said. "But yeah."

He finished with the cinch, sliding two fingers under to check the tightness.

"I'm gonna put my foot in the stirrup," he said. "She might step again. Same deal. You stay where you are. Don't wrap the rope around your hand."

"I'm not an action movie extra," she said. "I'm not trying to get dragged across the yard."

"Good," he said. "I'm fresh out of soft landings."

He put his left foot in the stirrup, weight shifting. Sage's ears flicked back. She danced half a step. Emma's muscles tightened, but she held. Caleb swung up smoothly, settling into the saddle.

From her angle, she could see why Hank had once said he'd been born there. His body seemed to find its balance automatically, shoulders aligning, hands going where they needed to be without conscious thought.

Sage snorted again, then blew out a breath that sounded suspiciously like resignation. Caleb patted her neck.

"See?" he said. "We're all still alive."

"For now," Emma replied.

He looked down at her, that familiar quick scan to make sure she was truly all right. Dust streaked her jeans. One of her sneakers had a smudge of something she probably didn't want identified. Her hair had escaped its tie again.

"You didn't have to say yes to this," he said.

"You didn't have to ask," she countered. "But I'm glad you did."

"I didn't ask," he pointed out. "Hank did."

"Semantics," she said. "You could've sent me back up the hill."

He paused, then nodded once. "Fair," he said. "You did good."

"That's twice today you've said that," she said, mock-astonished. "Careful, I'll get spoiled."

"Don't tell Hank," he said. "He's the one who likes to keep your ego in check."

"Please," she said. "He lives to compliment me. You're the grumpy one."

His brows rose. "I'm grumpy?"

"On a spectrum from 'sunny' to 'storm cloud,' you're at least a partly cloudy," she said.

"I'll take partly cloudy," he said. "Better than a full-on tornado."

She tilted her head, studying him. "You're not a tornado," she said. "Tornadoes don't worry this much about other people."

He looked away at that, down at his hands on the reins, the compliment landing somewhere he wasn't prepared to examine.

"Thank you," he said finally.

The simple sincerity of it made her chest feel unexpectedly tight.

Hank, leaning casually against the side of the barn a dozen yards away, pretended to fuss with a coil of hose while he watched them.

He saw the ease in their back-and-forth, the way she teased without malice, the way Caleb absorbed it, the way his shoulders loosened imperceptibly when she smiled at him. He saw the mare settle under

Caleb's weight, the truck parked neatly where it should be, the dust on Emma's legs.

He also saw the way his own chest eased at the sight.

He'd watched Caleb struggle under more weight than any one man should have to carry this early in life, war, grief, the ranch's financial razor edge, the breakup he'd never quite named out loud. He'd watched him turn work into both punishment and refuge. He'd seen the lines around his eyes deepen, the laugh lines fade.

This, this woman with ink on her fingers and calluses just starting to form on her palms, who could drive his truck and hold a horse and talk back without flinching, felt like a small miracle.

"Don't screw it up," he thought, not at either of them specifically, but at the universe, the way an old man might mutter at stubborn clouds when he needed rain.

Aloud, he said, "You two gonna stand around flirtin' all day, or you gonna earn your supper?"

Both heads snapped toward him.

"We weren't," Emma began, then stopped, flushing to the ears.

"Just gettin' chores done," Caleb said, tone even but a shade too fast.

"Sure," Hank said, letting it slide. "I got a trough down in the lower pen that's askin' for a scrubbin'. Emma, you wanna learn the fine art of algae removal?"

"Is that like latte art?" she asked.

"Exactly," he said. "Only smellier."

She sighed with exaggerated drama. "Living the dream."

As she handed off the halter rope and followed Hank toward the next task, she glanced back once.

Caleb was still watching her, one hand on the saddle horn, the other resting lightly on his thigh. When he realized she'd caught his eye, he tipped his hat in that small, restrained way of his, then nudged Sage forward.

The distance between cabin and barn remained the same. The hill hadn't moved; the fences hadn't shifted. But the space between them, the space measured in requests and offers, in small acts of asking and being asked, had changed.

For the first time, the help she'd given hadn't been just something she'd volunteered out of curiosity. Hank had engineered it, yes, but the chore itself required her. The truck wouldn't drive itself. The mare needed a steady hand.

Caleb had seen her step into those roles and not crumble. He'd seen the grit under the city edges. He'd seen that dirt on her sneakers didn't send her running for the cabin.

And she had seen, more clearly than ever, that he was willing to trust her with pieces of his world, small ones, practical ones, but pieces all the same.

It was a small shift, imperceptible if you only looked at miles or minutes. But for two people who had spent so long doing everything themselves, asking and accepting that kind of help was no minor thing.

High Meadow Ranch swallowed the rest of the day the way it always did, with more chores, more dust, more small victories and setbacks. But under the wide Colorado sky, something quietly significant had taken root: the knowledge, on both sides, that they could lean, just a little, without the whole structure collapsing.

Hank, watching from yet another convenient vantage point as they hosed out the trough together later, Emma shrieking when the spray splashed her jeans, Caleb laughing out loud for once, not just with that half-huff he usually gave, felt the knot in his chest loosen another notch.

"About damn time," he thought, again, with more warmth than exasperation.

He turned toward the house, already thinking about what he could cook for supper that would feed three instead of two.

Chapter Ten
Cracks in the Armor

By nine that morning, Emma had already broken one of her own rules.

She stared at the empty document on her laptop, the little word count in the corner cruelly proclaiming: 0.

Again.

The day hadn't started badly, not exactly. She'd woken to her usual view, the pale band of dawn stretching over the ridge, the sound of a distant engine as Caleb's truck fired up down at the house, the cabin floor cool under her bare feet. She'd made coffee, opened her laptop on the porch, wrapped herself in her old college sweatshirt, and told herself she would get a thousand words down before she even thought about checking her phone.

Instead, she'd made the mistake of rereading what she'd written the day before.

What had felt solid and alive yesterday now lay on the screen like something brittle and awkward. Dialogue that had seemed sharp read as stilted.

She tried to edit. Tweaked a line, cut an adjective, shifted a beat. The whole chapter sagged anyway.

By the time the sun had cleared the ridge and the first tractor passed below, she'd highlighted the entire section, nearly four thousand words, and hit delete.

The soft little whoosh of it vanishing felt both too quiet and too final.

She stared at the blank screen a moment, hand still hovering over the trackpad as if she could yank the words back through sheer will. Logic told her they weren't gone forever. Scrivener had backups. She had printed pages in the cabin. If she wanted to torture herself, she could resurrect every sentence.

Emotion told her she had just erased the only decent thing she'd managed to make in weeks.

"Okay," she said aloud, into the empty morning. "Melodrama much?"

Her voice sounded thin. Gus barked somewhere down by the barn, oblivious.

She set her fingers on the keys, determined to replace the vanished chapter with something better. For ten minutes, she typed nonsense, fragments of sentences that started strong and then petered out, descriptions she'd already used elsewhere.

Delete. Delete. Delete.

By ten o'clock, she had nothing new and the ghost of the deleted chapter lingering like an accusation.

Her phone, face down on the table beside her, buzzed.

She ignored it. Another buzz. Then a third, insistent. The familiar vibration of someone who knew to try more than once.

She sighed, picked it up, and squinted at the screen.

CALL FROM: MARTIN ELLIS.

Her editor.

Half of her wanted to fling the phone into the nearest pasture. The other half knew that if she sent him to voicemail, he'd simply call again. And again. And then email. And then possibly send a carrier pigeon up the hill.

She swiped to answer.

"Hey, Martin," she said, trying for breezy. "What's up?"

"Emma." His voice crackled through, brisk, city-smooth. She could hear the newsroom hum behind him, phones ringing, keyboards clacking, the muffled buzz of televisions always tuned to something urgent. "How's our mountain hermit?"

"Less hermit, more… raccoon," she said. "Living off scraps, avoiding daylight."

"Uh-huh," he said, firing right past the joke. "Listen, I'll cut to it. We've got something. Big."

He always said that. Everything was big. Everything was urgent. Breaking, developing, exclusive. She felt her shoulders tense reflexively.

"There's a story blowing up about the housing authority," he said. "Corruption, kickbacks, families getting screwed. We've been sniffing around it for months, but it just cracked wide open. I want you on it."

There it was, the old hit of adrenaline, the familiar flick of interest. Housing authority stories were the kind of thing she'd cut her teeth on. Names, documents, late-night phone calls. The high of chasing truth, the low of absorbing collateral damage.

"Martin, I'm on sabbatical," she reminded him. She could hear the weak note in her own voice.

"Technically," he said. "Unofficially, sabbaticals are flexible when the city's on fire."

"It's not literally on fire, is it?" she asked. "Because if it is, my cabin might actually be safer."

He exhaled, the sound of a man trying to be patient with someone not moving fast enough.

"Emma, you know this. This is what you do. You're good at it. You've got sources at Housing from the last zoning piece; you've got the instincts… we need you in the room."

"And my novel?" she asked before she could stop herself.

There was a brief pause. She could almost see him on the other end, blinking like she'd spoken another language.

"Your novel will still be there in a month," he said. "This story won't. We push now or someone else eats our lunch."

"I'm finally… I'm finally in it," she said, hating the small, pleading note in her own words. "It took me weeks to even get traction. If I yank myself out and go back,"

"You'll get a promotion out of this," he cut in, seizing on the argument he thought would move her. "You nail this, I can bump you to senior. Front page, big bylines. You can take another break after." He softened his tone slightly. "I know you've been fried, Em. I know. But this is why you got into this. To make things better. To hold people accountable."

She pressed the heel of her hand to her forehead, staring out at the pasture. A cow flicked its ear. The mountains sat solid and unconcerned about housing scandals.

He wasn't entirely wrong. She had gotten into journalism because she believed stories could change things. Some days, they did. When she'd uncovered that nursing home skimming its food budget to pad executive bonuses, the state had investigated. When she'd exposed a landlord neglecting heat in a low-income complex, heaters had miraculously been repaired within a week.

She could feel, in the way her heart sped up, how easily she could be pulled back in. The tempo of the newsroom. The sense of purpose. The clean, sharp satisfaction of catching someone in a lie and showing it to the world.

"You still there?" Martin asked.

"Yeah," she said. "I'm thinking."

"Think faster," he said, but there was a hopeful edge in his voice now. "We'd need you back in the office next week. The paper's covering your cabin through the end of the month, right? We'll eat the cost difference if we have to. I'll talk to accounting."

The idea of someone else paying for this place, of cutting short the time she'd bought with all that accumulated burnout, scraped at her.

"I..." she began, and realized she didn't know how to finish the sentence.

On the land below, a truck door slammed. She glanced down instinctively. Caleb and Hank were near the barn, loading something into the bed. A coil of irrigation pipe glinted in the sun.

"You don't have to decide this minute," Martin said, misreading her silence as strategic instead of paralyzed. "But I need an answer by tomorrow morning. I've got to assign bodies."

"Okay," she said dully. "Tomorrow."

He softened his tone a fraction. "Look, kid. I'm not trying to be the villain here. I know you needed a break. But you're one of my best. I don't want to see you… drift. We both know that doesn't look good on a résumé."

There it was again, that subtle shaming of rest. Drifting meant losing your edge. Slowing down meant falling behind.

"Got it," she said. "I'll call you."

She hung up before he could say anything else, thumb hovering over the screen for a moment longer than necessary.

The mountains didn't care that her résumé might suffer. The cottonwood leaves in the creek bed below didn't give a damn about career trajectories. But a part of her did, stubbornly, reflexively.

A bigger part, right this second, wanted to hurl the phone into the field.

Instead, she set it down very gently on the table and closed the laptop with equal care, as if handling something volatile.

The day had turned bright and sharp, sunlight glancing off the cabin's windows. A breeze kicked up, rustling the dry grasses.

She stood, suddenly feeling like the porch was too small, the air around her too thin.

Inside, the cabin felt no better. The sight of her printed pages, neatly clipped together on the table, made her stomach twist. They represented progress, yes, but also all the hours she'd poured into something that might never see a bookstore shelf, might never matter in the ways she'd been taught "real stories" mattered.

She grabbed her sneakers and jacket on autopilot and stepped back out, leaving the computer and phone where they sat.

The hill behind the cabin rose up invitingly. Beyond it lay a tangle of trails she'd only sampled so far, creek paths, deer tracks, little game trails Hank had pointed out on a map. "Good for clearin' your head," he'd said more than once, eyes knowing.

Her head definitely needed clearing.

She started up the slope, legs burning almost immediately, lungs catching the cold bite that still hung in the air at that elevation. The effort felt good, something for her body to do while her mind spun.

She didn't pay particular attention to which path she took. Left at the big rock. Right at the fallen log. Follow the faint impression of hoofprints here, the glint of water there. Her thoughts were loud enough to drown out any sensible instinct for distance.

A promotion. Front page.

Your novel will still be there in a month.

We both know drifting doesn't look good.

Except.

Except when had she last written something purely because she wanted to, not because it was urgent, or necessary, or someone else's idea of important?

Her sneakers skidded on loose gravel as the trail dipped unexpectedly. She caught herself on a scrubby pine, bark digging into her palm, then kept going.

The land flattened out a bit, opening into a small meadow she didn't recognize. Wildflowers dotted the grass in stubborn little clumps, purple, yellow, white. Beyond it, she heard the faint rush of water.

She walked toward the sound, pushing through a stand of aspen that shivered at her passing. On the other side, a narrow creek cut through the land, its banks soft and mossy in places, rocky in others. The water wasn't deep, but it moved with purpose, tripping over stones, chattering to itself.

She hadn't been to this part before. The creek she usually visited down near the cabin was wider, slower, its edges well-trodden. This stretch felt more tucked away, the banks less worn. The trail here was more suggestion than path.

She followed it along the water's curve until she found a flattish rock that jutted out just enough to sit on without actually getting her sneakers wet. She dropped onto it with a sigh that carried more than just physical exertion.

For a while, she just… listened.

The creek's sound filled the spaces in her head that had been occupied by newsprint and deadlines. The sun slanted through the trees, hitting the water in bright shards. Somewhere above, a bird called sharply, then fell silent.

Her mind, unaccustomed as it was too quiet, did not oblige her with peace.

What if Martin was right? What if she came back to Denver in September with nothing but a crappy first draft and a slightly better tan and found herself permanently side-lined on the big stories? There were a dozen younger, hungrier reporters who'd happily fill the space she left.

What if she stayed, and the novel never quite came together, and in five years she was… what? A failed novelist living in a cabin she couldn't afford, with a resume that had gone soft in the middle?

What if she went back now, saved her career, and woke up at fifty realizing she'd never once chosen something solely because she loved it, not because it looked good in a headline or on a LinkedIn profile?

Fear, it turned out, came in flavors.

She didn't realize she was crying until she tasted salt, unexpected, at the corner of her mouth. She swiped at her cheeks angrily.

"This is ridiculous," she said to the creek. "You're an adult woman, not a teenager in a coming-of-age movie."

The creek kept babbling, unimpressed.

She didn't know how long she sat there. The sun's angle shifted gradually, the air cooling by degrees that would matter up here once evening fell. Shadows lengthened, reaching from tree trunks toward the water.

At the ranch house below, chores ticked along on their usual schedule. The hours blurred together for Caleb as they did most days: feed, check water, talk to Jorge about a part he'd promised two weeks ago and still hadn't delivered, walk the fence line where a calf had tested it earlier in the week.

He kept half an eye, as he often did now, on the hill where the cabin sat.

He'd seen Emma step out that morning with her laptop and coffee. Later, when he and Hank had walked the pipe up past the barn, he'd glanced up; she'd been gone. Not unusual; she often moved inside, or down to the creek, or into town.

Still, he found himself looking again around midafternoon, more reflex than anything.

The porch was empty. No sweatshirt slung over the railing, no flash of movement behind the screen door. The cabin itself sat quiet.

"Seen our writer lately?" Hank asked at some point, as they coiled hose near the lower pasture.

"Not since morning," Caleb said. "She was up there with that computer."

"Hm," Hank grunted. "Hope it's goin' easy on her."

"Computers never do," Caleb said automatically.

"She'll figure it out," Hank said. "She's got some stubborn in her. Reminds me of someone else I know." He shot Caleb a look.

Caleb ignored it, on principle.

By late afternoon, clouds had started gathering at the edges of the sky, the kind that might turn into nothing or might decide to spit rain and lightning without much warning. Mountain weather played by its own rules.

He finished checking the pump and glanced up the hill again.

Still no Emma.

Fine, he told himself. She's allowed to take a drive. Town exists. So do hiking trails. She's not a kid.

Yet something lodged under his ribs wouldn't budge.

He checked the time: just past five. Summer meant long light, but up here dusk came quicker in the gullies and tree-choked creases. It was easy to get turned around a mile from home if you weren't paying attention.

He thought of that first week, when she'd wandered toward the creek and he'd found her sitting on a rock while the sky darkened, completely unfazed by the possibility of mountain lions or sudden storms.

"You wanderin' off into the trees again?" he'd asked then, half-teasing, half-serious.

"Just following the water," she'd said. "You'd come find me, right?"

He'd rolled his eyes, but something in him had filed the promise away even then.

By six, the knot under his ribs had tightened into something that felt suspiciously like full-blown worry.

"Hank?" he called, stepping into the barn where the older man was putting away tools.

"Yeah?"

"You seen Emma this afternoon?"

Hank wiped his hands on a rag, thinking. "Not since before lunch. She left a sandwich plate in the sink. Took her sneakers when she went out, I think. Why?"

"Just checkin'," Caleb said. "Clouds're comin' in. She's been explorin' those back trails."

Hank's gaze sharpened. "You think she went past the markers?"

"Maybe," Caleb said. "I don't know what she considers 'a little walk.'"

Hank glanced at the sky. "You want me to head up toward the cabin, see if she's back, while you check the creek?"

"I'll go toward the top creek," Caleb said. "If she went that far, she might be there. You see her at the cabin, light that porch lamp so I'm not wanderin' for nothin'."

"All right," Hank said. "Don't go fallin' in."

"Tryin' not to," Caleb muttered.

He grabbed his hat, his heavier jacket, and a flashlight just in case, then started up the slope, following the most commonly used path.

He'd walked these trails his whole life. As a kid, he'd raced up them with friends, daring each other to get closer to the rocky outcroppings that his mother had warned were "asking for broken ankles." As a teenager, he'd come up here to think, to breathe, to escape the claustrophobia of small-town gossip and his own restless brain.

Later, after deployments, after funerals, he'd walked them to try to bleed off the buzz of anxiety in his muscles.

Now, he walked them with his eyes scanning for any sign of someone who didn't yet know all their moods.

Broken grass. A footprint on a dusty patch. A scuff on a rock where a boot had slipped.

He found the first clear sign about halfway up, a sneaker tread imprint on the damp edge of the usual creek trail, smaller than his, heading north instead of looping back.

"Of course you did," he muttered, following.

The farther he went, the more the land closed in. Trees clustered closer to the water, their branches shading the creek even as the sky above still held some light. The path narrowed, became less deliberate and more opportunistic, roots and rocks demanding attention.

He found the meadow, a small open patch he hadn't visited in a while, and paused, heart ticking up. If she'd gone left, she'd hit the game trail that circled back. If she'd gone right…

He heard the creek before he saw her.

"…ridiculous," a voice said faintly. "You are an adult. Adults do not run away to cry on rocks."

He followed the sound, pushing through the last stand of aspen.

She sat on a flat rock by the water, hunched forward, elbows on her knees, jacket bunched around her. Her hair had come half loose, a messy halo around her face. Her cheeks looked damp, though it was hard to tell in the diffused light. Her sneakers dangled just above the waterline.

He had about three seconds to decide how to approach before she looked up and saw him.

"What are you doing up here?" she asked, surprise and something like embarrassment flickering across her features.

"Lookin' for you," he said, a little sharper than he meant to. The adrenaline of not knowing where she was hadn't completely drained yet. "Do you know what time it is?"

She glanced automatically at her wrist, then realized she wasn't wearing a watch. Her phone was somewhere back in the cabin, powerless and irrelevant.

"Um," she said. "Late afternoon?"

He stepped closer, boots crunching on the damp bank. "Try early evening," he said. "Sun's droppin'. Clouds are rollin' in. You're up near the top creek alone with no jacket worth a damn and no one knowin' exactly where you are."

She bristled, the embarrassment hardening into defensiveness. "I'm fine," she said. "It's not like I'm scaling Everest. I can see my cabin from that ridge. I'm not lost."

"That's not the point," he said. "Up here, you don't have to be lost to get in trouble. Weather changes fast. You twist an ankle, you take a bad fall, you meet somethin' with teeth… fine turns into not fine real quick."

"I'm not an idiot," she snapped. "I stayed near the water, I watched my footing,"

"And you didn't tell anyone where you were goin' or when you'd be back," he cut in. "No one's sayin' you're stupid, Emma. I'm sayin' you're not used to this land yet. And this land doesn't give a damn how smart you are."

She stood up, spine straightening. "Oh, I'm getting the full lecture, huh? Is this part of the Airbnb package? 'Two bedrooms, one bath, complimentary scolding if you dare walk too far'?"

He felt his jaw tighten. "I'm not scoldin' you for fun," he said. "I'm worried. There's a difference."

"Funny how worry sounds a lot like I know better than you," she said.

The hurt underneath her sarcasm bled through now. He saw it and finally registered that something besides the hike had her on edge.

He scrubbed a hand over his face, trying to temper his voice.

"Look," he said. "I get it. You needed air. I'm not askin' you to sit in that cabin and never leave. I just…" He gestured vaguely at the trees, the rocks, the sky. "I've pulled calves outta ravines up here. I've seen what a surprise storm can do. I don't want…"

He trailed off, the sentence hitting a wall inside him he hadn't realized was there.

"You don't want what?" she asked, softer now, some of the defensive spike gone.

"I don't want to find you at the bottom of something I coulda warned you about," he said finally. It came out rougher than he intended.

For a moment, the only sound between them was the creek.

Her shoulders eased a fraction. The flare of anger ebbed, leaving behind the raw exhaustion that had been driving her feet in the first place.

"I'm sorry," she said, unexpectedly. "I didn't… I wasn't thinking past the next bend. I just needed to move."

He watched her, suspicion shifting into concern.

"Bad day?" he asked.

She let out a breath that was half laugh, half choked-off noise.

"You could say that," she said. "I declared war on my own book, my editor tried to bribe me back to Denver with the promise of glory, and I managed to spiral so hard I ended up giving a pep talk to a creek. So, yeah. Not my best."

He blinked, thrown by the sheer density of that statement. "Start with the book," he said. "What happened?"

She sank back down onto the rock as if her knees had given out.

"I deleted an entire chapter," she said. "On purpose. It was the one I told you about. The one that actually felt right. Suddenly it didn't. So, I killed it. And now everything feels like a Jenga tower I pulled the wrong block out of."

He sat down beside her, leaving a careful amount of space. The rock was cool under him, the air cooler now that the sun had slipped lower.

"Maybe it needed to go," he said. "Sometimes you gotta tear down a fence and build it again right so it holds."

"You and your fences," she said, but there was no real bite in it. "And then Martin called."

"Your editor?" he guessed.

She nodded. "There's a big story brewing. Housing authority mess. Corruption, families getting screwed, all the greatest hits. They want me back early to help. Promotion if I say yes. Front page. The whole career advancement package."

He watched her face as she spoke. The conflict there was intense enough to be almost painful to look at.

"And you?" he asked. "Do you want to go back early?"

"That's the million-dollar question," she said. "Part of me… yeah. Of course. It's my job. I'm good at it. It matters." Her fingers twisted in the hem of her jacket. "Another part of me is screaming at the thought of walking back into that building and sitting under those fluorescent lights and feeling my brain fry all over again."

She stared at the water, eyes unfocused.

"I came up here because I was afraid," she admitted. "Afraid that if I didn't stop, I was going to wake up one day and realize I'd spent my whole life reacting to other people's emergencies and never once chosen something purely because I loved it. That I would have all these articles and no… life. No memories that were mine."

She swallowed.

"And now I'm afraid that if I don't go back and take this story, I'm going to tank my career, disappoint everyone who ever believed in me, and end up being the cautionary tale the younger reporters tell each other about not getting too precious with your dreams."

He let out a slow breath. "Sounds like you're scared either way."

"Exactly," she said, relief blooming at being understood. "It's like there's no version that doesn't end with me regretting something."

He was quiet for a moment, hearing the echo in his own chest.

"You're not alone in that," he said. "Fear doesn't disappear just because you pick one thing and stick with it."

She glanced at him sideways. "What are you afraid of?" she asked, genuinely curious.

He looked out at the creek. The trees on the far bank had darkened, their leaves turned almost black silhouettes against the dimming sky.

"Losing people," he said simply.

Her head tilted. "That's… very on-brand for you."

He gave a humorless huff. "It's the one thing I'm real good at, historically."

She waited, not pushing, just… leaving space.

He hadn't planned on saying more. His usual method of dealing with this particular subject was to keep it locked down behind work and sarcasm. But something about the way she sat there, shoulders sagged, knees drawn together, made the words easier than usual to find.

"You know the basics," he said. "Army. Two deployments. Came back different than I left. Lost some friends over there. Lost some after, in other ways."

He shifted, fingers tracing the edge of the rock.

"I thought if I came back here, I could make… I don't know, a deal with the universe," he went on. "You take your pound of flesh outta me over there, I come home, I build somethin' solid, I keep my head down, and you leave the rest of my life alone. Stupid, I know. But grief doesn't always think straight."

He swallowed.

"Then my dad got sick," he said. "Fast. Brutal. One minute he's bossin' me around from the tractor seat, next minute I'm signin' hospice papers." His jaw worked. "I watched that man fade out in the same room I used to get grounded in. Made me feel about six years old and ninety at the same time."

Emma's hand tightened on her own knee at the image.

"And Abby?" she asked gently. "You don't have to answer if,"

"She left," he said. "Not in a dramatic way. No throwin' plates or screamin'. Just… told me she couldn't do it. Couldn't be tied to a dying man, a broken man, and a ranch that was eatin' all of us alive. She wanted to see the world. So, she did. Good for her."

The bitterness slipped out at the end before he could catch it. He exhaled slowly, tempering it.

"I don't begrudge her that," he said, less sharp. "Not anymore. But it taught me somethin' I internalized a little too deep, maybe."

"What's that?" Emma asked.

"That if I love somethin', there's a decent chance I'm gonna lose it," he said. "To war, to cancer, to itchy feet. To whatever. So, I started… negotiatin' with myself. Limiting the number of things that mattered. Thinkin' if I kept my world small enough, maybe the next hit wouldn't land as hard."

"How's that working out for you?" she asked softly.

He gave a half-laugh. "Ask my blood pressure."

She smiled, brief and sad.

"So, when you say you don't want to find me at the bottom of a ravine," she said, "you mean… you don't want to add me to the list."

He looked at her then, really looked, the last of the day's light catching the worry in his eyes.

"Yeah," he said quietly. "I don't."

The simple admission sat between them like a fragile thing.

Her throat tightened. "You barely know me," she said. It wasn't an argument, just an observation.

"I know enough," he said.

"What, that I can't drive a truck straight and I talk too much when I'm nervous?"

"I know you came up here because somethin' in you was smart enough to say This is not sustainable," he said. "A lot of people ignore that voice until it's too late. I know you're willing to get dirt under your nails to help with a chore you don't technically have to do. I know you care about stories in a way that's… rare. And I know that when you're hurtin', you go quiet and start pickin' on yourself."

Her eyes widened a fraction. "Wow," she said. "Okay. That's… uncomfortably accurate."

"Comes from observation," he said. "I've got a lot of practice watchin' people try to outrun their stuff."

She pulled her knees closer to her chest, the edge of her sneaker scraping against the rock.

"I hate being scared," she admitted, voice barely above the creek's murmur. "It makes me feel… weak. Incompetent. Like I should know better by now."

He shook his head. "Fear's not weakness. It's information. It's your brain tellin' you, Hey, this matters. Don't screw it up."

"Seems like my brain is yelling that at everything right now," she said. "Stay, go, write, work. It's all urgent. All equally catastrophic if I choose wrong."

He tipped his head back, looking at the slice of sky visible through the trees. It had gone from blue to that in-between shade that wasn't quite dusk but wasn't day anymore either.

"You don't have to decide tonight," he said. "About your editor. Deadline or no. You can tell him you need more time."

"It's journalism," she scoffed lightly. "We don't do 'more time.' We do 'fifteen minutes ago.'"

"You're not a firefighter," he said. "No one's gonna die if you take an extra day."

"Tell that to a family losing their apartment," she said. "To kids sleeping in a car because the housing authority lost their paperwork."

He studied her face, seeing the way her sense of responsibility had twisted itself into a burden.

"You can't save everyone," he said.

"You sound like my therapist from two years ago," she said. "Did you secretly go to grad school in psychology?"

He snorted. "Hank's kitchen is my grad school. Look." He shifted, turning a little more to face her. "I'm not sayin' your work doesn't matter. It does. I'm sayin' your life matters too. And if you burn yourself down to embers chasin' every story, you're no good to anybody. Not to the people you're writin' about, and sure as hell not to yourself."

She stared at him, something in her expression caught between defensiveness and dawning recognition.

"That's... annoyingly reasonable," she said.

"I have my moments," he replied.

The wind picked up, threading through the trees, making the leaves hiss softly. The air had shifted; the first cool fingers of evening slid along the creek, raising goosebumps on her arms.

He noticed and shrugged out of his jacket without thinking.

"Here," he said, holding it out.

"I'm fine," she protested automatically.

"You're shiverin'," he said. "Take the jacket, Emma."

There was no scolding in his tone now. Just quiet insistence.

She took it, shrugging into the warmth. It smelled like him, hay and soap and something that might have been cedar. The fabric was worn-soft at the cuffs, the kind of garment that had been through too many seasons to count.

"Thank you," she said, voice smaller than she meant.

"Anytime," he said.

They sat in silence for a moment, the creek talking for them. The worst of the tension had drained, leaving behind a bone-deep tiredness in both of them.

"You said earlier you were afraid of wastin' your life," he said eventually. "Of lookin' back and seein' nothin' but work you did for other people."

She let out a humorless breath. "Yep. That looming existential dread. My favorite."

He nudged a pebble with the toe of his boot, watching it plunk into the water.

"Maybe the question isn't which choice eliminates the fear," he said. "Maybe it's which fear you're more willing to live with. Being seen as someone who stepped off the hamster wheel for a while, or bein' someone who never gave herself a chance to try somethin' that scared her in a different way."

She considered that.

"I hate that those are the options," she said.

"They're not the only ones," he said. "You could find a way to do both. Go back for the story, finish your book slower. Or tell your boss you'll help from here a little, but you're not comin' back early. The world's not as binary as our brains like to pretend."

She shook her head. "You're very wise for someone who spends his days arguing with cows."

"They make good conversationalists," he said. "They don't interrupt."

Her mouth quirked despite herself.

He glanced at the sky again and frowned.

"We should get movin'," he said. "Light's almost gone, and I've got no interest in explainin' to Hank why I left you up here to commune with the nocturnal wildlife."

"Isn't that part of the authentic mountain experience?" she asked, but she stood, joints creaking.

"We're closer to the overlook than the main trail from here," he said. "Come on, I'll show you somethin' before we head back."

"Overlook?" she asked warily. "Does this involve any climbing that might result in me falling dramatically to my death?"

"Not unless you're actively tryin'," he said. "It's not far. And it's worth it."

She studied his face, serious but soft at the edges now. The anger, the fear, the sharp lecture had melted into something else.

"Okay," she said. "Lead the way, shepherd."

He snorted. "Wrong species, but sure."

They turned away from the creek, following a narrower path that slanted upward through the trees. The incline set her thighs burning again, but the jacket kept the chill off. He moved ahead of her, occasionally reaching back to point out a root or a loose rock.

"Step there," he'd say. "Avoid that. Watch your head on this branch."

She found herself appreciating the guidance instead of resenting it this time. The earlier argument had moved something in her; she could see now that his instinct to warn came less from a desire to control and more from a long history of seeing things go wrong.

They broke out of the trees onto a rocky outcrop that jutted just enough from the hillside to offer a view.

Emma stopped.

"Oh," she breathed.

The land unfolded below them like a painting. The ranch house was a small, warm square of light in the dimming valley. The barn's roof caught what remained of the sun's glow, a dull metal sheen. The fields spread out in patchwork, dark green, pale gold, raw earth. The creek they'd left behind flashed silver where it wriggled through.

Beyond that, the town of Cottonwood Ridge lay even smaller, a handful of clustered lights, the faint suggestion of the main street.

Above, the sky stretched wide and deepening, blue sliding into a rich indigo. The first stars pricked through, tentative, then more confident as her eyes adjusted. The clouds that had gathered earlier now framed the view rather than obscured it, edges lit faintly from below by the last of the sun.

"It's…" she started, then laughed softly. "I need new words. I've used 'beautiful' so many times in my book it's lost all meaning."

"Pretty'll do," he said. "No one up here is grading your adjectives."

She stepped closer to the edge, but not dangerously so, wrapping the jacket tighter around herself. The wind picked up, cooler, carrying the faint scents of pine and earth.

"How did you find this place?" she asked.

"Chasin' cows," he said. "Where else?"

She smiled.

"Dad and I came up here a lot," he added, quieter. "When I was a kid, it felt like the top of the world. After… after he died, I stayed away for a while. Felt like it belonged to a version of me that didn't exist anymore."

"What changed?" she asked.

"Needed somewhere to put the grief that wasn't the barn," he said. "Or my bedroom. Or the bottom of a whiskey bottle. Came up here one night without really thinkin' about it. Sat right where you're standin' and realized the sky didn't look any different. It was… weirdly comfortin'."

She looked up. The stars were multiplying now; points of light scattered against the dark.

"When I was a kid, I used to lie on the roof of our garage and make up stories about the stars," she said. "I'd pick three and decide they were sisters, or lovers, or soldiers, or whatever. My dad would come out and tell me real constellation names, and I'd insist mine were better."

"What'd he teach you?" Caleb asked.

"Orion," she said. "Big Dipper. Little Dipper. Cassiopeia. The greatest hits."

He raised an arm, pointing.

"See that?" he said. "There's the Dipper. Handle there, bowl there."

She followed his finger, squinting until the familiar pattern emerged from the scattering.

"Got it," she said.

He shifted his hand a little. "And that bright one?"

She searched. "There?"

"'Fraid so," he said. "That's Denver. Light pollution. Even from out here, you can't escape it completely."

She laughed softly. "I kind of like that," she said. "A reminder that both worlds exist. That I'm not… completely cut off from either."

They stood in companionable silence, watching the line between day and night shift, the valley below slowly surrendering to shadow, the ranch lights becoming small, steady beacons.

After a while, her shoulders sagged, the combination of emotional exhaustion and fresh air catching up.

"Thank you," she said quietly.

"For what?" he asked.

"For coming up to find me," she said. "For… letting me be mad at you. For telling me why you were mad at me. For this." She gestured at the sky.

"Anytime," he said. He meant it more than he expected.

A breeze gusted, stronger, making her shiver despite the jacket. Without thinking too much about it, he stepped closer, shoulder brushing hers.

"You, okay?" he asked.

"Yeah," she said. "I'm… more okay than I was this morning."

"That's somethin'," he said.

Their arms touched lightly from elbow to wrist, the contact subtle but steady. Neither of them moved away.

"I don't know what I'm going to tell Martin," she admitted. "But I know I don't want to decide out of panic. Or fear. I want to decide… on purpose."

"That's a good start," he said. "He can yell. Bosses do. Yellin' doesn't mean you're wrong."

"You've clearly never met Martin," she said, but she smiled.

He turned his head to look at her. In the dim light, her features were softened, edges blurred. The traces of dried tears were still faintly visible, but there was something steadier in her eyes now.

"You're allowed to choose your life, Emma," he said. "Not just react to it."

The words landed in a place she'd been trying not to acknowledge, deep and tender.

"So are you," she replied.

He opened his mouth, then closed it again, surprised by the mirror.

Below them, the ranch lights glowed. Above them, the stars grew clearer as full dark settled in. The overlook held them, a small, shared island between their separate fears.

Omniscient eyes, watching from a wider vantage point than any single hillside could provide, noted the shift.

Cracks had appeared, not in the sense of damage, but in the sense of openings. The armor both of them had worn for years, his built from loss and responsibility, hers from ambition and constant motion, had split just enough to let honest words out and something softer in.

They didn't kiss. The story didn't need that beat yet. Instead, they stood there shoulder to shoulder, watching the sky, letting the silence between them feel less like absence and more like presence.

Eventually, he said, "We should head back before Hank calls in the cavalry."

"Do we have a cavalry?" she asked.

"His version is driving up here in the ATV and lecturin' both of us," he said. "You don't want that."

"Fair," she said.

They picked their way down the trail together. He walked slightly ahead, flashlight beam cutting a narrow path through the dark, occasionally reaching back a hand to steady her over a tricky section. The first time, she hesitated a fraction before taking it. The second time, she didn't.

When they reached the cabin, Hank's silhouette was just visible on the porch of the house below, leaning on the rail. At the sight of their two shapes against the sky, he gave a small two-fingered salute and turned to go inside, satisfied.

Emma paused on her porch, turning to face Caleb.

"Seriously," she said. "Thank you. For… all of it."

He tipped his hat, though he'd taken it off earlier and was now just holding it, the gesture more habit than function.

"You're welcome," he said. "Get some sleep. Maybe tomorrow you don't open your computer first thing."

"What, and break the sacred writer's ritual?" she said.

"Maybe your ritual can handle a day off," he said. "Go stack hay instead. Might be good for your book."

She tilted her head. "Are you… asking for help again?"

"Considerin' your track record with trucks and horses, I figure we're past the trial period," he said. "But yeah. If you're up for it."

Her chest warmed in a way that had nothing to do with the jacket.

"I'm up for it," she said. "See you in the morning, boss."

He snorted. "Don't call me that," he said. "Night, Emma."

"Good night, Caleb."

He walked down the hill, boots crunching softly. She watched until he turned toward the house and disappeared from view.

Inside, she shut the door, leaned her back against it, and exhaled.

The decision about Denver hadn't magically become easier. Her book hadn't suddenly finished itself. There were still emails waiting, and a blinking cursor in a document she'd eviscerated.

But something in her had shifted.

She'd let someone see her fear and hadn't crumpled. She'd heard his, and instead of using it as ammunition, she'd held it with care. They'd stood under the same sky that watched over all of it, the wars, the careers, the ranch, the creek, and for a few minutes, neither of them had been running.

She shrugged out of Caleb's jacket reluctantly, hanging it over the back of a chair to return in the morning. His warmth still clung to the fabric.

Then she picked up her notebook, flipped to a clean page, and wrote, without overthinking:

Tonight, I stood on a hill with someone who is terrified of losing and someone who is terrified of wasting, and for a little while, we were just two people watching stars. Maybe that's not the worst place to start a new kind of story.

Her armor wasn't gone. Neither was his. But the cracks in it, under the Colorado sky, were beginning to let the light in.

Chapter Eleven
A Past Revealed

The invitation came in Hank's usual sideways way.

Emma was on the porch that afternoon, bare feet propped on the railing, laptop balanced on her thighs, when she saw him trudging up the hill with something white and flapping in his hand.

"You got a very official summons," he called before he'd even reached the steps.

"Oh no," she said. "Is this it? Am I being evicted for overuse of metaphors?"

"Worse," he said solemnly, handing her the paper. "You're bein' asked to eat my cookin'."

She unfolded it.

On the sheet, in Hank's blocky handwriting, it said:

SUPPER. 6:30. NO EXCUSES. – H.

She laughed. "Did you really need to bring a written note?"

"Legal documentation," he said. "You reporters like paper trails, don't you?"

"I'm technically on sabbatical," she pointed out, but she was already mentally inventorying the meager contents of her cabin pantry for something she could bring. "What's the occasion?"

He shrugged, the casualness of his gesture undercut by a glint of satisfaction in his eyes. "You've been here a while. Figured it was time you tasted a proper ranch stew instead of that... what was it you made the other night?"

"Pasta," she said. "It was perfectly edible."

"Looked like somethin' you'd patch drywall with," he grumbled. "Anyway. Caleb'll be in around then. You should come down. Six-thirty. Don't be late. And wear shoes you can throw in the wash."

"That last part is ominous," she said.

He grinned. "You'll see."

He started back down the hill, whistling tunelessly. Emma watched him go, then glanced at her laptop.

The blinking cursor in her document felt less accusatory than usual. After the previous night on the overlook, something in her had… leveled out. She'd slept hard, dreamed of stars, and woken with her fear still there but no longer strangling.

She'd emailed Martin that morning with a carefully composed message: I need the full length of my agreed sabbatical. I can't come back early. I'm happy to consult by phone on the housing story, pass along my notes and contacts, but I won't be in the newsroom until September.

His reply had been shorter and less warm than his phone call: Your choice. We'll make do. Don't drift too far.

It stung. But the thing that surprised her more was that the sting didn't send her scrambling to reverse herself. She'd read the email, sat with the discomfort, and then turned the Wi-Fi off.

By late afternoon, she'd wrangled a few decent pages out of the day. Enough that she felt she could close the laptop with a sense of having at least shown up to the work, even if she hadn't conquered it.

At six-fifteen, she stood in front of the small mirror on the cabin wall, debating clothing choices with more intensity than the situation warranted.

It was just supper. Not a date. Hank would be there. It was probably half an excuse to get her to help with dishes.

She settled on jeans that had already surrendered their city crispness to ranch dust, a soft navy top, and the boots that had proven themselves least likely to betray her ankles. She pulled her hair into a loose braid and grabbed the small plate of brownies she'd cobbled together from a mix she'd found at the back of the cupboard.

"Peace offering," she muttered. "For insulting his stew in advance."

The walk down to the ranch house felt different in the falling light. She'd made the trip before, but usually for quick practical reasons, asking Hank about a tool, dropping off a borrowed book, helping carry something up. Now, with the sun low and the house lit from within, it felt… cozier. Inviting.

The ranch house itself had the easy sprawl of a building added onto as needed over decades. The original structure was a simple rectangle, but porches, a mudroom, and a side wing had grown from it like branches. The siding was weathered but freshly painted. A rocker sat on the front porch, its seat worn smooth.

She knocked once out of habit and then remembered Hank's instructions from earlier in the week: "You knock like that; you'll be standin' there till next Tuesday. Come on in. If you walk in on something you shouldn't see, it's our fault, not yours."

She opened the door and stepped into a wave of warmth, physical and otherwise.

The kitchen was the heart of the house, and that heart was beating loudly tonight. A big pot simmered on the stove, filling the air with the savory smell of beef and herbs. Cornbread cooled on the counter, its golden top cracked just enough to show soft crumbs. Dishes clinked; a radio in the corner hummed some old country song, low.

Hank stood at the stove, stirring, a dishtowel slung over one shoulder like a badge of office.

"Right on time," he said, glancing over. "If that's chocolate in your hand, you can come in. If it's kale, turn around."

"Brownies," she said, stepping fully into the room and closing the door behind her. "From a box. Don't get too excited."

He eyed the plate approvingly anyway. "Box chocolate's still chocolate," he said. "Set 'em over there."

Caleb was at the sink, rinsing something, carrots by the look of the peels in the basin. He turned at the sound of her voice.

"Hey," he said.

She offered the plate up slightly in greeting. "I brought a sacrificial dessert."

"Looks better than the time Hank tried to make tart," he said.

"That recipe was cursed," Hank protested. "And that stove runs hot."

"The stove did not make it taste like scrambled eggs," Caleb said.

Emma laughed, the ease of their teasing smoothing the small awkwardness she'd carried through the door.

"Can I help with anything?" she asked. "Or is this a sit-and-be-served situation?"

"Oh, you're helpin'," Hank said. "I may be retired from a lot of things, but I ain't runnin' a restaurant. You can set the table."

He nodded toward the doorway that led into the main part of the house. "Dining room's through there. Plates are in the hutch. Forks and knives in the drawer. Glasses… wherever Caleb left 'em last."

"Got it," she said.

She stepped through.

The dining room opened wider than she expected. A long oak table dominated the space; its surface marked with scratches and water rings that spoke of a thousand meals before this one. A runner lay down the center, faded but clean. The chairs didn't match, exactly, two at the ends with arms, six along the sides with slightly different backs, but they all belonged to the same family of furniture: sturdy, serviceable, meant to last.

A sideboard held a row of framed photographs. The mantel in the adjacent living room, visible through a wide archway, held more. Emma's eye was drawn to them the way a magnet finds iron.

She forced herself, briefly, to focus on the task at hand. Plates from the hutch, heavy ceramic with a chipped floral pattern at the rim. Forks and knives from the drawer, clinking softly as she counted them out. She laid them on the table, muscle memory from countless family dinners guiding fork, plate, knife in their familiar positions.

Only when the table was more or less set did she drift toward the photographs.

She told herself it was simple curiosity. Houses told stories, and these frames were clearly one of the main chapters. But she was also acutely aware of the fact that this was Caleb's story, not hers, and she had no right to rifle through it with her eyes.

She stopped at the first cluster.

A younger Hank grinned out at her from one of the old photos, hair darker, belly smaller, holding up a fish that had to have been at least twenty inches long if the camera could be trusted. Next to him, a man who had to be Caleb's father stood with one hand on the boy's shoulder, Carhartt jacket, weathered face, eyes crinkled in a way that looked familiar even in grainy print.

Between them, a small boy, six, maybe seven, held a fishing rod almost too big for him. The boy's smile was huge, reckless, his hair sticking up from under a cap. She recognized the bone structure even stripped of years: Caleb.

Another frame showed a teenage version of him, all elbows and height, leaning against the hood of a truck with grease on his hands, laughing at something out of frame. Tom, she remembered Hank using the name, stood nearby with a wrench, watching him with what could only be described as pride.

Her gaze moved along, tracing the progression. High school football photo, Caleb in a Broncos-blue jersey, number 42, helmet under his arm. A shot of him at what looked like a county fair, arm slung casually around the shoulders of another boy in a 4-H T-shirt, both of them squinting at the camera.

Then: the one that made her chest tighten.

Caleb in uniform.

The photo was faded along the edges, like it had sat in sunlight a bit too long. He stood in the middle of a group of other young men, all in matching Army fatigues, rifles slung, desert behind them stretching flat and unforgiving. Their faces were streaked with dust, smiles tired but genuine. Someone had scrawled a date in the corner with a black marker. It was over a decade ago.

Emma leaned in, studying his face.

He looked… so young. Younger than she'd expected, even accounting for the math. The boy in the fishing photo had become this man in green and tan, but the bridge between them suddenly felt shorter.

His jaw was smoother, no hint of the stubble shadow he usually wore now. His eyes looked straight at the camera, something clear and intense in them. The hint of humor that she'd come to recognize around his mouth was there, but under it a seriousness she suspected had been there long before the Army got a hold of him.

She found herself scanning the other faces, wondering which ones had made it home, which ones hadn't. Which names still lodged in his throat when he tried to talk about that time.

Her gaze slid to the next frame along the mantel, and her breath caught for a different reason.

Two teenagers stood by the old cottonwood tree she'd seen down near the north pasture. Snow dusted the ground around their boots. The girl, in a knit hat and puffy coat, cheeks red from cold, laughed at the camera, her mouth open, eyes bright. She had one hand on Caleb's chest as if she'd just pushed him, playfully.

Caleb, younger here than in the uniform photo, wore a jacket and a look that could only be described as love-struck. He'd been caught mid-laugh, head tilted slightly toward her, eyes creased at the corners. The way he looked at her in the split second the shutter caught was unmistakable.

His arm was around her shoulders. Her gloved hand hooked into his jacket.

Emma didn't need Hank's earlier hints to fill in the blank. This, clearly, was the ex. Abby.

She let herself look for one beat, two. Enough to register the energy of the moment, not enough to catalog every detail. Curiosity buzzed under her skin, what was she like? How long had they lasted after this photo? but she tamped it down. This was a stranger's life she was peeking into, not a puzzle to solve.

She moved on.

More photos. Tom in a hospital bed, thinner, smiling weakly, Hank on one side of him and Caleb on the other. The weight on Caleb's face there was heavier, even as he attempted a smile for the camera. A picture of Caleb with a trophy and a horse, his expression proud but sheepish. A group shot from what looked like a Fourth of July barbecue, kids waving sparklers in the dusk.

Each frame was a snapshot of a larger story, but she didn't go digging. She took them in as one takes in a painting in a gallery, respectfully, aware that there are brushstrokes you'll never notice and meanings you'll never fully understand.

"Table looks good," Caleb's voice said from behind her.

She turned, startled, almost bumping into him.

"I was just," she began, gesturing awkwardly toward the mantel.

"Being nosy?" he suggested lightly.

"Appreciating your interior design choices," she countered. "Very 'lived-in ranch chic.'"

He huffed a laugh. "Yeah, well, Hank's too stubborn to let me take any of this down, and I'm too tired most days to argue."

She glanced back at the photos, then at him. "They're nice," she said honestly. "You… look happy, in most of them."

"In most of them," he echoed. "Key phrase."

He didn't sound bitter, exactly. More resigned.

She caught herself about to ask about the uniform photo, about the girl, about the man in the hospital bed. The questions lined up neatly in her journalist brain, each one ready with a follow-up.

Instead, she pressed her tongue gently against the back of her teeth and let them dissolve.

His boundaries were not hers to push. He'd opened up to her on that overlook in his own way, on his own timing. That counted more than satisfying her curiosity tonight.

"Do you need me to get glasses?" she asked instead. "I didn't see any."

"In that cabinet there," he said, nodding toward the hutch. "Top shelf. Try not to drop 'em; they're older than both of us."

She went to fetch the glasses. He watched the side of her face for a second longer than necessary, the way her attention had lingered on certain frames not lost on him.

He could guess which ones.

When they settled at the table, Hank insisted she take the seat that had clearly been someone's regular spot once, third from the head, near the window, across from where Caleb sat. Hank took the end, where he could see both the kitchen and the front door, habit born of years of watching the comings and goings.

"Don't skimp on the stew," he told her as he ladled a generous portion into her bowl. "You're gonna need the energy for tomorrow's chores."

"You've been saying that every day," she said. "I'm starting to suspect there's no such thing as 'enough energy' for this place."

"Now you're gettin' it," he replied.

They ate, conversation meandering from the weather to the county fair plans to Hank's latest gripe about the price of fuel.

At one point, Emma told a story about a disastrous city council meeting she'd covered once where a microphone stuck on live had broadcast an official's whispered insult across the chamber. Hank nearly choked on his cornbread laughing.

"You should write for TV," he said. "Seems like there's a market for that kind of farce."

"I already did write for TV," she said. "They just called it news."

They moved on to lighter topics. Caleb chimed in here and there, offering dry commentary, asking the occasional question about her work. He didn't dominate the conversation, but the creative rhythm that had started between them, her open, rapid-fire observations, his measured, occasionally sly responses, slotted easily into the larger trio.

After stew and cornbread and second helpings, Hank pushed his chair back with a theatrical groan.

"You two handle the dishes," he declared. "These old bones cooked; they shouldn't have to scrub."

"That math seems suspect," Caleb said, but he started stacking bowls without protest.

Emma gathered glasses, balancing them carefully as she carried them into the kitchen.

Washing up felt oddly intimate and oddly comfortable at the same time. She stood at the sink, hands in warm, soapy water, while Caleb dried, leaning on the counter close enough that their arms brushed now and then.

"Did you always have all those photos up?" she asked, keeping her tone casual. "Or is that a recent thing?"

"Most of 'em have been there since before I can remember," he said. "Mom liked to document everything. Hank added a few over the years. I tried to take one down once and got the guilt trip of a lifetime."

"Which one?" she asked, then winced. "Sorry. You don't have to answer that."

"The football one," he said. "Junior year. I hated that haircut."

She laughed, grateful for the low-risk confession.

"You were cute," she said, then caught herself. "I mean, judging from the tiny, pixelated version I saw. Very... earnest."

His hand paused on the dish he was drying. "Cute, huh?" he said.

"Don't let it go to your head," she replied, cheeks warming. "I would never say that about a current photo."

"I'll try not to be crushed," he said.

They fell into a companionable silence then, plates clinking, water running. The kind of silence that felt less like an absence of talk and more like a shared activity filling the space.

Hank wandered in at one point, ostensibly to grab his glass from the table, but really to satisfy his lifelong habit of monitoring dishwashing quality.

"You two done bickerin' in there?" he asked. "Or do I need to come mediate?"

"We're very harmonious," Emma said. "Like an assembly line."

"Sure," Hank said. His gaze flicked past her toward the living room. "Emma, you ever see the photo of Caleb with that ridiculous mustache?"

"Hank," Caleb warned.

Emma's eyes widened. "Wait, there's a mustache photo? Where was that? I didn't see it."

"Good," Caleb muttered.

"She's talkin' about the mantel," Hank realized. "You been snoopin'?"

"She was lookin'," Caleb said. "I wouldn't call it snoopin'."

Emma raised her sudsy hands. "Guilty of looking," she said. "But I swear I only glanced. No magnifying glass involved."

Hank's expression softened for a beat.

"Those tell a lotta stories," he said. "Hard to resist. Just remember they're snapshots. Whole chapters left out in between."

"I know," she said quietly.

He nodded, satisfied with both the dishes and the answer, and drifted out again.

They finished cleaning up. Hank shooed Caleb away when he tried to help with the trash.

"I can shuffle a bag to the can, son," he said. "Go sit. Emma, you want coffee? Tea? Something to prove I own more than one beverage?"

"Coffee would be great," she said.

She ended up in the living room while it brewed, perched on the edge of one of the couches, brownies on a plate on the low table. The couch had that lived-in comfort that said many evenings had been spent here, watching games, falling asleep mid-movie. A throw blanket, clearly hand-knitted by someone with patience, draped over the back.

The mantel called to her again, but she forced herself to sit, hands wrapped around her knees, content to simply be in the space rather than catalog it.

Hank came in with coffee mugs a few minutes later, setting one in front of her, one near the other end of the couch, and one on the small table by his favorite armchair.

Caleb followed, dropping into the opposite corner of the couch, stretching his legs out. He looked tired in that bone-deep way she recognized now, but his eyes were awake.

Hank watched them both for a moment as they sipped, some equation he'd been working on in his head finally resolving.

"All right," he said, setting his mug down with a soft thunk. "I'm gonna go check the porch light. Make sure it doesn't short out. Again."

"You fixed it last week," Caleb said.

"Doesn't mean it won't betray us tonight," Hank replied. "I got trust issues with that thing."

He gave Emma a brief, assessing look, less of a warning, more of a question. She met it steadily. He seemed satisfied with what he saw.

"I won't be far," he said, and stepped out, leaving the door ajar so the evening cool could filter in.

Silence settled briefly between Emma and Caleb, softened by the lamp's warm glow and the comforting clink of ceramic on ceramic.

She considered asking him directly about the uniform photo, about the girl by the tree. The curiosity was still there, stronger now that she'd seen the layers of his life laid out in frames.

But the moment didn't feel like hers to claim.

Instead, she took a sip of coffee and said, "Thank you. For supper. And for letting me invade your living room."

"You're not invadin'," he said. "You're payin' rent."

"Yes, but there's no fine print about family dinners," she said. "I appreciate the bonus."

"You keep bringin' brownies, Hank'll adopt you outright," he said.

The thought warmed her more than the coffee.

They drifted into lighter talk again, Hank's idiosyncrasies, the virtues of cornbread with vs. without sugar, the best way to eat stew leftovers. Eventually, Caleb excused himself to go check on something in the barn, "Won't be long; just want to make sure I latched the side door. Wind's pickin' up", leaving Emma alone with her mug.

Hank slipped back in from the porch a minute later, closing the door gently behind him.

"Barn check?" he asked, nodding toward where Caleb had gone.

"Apparently," Emma said. "He said he'd be right back."

"He will," Hank said. He lowered himself into his armchair, joints protesting. "That boy's got a checklist for the checklist."

She smiled, then hesitated. The question she'd been swallowing all evening pressed at the back of her throat.

"Hank?" she said. "Can I… ask you something?"

"Depends on the something," he said easily. "But you can try."

She glanced toward the mantel, where the photos waited out of sight.

"I saw the pictures," she said. "Of Caleb. In uniform. And… younger. With a girl by the tree."

Hank's gaze flicked to the archway, reading the angle of her glance even without seeing the frames.

"Yeah," he said. "Those have been there a while."

"I'm not trying to pry," she said quickly. "I know it's not my business. It's just… it helps sometimes to understand not just who someone is now, but how they got there. Especially when you're… living on their land."

"You're writin' about us," he said, not unkindly. "In your own way."

She opened her mouth to deny it, then shut it again. Lying to Hank felt both impossible and unwise.

"Not exactly," she said. "But… yes. Maybe a little."

He sipped his coffee, eyes thoughtful.

"You're not the first person to look at that wall and think, There's more to this than he lets on," he said. "And you won't be the last."

"If you don't want to talk about it, I understand," she said.

He considered her for a long moment, weighing. He'd been the guardian of Caleb's story for years, choosing carefully when and how to share it. Not to protect Caleb's pride; the man had less of that than most. But to protect his right to define himself in the present, not forever as the sum of his past hurts.

He saw something in Emma's face that tipped the balance. Not prurient interest. Not the hungry curiosity of a reporter sniffing a lead. Something gentler. A desire to understand so she could be kinder.

"All right," he said slowly. "I'll tell you a little. My version, anyway. Just remember, it is a version. You want the whole thing, you ask him."

"I won't… dig," she said. "I just… want context."

"Context," he repeated, amused. "Fancy word for gossip."

She flushed. "Ethical gossip."

He chuckled, then settled back in his chair, mug cradled in both hands.

"You saw the uniform photo," he said. "That was taken halfway through his first deployment. Afghanistan. He was, what, twenty-two? Twenty-three? Somewhere in there. Barely older than the kids who come up here now to ask if they can rent a cabin for a bachelor party."

Emma thought of the clear eyes in the photo, the dust on his face.

"He enlisted right outta high school," Hank went on. "Didn't surprise me. The boy had a whole lot of restless in him back then. Smart, but not the sit-behind-a-desk kind. This place… he loved it. Always did.

But the walls felt closer when he was nineteen than they do now. He wanted somethin' bigger. Thought the Army would give him that."

"Did it?" she asked.

Hank's mouth thinned. "In some ways," he said. "He got to see more of the world than most folks in this valley ever will. Learned what he was capable of. Learned what other people are capable of, too. Some of it good. Some of it…" He shook his head. "Some of it you don't come back from all the way."

She nodded. She'd interviewed enough veterans in her reporting days to know the gaps between what the brochures promised and what the desert delivered.

"He came back older," Hank said simply. "And I don't mean the number. You can see it in his eyes in those pictures. Before he left, his biggest worry was whether his truck would start or if he'd make it back from a date before his curfew. After… he'd seen things that made them worries seem small."

"And the girl?" Emma asked quietly. "Abby?"

"Abby," Hank confirmed. "High school sweetheart. Good kid. Smart. City in her bones. They were thick as thieves all through school. She was there through boot camp, through the first deployment. They really did try."

He shifted, looking down into his mug, as if the story might be written there.

"Thing is," he said, "they were tryin' to build a future on two very different sets of needs. She wanted out. Not just out of the ranch, out of the town, the state, maybe the country. Wanted to move, see things, never put roots down deep enough to feel trapped. Caleb… he wanted somethin' solid. A place he could come back to, with someone who'd be here when the dust settled."

He glanced up at Emma. "And then his dad got sick. That's the other photo you saw in there. Tom in the hospital."

She remembered it, the thin man in the bed, Caleb's hand on the rail, the weight on his face.

"Cancer doesn't care about your plans," Hank said. "It's greedy. It eats time first, then money, then whatever peace you had left. Caleb came home on emergency leave. Thought he'd get Tom through the worst of the treatments and be back overseas. Except worst turned into last. Treatments turned into goodbyes."

He paused, throat working.

"I'd known Tom since we were kids," he said. "Watched him build this place from nothin' with his own hands. Watchin' him fade like that… that was its own kind of war."

He took a breath, steadying himself.

"Caleb came home a soldier and became a caretaker in the span of weeks. He went from leadin' a squad to helpin' his old man up the stairs. From patrols to paperwork. And bein' twenty-something on top of that. It's a hell of a thing."

Emma's heart ached at the image, Caleb, already carrying the desert in his bones, now shouldering his father's illness, the ranch's precarious finances, a relationship stretched to breaking.

"And Abby?" she prompted gently.

"She tried," Hank said again, and this time there was no skepticism in it. "She brought meals. Sat at the hospital. Held his hand. But she was young too. And scared. Scared of hospitals, scared of death, scared of bein' tied to a future where every day was about chemo schedules and hay prices instead of passports and grad school."

He rubbed a thumb along a chip in his mug, remembering.

"She told him one day she couldn't be his wife under those conditions," he said. "Not right then. She said she didn't know how to be half-here and half-out there, and he couldn't be half-in on this place without everything fallin' apart. She was… honest, I'll give her that. Didn't sneak around. Didn't drag it out. Just looked him in the eye and said she needed somethin' else."

He met Emma's gaze.

"She wanted things he couldn't give her then," he said. "And he couldn't be the man he is now without walkin' through that fire first."

Emma sat with that for a moment, the weight of it settling.

"That doesn't make her the villain," Hank added. "Much as I wanted to paint her that way at the time. I was mad as a wet hen on his behalf. But anger fades. Perspective doesn't."

He leaned back, the chair creaking.

"She left," he said simply. "He stayed. Buried his dad, took over the ranch full-time, dug in. And he made a deal with himself somewhere along the way: he'd keep this place alive if it killed him. And he'd be damn careful about who he let close enough to watch if it did."

"You mean… relationships," she said quietly.

"Relationships, friendships, anything that required him to admit he might need someone," Hank said. "He's not afraid of work. He's not afraid of debt. But ask him to risk his heart again? That's another story."

She thought of the way he'd appeared at the creek, the sharpness of his tone when he'd found her, the haunted flash in his eyes when he'd said, I don't want to find you at the bottom of something I coulda warned you about.

"That's why he gets so… intense," she said slowly. "About safety. About… not wandering off."

"Part of it," Hank said. "Some of that's just good sense. Up here, you respect the land or it reminds you who's boss. But yeah. Some of it's him tryin' to out-maneuver that fear of loss. If he can keep track of everyone and everything, maybe he won't get blindsided again."

"Except life doesn't really work like that," she said.

"Don't I know it," Hank replied.

She tapped her fingers lightly against her mug, thinking.

"In the city," she said, "if a guy acted like that, insisted on knowing where you were, got angry if you didn't check in, it'd be a red flag. Controlling. Dangerous."

Hank nodded slowly. "In some contexts, you'd be right," he said. "I've seen my share of men who use 'worry' as an excuse to keep their thumb on someone. Keep 'em small. Make 'em need permission to breathe."

"And Caleb?" she asked.

"Caleb's different," he said. "He wants the people he cares about to be safe. That's not the same as wantin' them to be small. He might come on too strong sometimes, especially when something triggers that old fear. You saw a bit of that at the creek, I'm guessin'. But he's not… possessive. He doesn't see people as things that belong to him. He sees 'em as… responsibilities he doesn't want to fail."

She thought of the way he'd told her, You're allowed to choose your life, Emma. Not just react to it.

"He's been accused of being controlling before," she said. The words slipped out before she could stop them.

Hank's eyebrows rose. "Abby's words get around," he said. "Small town. She told her version to a few folks. Word stuck. Her dad is… a piece of work. Real controlling. She saw echoes of that in Caleb's protectiveness and decided she didn't want a repeat."

"Do you think she was wrong?" Emma asked.

"I think she was scared," Hank said. "And when you're scared, you start seein' ghosts of old pains in new places. Could Caleb be intense? Sure. Did he maybe grab onto her a little tighter when the world was fallin' apart around him? Probably. He'd just come back from people tryin' to kill him, his old man was dyin', the ranch was teeterin' on the edge. Of course, he wanted to hold onto the one good thing that still made sense."

He lifted one shoulder.

"But I also watched him respect her 'no,'" he said. "Respect her decision to leave. He didn't beg. Didn't threaten. Didn't call her names. Just… let her go. Hurt like hell, but he did it. That's not how a controlling man behaves. That's how a man behaves who knows he can't force somebody to stay without breakin' 'em and himself in the process."

Emma's chest tightened.

"So, when he worries," she said, "he's not… trying to manage me. He's trying to not have to bury someone else."

"That'd be my read," Hank said. "Doesn't mean you have to like how it comes out every time. You can set your own boundaries. Tell him when it crosses a line for you. He's not perfect. But if you do, he'll listen. That's the difference."

She let out a slow breath she hadn't realized she was holding.

"Why are you telling me all this?" she asked. "I mean, I appreciate it. But… why me?"

Hank's gaze softened.

"Because you're not just passin' through," he said. "Most folks who rent that cabin treat this place like a pretty backdrop for their vacation photos. They don't see the work. They don't see the cracks. You… do. And you care. I see the way you watch him. Not like he's some rugged postcard. Like you're tryin' to figure out how his pieces fit."

She swallowed, feeling suddenly transparent.

"And because," Hank went on, "I've watched that boy take hits from life like he was built for it. I've watched him keep standin' when a lesser man would've found a barstool and stayed on it. He deserves someone in his corner who understands that his rough edges came from tryin' to hold everything together, not from enjoyin' breakin' things."

He leaned back, the chair groaning.

"I'm not sayin' you're that someone or you owe him anything," he added. "You got your own life to sort. But if you do find yourself in his orbit, I'd rather you had the full picture than some half-truth you picked up in town."

She nodded, throat tight.

"Thank you," she said quietly. "I… that means a lot. That you trust me with that."

He waved a hand, uncomfortable with gratitude that heavy.

"Don't make it a bigger thing than it is," he said. "I'm just an old man runnin' his mouth in his own living room."

But the truth was, it was a big thing. A piece of a puzzle she hadn't even realized she was actively assembling.

Footsteps sounded in the hallway. Caleb appeared in the archway, wiping his hands on a rag.

"Side door was latched," he reported. "You two talkin' about me?"

"Always," Hank said.

Emma took a breath, smoothing her expression.

"Only the good parts," she said lightly.

Caleb squinted at the two of them, aware in that bone-deep way people are when they've been the topic of conversation.

"Should I be worried?" he asked.

"Not unless your ears are burnin'," Hank said. "You want coffee? Emma and I have solved approximately half the world's problems while you were out there."

"I'll pass," Caleb said. "If I drink more, I'll be up all night thinkin' about that south fence."

"Don't pretend you won't be up anyway," Hank said.

Caleb rolled his eyes affectionately and dropped onto the far end of the couch again.

Emma felt the weight of the new information nestle into her understanding of him, like a puzzle piece finally finding its notch.

She saw now, more clearly, how the man who'd walked up to the creek angry and afraid was also the boy who'd watched his father fade and his fiancée leave. She understood how the soldier in the photo, surrounded by dust and brothers-in-arms, had become the rancher who checked the side door twice before bed.

She still hadn't seen him act controlling. Protective, yes. Intense, occasionally. But his worry curved outward, away from himself. It didn't feel like a cage; it felt like an offer of shelter he didn't quite know how to extend without sounding like a lecture.

As they drifted into conversation again, this time about nothing more consequential than whether Gus actually understood the word "no", she stored Hank's words carefully.

She wanted things he couldn't give her then. And he couldn't be the man he is now without walking through that fire first.

She turned them over in her mind like river stones, smoothing them with repetition.

Omniscient eyes noted the shift in her posture, the subtle way she relaxed slightly when Caleb's hand brushed her knuckles reaching for the brownie plate, the way her laugh at his dry comment held a new layer of tenderness.

She did not, that night, tell him what Hank had shared. She did not rush to reassure him that she understood. That would come later, when ghosts from the past started to step back into the present with opinions of their own.

For now, she simply sat on his couch, in his house, under the watchful gaze of the photos on the mantel, and let the story of who he'd been deepen her appreciation for who he was.

The armor he wore, she realized, wasn't just about keeping people out. It was also about holding together the pieces of himself that had been through more than most people ever would. Seeing the seams didn't make him seem weaker; it made the structure of him make sense.

She sipped her coffee, listened to Hank grumble good-naturedly about the porch light again, and thought, without quite naming it:

I'm glad I walked onto this land.

Chapter Twelve
Town Night & Almost Kiss

Cottonwood Ridge wasn't a big town, but it knew how to look busy on a Friday night.

By six, Main Street glowed with that particular kind of small-town energy, pickup trucks angled in along the curb, kids darting between their parents and the ice cream stand, the faint smell of burgers and fryer oil drifting from the diner. The neon OPEN sign in the front window of Pages & Pours flicked on, followed a beat later by the rusty neon of The Spur down the block sputtering to life.

Hank had a theory that the town ran on three things: caffeine, feed, and whatever passed for live music out here. Tonight, all three were in play.

"Need anything?" Emma asked, hovering in the cabin doorway with her keys in hand.

She'd spent most of the afternoon wrestling a single paragraph into existence, deleting it, and then writing it again from a different angle. It wasn't a bad writing day, exactly, just one of those days where nothing came easy and the cabin walls had begun to close in.

Town, with its lights and noises and shelves of books, sounded like relief.

"Bring me back a new hip," Hank said from where he was tightening a bolt on the ATV. "Barring that, we're low on coffee. You goin' by the bookstore café?"

"Pages & Pours," she said. "Yes. Because I am a weak woman who requires both books and caffeine to survive."

"Get the house blend," he said. "Tell 'em it's for me; they'll give you the big bag, not the tiny city one."

She smiled. "Anything else?"

"Nah," he said. "We're runnin' to the feed store in a bit. Caleb's makin' a list like we're goin' to war."

"Isn't that your default mode?" she teased.

"Man likes to be prepared," Hank said. "Keeps us from runnin' outta things like salt lick and baling twine."

Emma tucked that detail away with all the others. "Okay. I'll be back later. Don't burn the place down."

"We'll try not to," Hank said. "You watch yourself in town. Friday nights folks get rowdy."

"In Cottonwood Ridge?" she asked, amused. "What do they do, order a second slice of pie?"

Hank just grinned. "You'll see."

She headed out, the drive down the gravel lane familiar now. The road into town wound along the base of the hills, cottonwoods and willows lining the creeks. The sky was sliding toward evening, all soft blue and streaks of peach. Her car's radio fuzzed in and out between stations; she turned it off and rolled the window down, letting the wind tangle her hair.

Pages & Pours occupied a narrow brick building on Main, front half bookstore, back half coffee shop, with a few mismatched tables bleeding into the stacks. A bell over the door jingled when she stepped in.

"Hey there," called the woman behind the counter, wiping espresso grounds from her hands. Libby, if Emma remembered right, owner, barista, and resident recommendation engine. "Back for another hit?"

"You're my dealer," Emma said. "I'm powerless to resist."

"Wi-Fi's slow today," Libby warned. "Storm messed with it yesterday."

"I'm pretending the internet doesn't exist," Emma said. "I just need coffee and a place that isn't my own four walls."

"We can do that," Libby said. "House blend?"

"And a blueberry muffin if there are any left," Emma added, eyeing the glass case.

"For you?" Libby said. "I hid one behind the scones. Don't tell the locals."

Emma felt absurdly honored. "My lips are sealed."

She took her mug and plate to a small table near the front window, one that looked onto Main Street. Sunlight slanted through the glass, catching dust motes and the occasional passing truck.

Her notebook came out instead of the laptop. After the emotional excavation of the past few days, the creek, the overlook, Hank's stories, she didn't have the bandwidth for screen glare. Pen on paper felt more honest tonight.

She scribbled for a while, half novel, half journal. Snatches of dialogue, a description of the way the light had looked on Caleb's face when he'd pointed out the Big Dipper.

At one point, she caught herself writing his name and crossed it out, replacing it with "C." That wasn't much better. She underlined that and then drew a tiny cow beside it, as if that somehow turned it into fiction.

Outside, the town's rhythm rolled on. A group of teenagers gathered in front of the ice cream counter, jostling each other. A couple in their sixties ambled past holding hands. A dog tied to the lamppost across the street sighed dramatically every time someone walked by without petting it.

She was so caught up in watching that she almost missed the familiar truck pulling into a spot just down from the bookstore.

The old green pickup eased in behind the feed store, back end loaded with empty tubs. Caleb climbed out, shutting the door with the habitual slap of someone who'd closed that door a thousand times. He wore a button-down tonight instead of a T-shirt, plaid, sleeves rolled, jeans that had seen better days, hat brim low.

Her stomach did a small, traitorous flip.

Of course he'd be here. Hank had said feed store run. And Friday nights in Cottonwood Ridge had a pattern: feed store open late for the ranchers coming in from chores, The Spur serving burgers and beer next door, a live band or at least a decent playlist on the speakers.

He disappeared into the feed store, door chiming behind him.

Emma looked back down at her notebook, heart beating a little faster than before. She hadn't exactly been avoiding seeing him outside the ranch, but this was different. Neutral ground. No excuse of a chore or a shared coffee pot.

You could go say hi, she thought. It's not illegal.

Her feet, however, remained stubbornly under the table.

She wrote another paragraph. Drank more coffee. Watched as the sidewalk traffic thinned slightly, the demographic shifting from families to people her age and older. The sun finally slid fully behind the ridge, the sky deepening toward indigo. Streetlights flicked on.

At some point, she became aware of music threading faintly through the glass, guitar, drums, a fiddle cutting clean lines through the mix. She recognized the direction: The Spur. Friday night band.

She glanced that way and caught a glimpse through The Spur's open door: strings of lights, a small stage in the corner, people already occupying the handful of tables.

Her chest tightened with a mix of intrigue and nerves. Dancing had never been her thing. Not like this, anyway. Not the kind of dancing where everyone knew the steps but her.

She turned back to her notebook and drew a star in the margin instead.

Down the block, in the feed store, Caleb was having his own version of an ordinary Friday night.

He leaned on the counter while Eddie, who'd been managing the place since before Caleb was born, rang up the list, mineral blocks, chicken feed, a new nozzle he'd been putting off buying for weeks.

"Got your hands full?" Eddie asked, squinting at the receipt.

"More mouths every spring," Caleb said. "Feels like anyway."

"Means you're doin' somethin' right," Eddie said. He slid the bags along. "Hank still alive?"

"Stubbornness and coffee," Caleb said. "He'll outlast all of us."

"Tell him to get his hide in town one of these nights," Eddie said. "Haven't seen him two-step in too long."

Caleb snorted. "Last time he did, he put his back out and blamed me."

"Old men gotta have someone to blame," Eddie said. "You takin' in the band tonight?"

"Maybe," Caleb said. "We'll see how heavy the feed feels once I load it."

Eddie gave him a look. "Even you can take a night off, son," he said. "Bar's five steps that way."

Caleb didn't argue, but he didn't commit either. He hefted the bags one by one into the bed of the truck, muscle memory doing most of the work while his mind drifted.

The past week sat in him like a stone he'd turned over so many times it was starting to grow smooth. Emma at the creek, eyes bright with unshed anger and fear. Emma on the hill, face tipped up to the stars, shoulder warm against his. Emma in his living room, mug cradled, listening as Hank filled in some of the blanks.

He'd caught the glance between her and Hank when he'd walked back in, knew with bone-deep certainty that they'd been talking about him. And yet, he hadn't felt exposed in the way he usually did when small-town gossip circled. Instead, it had felt like a piece of weight shifting from one shoulder to three, spread out.

He slammed the tailgate shut and wiped his hands on his jeans. The band's music drifted clearer now, someone covering an old George Strait song, the familiarity of it wrapping around him like an old jacket.

The Spur was only a few doors down, its side entrance practically spitting distance from the feed store's back ramp. He could picture the interior without looking: narrow bar along one wall, small dance floor cleared in front of the stage, tables crowded with folks from every corner of the county. Friday nights like this had been his social life once, before things got heavier and the ranch's demands had multiplied.

He told himself he'd just go in for one beer. Maybe a burger. Listen to a song or two. Remind himself he could exist in a room that wasn't either his kitchen or a barn.

He rounded the corner to the front, boots clicking on the sidewalk.

That's when he saw her.

Through Pages & Pours' wide front window, lit by the warm glow inside, Emma sat at a small table, pen moving. Her hair fell forward as she bent over the notebook, profile intent. A half-eaten muffin sat on a plate; her coffee mug was nearly empty.

Something unspooled in his chest, unexpected and too quick. The same feeling he got sometimes seeing the first calf of the season stand on wobbling legs, a mix of JOY and caution.

He stopped without meaning to, gaze snagged. After a second, he realized he was just… standing there on the sidewalk staring like an idiot. He forced himself to move, cutting across toward The Spur, telling himself he'd pretend he hadn't noticed her if she looked up.

He made it almost to the bar door before a familiar voice cut across the music.

"Thought that was you."

Hank.

Caleb turned to see the older man leaning against the brick wall between The Spur and the bookstore, hands tucked into his jacket pockets. He'd clearly come into town on his own, truck parked a few spaces down, cap pulled low.

"You followin' me now?" Caleb asked.

"Please," Hank said. "I was checkin' the produce at the grocery. Making sure they still put the lettuce in the right place. Man's gotta have hobbies."

Caleb huffed. "You hate lettuce."

"I hate badly organized lettuce," Hank corrected. He tipped his head toward the bookstore window. "She's here."

Caleb didn't have to ask who "she" was.

"Yeah," he said. "I saw."

"You goin' in there?" Hank asked.

"It's a bookstore," Caleb said. "You know my stance on readin' for fun."

"Sad, really," Hank said. "All those words, wasted on a man who thinks manuals are literature."

He nudged his chin toward The Spur's door, where the music had kicked up a notch. A couple walked in laughing, hands linked.

"They're playin' tonight," Hank said. "Tanner's band. They ain't half bad. You could do worse things with an evenin' than dance with a pretty girl."

Caleb's mouth twisted. "I'm not much of a dancer."

"Hell of a rider though," Hank said. "Balance is balance. Feet instead of hooves. You'll figure it out."

Caleb glanced back at the bookstore window. Emma had put her pen down, fingers massaging the bridge of her nose. The expression on her face was familiar, mental fatigue, the kind that came from wrestling invisible problems.

"She might not wanna dance," he said. "She might want a quiet night with her coffee and her... French poetry or whatever she reads."

Hank gave him a look. "You ever ask her what she wants this evenin'?"

Caleb exhaled. "No."

"Then you don't know," Hank said. "Go ask. Worst thing that happens is she says no and you go back to drinkin' alone. Lord knows you've done that enough."

Caleb shot him a dry look. "You always this pushy?"

"Only when I'm right," Hank said. He clapped a hand on Caleb's shoulder, solid and warm. "Go ask her if she wants to see how these folks dance."

The words landed like a gentle shove.

Caleb stood there another half second, weighing. Pride, fear, self-consciousness all put in their bids. Then he pictured Emma alone at that little table, headlights passing across her face, the band playing next door while she sat there trying to shut her own thoughts up with caffeine.

Before he could talk himself out of it, he turned and walked toward the bookstore.

Inside, the bell over the door jingled again.

Emma looked up automatically, pen mid-scratch. Her eyes widened a fraction when she saw him.

"Hey," she said, surprise softening into something warmer. "Fancy seeing you here."

"Feed store," he said, lifting an imaginary bag with one hand. "Figured I'd check in on the town's caffeine addict while I was here."

"That's very neighborly of you," she said. "You want to sit?"

He glanced at the small chair opposite her, then down at himself, barn jacket, boots, the perpetual faint dust. "I might break that thing," he said.

"That's just an excuse," Libby's voice chimed from behind the counter. "It held Hank once and he's built like a tractor. You're fine."

Caleb gave her a mock-glare. Libby just smiled and kept wiping down the espresso machine.

He pulled the chair out and sat. It creaked a little but held.

"What are you workin' on?" he asked, nodding toward the notebook.

"Vague existential dread and women making questionable choices about love," she said.

"So… your book," he said.

"Basically," she said. "Sometimes I can't tell where my stuff ends and the story begins."

He studied her for a beat. "You, okay?" he asked, voice low enough that Libby couldn't easily eavesdrop even if she wanted to.

She hesitated. "I emailed my editor this morning," she said. "Told him I'm not coming back early."

"And?" he asked.

"And he was… not thrilled," she said. "But he'll live. I keep reminding myself of that. No one died because I chose to not burn myself out on a housing scandal."

"Good," he said simply.

"Good that he'll live or good that I'm… selfish?" she asked, half teasing, half genuinely unsure.

"Good that you chose somethin' for yourself," he said. "You can call it selfish if you want. I call it sane."

Her chest loosened a fraction.

"Thank you," she said softly.

He glanced toward the window, where The Spur's neon glowed faintly red in the dusk.

"Listen," he said, clearing his throat as if about to deliver a weather report instead of an invitation. "Tanner's band is playin' at The Spur tonight. They're not bad. Little loud. Lotta twang. Thought maybe…"

He shifted, clearly out of his comfort zone.

"Thought maybe you'd want to see how these folks dance," he finished, the last part coming out with a faint echo of Hank's phrasing.

Emma's eyebrows went up, a smile tugging at the corner of her mouth before she could stop it.

"Are you asking me out, Mr. Walker?" she said lightly.

"I'm askin' if you wanna go listen to some music and, if you want, let me step on your toes a few times," he said. "No pressure."

She considered making a joke, deflecting. Dancing wasn't her thing; she'd established that early in her adult life after a particularly humiliating wedding reception. But the thought of staying at this little table while he walked back out into the night alone, when there was a chance, a small, terrifying, exhilarating chance, of something else, felt worse.

Her heart thudded once, hard.

"I'd like that," she said.

He exhaled, almost imperceptibly. "All right then," he said. He stood, chair scraping gently. "You need to settle up?"

She glanced toward the counter. Libby was already waving a hand.

"Go," Libby mouthed. "You can pay me later."

Emma laughed. "Apparently my tab is good."

"Must mean you tip well," Caleb said.

"Or she's investing in the entertainment of watching me attempt to dance," Emma replied.

They stepped out into the cool evening, the bell jingling behind them. The street had quieted a bit, though there were still clusters of people moving between the diner and the bar, laughter rolling.

The Spur's front door stood open, music spilling out. As they approached, Emma's pulse kicked up again.

"Just so you know," she said as they crossed the threshold, "my dancing experience consists mostly of swaying awkwardly at concerts and that one Zumba class I went to with a friend in college."

"You're overqualified," he said. "Most guys here just rock back and forth and hope their partner covers for 'em."

Inside, The Spur looked exactly the way Hank's stories had led her to expect. Wooden floors, scuffed and polished by years of boots. A long bar along one side, bottles lined up behind it, bartender moving efficiently. A handful of high-top tables scattered around, most occupied. The stage in the corner held a four-piece band, guitar, bass, drums, fiddle. Tanner, a wiry man in a ball cap and T-shirt, leaned into the mic, voice smooth.

"Evenin', Caleb," the bartender called as they stepped in.

"Hey, Dale," Caleb said. "You know Emma?"

"Seen her in at Pages & Pours," Dale said. "Ma'am."

"Hi," Emma said, acutely aware of how obvious she must seem, stepping in with Caleb at her elbow.

"You want a beer?" Caleb asked her. "Or somethin' else?"

"Beer's good," she said. "Whatever you're having."

He ordered two longnecks, handed one to her, and gestured toward the edge of the dance floor where a few couples already moved in time with the song, a mid-tempo number, perfect for two-stepping.

They stood watching for a moment, older couples who clearly knew each other's movements by heart; younger ones still figuring it out, laughing when they misstepped. The air inside was warm, edged with sweat, perfume, and something that might have been barbecue.

"You still sure?" he asked, voice near her ear to be heard over the music.

She tightened her grip on the bottle. "About dancing?" she said. "No. But I'm not running."

"That's somethin'," he said.

He set his beer down on a nearby ledge. She did the same, hands suddenly feeling very empty.

"Okay," he said. "Here's the deal. I'll lead. You follow. If you don't know what that means yet, that's fine. Just move when I move. When in doubt, step. Nobody's keepin' score."

She laughed, nerves spiking into something almost giddy. "I reserve the right to mock you mercilessly if you screw up," she said.

"Fair," he said.

He held his hand out to her.

She hesitated only a heartbeat before placing her fingers in his. His palm was warm, rough. He guided her onto the floor, weaving between couples with an ease that suggested he'd done this plenty of times.

They stopped near the edge, not in the thick of things but not too far away either. He placed her right hand on his shoulder, his left hand settling lightly at her waist. The contact sent a quick, surprising jolt through her.

"Relax," he murmured.

"That's a lot to ask," she said, trying to ignore how aware she suddenly was of every point where they touched.

He smiled, small but genuine. "Just listen," he said.

The band slid into the chorus. He shifted his weight, stepped forward, then sideways. She stumbled the first time, her feet a half-second behind his. She stepped on his boot.

"Sorry," she blurted.

"Cost of doin' business," he said. "Try again."

They found the pattern slowly. Step, together, step, tap. Turn. Her body resisted at first, wanting to anticipate, to control. But the music had its own logic, and his lead was steady without being forceful. When she let herself stop overthinking, her feet began to fall into place.

After a minute, it almost felt like they were gliding.

"There you go," he said. "You're doin' it."

"Don't jinx it," she said, but she couldn't help the smile that spread across her face. Something inside her unwound a notch.

They moved through the space, the other couples swirling around them. Laughter bubbled up every time they nearly collided with someone else or she veered off rhythm and he had to gently steer her back.

"Who taught you to do this?" she asked, breathless between verses.

"Mom," he said. "Tom, some. Hank, when he was in a sentimental phase. This is pretty much the only way this town knows how to dance. Figured I should keep up."

"I had no idea you were so cultured," she said.

"Don't go spreadin' rumors," he replied. "I've got a gruff country image to maintain."

She laughed, the sound genuine and free.

Halfway through the song, something shifted. Her hand on his shoulder relaxed, fingers no longer gripping fabric like a lifeline. His hand at her waist settled a little more firmly, guiding without gripping. Their bodies, tentative at first, began to anticipate each other's weight, moving in tandem.

He caught the scent of her shampoo, something faintly floral, clean. She could feel the solid warmth of his chest under her palm, the steady rise and fall of his breathing. The world narrowed to the circle of their shared space and the music threading through it.

When the song ended, they both stepped back slightly, a little flushed.

"You survived," he said.

"Barely," she replied. "I expect a medal."

"The medal is we get to do it again," he said, nodding toward the stage as the band launched into another number, this one slower.

"Now you're pushing your luck," she said, but she didn't move to leave the floor.

The slower song shifted the energy in the room. Couples drew closer. The two-step became less about footwork and more about sway, connection.

He slid his arm a fraction higher on her back, hand settling between her shoulder blades. Her hand on his shoulder drifted slightly closer to his neck. Their joined hands lowered a bit, bringing them nearer.

"Tell me if this is too close," he said quietly.

She met his eyes. The offer was there, clear, opt out if you need to. She could feel the edges of his own restraint.

"It's okay," she said. "I trust you not to fling me into a jukebox."

"No jukebox-flingin'," he agreed.

They began to move again. The slower tempo gave her brain more space to notice things. The way his thumb traced small, absent circles against her back. The way his gaze kept flicking from her face to somewhere over her shoulder and back, as if he were trying not to stare and failing a little.

The song's lyrics talked about second chances and long roads back. Too on-the-nose, she thought, if she were writing this. But she wasn't; she was living it, and life had no qualms about leaning into cliche.

"You're not bad at this," she said softly.

"I've had practice," he said. "You're pickin' it up quick."

"Don't sound so surprised," she said.

"I'm not surprised," he said. "I just… like seein' you find your feet here. Literally and otherwise."

Her throat tightened at that.

"You make it easier," she said before she could overthink it. "Being here. Doing chores. Talking me off ledges."

He huffed a small laugh. "You make it harder," he said.

She blinked. "Harder?"

"Not in a bad way," he said quickly. "Just… I'd spent a lotta years makin' my life real simple. Work, sleep, repeat. Then you show up with your notebooks and your questions and your city boots, and suddenly I'm thinkin' about things like whether Hank's stew is fit for company."

"Hey, I like his stew," she protested. "You saying I have standards?"

"I'm sayin' you have options," he said. "You could be anywhere. You chose here. That… matters."

The way he said it made her chest ache.

She swallowed. "You know I'm not just… killing time, right?" she asked, voice low. "That I'm not here because I ran out of places to go?"

"I know," he said. "I see the way you look at this place. At the work. At… us."

The word hung between them, almost unnoticed in the swirl of music, but not by them.

She held his gaze. The room around them blurred a little, noise fading to a softer hum.

His eyes were darker in the low light, lashes casting faint shadows. There was a question in them now, the same one beating wildly in her chest: Is this more than borrowed time? Are we allowed to let it be?

Her heart answered before her mind could.

The song's bridge hit; the band drew out a fiddle note that made the hairs on her arms rise.

They were close enough now that she could feel the warmth of his breath when he spoke.

"I like this," he said quietly. "Dancin' with you."

"I do too," she said.

The honesty cracked something open. Even the armor he'd spent years welding around himself couldn't fully deflect the vulnerability of the moment.

His gaze dropped, almost of its own accord, to her mouth. Hers flicked to his, then back up. Time stretched thin.

He leaned in the smallest fraction, as if pulled. She couldn't have said who moved first. The world narrowed to the space between them, that last inch of air suddenly thick.

Her lips brushed his.

It was barely anything, so light it might have been an accident if not for the way both of them froze at the contact. Heat jolted through her, sending sparks along nerves she'd thought were dormant. His hand at her back tightened, just for a second.

Then,

"Last call, folks!" the bartender's voice boomed over the music, cutting through the moment. The band slid into an outro, laughter erupting from a table near the bar as someone knocked over a chair.

The spell snapped like a taut rope cut too suddenly.

Emma pulled back a hair, breath hitching. Caleb straightened just enough to put a sliver more space between them, jaw tight.

"Sorry," he murmured, though it wasn't clear whether he was apologizing for leaning in or for stopping.

"You didn't..." she began, then stopped. Words felt clumsy compared to what had just passed between them.

The song ended. Applause broke out. People started drifting off the floor, heading toward the bar or the door, conversations swelling.

"We should," he said.

"Yeah," she said at the same time.

They both half-laughed, the sound shaky.

He stepped back, letting his hand fall from her back reluctantly. The loss of contact was immediate, a small shock.

"Do you want another drink?" he asked. It was the safe question, the neutral ground.

She glanced at the bar, the people stacking empties and counting tips.

"I think if I have another beer, I'll fall asleep on your barn floor tomorrow," she said.

"Can't have that," he said. "Hank'd never let me live it down."

"Or he'd take a picture for future blackmail," she said.

"Also likely," he agreed.

They retrieved their bottles, now half-warm, and set them on the bar. Dale gave Caleb a knowing look but didn't say anything beyond, "You drivin' safe?"

"Always," Caleb said.

They stepped out into the cooler night air. The contrast made Emma shiver. The sky above Main was clear, stars faint against the glow of the streetlights, but still there.

"That wasn't so bad," she said, aiming for lightness and landing somewhere between.

"You didn't break any toes," he said. "I call that a success."

She smiled. Then, caught by the courage that sometimes comes only at the edges of exhaustion and beer, she added:

"And for the record, I didn't hate that either."

His eyes met hers, something raw and grateful flickering across his face.

"Me neither," he said softly.

For a moment, they stood there on the sidewalk, traffic a distant whoosh, the town's hum fading as people drifted home. The almost-kiss hung between them like a secret, fragile and electric.

He cleared his throat, practical instinct reasserting itself.

"You want me to follow you back?" he asked. "Road's dark. Deer like to test bumpers."

She shook her head. "I'll be careful," she said. "Besides, you've already saved me from one creek this week. Don't want to overuse my damsel-in-distress quota."

He smiled, but his worry didn't entirely dissipate. "Text Hank when you get in," he said. "Or turn on the porch light. We'll keep an eye out."

She nodded. "Deal."

They walked to their respective vehicles parked along the curb. For a second, she thought about leaning over and kissing his cheek in some half-measure of gratitude and recklessness. But the moment didn't quite feel right for that. They were balanced on a knife edge; one wrong move and the careful slow burn might turn into something else too fast.

Instead, she put her hand briefly on his forearm, squeezing once.

"Thank you for asking me," she said. "To dance."

"Thank you for sayin' yes," he said.

They parted then, her to her sedan, him to his truck. Engines turned over. Headlights washed the street.

As Emma pulled out and headed toward the dark stretch of road leading back to High Meadow, she caught a glimpse in her rearview mirror of the green truck's lights behind her, not tailgating but not letting much distance build either.

He said he wasn't following her. He was just… driving home the same way.

Omniscient eyes knew better.

When she turned onto the gravel lane that led up to the cabin, his headlights continued straight toward the ranch house. She watched his taillights in her side mirror until they disappeared around the curve.

At the cabin, she killed the engine and sat in the quiet for a moment, hands still on the wheel. The night pressed close, crickets, the rustle of grass, the faint sound of a cow lowing somewhere far below.

Her lips still tingled faintly where they'd brushed his. She touched them, almost disbelieving.

"What are you doing, Emma?" she whispered to the dark.

She didn't have an easy answer. But she knew this: the orbit she and Caleb were in now wasn't casual. It wasn't a fling to fill a summer. The way her heart had leapt at his invitation, the way his had cracked open a little on the dance floor, it all pointed in one clear direction.

She turned on the porch light, a small beacon in the night. Down at the ranch house, Caleb, stepping onto his own porch, saw it flare and felt the knot in his chest ease, just a bit.

They both went to bed that night acutely aware of how far they'd fallen already, past neighborly curiosity, past convenient company, into a depth that made the next steps both terrifying and inevitable.

Under the Colorado sky, the slow burn had found its spark. The fire, though still controlled, was very much lit.

Chapter Thirteen
Choosing Each Other

The call came just before dawn.

Emma woke to pounding on the cabin door, a sharp, urgent rhythm that cut straight through the sleep fog. For half a second, she thought it was the Denver landlord she'd once had who used to bang on doors for late rent, and her heart lurched. Then she registered the cold blue of early morning seeping around the edges of the curtains, the faint smell of pine, and the sound of Gus barking below.

She scrabbled for her phone. 4:37 a.m.

"Emma!" Caleb's voice, rough and louder than she'd ever heard it, came through the wood. "You awake?"

Her brain flipped from dream to now in a heartbeat.

"Yeah!" she called, already halfway out of bed. "One second!"

She yanked on jeans, shoved her arms into the flannel shirt hanging on the back of a chair without bothering to button it, and jammed her feet into boots. Her hair went into a messy knot that would've made her Denver friends nervous about being seen in public; here, she didn't have time to care.

She threw the door open.

Cold air slapped her awake. Caleb stood on the porch, hat low, jacket half-zipped, breath white in the dim light. His eyes, usually steady, were bright with something sharper.

"Sorry to bang on you like that," he said, already turning as if expecting her to follow. "We got a situation. First-calf heifer down in the east lot. Calf's comin' wrong. Hank's out there with her now, and I need another pair of hands."

Her brain caught enough of that to latch on to the important part. "What do you need me to do?" she asked.

He looked back at her, double-taking at her bare hands. "Grab gloves," he said. "The work kind. And a jacket you don't mind ruinin'. Meet me at the barn."

She snatched the thick work gloves Hank had insisted she keep by the door for "when the real chores start, city girl" and shrugged on her heaviest jacket. By the time she reached the path, Caleb was already halfway down the hill, moving in that long, efficient stride that ate ground. She jogged to catch up, gravel crunching under her boots, breath puffing.

"What's a… first-calf heifer?" she asked, lungs burning. "And how wrong is wrong?"

"First-time mama," he said without slowing. "She's young and nervous, calf's not lined up right. If we don't get it turned, we could lose both."

The words landed with icy clarity.

Lose both.

The barn loomed out of the half-light, yellow glow spilling from its open doors. The sky above was only just beginning to pale at the edges; stars still clung to the dark.

Inside, the air hit her warm and wet and full of earthy smells, hay, manure, animals breathing. Hank's voice came from the far end, sharp and calm, talking to someone, or something.

"Easy, girl. That's it. Breathe. We're gonna help you."

They rounded the corner of the aisle.

A brown-and-white heifer lay on her side in the straw of a small pen, flanks heaving, eyes wide and rolling. Her back pressed against the wooden wall, legs kicked out in front. A slick bulge of membrane and hooves pushed at the air behind her tail, the angle all wrong even to Emma's untrained eye.

Hank knelt near her hindquarters, sleeves rolled up, arms bloodied to the elbow, leaning in. There was a grim set to his jaw Emma hadn't seen before.

"'Bout time," he said without looking up as Caleb slipped into the pen. "She's tryin', but she ain't got the room. I got ahold of one leg, but the other's tucked. Can't get enough leverage on my own without rollin' her and I'm not keen on gettin' my ribs kicked in today."

"Okay," Caleb said, already moving to the heifer's head. "Emma, in here with me. Close the gate behind you."

She did as told, heart pounding so hard she could feel it in her ears. The straw rustled underfoot, damp in spots. The animal's harsh breaths filled the space.

Caleb knelt by the heifer's head, one hand on her neck, voice low and steady. "Easy, Daisy," he murmured. "You're doin' good, girl. We're gonna get your baby out. You just hang on."

Emma stood there in the middle of the pen, hands fisted inside her gloves, staring at the scene: Hank elbow-deep in the back end of a laboring animal, Caleb talking to her like she could answer, the heifer herself half out of her mind with pain and fear.

"What do you need me to do?" she asked again, louder this time to cover the wobble in her voice.

Hank flicked his eyes to her briefly, reading her. "You squeamish?" he asked.

"Define squeamish," she said. "I'm not going to faint, if that's what you mean."

"Good enough," he said. "Come kneel here by me. When I tell you, I'm gonna need you to pull on this rope. Not like you're tryin' to win a tug-o-war at the county fair, steady, even. You're basically replacin' a contraction when she gets too tired."

"Okay," she said, moving into position. The smell was stronger here, metallic, wet. She swallowed hard and focused on the rope looped around something inside the heifer.

He guided her hands. "Here," he said. "Feel that? That's the front leg. I've got the other. We're gonna line 'em up and get this little one out. You just do what I say and watch your head. She kicks, you duck."

"Great," she muttered. "No pressure."

Caleb heard the wry note and felt something like pride flicker under his worry. Most people who weren't born into this kind of work took one look at a scene like this and backed right out of the barn. Emma had stepped in and asked for instructions.

"All right," Hank said, voice tightening as he maneuvered inside. "She's pushin' again. That's it, girl. Emma, when I say pull, you pull. Caleb, when we get shoulders clear, I'm gonna need you up here to grab and pivot if we're gonna keep the sac from hangin' up."

"Got it," Caleb said. He moved to where he could pivot quickly between head and hindquarters.

Time narrowed to the small universe of the pen.

The heifer groaned, whole body clenching. Hank braced. "Okay, pull now," he grunted.

Emma leaned back, gripping the rope, using her body weight more than her arm strength. The resistance on the other end was startling, wet and heavy, and then, as the calf slipped a little, there was movement. Hank adjusted.

"Good," he said. "Again. Easy. Don't jerk. That's it. You're doin' great."

Sweat sprang on Emma's forehead despite the chill. Her boots slid slightly in the straw as she tugged. The rope bit into her gloves.

"Here we go," Hank said between his teeth. "Head's comin'. C'mon, baby, work with me."

The heifer strained, a low, guttural sound tearing out of her. Caleb kept up a stream of murmurs at her head, hand on her neck, feeling each contraction in the muscles under her hide.

"You got this, Daisy," he whispered. "One more. One more, girl."

Emma felt something give on her end. The rope went slack for a split second, then the weight shifted, heavier.

"There," Hank barked triumphantly. "Head's free. Nose, mouth… all right, Emma, let go the rope, slide back. Caleb!"

Caleb was already moving, sliding from the heifer's head to her hindquarters in two strides, dropping to his knees beside Hank.

A slick, dark shape emerged fully in a rush, calf hitting the straw with a wet thud, limbs limp, head lolling.

For one horrible second, it didn't move.

Emma's breath caught. "Is it,?"

"No time for questions," Hank snapped, not unkindly. "Caleb, clear the nostrils. Emma, get that sack off its face. Rub like hell."

The membrane clung to the calf's muzzle. Emma plunged her gloved hands into the mess without thinking, pulling the sac away, peeling it back over the tiny head, revealing a nose, a mouth, a tongue too still.

She grabbed a fistful of clean straw, rubbing the calf's chest, its sides, anything to coax a response. Hank reached down, grabbed the oversized newborn by the hind legs, and lifted, letting gravity help drain fluid from its lungs and nose.

"Come on, kid," Caleb muttered, fingers sweeping the calf's nostrils, mouth. "Breathe."

The calf coughed, a small, wet sound. Emma's heart leapt into her throat.

"That's it," Hank urged. "Again."

She rubbed harder, straw scratching at her wrists. Her arms already ached from the earlier pulling, but adrenaline drove her.

The calf took a ragged breath, then another, each one a little stronger. Its chest rose, fell. A tremor ran through its legs.

"There you go," Hank said, relief threading through his tone. He lowered the calf back to the straw gently. "Welcome to the party."

Emma laughed on a half-sob. Caleb sat back on his heels, head tipping forward for a second as if in silent thanks.

The heifer lay panting, eyes rolling back to see what had just come out of her. Caleb reached over, hand smoothing along her flank.

"You did good, girl," he said softly. "You did real good."

The calf, still slick and steaming in the cool air, made a half-hearted attempt to lift its head and failed, nose flopping into the straw. Emma's chest squeezed.

"Is it okay?" she asked, voice shaking.

"Looks good," Hank said. "Little slow gettin' started, but he's breathin' on his own now. Heart's strong. He just had a rough ride."

"He," Emma repeated. "It's a boy?"

Hank peered. "Yeah," he said. "Little bull. Big one too. No wonder his mama had trouble."

Emma sat there in the straw, gloves sticky, knees damp, heart pounding, and felt a rush of something fierce and protective that surprised her. This calf was just a stranger, an anonymous life in the grand scheme. And yet, in the space of ten minutes, she'd gone from sleeping to fighting for fighting for a calf's life.

Caleb looked up at her. There was hay stuck to his sleeve, a streak of something on his cheek, his hat knocked slightly askew. He'd never looked less composed, and somehow never more intensely himself.

"You, okay?" he asked.

Emma took inventory. Sweating, yes. Shaking a little. Knees soaked. Heart doing acrobatics. But under all that, a solid, surprising yes.

"I'm… weirdly great," she said, laughing breathlessly. "And disgusting. But great."

Hank chuckled. "That's ranch life for you," he said. "Congratulations, you just helped deliver your first calf."

Emma stared at the tiny creature, still trying to coordinate its limbs. "I didn't," she began.

"You did," Caleb said quietly, cutting through her self-dismissal. "You held that rope when we needed another pull. If you hadn't, we might've lost him. Or Daisy. Or both."

The idea made her stomach drop and soar at the same time.

The calf bleated, a thin, uncertain sound. Emma's heart clenched.

"Okay," Hank said, shifting stiffly to stand. "Mama's got some work to do now. We'll give 'em a minute. Then we'll see if Romeo here can figure out how to stand without fallin' on his face."

He stepped carefully out of the pen, flexing his fingers to get blood flowing again. Emma moved to follow, but Caleb caught her wrist lightly.

"Stay a second," he said. "Let him get a whiff of you. You're part of the herd now."

She blinked at the phrasing, at the warm ring of it. "Part of the herd," she repeated.

He smiled just enough to soften the line of his mouth. "Come on," he said. "Help me rub him down a little more."

They worked together in the straw, shoulder to shoulder, using towels Hank handed through the gate. The calf wriggled and snorted, attempts at standing becoming more serious.

At one point, the calf pitched forward, front legs collapsing. Emma instinctively reached out, catching its head before it bashed the boards.

"Easy, little man," she murmured. "You just got here. No concussions allowed."

Caleb watched her hands cradle the newborn's head, watched the way her voice shifted, softening, steadying. Something inside his chest moved, slow and seismic.

He'd seen people help with births before, neighbors, family, hired hands. It was messy, intense, occasionally traumatic. Some folks handled it; some didn't. What Emma had done tonight went beyond handling. She'd stepped into a situation way outside her experience and met it head-on, not because she had anything to prove, but because the alternative, being a bystander, was unacceptable to her.

She wasn't fragile. She wasn't there for scenic sunsets and cowboy photo ops. She was in this, straw and all.

The calf finally managed to get all four legs under him at once, swaying like a drunk on an icy sidewalk. He took a step, then another, guided by some primal magnet toward his mother's udder.

Daisy lifted her head enough to nuzzle him, licking at his wet hide in rough, vigorous strokes.

"There you go," Hank said from the rail, satisfaction warming his voice. "Nature doin' her thing."

They watched until the calf latched clumsily, then more confidently, the rhythm of suckling filling the pen.

"Okay," Hank said, clapping his hands softly as if closing a meeting. "We're outta their way now. They got this part."

He nodded toward the barn aisle. "Come on. Let's get you two hosed off before you start attractin' every fly in the county."

Emma peeled off her gloves, fingers trembling with a mix of adrenaline and fatigue. As she followed the men out of the pen, she caught one last look at the pair: Daisy, eyes half-closed in exhausted relief, and the calf, pressed close to her side, tail twitching.

She felt unexpectedly emotional. "He's… kind of perfect," she said.

"Give him an hour," Hank muttered. "He'll be tryin' to crawl under the fence and ruin my morning."

But his gaze softened as he said it.

In the aisle, the cold hit harder now that the adrenaline was ebbing. Emma suddenly became acutely aware of how damp and chilled she was. Her jacket was smeared with fluids she didn't want to think too hard about; her knees were soaked through.

Caleb led the way to the wash area, where a hose hung coiled above a drain, a rack of towels nearby.

"Hands first," he said. "Cold water. Sorry."

"It's fine," she said. "I've already lost feeling in my soul; my fingers can go next."

He turned the tap, water sputtering before flowing. She thrust her hands under, hissing as the chill bit.

"Just pretend it's a fancy spa treatment," Hank suggested. "Exfoliatin' with hay."

"Ten out of ten, would not recommend," Emma said, but she scrubbed diligently, watching the evidence of the last hour swirl down the drain.

Caleb washed too, forearms reddening under the stream as he worked. They kept bumping into each other in the narrow space, hips, elbows, shoulders, each contact sending little sparks of awareness through Emma's already keyed-up system.

By the time they'd gotten as clean as the hose would allow and dumped their ruined jackets into a corner bin "for later triage or arson," as Hank put it, exhaustion started to seep through the cracks adrenaline had left.

"What time is it now?" Emma asked, wringing out her braid.

Caleb checked his watch. "Six-something," he said. "Sun'll be up soon. Morning chores won't wait just 'cause we've been up playin' midwives."

Hank groaned theatrically. "Speak for yourself," he said. "Old men need naps. You kids handle the rest."

"You're not that old," Emma protested.

"Tell that to my knees," Hank said. "I'm gonna grab an hour in the chair upstairs. You two make sure Daisy Junior doesn't try to escape. And drink water, for God's sake. Y'all look like you ran a marathon in a steam room."

He shuffled off toward the small apartment above the barn, muttering something about coffee and the betrayal of joints.

The barn quieted.

Outside, the first birds had started their tentative chirps. Light seeped under the big doors.

Emma leaned back against a stall door, letting her head rest on the cool wood. Her whole body hummed, a strange mix of exhausted and wired.

Caleb watched her for a moment, then grabbed a water jug from a nearby shelf and poured into two beat-up plastic cups.

"Here," he said, handing her one.

She took it, fingers brushing his. "Thanks."

They drank in silence for a minute, the water stark and metallic, tasting better than any latte she'd ever had.

"I'm impressed," he said finally.

She blinked. "By what? My ability to get bodily fluids in my hair?"

"By the fact that you didn't flinch," he said. "Most people would've backed right outta that pen. You stepped in and did what needed doin'."

She shrugged, suddenly shy. "You asked for help," she said. "I wanted to be… helpful."

"You were more than that," he said. "You were part of the team. We wouldn't have done that as clean without you."

The simple, matter-of-fact affirmation sent warmth flooding through her that had nothing to do with the barn's temperature.

"Thank you," she said quietly.

He leaned against the stall across from her, mirroring her posture. In the half-light, with the barn mostly empty, he looked younger and older all at once. Lines of fatigue ran around his eyes, but there was a softness there too, a rawness he didn't usually let show.

"How are you feelin'?" he asked. "Really."

She considered.

"Tired," she said. "Like… bone-tired. But also… alive? That sounds dramatic, but… You know when you write a piece and you feel like it might actually change something? How there's this weird hum in your chest afterwards? It's like that. Only smellier."

He smiled. "That's a good sign," he said. "Means this kinda work might suit you more than you thought."

"I'm not sure 'emergency cow obstetrics' was on my life plan," she said. "But… yeah. There's something about it."

She hesitated, fingers tracing the rim of her cup.

"I was always supposed to be the observer," she went on. "You know? The one who writes about other people's stories. Today I was… in the story. Not taking notes. Just… there. That felt… right."

"Then maybe your life plan needed rewritin'," he said.

She looked at him, the words landing softly.

"Maybe," she said.

He held her gaze. The space between them, quiet and full of hay dust, felt charged in a new way. Not just with adrenaline or leftover fear, but with something deeper. A recognition.

He'd watched her run up that hill half-asleep and show up ready. He'd watched her put her hands into a situation that terrified most grown men and just… follow instructions. He'd seen her fight for life tonight, not as someone looking for a story, but as someone who couldn't stand to let something that depended on her slip away.

Whatever this was building between them, this slow, steady burn, it wasn't built on surface things. It was being forged in places like this: a barn at dawn, straw sticking to their clothes, hearts still tripping from a near-loss.

His chest ached, in that old familiar way that usually signaled danger. Attachments lead to loss. You let someone in and the universe takes them. But alongside that ache now was something else. Something stubborn and undeniable.

He didn't just like her. He didn't just enjoy her company. He was… in deep.

The realization stole his breath more than any sprint up a hill ever had.

He swallowed, suddenly aware of the thinness of the air in the barn. Of the way she'd wrapped her arms around herself against the lingering chill, shoulders hunched.

Without thinking too much about it, he shrugged out of his clean-ish overshirt and tossed it to her.

"Here," he said. "You're shiverin' again."

"I'm fine," she started, then stopped herself mid-reflex. She slid into the shirt instead, rolling up sleeves still warm from his body. It hung on her, swallowing her smaller frame.

"Thank you," she said, voice quiet.

"You gotta stop thanking me for basic decency," he said.

"Maybe I'm just not used to it," she said, then winced. "That came out more tragic than I meant."

"Nah," he said. "Makes sense."

Silence fell again, but it wasn't heavy. It was full.

A calf bawled in a nearby pen. Somewhere in the rafters, a bird rustled.

He pushed off the stall, took a step closer without fully deciding to. The gap between them shrank until they were a few feet apart, enough space to back out, not enough to pretend they were just two coworkers debriefing.

"Emma," he said.

She looked up, eyes tired and bright. There was straw in her hair, a smudge on her cheek she hadn't noticed. She'd never looked less like a polished city reporter, and never more beautiful.

"Yeah?" she said.

He searched for something safe to say and came up empty. Everything that rose wanted to breach the walls he'd built carefully over years, words like I'm glad you're here and You scare me and I'm falling.

What came out instead was softer, but truer than anything on the surface.

"I keep thinkin' I've got you figured out," he said. "And then you go and… do this."

"Deliver your calf?" she asked, one corner of her mouth lifting.

"Show up," he said simply. "In the hard parts. Not just the pretty ones."

Her breath hitched. Something in her loosened at the same time.

"You do that too," she said, matching his honesty. "Show up. Even when it's… inconvenient. Or scary. Or early," she added, glancing toward the barn doors. "I've never met anyone who makes it feel… less terrifying to be afraid."

He stared at her, that landing in a place he'd kept boarded up since his dad died.

"Emma," he said again, but there was more in it this time, her name carrying a weight it hadn't before. A plea, a confession, a warning.

She stepped closer without fully deciding to, drawn by something she didn't want to examine too closely yet. One more step and she was within reach, his heat a presence in the chilled air.

They stood there, close enough now that she could see tiny flecks of green in his hazel eyes, close enough that he could count the faint freckles at the edge of her jaw.

The barn faded. The calf, the cows, the world beyond the doors, their sounds dropped away to a dull hum under the roar of blood in their ears.

He lifted a hand, slow enough that she could have flinched away if she'd wanted to. He brushed the pad of his thumb gently across her cheek where the smudge was.

"Straw," he said, voice rough. "You missed some."

"Occupational hazard," she whispered.

His hand didn't drop. It drifted, almost of its own volition, to the edge of her jaw, fingers curving lightly around the back of her neck. She inhaled, the air catching.

"This is probably a bad idea," she said, but there was no conviction in it.

"Probably," he agreed.

Neither of them moved away.

Her hands came up halfway between them, hovering as if she wasn't sure whether to push him back or pull him closer. When he didn't close the distance immediately, she made the choice for both of them.

She slid her hands up his chest, fingers curling in his shirt near his shoulders, and rose onto her toes.

The first touch of his mouth on hers was nothing like the almost at The Spur.

There, they'd been interrupted by noise and light and outside eyes. Here, in the hush of the barn, there was no band to blame, no bartender to shout last call at them. Just the soft exhale they both gave as their lips met, relief and surprise mixed.

The kiss started gentle, tentative, like both of them were testing ice they weren't sure would hold. His thumb stroked once along the line of her jaw, the touch reverent. She tasted salt and coffee and the undefinable something that was just him.

The world narrowed to the point of contact.

Then something in both of them shifted.

The tension that had been building for weeks, the glances across fence lines, the almost-kiss in town, the shared hilltop under the stars, the creek argument and its aftermath, poured into the space between their mouths.

The kiss deepened without either of them making a conscious choice. His hand slid into the back of her hair, fingers tangling gently. Her hands fisted in his shirt, pulling him closer.

He angled his head, finding a better fit, a truer connection, and the small sound she made into his mouth nearly undid him. He'd forgotten this, a kiss that felt less like fireworks and more like coming home after a storm.

Emma melted and burned at the same time.

She'd kissed people before, obviously. There had been fun, adrenaline-fueled hookups in college, wine-fuzzy affection with boyfriends who liked to talk about "power couples" and "networking." None of it had felt like this, like her whole nervous system was reorienting itself around one person.

This kiss held everything they hadn't said out loud yet: I see you. You scare me. I want this anyway.

Time went strange. It could have been seconds, could have been minutes. All she knew was the press of his chest, the warmth of his palm at the base of her skull, the way his breathing hitched when she leaned in instead of pulling back.

At some point, the need for oxygen broke through.

He lifted his head slightly, foreheads bumping. Their noses brushed. Both of them breathed hard, the sound loud in the quiet barn.

"Sorry," he said, voice hoarse, even though he didn't move his hand. "I,"

"Don't," she said quickly, hand tightening in his shirt. "Don't apologize."

He searched her face, needing to be absolutely sure.

"You, okay?" he asked. "Really?"

She let out a shaky laugh that was half-sob. "I'm… so far from okay," she said. "But not because of that."

His thumb brushed along her cheekbone. "I shouldn't,"

"I kissed you back," she said, cutting off the self-recrimination she could hear revving up. "Fully consenting adult. No regrets."

He exhaled, the tension in his shoulders easing a fraction.

"Okay," he said.

"Okay," she echoed.

They stood there, still close, neither quite ready to break the contact completely. The air between them felt different now, charged but clear. No more pretending this was a maybe. This was a yes, whatever shape it took.

Inside his chest, something heavy settled into place with a strange, quiet certainty.

He loved her.

The phrasing startled him, sharp and undeniable. He'd been circling it, refusing to name it, because naming things made them real, and real had a way of becoming vulnerable. But standing here in the barn, her hands still clinging to his shirt, the smell of straw and new life around them, there was no point in lying to himself.

He loved that she'd come up here to save herself before she broke. He loved that she balanced her fear of wasting her life against her fear of being judged and chose herself anyway. He loved her stubbornness, her curiosity, her willingness to get messy for something that mattered.

He loved her.

The realization scared him in that old, familiar way. But it also flooded him with something like peace. Not the absence of fear, but its companion, meaning.

Emma, her forehead still resting against his, was having her own quiet revelation.

She loved him.

It unfolded in her like a slow sunrise, not a lightning strike. All the scattered moments clicked into place: his steady hand on her elbow crossing a rocky patch; the way he'd shown her the sky as if it were a gift he wanted to share; the way he'd listened to her fear about Denver without trying to fix it; the way he'd trusted her tonight, not as a guest, but as a partner in the thick of a crisis.

She loved the way he moved through the world, wary but kind, protective but not possessive, rooted and yet open enough to let her see the soft parts he'd locked away. She loved his dry humor, his careful words, the flashes of unguarded laughter. She loved that he made her feel more like herself, not less.

She loved him.

It terrified her. It thrilled her. It felt inevitable in retrospect.

Neither of them said the words. They didn't need to, not yet. The timing would come later; in some other scene the story hadn't reached. For now, the truth of it sat quietly between them, making everything sharper.

A sound from the pen, Daisy shifting, the calf letting out a questioning bleat, broke the moment gently.

Emma drew back a little, hands sliding down from his shoulders, leaving heat in their wake. He let his hand fall from her hair slowly, fingers tracing the last few inches like he was reluctant to let go.

"We should probably…" she said, gesturing vaguely toward the rest of the barn, cheeks flushed.

"Yeah," he said, voice still rough. "Cows don't care about our… whatever this is."

"Very rude of them," she said.

He huffed a laugh, the sound lighter than she'd heard from him in a long time.

"We'll check on Daisy and the little guy," he said. "Then you're goin' back up that hill and takin' a nap. I'll handle the rest of morning chores. You've done enough for one day by five a.m."

"Look at you, trying to tell me what to do," she said lightly, but there was no sting in it.

"Consider it a strong suggestion," he said. "You can veto it if you want, but I reserve the right to tell Hank I tried."

She smiled, heart full.

"Okay," she said. "Nap. After we say goodbye to my first patient."

They moved back toward the pen, walking side by side. Their shoulders brushed once, twice. Neither of them pulled away.

Inside, Daisy blinked at them, calmer now, chewing slowly. The calf, still wobbly, nursed with determination, tail twitching.

Emma leaned on the rail, watching. Caleb stood close enough that she could feel the warmth of him along her arm.

"What are you gonna call him?" she asked.

"Hadn't thought that far ahead," he said. "You did some of the heavy liftin'. You want the honor?"

She considered, mind flipping through names. None of them felt right, too cute, too obvious.

"How about Lucky?" she said finally.

"Lucky," he repeated. "Fittin'."

He glanced at her. She glanced back.

Lucky calf. Lucky timing. Lucky that a burnt-out city reporter had clicked on a cabin listing one night instead of booking a flight somewhere far away.

As they stood there in the slowly brightening barn, watching the little bull find his legs in a world that had almost not included him, the midpoint of their summer, of their story, clicked into place.

Externally, they were still just a rancher and a temporary tenant, coworkers in the loose sense, friends who'd danced and kissed and delivered a calf together.

Internally, they had chosen.

They might not have said the words. They might not have drawn up a plan. There were still exes to stir up trouble, careers to reckon with, choices to make about where to live when the leaves turned.

But in the quiet recesses of their hearts, under armor that had cracked open just enough, a decision had been made.

I'm in this. I'm in this with you.

Under the Colorado sky, as dawn edged over the hills, Emma and Caleb stood in a barn that smelled of hay and new life and the end of one kind of loneliness. The story had tipped, almost imperceptibly, from "maybe" to "yes."

Whatever came next, for the ranch, for her writing, for them, they would face it changed by this morning.

They had both, in their own stubborn, careful ways, chosen each other.

Chapter Fourteen
Summer Bloom

The days after Lucky's birth fell into a new kind of rhythm, one that made the weeks before feel like a rough draft.

The morning after the barn, Emma slept harder than she had in months. When she finally pried her eyes open, the light in the cabin was already bright and high, pouring in around the edges of the thin curtains. The clock on her nightstand blinked 10:23 accusingly.

For a second, panic surged, she'd overslept, missed a meeting, a deadline, a call. Her body tensed, ready to launch.

Then reality drifted back in like dust motes.

No newsroom. No daily brief. No editor peering over the top of her monitor with another "quick turnaround" that would swallow her afternoon whole. Just the cabin, the ranch, the faint bleating of a calf somewhere down the hill.

She lay there, letting the panic ebb and something gentler take its place.

The memory of the barn slid in, almost embarrassingly vivid. The heifer's straining sides. Lucky's first breath. Caleb's rough hand in her hair, the warm press of his mouth on hers in the quiet afterward. The way something in her had shifted like a fault line finally giving way.

She touched her lips, half-expecting to find some visible marker. They were just lips. Slightly dry. No sign at all of the way her heart had been reengineered under them.

The porch creaked. She stiffened, then relaxed as Hank's cough rattled through the thin wall. She heard his muttered commentary, something about "kids these days sleeping till noon", and the porch chair protesting under his weight.

The reassurance of that ordinary sound steadied her. Life, as it turned out, persisted even after major emotional tectonics.

She pulled herself out of bed, showered, and scrubbed away the last of the barn from her skin. When she stepped out onto the porch with her notebook and a mug of coffee, the day had settled into that particular late-morning laziness of summer, warm, but not yet oppressive, the sky a high, endless blue.

Hank tipped his hat without getting up. "Look who joined the land of the livin'," he said.

"I think I transcended," she said, sinking into the chair beside him. "Ascended, descended… something."

He snorted. "You earned that sleep," he said. "You did half my work this morning."

"Liar," she said. "You were up at dawn doing six people's jobs."

"Now who's the liar?" he asked. He studied her face for a second, the way her gaze flicked reflexively toward the barn, her fingers wrapped around the mug.

"He headed out with the tractor a bit ago," he said casually, answering the question she hadn't quite asked. "Fixin' the upper pasture fence. He'll be back around lunchtime. Lucky and Daisy are doin' fine, in case you're about to go peek in your patient chart."

"I was thinking about it, actually," she admitted.

"Later," Hank said. "You look like a strong wind could knock you over. Sit. Write your… cowsmopolitan article."

She laughed. "God, don't give my old editor ideas."

They sat in companionable silence for a while, the only sounds the creak of wood, the hum of insects, the occasional far-off clang of metal on metal.

Emma opened her notebook, intending to pick up where she'd left off on the novel.

Instead, she flipped to a fresh page.

At the top, she wrote:

Chapter Title Ideas That Don't Sound Like a Soap Opera.

She scribbled half a dozen terrible options, each crossed out more dramatically than the last. The exercise loosened something, got ink flowing.

From there, the words came easier than they had in weeks.

She wrote about the way the light hit the east pasture at dawn, turning everything silver. About the way Lucky had blinked at her this morning over the fence, ears too big for his head. About Hank's half-muttered prayers over the coffee pot.

The "honeymoon" phase didn't arrive with balloons or fireworks. It showed up in smaller, quieter ways.

It was there in the way their conversations picked up where they left off, less guarded now, more playful. In the way Emma started appearing at the barn or the pasture without needing to be asked, work gloves already on. In the way Caleb, without making a big production out of it, began to factor her presence into his mental calculus of the day.

She still wrote every morning, habit and need driving her. But now, the hours after that belonged as much to the ranch as to the blank page.

One afternoon, she caught herself thinking of it as "our" work and had to put her pen down to breathe through the implications.

They never talked about the kiss in the barn in grand, sweeping terms. There was no debrief, no Relationship Summit where they defined terms. The closest they came was the next day, when he'd walked her up halfway to the cabin and stopped, hands shoved in his pockets.

"About… that," he'd said, chin jerking toward the barn.

"The calf?" she'd said, knowing exactly which "that" he meant.

"Among other things," he said.

She'd taken pity on him.

"We wanted to," she said. "I'm not drunk. You weren't… pity-kissing your tenant. I'm okay with what happened."

He'd nodded, some of the tension easing. "I don't… move fast," he'd said. "Not anymore. I don't… I'm not lookin' for somethin' casual. Just so you know. If that changes how you… plan your summer."

Her heart had pounded so hard she'd been sure he could hear it.

"I'm not really built for casual either," she'd said. "Not anymore. And I didn't come up here looking for a summer fling, if that's what you're worried about."

"I was worried about a lotta things," he'd admitted. "Hurtin' you, for one. Or you wakin' up one day and realizin' you traded one trap for another."

"This place doesn't feel like a trap," she'd said softly. "You don't feel like a trap."

He'd looked like he wanted to argue and kiss her at the same time. He chose neither, exactly. He'd touched his fingers lightly to her wrist instead, a small, steady contact.

"Okay then," he'd said. "We'll… figure it out as we go."

That was their unofficial, fragile agreement. No labels. No timelines. Just a mutual understanding that whatever this was, it wasn't an accident and it wasn't nothing.

Days blurred, tethered by small rituals.

There was the mid-morning coffee at the ranch house, where Emma would wander down after a writing session and find Hank and Caleb debating weather patterns like two meteorologists without degrees.

"South fence'll wash out if we get another storm like last week," Hank would grumble.

"Only if the creek jumps the bank," Caleb would counter.

"There's your next investigative piece," Hank would tell Emma. "Rural water mismanagement in the arid West. Film at eleven."

"Do I get to use phrases like 'blistering exposé'?" she'd ask.

"Only if you say 'em in that fancy anchor voice," Hank would say.

"You know I was a print reporter, right?" she'd respond.

"Waste of good cheekbones," Hank would mutter into his mug.

There were the late afternoons when the heat broke enough to make outside work less punishing. Emma found herself volunteering more and more.

"I can help with that," she'd say when she found Caleb loading fence posts.

"Ever stretch barbed wire?" he'd ask.

"How hard can it be?" she'd say.

He'd give her a look that said, Famous last words. Then he'd show her anyway.

The first time she unrolled barbed wire, she nearly lost a glove to it. Caleb stepped in behind her, calloused hands guiding hers on the spool.

"Don't fight it," he said, voice close to her ear. "You're not tryin' to wrestle a snake. Let it unwind, keep tension, but don't yank. It'll win if you do."

"Is that another one of your metaphors for life?" she asked, heart doing odd things at the feel of him behind her.

"Maybe," he said. "Or maybe I just don't want you to get eighty-seven little cuts."

"Look at you," she said. "Respecting my autonomy and my skin."

"High bar," he said dryly.

She laughed, the sound echoing over the pasture.

They worked well together.

Emma learned how to read Caleb's "barn voice", short, precise instructions that carried the weight of someone used to giving orders that mattered. At first, the sharpness set her nerves on edge, old instincts flaring, men who raised their voices in Denver usually weren't trying to keep anyone alive except themselves.

But here, in the context of dropping hay bales and unpredictable animals, she began to understand. His intensity wasn't about control; it was about safety. When he barked, "Move," it wasn't to show dominance; it was because a half-second delay could mean a hoof to the ribs.

The more she saw that, the more she trusted the cadence.

And he, in turn, learned to trust her judgement. He stopped hovering when she drove the truck through the lower pasture, stopped double-checking every knot she tied. He'd still offer gentle corrections when needed, but there was a growing confidence in his tone when he said, "Can you handle the north water trough while I finish this?"

She'd nod, and he'd turn away without looking back every other second. That small act of faith felt like its own kind of intimacy.

The more time they spent side by side in the work, the more space opened for talk.

Not just about weather or feed prices, but about the trenches they'd each crawled through to get here.

One evening, they loaded hay into the loft as the sun slid low, turning everything amber. Dust motes floated in the beams of light, the air thick with the sweet, dry smell of the bales.

Emma stood on the bed of the truck, wrestling one of the squares toward the edge. Caleb stood below, arms raised to catch.

"You're gonna throw your back out," he said, watching her stance.

"You're gonna insult my core again," she said. "I'm insulted."

He smirked. "You think you had a core before you came here?"

"Hey, I did Pilates," she said. "Once."

"There it is," he said. "You done braggin' or you gonna toss that bale?"

She grunted and shoved. He caught it easily, tossing it onto the growing stack with practiced grace.

They fell into a rhythm. She shoved bales, he caught, stacked, repeated.

At one point, she paused to wipe sweat from her forehead with the back of her wrist. "You ever miss it?" she asked.

He caught the next bale automatically. "Miss what?"

"The Army," she said. "Deployments. Your… other life."

He set the bale down and straightened, rolling his shoulders.

"Yes and no," he said after a moment. "I miss the guys. The… clear purpose. You wake up and there's no question what your job is. You're trainin', you're on patrol, you're on guard. You're workin' toward something, even if the somethin' gets muddied by politics."

He reached for another bale, more to have something to do with his hands than out of necessity.

"I don't miss… always bein' on," he said. "Never really breathin' deep. Sleepin' with one ear open. The way your muscles forget how to unclench."

"You sleep better now?" she asked.

He glanced up at her, surprised she'd picked that detail out of everything he'd said.

"Most nights," he said. "Took a while. At first, after I came back, my body didn't know what to do with quiet nights. I'd hear the wind and my brain would go, That's not right. Something's wrong. Took months before I stopped expectin' a mortar every time a truck backfired."

She swallowed, the weight of that sinking in.

"How long were you over there?" she asked.

"Two tours," he said. "Year each, give or take. There was this stretch in the middle where it felt like I was never not in the sandbox. Time blurs when every day's dust and heat and waitin'."

He didn't talk about specific missions or firefights. Not yet. But he let slip small pieces, enough for her to glimpse the landscape he'd walked.

"You ever write about it?" she asked.

He huffed a laugh. "No," he said. "I barely talk about it. Hank knows some. Tom knew. Abby…" He trailed off, then shook his head. "She saw the headlines, heard the news, but that's different. It's like watchin' a fire on TV instead of feelin' the heat."

"You don't have to tell me anything you don't want to," she said quickly. "I'm not mining you for content."

"I know," he said. "That's the only reason I'm sayin' anything at all."

He caught her eye, something unguarded there.

"The worst part wasn't the bad days," he said. "The ones where it all went sideways. Those, at least, had clarity. You knew what you were supposed to do: keep as many people alive as you could. It was the in-between that got me. The boredom, the petty orders, the sense that you're expendable to folks who only see numbers on a briefing sheet."

She nodded, the journalist in her recognizing the story behind the story.

"Sometimes I'd look up at the sky over there," he said, "and think, It's the same sky. Folks back home are under this same blanket. And I'm… here, sprawled under it in a whole different world. It messed with my head."

He shrugged, the movement trying to shake off the weight of the memory.

"Now I look up and I'm… grateful," he said. "To be under the same sky but… here. With trees. And cows. And one very insistent writer who keeps showin' up with a notebook and a million questions."

"Only a million?" she asked, voice lighter than she felt.

"Maybe two," he conceded.

She leaned on the back of the truck, watching him.

"Thank you," she said.

"For what?" he asked.

"For telling me that," she said. "For… trusting me with it."

He shifted, a little uncomfortable under the earnestness, but didn't deflect.

"You share plenty with me," he said. "Seems only fair."

She snorted. "I mostly rant about clickbait and my editor's obsession with listicles," she said.

"I don't know what that first word means," he said. "And I thought listicles were what you needed surgically removed if you sat wrong on a saddle."

She choked on a laugh. "That's… definitely not it," she said. "You might be confusing listicles with testicles."

"Semantics," he said.

"Not really," she said, but she was smiling.

He wiped his hands on his jeans. "So, tell me more about your... world," he said. "The one with the blinking cursors and the people yellin' about page views."

So, she did.

They took a break, sitting side by side on the tailgate, legs swinging. Emma told him about chasing stories in Denver, the housing protests, the budget hearings that went past midnight, the small victories when an article actually moved a needle.

She told him about the flip side too. The editor who'd started assigning more and more "engagement pieces", clicky headlines and shallow content designed to keep people scrolling, not thinking.

"I got into it to tell stories that mattered," she said. "Not to moderate comment wars and parse the difference between 'Ten Ways to Tell If Your Boss Is a Narcissist' and 'Nine Ways.'"

He made a face. "Folks need an article to tell 'em that?" he asked.

"You'd be amazed," she said. "Or maybe you wouldn't. People like being told how to live."

He glanced at her. "You do?"

She thought about it. "I used to," she said. "It was easier. There's comfort in a list. In steps. 'Do this and you will be happy.' But it's... hollow. It doesn't leave room for real life. For mess. For... calves born sideways at four in the morning."

He considered that.

"So, what do you want to write instead?" he asked.

The question landed like a pebble in deep water, rippling out.

She looked out over the pasture, the hills beyond. The air had cooled, the sun now a soft glow behind the ridge.

"I want to tell stories that make people feel less alone," she said slowly. "That make them look at their own ordinary life and see... beauty. Worth. I want to write about people like you and Hank. And Daisy and Lucky. About... quiet bravery. Small choices that add up to big changes."

He listened like it mattered, like he wasn't just humoring her.

"I want to write books," she went on. "Not just articles that disappear into the feed ten hours later. Stories that someone might pick up in ten years and still feel… something."

She laughed softly, self-conscious.

"Sorry," she said. "That sounds pretentious out loud."

"Doesn't," he said. "Sounds like you found somethin' worth sweatin' for."

He bumped her knee lightly with his.

"For what it's worth," he added, "I'd read your book."

"You hate reading," she pointed out.

"I'd make an exception," he said.

The simplicity of that made her chest ache more than any grand declaration could have.

Evenings became their own kind of sanctuary.

Some nights, they ended up on her cabin porch, watching the sky go from gold to purple, the first stars winking into place. He'd bring a beer; she'd bring tea or wine, depending on the day. They'd sit side by side, shoulders not always touching but always aware.

"City sunsets are loud," she said one night, legs curled under her. "All neon and sirens and reflective glass. This is… quieter."

"Quieter's not always better," he said. "But it's honest. Sky doesn't do anything just 'cause someone paid for a billboard."

She smiled. "Listen to you," she said. "Poet."

"Tell anyone and I'll deny it," he said.

Other nights, they ended up at the ranch house kitchen table, Hank serving as both buffer and instigator.

He'd toss out a question, "So if the internet went away tomorrow, would you be out of a job?", and then sit back, enjoying the way Emma and Caleb argued their way toward some shared understanding.

"You'd still have storytellers," Emma said once. "People have told stories since they were drawing on cave walls. The tools change. The need doesn't."

"You think that's what you are?" Hank asked. "A cave-wall scratcher?"

"Sure," she said. "Except my cave wall crashes twice a day and needs software updates."

"See, that right there is why I like fences," he said. "They stay where you put 'em unless a cow runs through 'em. Which, to be fair, happens more'n I'd like."

Caleb shook his head, smiling into his coffee.

The affection in those nights, it crept up on them like ivy. Emma found herself learning the little things: how Caleb took his coffee (black, unless Hank was making it, in which case he took it however it came); how he always rinsed his plate before putting it in the sink, even when Hank told him not to bother; how he read the weather as easily as she read a headline.

Caleb, in turn, learned that Emma hummed when she concentrated, a tuneless little sound that escaped without her noticing. That she preferred pens that bled a little. That she talked in her sleep, sometimes, on the nights he'd walked her up and lingered at the bottom of the cabin hill, listening to the rise and fall of her voice through the window light.

They accumulated these tiny data points with the quiet hunger of people who knew, even if they weren't saying it yet, that these details would matter. That if this broke, these would be the pieces that hurt to remember.

Nothing about it was officially defined. When people in town saw them together, at the feed store, at Pages & Pours, at The Spur on another Friday night, there were looks. Emma felt them, could almost hear the unspoken questions.

Hank certainly saw it. More than once, he opened his mouth like he was about to say something, then shut it again, satisfied for now to play the part of old man on porch, watching history maybe repeat in a better way.

"You should see you two from where I'm sittin'," he muttered to himself one afternoon, as Emma and Caleb walked down to the creek, laughing at some shared joke. "Like watchin' wildflowers decide to bloom in a place that's seen nothin' but frost."

He wouldn't tell them that, of course. It would spook them. Better to let the summer do its quiet work.

One evening, near the end of June, they found themselves back at the creek where they'd had their first real fight.

The air was thick with the smell of sun-warmed water and wild mint. Cottonwood fluff drifted lazily. The rock where Emma had sat that day, angry, scared, shaking, looked harmless now, just another boulder.

She waded ankle-deep along the bank, jeans rolled up, toes digging into the cool mud. Caleb stood a little back on the shore, boots planted, watching her.

"You okay out there?" he called.

"You gonna yell at me if I go to mid-calf?" she asked.

"Depends," he said. "You plannin' on fallin' in?"

"Not today," she said. "I have someone to kiss goodnight and I'd prefer to not smell like creek sludge."

His pause was brief but noticeable. They'd kissed several times since the barn, soft, sweet, lingering touches before parting, in the shelter of porches and the shadows of barns. But she'd never framed it quite that directly.

He stepped closer to the edge, sunlight catching in his eyes. "That so?" he asked, voice low.

She turned toward him, water lapping at her ankles. "Maybe," she said. "Depends if he behaves."

"Hard ask," he said. "Whoever he is."

She snorted, waded back to shore, and hopped onto the grass, shaking water from her feet. He offered his hand without thinking; she took it without hesitating, letting him steady her onto the bank.

They stood there, close, fingers still linked.

"I'm glad we came back here," she said, looking at the curve of the creek.

"Me too," he said. "Gives me a chance to have somethin' other than you bein' mad at me in my mental file for this spot."

"I wasn't just mad," she said. "I was… scared. And I took it out on you."

"I was scared too," he said simply. "And I took it out on you. We're even."

She smiled, the memory already softened by everything that had come after.

They sat on the rock together this time, shoulders touching. She leaned her head briefly against his shoulder, feeling the steady rise and fall of his breathing.

"Do you ever think about… after?" she asked. "Like… after summer?"

He was quiet for a moment. The water gurgled over stones, unbothered by human timelines.

"All the time," he said. "And not at all."

"That's not an answer," she said, amused and aching at once.

"It's the only honest one I got," he said. "Part of me wants to pin it down. Make a plan. Know exactly how this goes so I don't get blindsided again. And part of me knows life doesn't give a damn about my plans. So, I'm tryin' to… be here. While you're here."

She swallowed. "I don't have it figured out either," she said. "The… logistics. The money. The 'what does my family say when I tell them I fell for a rancher and want to live three hours from the nearest newsroom.'"

He made a small sound that was almost a laugh. "You fall for a rancher, huh?" he said.

She elbowed him lightly. "Don't get cocky," she said. "It's theoretical."

"Sure," he said, but there was a softness in his eyes that said he'd heard it for what it was.

She reached over, laced her fingers through his again.

"I'm not making any promises I can't keep," she said. "But… I'm not treating this like a summer fling. So, you don't have too either."

He squeezed her hand, the grip firm.

"Good," he said. "'Cause I wouldn't know how."

They sat there until the shadows lengthened, talking about everything and nothing, her brother's ridiculous baby names, Hank's rumored dancing prowess in his youth, the best pie in Cottonwood Ridge (a heated debate between the diner and the church ladies' bake sale). They built a small, shared mythology of the place, layering their inside jokes onto the landscape.

On the walk back, he stopped halfway up the hill, tugging her gently to a halt.

"What?" she asked.

He nodded toward the horizon. The sun was a low disk, the sky around it streaked in shades of rose and orange. The ranch spread below them, fields a patchwork of green and gold.

"This is why I stayed," he said quietly. "After everything. This. I thought I'd be alone up here. Turns out I was wrong."

She looked at the view, then at him.

"Me too," she said.

He turned toward her, the last light clustering around the edges of his hat, casting his face in soft shadow. He reached up, cupped her cheek with one calloused palm. She leaned into it, heart full to the point of ache.

He kissed her there, in the open, not hiding in the barn or behind a cabin door. It was slow and sure and unbelievably tender. Not a question this time, but an answer.

The world didn't explode. No thunder rolled. A cow slowed down in the pasture; a bird called overhead. Life went on, but her internal landscape shifted again, subtly, to accommodate the new truth:

This isn't a maybe.

It was fragile. It was unofficial. There were a hundred ways it could still crack, distance, fear, old wounds, new opportunities. But it was also becoming the axis her days turned on.

She pulled back, resting her forehead against his for a moment.

"Thank you," she whispered.

"For what?" he asked, because he needed to hear it, even if he didn't know why.

"For letting me see this," she said. "The land. The work. You."

He swallowed, the simplicity of her gratitude hitting him harder than any compliment she could have crafted.

"You're welcome," he said.

Summer moved forward.

Lucky grew, legs less wobbly, curiosity more dangerous. Emma kept writing, pages stacking up, the story in her laptop increasingly populated by people who sounded suspiciously like the ones in her life. Caleb kept fixing fences, tending cattle, balancing books. Hank kept dispensing advice she pretended not to need and they pretended not to seek.

Underneath all of it, a quiet understanding deepened.

They hadn't said love out loud yet. They hadn't promised forever. But on long days under the sun and quiet nights under the Colorado sky, they were, in ways both small and monumental, already living like people with something precious to lose.

Chapter Fifteen
The Ex in Town

By late July, Emma had fallen into a comfortable ritual with Pages & Pours.

Once or twice a week, usually when the words in her cabin refused to line up into anything useful, she'd drive into Cottonwood Ridge, park in her now-favorite spot beneath the crooked streetlamp, and sink into the hum of the little bookstore café. There was something about the murmur of other people's conversations and the smell of coffee that loosened the stubborn parts of her brain.

That morning, the heat had settled over High Meadow Ranch early, pressing on shoulders and tempers alike. Caleb had been up before dawn checking water lines; his brow furrowed at the weather forecast on his phone.

"Week of this and the grass is gonna crisp," he'd muttered, thumb tracing the little sun icons. "Might have to rotate the herds more."

"You gonna yell at the sky again?" Hank had asked, pouring coffee.

"Didn't work last time," Caleb said. "Thought I'd try glaring instead."

Emma had watched him, the way he carried the weight of the land in the lines of his shoulders, and felt that now-familiar pang of both admiration and worry.

"Go," Hank had said to her when she'd mentioned town. "Before he drafts you into hose duty. Bring me back somethin' sweet that isn't that gluten-free nonsense Libby tried to pawn off on me last week."

"It was a perfectly good muffin," Emma had protested.

"It tasted like sadness," Hank had said. "And regret. Get a cinnamon roll."

So, she kissed Caleb on the cheek at the back door, quick, conscious of Hank's pointed nonchalance at the sink, and promised to text when she got to town.

"Be careful," Caleb had said, as he always did.

"I will," she'd answered, as she always did.

The drive in felt like any other summer trip. Fields rolled past in shades of gold and green. The sky was that particular sharp blue that made everything beneath it look both smaller and more precious. She hummed along to the radio, the old country station drifting in and out.

She felt… good. Tired in the way work made you tired, not in the way burnout did. The barn kiss still lived just beneath her skin, a quiet, steady warmth.

Pages & Pours was pleasantly busy when she stepped inside, bell chiming. A couple of tourists in matching hiking gear hovered nervously near the local interest shelf. Two older women argued amiably about a book club pick in front of the new releases. Libby, hair up in a messy knot, danced between the espresso machine and the pastry case with practiced ease.

"Hey, Emma," she called. "You're in luck. Fresh cinnamon rolls. I made 'em before the heat made the dough revolt."

"Bless you," Emma said. "One of those, a house blend, and… a bottle of cold brew to go for Hank, or he might disown me."

"On it," Libby said. "Sit wherever. The couch is finally free of teenagers."

Emma claimed the battered leather couch near the back with a little thrill of triumph. She set her bag down, pulled out her notebook and laptop, and was just settling in when Libby arrived with her order balanced expertly on a tray.

"You need Wi-Fi today?" Libby asked. "It's having a moody morning. Mercury in retrograde or some such."

"Maybe that's a sign," Emma said. "I'll try to write without three open tabs for once."

"That's the spirit," Libby said. She glanced toward the door as the bell chimed again. "Morning, Abby."

Emma didn't look up right away. The cinnamon roll smelled like heaven, and hacking through the first, sticky layer of icing seemed like the most pressing matter in her universe.

It took her a second to place the name.

Abby.

She'd heard it before. In Hank's living room, his voice softer when he'd said, Abby tried. Abby was scared. In Caleb's more guarded mentions, my ex, my high school sweetheart, she wanted something else. The girl in the photograph by the cottonwood tree, frozen mid-laugh in a snow-covered world ten years gone.

Emma's pen stilled. She turned a page in her notebook she hadn't written on, keeping her movements casual, and glanced up.

The woman at the counter was only a few years younger than Emma remembered from the photo, but time had done what it always did, it had sharpened some features, softened others.

She was pretty in a way that read as effortless: long dark hair pulled into a low ponytail, jeans that actually fit, a white T-shirt with a small logo over the pocket, dusty sneakers. No makeup that Emma could see. She carried herself with an ease that said she knew her way around this town and out of it.

"Hey, Lib," Abby said. "Can I get an iced latte? And one of those cinnamon rolls before that old man from the ranch gets them all?"

"Hank's got spies," Libby warned. "He'll know you stole his sugar."

"He always knows," Abby said, smiling. Her voice had a familiar cadence, that particular Western lilt Emma had come to associate with Caleb and Hank and half the people in Cottonwood Ridge.

Face-to-face, Abby didn't look like the villain Emma's more insecure moments had conjured. She looked… human. Tired around the edges in the way adults got tired. There was a faint line between her eyebrows that hadn't been there in the photo, the mark of someone who'd spent time frowning at screens or road maps or both.

Libby handed over the iced latte and cinnamon roll. Abby turned, scanning the café for a seat. Her gaze skimmed the room, passed briefly over the tourists and book club duo, then landed on Emma.

Recognition didn't flash immediately. Why would it? To Abby, she was just another stranger in town… until she wasn't.

Emma saw the moment gossip kicked in. Abby's eyes narrowed a fraction, then widened with something like aha. Her mouth curved, not quite a smile, not quite anything else.

She walked toward the couch, cinnamon roll on a small plate, iced latte sweating in her hand.

"Mind if I sit?" she asked, nodding toward the armchair angled near the couch.

"Go ahead," Emma said. Her heartbeat had picked up, but her voice sounded normal to her own ears.

"Thanks," Abby said, settling into the chair with a practiced flop. "Libby's right; that couch is a teenage nest most days. Gotta grab it when you can."

Emma smiled, noncommittal. Inside, her mind was already spinning, cataloging details, bracing for… something.

"So," Abby said after a sip of her latte, "you must be Emma."

There it was.

Emma blinked. "I am," she said slowly. "Have we… met?"

"Not officially," Abby said. "I'm Abby."

She let the name hang there, waiting to see if it landed.

It did. Emma felt something small and involuntary tighten in her chest. She wasn't sure if it showed on her face, but Abby's eyes flickered with satisfaction all the same.

"I've heard your name," Emma said, keeping her tone neutral.

"Small town," Abby said with a little eye roll. "Names travel faster than trucks."

Emma huffed a small laugh at that. "That they do."

"Saw your car go up the High Meadow road," Abby went on, tearing a piece off her cinnamon roll. "And everyone at the diner apparently decided that meant Caleb finally joined the twenty-first century and got himself an Airbnb guest."

"Apparently," Emma said.

Abby studied her with open curiosity now, gaze taking in the worn jeans, the flannel shirt, the faint line of sunburn at Emma's collarbone where she'd forgotten sunscreen a few days ago.

"You're not what I pictured," Abby said.

"Oh?" Emma asked. "What did you picture?"

"More... Patagonia," Abby said, waving a hand as if conjuring someone. "Less... actual working boots. No offense."

"None taken," Emma said. "I came up here very much as a Patagonia person. The boots are a more recent development."

Abby smiled, genuine amusement flashing. "Ranch'll do that to you," she said. "You here for the week? Weekend?"

"For the summer," Emma said.

Abby's eyebrows rose a fraction. "Whole summer," she repeated. "That's... a commitment."

"I needed a break from the city," Emma said. "And the cabin was... available."

"Caleb doesn't usually rent it out that long," Abby said, as if in passing. "He likes his space. Guess he's loosening up."

Emma let that sit. This conversation could tip into defensive sparring easily if she let it.

"How long are you in town for?" she asked.

"Just the summer," Abby said. "Home base is Fort Collins now. I do freelance marketing for outdoor brands." She made a face. "I get paid to come up with taglines like 'Find Your Wild.' I am part of the problem."

Emma grinned despite herself. "As someone who has written 'Five Ways to Refresh Your Morning Routine' for a living," she said, "I will not throw stones."

"Journalist, right?" Abby asked. "Libby said something about that."

Emma's skin prickled faintly. Of course, Libby had mentioned it. She probably told people what everyone did for a living without thinking about it, just small-town chatter.

"Yeah," Emma said. "Kind of on sabbatical at the moment. Working on a novel."

"Wow," Abby said, leaning back. "Ambitious. Miles above my 'sell more backpacks' agenda."

She took another drink of her latte, ice clinking.

"So," she said, casual as a cat stretching in a patch of sun, "how are you liking the ranch?"

There it was, the subtle pivot.

Emma chose her words carefully. "It's... different," she said. "Harder work than I expected. But good. Beautiful. Quiet in a way I didn't know I needed."

Abby's mouth quirked. "Yeah," she said softly. "It'll get under your skin if you're not careful."

An odd note there. Fondness? Resentment? Both?

"I grew up out there," Abby went on. "My folks' place is on the other side of town, but I spent more time at High Meadow than at home some years."

She smiled, and the picture that had hung on the mantel came to life a little, girl by the cottonwood, snow on the ground, boy beside her.

"You and Caleb went to school together," Emma said. It wasn't a question.

"From kindergarten," Abby said. "We were each other's science partners, prom dates, debate team rivals... you name it. Everyone in town just kind of assumed we'd... you know." She made a little finger-twisting gesture that could have signaled braiding or tying a knot. "I guess we did too."

Emma nodded, throat tight. This was the part of the story she'd heard in pieces, filtered through Hank and Caleb and the photos on the mantel. Now she was hearing it from the source.

"What happened?" she asked, because not asking would be stranger.

Abby's gaze drifted toward the window, where a pickup rolled slowly down Main.

"Life," Abby said. "War. Cancer. The usual."

She laughed lightly, but it didn't reach her eyes.

"Caleb always belonged to that ranch," she said. "Even when he swore up and down, he was going to join the Army and never look back, I knew he'd come home. It's… in his bones, you know? That land. Those hills."

Emma did know. She'd seen it in the way he looked at the fields at dusk, in the way his shoulders eased on horseback.

"I thought I could… fit into that," Abby went on. "We got engaged right after he came back from basic. It was all very… small-town fairy tale. Boy goes to war, girl waits at home, they get married, build a life. Except real life wasn't… that clean."

She took a breath, the work of compressing years into sentences evident.

"When his dad got sick, everything changed," she said. "It was like the ground shifted under us. He came back different from deployment, older, harder, and then he had to start watching the man who'd taught him everything fade. He was grieving, scared, angry. He had all this protective energy and nowhere to put it except on the things he could still… control."

Emma's pulse elevated. The word hung there between them like a signpost.

"Like what?" she asked carefully.

"Like me," Abby said simply. "Like us."

She tore another piece from her cinnamon roll, hands steady.

"He started… tightening," she said. "I couldn't drive to Fort Collins to see friends without a full itinerary. He'd freak out if I didn't text when I got there, when I left, when I stopped for gas. He hated when I went out at night in town without him. He'd say it was about safety, drunk guys, the back roads. And maybe part of it was. But it felt like every move I made had to be run through his 'risk assessment.'"

She smiled ruefully. "He'd stand in the kitchen and talk about 'force protection' when I wanted to go camping with my girlfriends. I know that was his job over there, but I wasn't his mission. I was supposed to be his partner."

Emma's stomach tightened. The scenario sketched was disturbingly easy to imagine, a scared young man, everything he loved under threat, grabbing harder at whatever he thought he could keep safe.

"He acted too much like my father and not my fiancé," Abby said quietly.

The line dropped into the space between them like a stone in a pond. Ripples moved outward.

Emma remembered Hank's version, her dad is… a piece of work. Real controlling. She saw now how those blurry phrases sharpened.

"My dad's old-school," Abby explained, as if picking up Emma's thought. "Ministry man, big on headship and submission and all that. He means well, but he likes his women… small. My mom never went anywhere without letting him know where, when, why, with whom. I grew up thinking that was normal until I got to college and realized it… wasn't."

She shrugged one shoulder.

"So, when Caleb came back and started echoing those same patterns, even if his reasons were different, it felt like I was trading one cage for another," she said. "He'd never hit me or yell at me; he's not that guy. But the constant… monitoring? The intensity? It wore me down. I couldn't breathe."

Emma thought of Caleb's sharp worry at the creek, his voice a little too loud around the edges. She thought of how Hank had framed it, there's a difference between a man wanting to keep you safe and a man wanting to keep you small. She thought of how Caleb had, even there, apologized when he'd gone too far.

"Did you tell him that?" Emma asked. "That you felt... caged?"

"I tried," Abby said. "But he was drowning. Between his dad, the ranch, the nightmares he wouldn't talk about... I don't think he could hear me. To him, my wanting to go to grad school or take a job in Denver looked like me walking into danger, not me... having a life."

Her eyes flicked back to Emma's face, gauging.

"He'd say things like, 'I just want to know you're safe,'" she said. "And I'd hear, 'I don't trust you to make your own decisions.' Maybe that's my baggage. Maybe I was unfair. But I know how it felt."

Emma nodded slowly. It was easy, listening to her, to see the validity in her fear. To see the twenty-something version of Caleb, raw and unprocessed, overcorrecting in all the wrong ways.

"How did it end?" she asked softly.

Abby's mouth twisted. "Badly," she said. "I broke it off while his dad was mid-treatment. Timing was... not ideal." Guilt flickered in her expression. "I told myself I was doing him a favor. That it was better to rip the bandage off than drag it out while he was already in hell. But the truth is, I was scared. I didn't want to wake up in ten years with kids and a mortgage and realize I'd built my life around someone else's fear."

She leaned forward a little, elbows on her knees, cinnamon roll forgotten.

"I'm not telling you this to... badmouth him," she said, and for a moment, Emma believed that. There was genuine pain here, and regret, and a kind of nostalgia that hurt. "He's a good man. He cares more deeply than anyone I've ever met. That's part of the problem. His protectiveness, it can be... a lot."

She held Emma's gaze with a steady seriousness now.

"I'm just... saying be careful," she said. "It's easy to confuse that intensity with passion at first. To feel... special. Chosen. 'He worries because he loves me.' That's what I told myself. And maybe it was true. But love that big, without... boundaries, it'll swallow you. It almost swallowed me."

Emma's hand tightened on her coffee mug without her realizing it. The heat grounded her.

She thought of the ways Caleb had worried about her, asking her to text when she got in, checking the weather before she went for hikes, reminding her to carry a flashlight if she walked back from the ranch house after dark. It had never felt like surveillance. It had felt... like being seen. Cared for.

But Abby's words wormed in around the edges, finding old fears and tapping them lightly, like checking for hollow spots.

"You don't... think people can change?" Emma asked.

"Oh, I do," Abby said. "I have. He has, probably. We were kids trying to play at being adults. I'm sure he's... calmer now. Time and land will do that. But... people's patterns are sticky. Especially under stress."

She gestured vaguely, as if encompassing the ranch, the drought, the perpetual financial balancing act.

"You're here for a summer," she said. "He's here... for life. He's got a way he does things. You step into that, it's easy to lose track of where you end and he begins."

She softened it with a small, self-deprecating smile.

"Listen to me," she said. "I sound like some bitter old ex on a talk show. That's not what I want. I just... saw your car on that road, heard your name at the diner, and couldn't shake the feeling that... I should say somethin'."

She sat back, exhaling. "Take it with all the salt in the shaker," she added. "You're your own person. Maybe your experience will be totally different. Maybe he learned from... us. God knows I've learned from it."

Emma's mind felt like the café's ceiling fans, whirring, trying to move thick air.

She could feel the shape of Abby's story, the pain of it. It wasn't hard to imagine being that younger woman, watching her fiancé tighten his grip as his world went sideways, hearing echoes of a controlling father where maybe there were none, or maybe there were some.

At the same time, she had her own data points. Caleb stopping himself mid-lecture at the creek. The way he'd apologized when his worry had come out like anger. The way he'd told her, I don't want you to give up your life for some ranch in the middle of nowhere... unless it's what you truly want.

He'd never checked her phone. Never demanded itineraries. Never told her no about town or hikes or time alone. He'd worried, yes. But he'd also listened when she'd said, I'm okay.

Still, the old reflexive fear, of being small, of being subsumed, stirred. Her relationship with her own parents had its minefields. Her father was less domineering than Abby's by the sound of it, but he had his opinions about what constituted a "real job" and a "real life." She'd spent years trying to live up to someone else's idea of success.

The thought of trading one set of expectations for another, even gently-intentioned ones, made her throat tighten.

Abby watched her, something almost like compassion in her face now.

"You look like I just dumped a bucket of mud on your nice picnic," she said lightly. "I'm sorry. I really am. I'm not trying to scare you off. I just... would've wanted someone to give me the full picture back then. And nobody did. Everyone loved the idea of 'Caleb and Abby' too much to... see the cracks."

"I appreciate the honesty," Emma said, and she meant it, even as she sorted the truth from the projection. "It's... a lot. But... thank you."

Abby nodded. "Of course," she said. "You're... clearly not an idiot. You'll figure out what's right for you."

She glanced at her watch and winced. "I should get going," she said. "My mom's expecting me for lunch and she'll call out the National Guard if I'm late."

She stood, gathering her things. She hesitated, then reached into her bag and pulled out a small card, sliding it onto the table beside Emma's notebook.

"My number," she said. "If you ever want to talk. About… anything. Ranch life, small towns, good hiking spots, whatever. I'm in and out all summer."

Emma glanced at the card, then back at her. "Thanks," she said again.

Abby smiled, something unreadable in it. "Enjoy your cinnamon roll," she said. "And… be careful with him, okay? He doesn't always know how big he is."

The phrase lodged in Emma's chest.

She watched Abby walk out, the bell chiming behind her. Through the front window, she saw her cross the street, pause to pet the lamppost dog, then climb into a Subaru with a roof rack plastered in national park stickers.

Emma sat back on the couch, the chatter of the café suddenly a little too loud. Her cinnamon roll had cooled. Her coffee had gone lukewarm. Her notebook sat open and blank in front of her, pen balanced across the page.

"Everything okay?" Libby's voice floated over. Emma looked up to see her hovering, concern in the tilt of her head.

"Yeah," Emma said automatically. "Just… a lot on my mind."

Libby's gaze flicked to the door Abby had exited, then back. "She talk your ear off?" she asked, tone neutral.

"A bit," Emma said. "She… knows Caleb."

"Everybody here knows Caleb," Libby said. "Some better than others."

There was a wealth of information in the pause.

"I'm not gonna pry," Libby added. "Just… don't let other people's ghosts live rent-free in your head, okay? This town loves a rerun. Doesn't mean you owe anybody a sequel."

Emma managed a smile. "I'll… keep that in mind."

Libby squeezed her shoulder gently and retreated to the counter, leaving Emma alone with her thoughts and too-cool coffee.

She tried to write. She really did.

She stared at the blinking cursor on her laptop. Typed a sentence. Deleted it. Wrote in her notebook instead. The words that came out were flat, tinny.

After half an hour of fighting it, she gave up. She closed the laptop, shoved her notebook back in her bag, and stood.

The drive back to the ranch felt longer than usual. The scenery hadn't changed, the same hills, the same sky, the same patch of road where the asphalt cracked in a jagged line. But her mind ran loops too fast and too tight.

Be careful with him. He's… intense. Controlling, even. He acted too much like my father and not my fiancé.

She turned the phrases over, trying to see them from every angle. Some parts slid off, unable to stick to the Caleb she knew. Other parts found shallow grooves, places where they might nest and grow if she let them.

By the time she turned onto the long gravel lane up to the cabin, her chest felt tight.

Gus barked at her arrival, his usual greeting. Hank emerged from the side of the ranch house, wiping his hands on a rag. Caleb was nowhere in sight, probably out in the fields.

"You're back later than I expected," Hank called as she got out of the car. "Town hold you hostage?"

"Something like that," she said, trying for lightness.

"Cinnamon roll?" he asked, hopefully.

She lifted the paper bag. "Peace offering," she said.

He took it, then squinted at her. "You all, right?" he asked bluntly.

"Just tired," she said. "It's hot."

He didn't look convinced. Hank had known her only a few weeks, but he was already cataloguing her tells, how her shoulders hunched when she was overwhelmed, how her jokes got sharper when she was scared.

"Mm-hm," he said. "Well, try not to melt. Caleb's up in the north pasture if you're lookin' for him. Said he might be a while. Water line issue."

"I'm gonna… go write for a bit," she said. "Then maybe I'll go up there."

"You do what you need," he said. He waved the bag. "I'll be in the kitchen communin' with this cinnamon roll."

She walked up the hill toward her cabin, the air heavy around her. The porch boards creaked under her weight. Inside, the space felt smaller than it had that morning.

She set her bag down, closed the curtains halfway against the glare, and sank onto the edge of the bed.

She should have trusted her first instincts, about Caleb, about herself. She should have been able to hold his actions up against Abby's words and say, no, this is different. And part of her could. But another part, old, raw, attuned to red flags, couldn't help but picture the younger version of him, the one in the photos, and see how easily good intentions could calcify into control.

He hadn't done that with her. Not yet. Maybe he wouldn't. Hank certainly seemed convinced that he'd learned from the past. But people's patterns were sticky, Abby had said. Especially under stress.

And life on a ranch was nothing if not stressful.

She lay back on the bed and stared at the ceiling, listening to the faint hum of insects outside.

Omniscient eyes, if they'd been in the room, would have noted that the unsettled feeling twisting in her gut wasn't just about Caleb. It was also about her. About the fear that she was once again building a life around someone else's gravity. That she might, without realizing it, slip back into a familiar pattern, adapting, accommodating, making herself smaller so someone else could breathe easier.

She didn't want that. Not here. Not now. Not with a man who had already shown her he respected her choices.

And yet, Abby's words clung like burrs.

Be careful with him.

She closed her eyes, exhaled hard, and tried to separate what belonged to the past and what belonged to the present.

Caleb, miles away in the north pasture, had no idea that an old ghost had just brushed its fingers along the edges of what he and Emma were building. He was knee-deep in mud, hands on a pipe wrench, cursing quietly at a stubborn valve. He'd look up later, see the cabin light on, and feel that now-familiar pull toward the hill.

For now, the story let the tension sit, coiled and quiet, in the small cabin under the wide Colorado sky.

Emma had met the ex. And though she left Pages & Pours unsettled but not convinced, a hairline crack had been laid.

What she did with it, and what Caleb did when those old shadows began to move, would determine just how much there was to lose.

Chapter Sixteen
Seeds of Doubt, Voice of Wisdom

The afternoon slid by in pieces.

Emma tried to write. The words came out crooked.

She sat at the little cabin table with her laptop open, the blank document glaring. The conversation at Pages & Pours looped in her head like a bad song, Abby's voice playing over the hum of the refrigerator.

Be careful with him.

He's… intense. Controlling, even.

He acted too much like my father and not my fiancé.

Emma closed the laptop, opened her notebook instead, and stared at a page full of neat blue lines. She wrote "Lucky" in the margin, then doodled a little clumsy calf with legs too long. The drawing made her smile for half a second before it twisted into something else.

He's a good man. He cares more deeply than anyone I've ever met. That's part of the problem.

She got up, made tea. Sat back down. Got up again, paced the narrow length of the cabin, the boards creaking under her feet. Outside, the day burned bright and cloudless. In here, everything felt slightly off-kilter.

She tried to give herself a stern, rational lecture.

You know him.

She listed the evidence like she was building a case:

He'd never checked her phone.

He'd never told her not to go into town.

He'd never said, "You can't," about anything except sticking her hand in an electric fence.

He worried. That was true. He reminded her to text when she got home, to carry water on hikes, to let someone know where she was going. He'd barked at her at the creek, voice a little too sharp.

But when she'd pushed back, when she'd told him she needed to live her own life, he'd listened. He'd apologized. He'd taken a breath and stepped back instead of closing in.

Still, the seed was there now, lodged under her skin.

Be careful.

She walked out onto the porch, looking for air.

From up here, she could see part of the lower pasture, a patch of pale grass and darker cattle moving like slow thoughts. The heat shimmered over the fields. Somewhere down there, a truck engine revved, a distant mechanical growl that meant work.

As if conjured by her thoughts, Caleb appeared a few minutes later on the path below, a small dot resolving into a tall man in a sweat-darkened shirt, hat pushed back.

He paused at the foot of the hill and shaded his eyes, looking up. Even at this distance, she knew the shape of his stance, the slight tilt of his head when he was checking on something that mattered to him.

Her.

"Hey!" she called, leaning on the porch rail.

"Hey yourself," he called back. "You make it back in one piece?"

The question, familiar as breathing now.

"Yes," she said. "No dramatic coffee shop accidents."

"Good," he said. "You drink enough water? Roads were throwin' heat like a skillet when I came in."

Normally, the mild fussing would have made her feel… held. Today, the words brushed up against the rawness of Abby's cautions and stung.

"I'm sufficiently hydrated," she said. "Promise."

He came up the hill, boots crunching on the gravel. Up close, the sun had deepened the tan at his throat, a line of lighter skin visible where his shirt collar usually sat. Sweat had plastered a few strands of hair to his temple.

"Storm might roll in later," he said, glancing at the horizon automatically. "You hear any thunder, you stay up here, okay? Don't go walkin' ridgelines."

"There's not a cloud in the sky," she said.

He nodded toward the west. "See that line?" he asked. "Heat haze, yeah, but there's a darker band under it. That's moisture stackin' up. Out here, storms can blow in fast. Lightning likes high ground and idiots with metal water bottles."

She followed his gaze. To her eyes, the sky was just blue, shifting toward paler at the edges. To him, it was a forecast, a collection of patterns years in the reading.

"I'll... keep an eye out," she said.

"Good," he said. His gaze flicked over her, checking without seeming to. "You, okay? You look... tired."

"I'm fine," she said. The word came out too fast. She forced a smile. "Just fried from the heat."

"Don't forget the snakes, either," he added, eyes scanning the scrub near the porch out of habit. "They like to coil up in warm spots near rocks this time of day. If you go wanderin', wear boots and watch where you put your hands."

The caution was familiar. She'd heard some variation of it from him a dozen times since she'd arrived. He'd shown her a rattler's shed skin once, explaining fang placement with a stick while she'd tried not to imagine the live version.

Today, under Abby's words, it sounded different. Like an invisible list of dangers only he had the key to, and she was a variable to be managed.

You step into that, it's easy to lose track of where you end and he begins.

She hated that the thought even appeared. Hated that she looked at his concern and saw not just care, but potential threat.

"You're very consistent with the safety briefs," she said, trying for light.

"Yeah, well," he said, mouth twitching, "occupational hazard. They drilled 'risk management' into us so hard I see potential hazards in a church pew."

She laughed because that was objectively funny. The sound eased some of the tension between them, but inside, the conflict remained.

He reached the porch and set a hand on the rail near hers, close enough that their fingers almost brushed.

"How was town?" he asked. "Libby talk you into more books you don't have time to read?"

"It was good," she said. "Got some writing done. Saw… people."

He caught the slight hitch. "Anybody give you a hard time?" he asked, tone sharpening just a little.

There it was again, that alertness, that tilt forward.

"Nothing dramatic," she said quickly. "It's fine."

He studied her for a beat, torn between pushing and letting it go. His instinct, honed by years of needing to know what he was walking into, leaned toward the former. The part of him that had learned how to not crowd people he cared about tugged the other way.

"Okay," he said finally. "If you say so."

He straightened. "I'm gonna grab a quick shower," he said. "Then we're movin' the lower herd to the north lot before it gets too late. If you want to come, bring a hat. You'll fry out there."

"I might stay up here," she said. "Try to wrangle some words. But thanks."

He nodded. "All right," he said. "Text Hank if you need anything. Service is better down there."

He hesitated, then leaned in and pressed a quick kiss to her forehead. It was a small, tender thing, his lips warm from the sun. Normally it would have grounded her. Today, it landed and echoed, rippling through the tangle of worry.

He went down the hill. She watched him, the broad line of his shoulders, the easy way he moved even when tired. He paused once, halfway, and looked back, as if checking she was still there. She lifted a hand. He tipped his hat, then kept walking.

Alone again on the porch, she exhaled slowly.

That had been… nothing. Just Caleb being Caleb. The same man who'd told her, I don't want you to give up your life for this place unless, you're sure. The same man who'd sat on her porch railing at midnight and listened to her talk about feeling like a hamster on a news-cycle wheel.

So why did her stomach twist like she'd seen a warning sign?

Because someone had handed her a story where he was dangerous and told her to read her life through it.

She closed her eyes, willing the narrative to loosen its hold.

Maybe talking about it would help.

Not with him. Not yet. Not with her thoughts this jumbled. The last thing she wanted was to hurl Abby's words at him raw, to watch his face shutter and his shoulders stiffen.

There was someone else, though. Someone who'd known him longer than anyone but Abby. Someone who loved him without sugarcoating his faults.

Hank.

The kitchen of the ranch house smelled like coffee and cinnamon and something frying. Hank stood at the stove, spatula in hand, coaxing eggs around in a skillet. The radio on the counter played a low, crackly classic rock station.

"You look like a woman with a question," he said without turning when Emma stepped into the doorway.

She blinked. "That obvious?"

"Only to the highly trained," he said, flipping an egg. "Or to an old man who's seen that exact expression on more faces than he can count."

She hovered near the table, fingers fiddling with the edge of Hank's folded newspaper. "Do you have a minute?" she asked. "I can come back if,"

"Sit," he said. "If I can fry an egg and hear you out at the same time, maybe my ex-wife'll finally forgive me for bein' a terrible multitasker."

Emma slid into a chair. The cheap vinyl stuck faintly to the backs of her knees in the heat.

Hank slid a plate in front of her, a fried egg, a slice of toast, one of the cinnamon rolls she'd brought earlier hacked in half for sharing.

"Eat somethin'," he said, setting his own plate down across from hers. "You think better when your blood sugar's not in the basement."

She picked at the toast, appetite dulled by nerves.

Hank took a bite of egg, chewed, swallowed, then fixed her with that steady, pale blue gaze.

"All right," he said. "What's got your brain runnin' circles? And don't say 'nothing,' unless you want me to start guessin' and really embarrass us both."

She huffed a laugh despite herself. "I… ran into Abby in town," she said.

One of his eyebrows went up. "Ah," he said. "And there it is."

"You knew she was back?" Emma asked.

"Been in and out all summer," he said. "Her folks drop her name at church like she's still nine and just got an A on a spelling test. And this town couldn't keep a secret if you stapled it shut. Least of all when it comes to Caleb Walker's love life."

He paused, fork hovering midway. "Did she… talk to you?" he asked. "Or just stare across the room all soulful-like?"

"She talked," Emma said. "At Pages & Pours. She recognized me from…" She gestured vaguely in the direction of the ranch.

"From me and my big mouth," he guessed. "Folks've been speculatin' about 'the girl up at Caleb's' since you pulled off the highway."

"It's fine," Emma said automatically. Then, because it wasn't, she added, "She seemed… nice. At first."

He snorted. "She is," he said. "Mostly. Nice doesn't mean harmless."

Emma took a breath. "She… told me some things," she said. "About when they were together. About how he was… after he came back. And when his dad got sick."

He set his fork down, attention sharpening.

"She said he was… intense," Emma went on. "Protective, I guess. That he wanted to know where she was all the time. That he freaked out when she wanted to go places without him. That she felt like he was acting more like her father than her fiancé."

Hank's jaw tightened just a hair at that last part.

"And?" he prompted when she trailed off.

"And I can't… quite match her story with the man I know," Emma said. "But I also can't totally dismiss it. Which is… messing with my head."

She looked down, tracing a crumb on her plate with one finger.

"I've seen how he is," she said. "He worries. About everything. About me driving in the dark, about weather, about snakes and mountain lions and… rogue tumbleweeds. And most of the time, that feels… good. Like someone has my back." Her throat worked. "But now I keep hearing her voice in my head, saying, 'Be careful. It feels like love until it feels like a cage.'"

The room was quiet except for the faint buzz of the radio.

Hank didn't rush to fill it. He let the silence stretch, the way someone who was comfortable with hard things did.

"You want to know if he was ever… too much with her," he said finally. "Whether she's got a point, or whether she's sellin' you a story."

Emma met his eyes. "Yes," she said. "And I know you care about him. I'm not asking you to… trash him. I just… need more context than the worst version of the story."

He nodded, lips pursed. "Fair enough," he said. He wiped his mouth with a paper napkin, folded it carefully, buying time.

"You gotta understand somethin' first," he said. "When Caleb came back from that second deployment, he was… rewired. Not broken. But different. The Army drills a certain way of seein' the world into you. You spend long enough over there, your dial for danger gets stuck on high."

He tapped his temple lightly.

"I still remember the first week he was back," Hank went on. "We went into town for groceries. Some kid dropped a pallet in the back and the noise sounded just wrong enough that Caleb hit the deck before his brain caught up. Whole store frozen, him sprawled on the floor with a bag of flour in his hands. He laughed it off, but his eyes…" He shook his head. "They don't train you how to turn that off. They just send you home and say, 'Good luck.'"

Emma pictured it, the sharp startle reflex, the way Caleb's shoulders sometimes twitched at distant bangs.

"So yeah," Hank said. "For a while there, he needed to know where the people he cared about were. It wasn't about ownin' 'em. It was about bein' able to predict threats. He thought if he could track variables, he could prevent bad outcomes."

He gave her a dry look. "Sometimes it was helpful," he said. "Like when he insisted, I take the truck instead o' the old Ford on an icy night and I would've ended up in a ditch otherwise. Sometimes it was… a pain in the backside."

"Like with Abby," Emma said softly.

"Like with Abby," Hank agreed. "Now. Was he… too much sometimes?" He held up a hand before she could answer. "Yes. I'm not gonna sugarcoat that. He'd get twitchy if she drove up to Fort Collins late and didn't text at the usual time. He'd stay up until she checked in, then fall asleep in a chair like his old man used to do waitin' for him to come back from dates. He'd grumble about bars and crowds and fellas with too many tattoos hittin' on her. A lot of that wasn't about her. It was about him. About this…" He tapped his chest. "Fear he was gonna lose someone else and it was gonna be his fault for not seein' it comin'."

Emma's throat tightened. She remembered him at the creek, fear spilling out as anger when he'd found her too close to the edge at dusk.

"But here's what he didn't do," Hank said. "He didn't tell her she couldn't go. He didn't take keys or phones or say, 'You're not allowed.' If she wanted to go visit friends, she went. If she wanted to dance with someone else at The Spur, she did. He might've stood in the corner glowerin' into his beer, but he let her make her own mistakes."

He took a sip of coffee, eyes distant with memory.

"I watched him," Hank said. "Because I know what real control looks like. My daddy had a temper when he drank; I've seen men who hit and then cry after, who call it love when it's just fear and ego. Caleb's not that. He was clingy, sure. Overprotective, sometimes. But he always… stopped at the line. If she said, 'You're smotherin' me,' he tried to back off. Didn't always get it right. But he tried."

Emma let that sink in. It painted a picture that matched what she'd seen, someone operating with the volume turned up too high, fumbling for the dial.

"Abby's daddy is a different story," Hank said, voice going a shade drier. "He's got this… theology he likes to wrap around his need for control. Talks about headship and submission and whatnot. Says he wants what's best for his womenfolk, but what he means is he wants 'em where he can see 'em. That man would've mapped that girl's day down to the minute and called it 'providin'.'"

There was no anger in his voice, just a weary familiarity with the type.

"So, you've had this young woman," he went on, "growin' up under that thumb. And then she falls in love with this boy who goes off to war, comes back with his danger dial stuck on red. He's scared; she's scared. He says, 'Please text me when you get there, because if you wind up in a ditch I don't know how I'll live with myself.' She hears, 'I don't trust you to drive.' He says, 'I'm worried about you goin' to that concert alone. Lotta drunk folks and no backup.' She hears, 'You can't have a life outside me.'"

He held out his hands, palms up, weighing invisible scales.

"They weren't speakin' the same language," he said. "Their wounds were talkin' to each other."

Emma swallowed hard. She could see it now: two frightened young people, both dragging their pasts into the space between them, mistaking each other's flinches for attacks.

"Did you ever… talk to him about it?" she asked. "Back then?"

"I tried," Hank said. "Lord knows I tried. Told him more than once, 'Son, you can't bubble-wrap the people you love. They'll suffocate and you'll hate yourself when they break out.' He'd nod like he understood. Sometimes he'd ease up. Sometimes somethin' would happen, a close call with his dad, a bad dream, and he'd revert, 'cause that felt safer than standin' there empty-handed."

He sighed, rubbing a hand over his face.

"I told Abby, too," he said. "Told her he was changed, that he needed time to figure out who he was now. Told her she had every right to need space. Told 'em both they might need help bigger than my kitchen table could provide." He smiled wryly. "Twenty-somethin's in love don't listen real well, on the whole."

Emma managed a faint smile in return.

"So, when she says he was… controlling," Emma said carefully, "you'd say…?"

"I'd say she's tellin' the truth as she lived it," Hank said. "And also missin' some truth about where it came from. He didn't want to own her. He wanted to keep every bad thing she'd ever known from touchin' her. Same with his mama, his dad, me. Anybody he loved, he slapped armor on in his head."

He leaned forward slightly, elbows on the table.

"And I'd also say," he added, "that he's not the same man now that he was then. Losing her, losing his dad, nearly losing the ranch… that humbled him. He did some work. Talked to a counselor the VA hooked him up with. Learned a little about what's his to carry and what ain't."

Emma's eyes widened. Caleb hadn't mentioned therapy. Somehow, the knowledge that he'd gone felt… important. A sign that he hadn't just white-knuckled his way through.

"He still gets twitchy," Hank said. "You've seen it. He'll go quiet when he worries. His voice'll get sharp if he thinks you're courtin' danger. But have you ever," He paused, choosing his words. "Have you ever felt like you couldn't say no to him?"

She thought back.

At the creek, when she'd bristled at his tone, she'd told him he wasn't her father, that he didn't get to dictate the radius of her life. He'd gone still, taken a breath, and softened. He'd apologized. He'd shown her the overlook instead of dragging her home.

When she'd said she was considering quitting the paper, he'd tested her decision, not to undermine it, but to make sure she wasn't doing it for him. He'd told her, I don't want you to wake up ten years from now and hate this place because of me.

"No," she said slowly. "I haven't."

"Ever felt like you couldn't walk down that hill and get in your car if you wanted to?" he pressed.

Images flickered, her packing for town, Caleb asking where she was going, then kissing her and telling her to have fun. The quiet understanding that if she chose to leave at the end of summer, he wouldn't chain himself to her bumper.

"No," she said again. "That's... never been in question."

"Do you feel like you're makin' yourself smaller to fit him?" Hank asked. "Quieter. Less you."

She thought about that one harder.

If anything, she realized, she felt more like herself up here than she had in years. She laughed louder. Cursed more. Wrote messier first drafts. She argued with him and with Hank and with the radio. She wore less makeup, more flannel. She said what she thought and got called on it when she was wrong.

"No," she admitted. "I feel more... me."

"There's your data," Hank said gently. "Not what I say. Not what Abby says. What your life with him actually looks like."

He sat back, the chair creaking.

"There's a difference," he said softly, "between a man wantin' to keep you safe and a man wantin' to keep you small."

The words rang through her, familiar. He'd said them before, weeks ago, when he'd first told her about Caleb and Abby. Back then, they'd sounded like folklore, something carved into a barn beam for future generations. Now they landed different, sharper.

"A man who wants to keep you small," Hank went on, "will chip at you. Little digs when you succeed. A hand on your shoulder when you speak up, pushin' you back down. He'll make his fear your fault. Blame you for makin' him worry, for bein' too pretty, too loud, too much."

He looked at her over the rim of his mug.

"You seen any of that in him?" he asked.

She thought of Caleb, proud and a little awed when she'd told him about her front-page investigative piece. Of him reading her chapters slowly on the porch, lips moving, then looking up and saying, I like the way you make people feel real. Of him telling her, half teasing, half serious, that her stubbornness was one of his favorite things about her.

"No," she said again, stronger this time. "He… doesn't make me feel too much. He makes me feel… enough."

"Then don't let someone else's ghost tell you who he is now," Hank said quietly. "Or who you are."

Emma blinked hard. Emotion pricked behind her eyes, unexpected and sharp.

"I'm not sayin' ignore your gut," he added. "If he ever does pinch you down, if he ever starts makin' you doubt your own mind on the regular, you come sit right back at this table and we'll have a different talk. I'm not so old or sentimental that I won't tan his hide if he starts down the wrong road."

She laughed, watery. "I'd pay to see that," she said.

"You and half the county," he said dryly.

He sobered.

"But I've watched that boy for more years than either of you would like me to say out loud," he said. "And what I see now is a man who's learned some hard lessons. He still worries too much. He still scans every room. But he knows better than to grab so tight he breaks what he's holdin'. You're good for him. You make him laugh more than I've heard in… a long time. Don't let somebody who left tell you what stayin' oughta feel like."

The line hit deep.

Emma let out a long breath she hadn't realized she'd been holding.

"Okay," she said softly.

Silence settled again, but it was different now, less jagged.

She picked up her fork and took a bite of egg, more to give herself a task than out of hunger. The flavor surprised her, simple, good.

"Does he know she's… talking to me?" she asked after a minute.

"Not unless she told him," Hank said. "And if she did, I imagine it was in the form of, 'I tried to warn her.'"

Emma winced. "Great," she muttered. "Love being the next episode in the town's favorite soap opera."

"Welcome to Cottonwood Ridge," Hank said. "Population: people who talk. You don't owe any of 'em a damn thing."

She nodded, letting that settle.

"I feel bad for her," she admitted. "It's clear she went through… stuff. With her dad. With Caleb. With herself. But I also… don't like that she put that on me. On us."

"Empathy's good," Hank said. "But empathy without boundaries'll have you pickin' up everybody else's baggage till you can't walk. You can feel sorry for her and still say, 'That's not my road.'"

Emma toyed with her napkin, folding it into smaller and smaller squares.

"Should I… tell him?" she asked. "About what she said?"

Hank considered. "Not from a place of pointin' fingers," he said. "But yeah. Eventually. Secrets rot. Better he hear it from you than from some sideways comment at the feed store. But you don't have to do it today. Or when you're still chewin' on it raw. Let it settle. Talk to him when you know what you feel, not just what you heard."

She nodded, relieved he hadn't said, March down there this second and demand answers.

"Okay," she said.

He pushed his plate away and stood, stretching.

"In the meantime," he said, "I got a gate hangin' crooked on the west side that's been mockin' me all mornin'. You wanna distract your brain, come hold it while I try not to take the skin off my knuckles. Nothin' like cussin' at hardware to quiet the mind."

She smiled, the invitation exactly what she needed. "Yeah," she said. "I think I'd like that."

They worked the rest of the afternoon side by side, wrestling with hinges and bolts, arguing amiably about the right way to shim a sagging post. The physical effort, the small victories, the easy banter, each helped scrape Abby's words out of the grooves they'd tried to carve.

Later, as the sun dipped low and the air cooled, Emma walked back up the hill to her cabin. She felt tired, but in a different way now. Less like someone carrying an unfamiliar burden, more like someone who'd set part of it down.

On the porch, she paused, looking down toward the ranch house.

Caleb stood by the corral, one arm draped over the top rail, hat tilted back as he watched Lucky tearing around in clumsy loops. The little bull calf skidded, legs splayed, then regained his balance and took off again like a kid on a sugar high.

Caleb laughed, out loud, unguarded. Even from this distance, Emma could hear it. It tugged at something in her chest.

He looked up, as if sensing her eyes. When he spotted her, he raised a hand. She lifted hers in return.

She thought of Abby's warning, of Hank's steady words, of her own lived experience.

There's a difference between a man wanting to keep you safe and a man wanting to keep you small.

Caleb Walker, for all his sharp edges and scars, had never asked her to shrink. If anything, he seemed baffled and a little in awe when she expanded, when she spoke her mind, when she charted her own course.

The seed of doubt Abby had planted was still there, but it was no longer the only thing growing. Hank's context, her own memories, the way she felt in her own skin around Caleb, they sent roots deeper, anchoring her.

She still had questions. She still intended to talk to him, to lay the shadows between them in the open where they could see them together. But the panic had ebbed.

As she watched him lean over the rail to scratch Lucky's head, murmuring something that made the calf butt his hand, Emma felt that quiet, stubborn truth settle back into place.

Whatever flaws he had, whatever ghosts still walked his nights, Caleb didn't want to cage her. He'd rather stand outside the gate, keeping watch, than slam it shut.

Under the Colorado sky, the voice of doubt had spoken. So had the voice of wisdom. For now, she chose to believe the one that knew them both.

Chapter Seventeen
Distance and Misreading

The first hint that something had shifted didn't come from Caleb or Emma.

It came from the feed store.

Caleb had gone into town two days after Emma's coffee with Abby, list in his pocket and a thin coil of tension between his shoulder blades. July had settled into one of those stretches where the heat didn't break at night, just sagged darker and thicker. The cows panted in the shade. The dust on the road tried to climb into his truck.

He told himself he was there for mineral blocks and fly tags. That was true enough.

The bell over the feed store door jingled as he stepped inside, hat pushed back against the cooler air. The place smelled like fertilizer, leather, and old coffee. A couple of ranchers he knew by sight nodded in that laconic way men around here said hello.

"Hey, Caleb," Gary behind the counter called. "Got those salt blocks you asked for in the back."

"Appreciate it," Caleb said, heading toward the aisle with fencing supplies. He passed a rack of dog toys and paused long enough to grab a new ball for Gus; last one had died an honorable death in the jaws of an enthusiastic heeler.

He was comparing two brands of fly tags, mentally running through prices, when he heard his name from the front.

"Caleb Walker's really gone modern, hasn't he? Airbnb and all."

He recognized the voice, Nancy, who ran the florist next door and knew just about everything that went on within a twenty-mile radius.

He wasn't trying to eavesdrop, exactly. The store was small. Voices carried.

"Libby said that girl from Denver was in the shop again," Nancy went on. "Emma, right? Smart. Pretty. Asked all the right questions about the town. Abby says,"

The rest blurred. The word Abby alone was enough to raise the hair on the back of his neck.

He stepped around the end of the aisle and into view. Both women at the counter started slightly, caught mid-gossip. Nancy recovered first, smiling too brightly.

"Well, if it isn't the man himself," she said. "Speak of the devil and he shall appear."

"I'm hopin' that's just a figure of speech," Caleb said, setting his fly tags on the counter. He kept his tone mild, but his pulse had picked up.

Nancy laughed, flapping a hand. "We were just saying Emma seems like a nice girl," she said. "Abby ran into her at Pages & Pours the other day. Said they had a good chat."

The sentence landed like a fist below his ribs.

"Yeah?" he said, keeping his face neutral.

"Oh yeah," Nancy said, oblivious to the shift in his posture. "This town's too small for people not to bump into each other. Abby said she tried to give her some friendly advice." She waggled her eyebrows as if this were charming. "You know, 'been there, done that, bought the cowboy.'"

The joke scraped across something raw inside him.

"Is that right," he said.

He pictured Abby at one of those little tables, leaning forward, voice soft and earnest. He could almost hear the phrasing: be careful. He's intense.

Of course she'd mean well. Or tell herself she did. Abby had always framed her doubts as concern, for him, for herself, for what they might become. That didn't mean the words wouldn't sour when they landed in the wrong place.

He slid cash across the counter, jaw tight.

"Just so you know," Nancy said, unable to help herself, "people are glad to see you… movin' on. You were a sad postcard for a while there. It's good to see some… fresh color up at High Meadow."

"Appreciate the input," he said, a little cooler than usual.

He carried his purchases out to the truck without really feeling the weight of them. The sun hit him like an open oven. He stood for a moment in the brightness, palms pressed to the warm metal of the tailgate, breathing.

Abby had talked to Emma. About him. He didn't know exactly what she'd said, but he knew the shape of it. The contours of the story were familiar. He'd heard them in the bruised silence of their breakup, in her father's clipped phone call, in his own nightly catalog of mistakes.

Too much. Too intense. Too controlling.

The words he'd used on himself for years.

He'd thought, hoped, that whatever narrative Abby carried now lived mostly in her own head, far from his pastures. Hearing that she'd handed a version of it to Emma made his stomach twist.

He pictured Emma, sitting in the coffee shop, listening with that tilted-head attention she had. He imagined her trying to reconcile the man she'd been living with, the one who worried and apologized and tried, with the boy Abby described.

What if she believed it?

What if she looked at him and saw not a man doing his damndest to learn, but an inevitable pattern? A cage waiting to snap shut?

The thought lodged under his chest like a stone.

He drove back to the ranch on autopilot, the road a blur. His mind kept circling the same patch of territory, Abby's caution, Emma's face, Hank's kitchen table. The world outside narrowed to the confines of his truck cab and the memories he'd spent years trying to file away.

By the time he pulled into the drive, his overactive caution had latched onto a plan.

If his intensity had helped drive Abby away, maybe the answer, this time, was to step back. To give Emma more space than she thought she needed. To not crowd, not hover, not ask for check-ins that could look like leashes.

He could manage his own fear without making it her problem.

He owed her that much.

From Emma's vantage point, the shift was quiet, almost imperceptible at first.

Small things.

Caleb still showed up to move cattle, still ate dinner with Hank, still texted occasionally if he was going to be late. But the daily rhythm they'd slid into, a quick swing by her porch in the evening, a shared coffee in the ranch kitchen mid-morning, a kiss stolen in the shadow of the barn, got… patchier.

The first day, she chalked it up to chores.

He didn't come up the hill at dusk like he usually did. She waited on the porch with her mug, watching the sun bleed out behind the ridge, expecting to hear his boots on the steps, his hand on the railing. When the light faded and the only sounds were birds and the wind, she went inside and told herself he'd gotten hung up fixing a line.

The second night, she spotted his truck lights flashing briefly near the north lot just as the sky went from purple to black. Her phone buzzed with a text.

Storm's movin' in fast from the west. Stay inside tonight, okay? Don't want you caught in lightning if you wander.

She stared at it, that familiar mix of concern and command. Her thumb hovered over the keyboard.

Abby's voice slid in uninvited.

He always knew how to make a girl feel trapped.

Emma closed her eyes, anger and affection colliding.

He was right, objectively. Thunder had been rumbling in the distance for a while. She'd spent enough time watching the sky with him to see it now, the low, dark line of clouds marching toward the ranch, the sudden chill that meant rain wasn't just a rumor.

She typed,

Got it. I'll stay put. Thanks for the heads up.

Then hesitated.

Beside the gratitude, she added,

You can come up if you want. I make a mean storm-watching playlist.

The typing dots appeared, blinked, disappeared. Reappeared. She exhaled slowly.

Finally, his reply popped up.

Thanks, but I better stay with the herd. Don't like leavin' 'em in this if I can help it. Rain on the north lot gets slick. Another time.

It wasn't cold. It was practical. Exactly what he would have said two weeks ago, before Abby, before Hank's kitchen conversation.

It still landed like a small door closing.

She set her phone down harder than necessary on the table and paced the narrow cabin, the rising wind rattling the windows. Her brain obliged by spinning alternate translations.

He's busy.

He's being responsible.

He doesn't want to see you tonight.

He's pulling back.

He's realized this is temporary and he shouldn't get attached.

The storm broke, sheets of rain hammering the roof, lightning etching the hills in white. In the occasional flashes, she could see the pasture, silver and black, the vague shapes of cattle huddled.

Somewhere out there, in that mess, he was probably soaked through, mud to his knees, keeping watch. She could picture him clearly, hat pulled low, jaw set, eyes scanning.

The image made her chest ache with something that had nothing to do with Abby's warnings. This was who he was at his core, a man who stood out in storms because he believed being there made a difference, even when it didn't.

She pressed her forehead to the cool glass and closed her eyes.

Don't be ridiculous, she told herself. He's doing his job. Not giving you the silent treatment.

But the unease lingered, a hairline crack in the easy confidence they'd been building.

Down in the pasture, Caleb wiped rain from his eyes and tried not to think about a cabin on a hill.

The herd had clustered instinctively against the windward side of a stand of scrubby trees. Lucky pressed against Daisy's flank, occasionally startled by thunder and trying to climb under her with oversized determination.

"Same, kid," Caleb muttered, adjusting his jacket.

His phone buzzed in his pocket. He fished it out with wet fingers, nearly dropping it in the mud.

You can come up if you want. I make a mean storm-watching playlist.

He stared at the text, the words haloed by droplets on the screen. Warmth shot through him entirely unrelated to the weather.

He wanted that so badly it hurt. To sit on her porch while the sky went wild, to feel her shoulder leaning into his as she narrated cloud shapes, to let the barn and the fences and the dripping cattle be someone else's problem for an hour.

He also knew he wasn't the man who left his herd in a storm. Not twice, not after the one-time years ago when he'd come back to a fallen tree and a terrified bunch of animals pressed against broken wire.

You don't get to clock out, his father had said, not unkindly. This place asks what you're made of every day.

He thumbed a quick reply. Tried to keep it light.

Thanks, but I better stay with the herd. Don't like leavin' 'em in this if I can help it. Rain on the north lot gets slick. Another time.

He hovered over the keyboard, wanting to add more.

I miss you.

I'd rather be there.

This isn't me avoidin' you, I swear.

He deleted each version. They all sounded like excuses. Instead, he tucked the phone back into his pocket and turned his focus outward, scanning the fence line with his flashlight beam.

Lightning crackled closer. Thunder chased it, loud enough to shiver his bones. He thought of her up there, probably pacing, probably overthinking, and felt a fresh stab of guilt.

Give her space, he reminded himself. Don't make her feel like you're keeping tabs. She doesn't need your running commentary on her evening.

It didn't occur to him that as he pulled back to avoid smothering her, she might interpret it as something else entirely.

The omniscient eye, if invited in, could have laid their internal monologues side by side and shaken its head at the symmetry: both of them wanting to lessen the other's burden, both of them padding their love in silence like delicate glassware, both of them missing how the careful distance read as doubt.

But omniscient eyes, however wise, don't get to intervene. They only watch.

The storm rolled over the ranch, dumped its anger, and drifted east. The hills steamed in the sudden cool. Cows shook off water. Caleb's jacket stuck to him in cold patches.

By the time he trudged back toward the house, his muscles ached. His eyes kept drifting up the hill even when he told himself to look at his own feet before he trip-slid into a gopher hole.

He could see a rectangle of light in Emma's cabin window. A shadow moved against it. He looked away deliberately, telling himself that not every moment of her evening needed to be his business.

The next morning was bright and clear, the world scrubbed. The air smelled like wet earth and sage. Emma woke later than she meant to, hair gluey on one side from falling asleep on the couch instead of the bed. She'd dozed off at some point midway through a movie she didn't remember starting, storm noise and her racing thoughts finally exhausting each other.

She showered, pulled on clean jeans, and told herself she wouldn't read into anything.

Down at the ranch house, Hank greeted her with his usual cheerfully grumpy commentary about weather and aging knees. Caleb sat at the table, a mug cupped in both hands, looking freshly showered but tired around the eyes.

"Morning," Emma said.

"Hey," he replied, voice easy. "Storm keep you up?"

"Some," she said. "You?"

"Cows sang the song of their people all night," he said. "Lucky spent half of it tryin' to climb into Daisy's ribcage."

"That's because you named him Lucky," Hank said, dropping a plate of eggs on the table. "He assumes the universe'll bend for him."

"It did the day he was born," Caleb said.

Their eyes met briefly, a shared flash of that morning in the barn.

Emma felt it like a physical thing and looked away too quickly, suddenly aware of an entire silent conversation she wasn't sure how to start.

"Got any big plans today?" Hank asked her, breaking the moment.

"Writing this morning," she said. "If the words cooperate. Maybe help with whatever this afternoon, if you need an extra pair of hands."

"Always need hands," Hank said. "But don't you let this place eat your summer if that's not what you want."

"I like helping," she said. "It… clears my head."

Caleb's thumb traced the rim of his mug. He heard the offer and ran it through his new, over-cautious filter.

Don't drag her into your world if she doesn't truly want it. Don't assume. Don't make the ranch her problem.

"You don't have to," he said, a little too quickly. "With the heavy stuff. We got it. Your book matters too."

"I know I don't have to," she said. "I want to."

He nodded, but part of him still held back. "We'll see how the day shakes out," he said. "Don't plan your hours around our mess."

"What if I want to plan some of them around your mess?" she asked lightly.

Hank's eyes flicked between them, catching the subtle misalignment, a question offered, an answer that missed the mark by just an inch.

"I just don't want you feelin' obligated," Caleb said.

She smiled, but it wobbled at the edges. "I'll let you know if I start," she said.

To her, his insistence read like a reluctance to include her. A line drawn, this is my sphere, that is yours. It pricked at the part of her that wanted to be not just his guest, but his partner. The part that had sat in Hank's kitchen and thought, We're in this together.

To him, it felt like penance. Like practicing not snapping his fears around her like a leash. If he could keep from drawing her too close, maybe he'd avoid the sin Abby laid at his feet.

Both thought they were being considerate. Neither saw the distance they were adding, one careful inch at a time.

Over the next several days, the pattern held.

Emma would appear at the barn, gloves in hand, saying, "Need help?" Caleb would look up, torn between gratitude and restraint.

"Only if you really want to," he'd say. "Otherwise, Hank and I got it."

Which, to his mind, was the opposite of pressure. He'd spent years giving orders that couldn't be refused; now he was trying to offer options.

To Emma, the repeated caveat started to sound like, I don't want you here if it's any trouble. You're an extra, not essential.

She'd hang back more often, hearing implied rejection where none was intended.

"All right," she'd say, hearing a note of forced brightness in her own voice. "I'll go wrestle my chapter instead. Holler if you need me."

They both watched her walk away, the line of her shoulders a little stiffer, the swing of her ponytail a little too casual, and both misread it.

Caleb saw a woman rightly prioritizing her own work, not letting herself get subsumed by his responsibilities. Relief warred with sadness.

She's not building her life around your schedule, he told himself. Good. That's healthy. That's what you wanted for her.

Emma saw a man who didn't reach for her help. A man who had, once, pulled her into the thick of things, into storms and births and fence repairs, and was now carefully doing things without her.

He's pulling back, she thought. Maybe Hank was wrong. Maybe Abby's story is still truer than I want it to be.

She fought that thought, reminding herself of Hank's words, of her own experience. But it lingered, showing up at odd moments like a bad headline in her mental feed.

They still had good moments.

Even distance couldn't erase the gravity between them entirely.

One evening, she did end up in the north pasture with him, Lucky chasing her shoelaces while Caleb fixed a mineral feeder. They ended up lying on their backs in the grass, watching satellites crawl across the sky.

"You know, in Denver I couldn't see half these stars," she said.

"In Baghdad, I thought the stars were pendin' court-martial," he said.

She laughed, rolling her head toward him. "How do you make every romantic moment weird?" she asked.

"Talent," he said.

Another afternoon, he found her in the cabin, hunched over her laptop, and silently set a plate of sliced peaches on the table beside her.

"You looked like you were forgettin' to eat," he said, leaning in the doorway.

She blinked up, brain slow to shift gears. "You're very judgey for someone who runs on coffee and beef jerky," she said.

"I never claimed model status," he said. "Eat the fruit, woman."

She did. The sweetness surprised her tongue, sticky and bright. She smiled at him around a mouthful.

"Thank you," she said.

He shrugged, one corner of his mouth lifting. "Somebody's gotta keep you from wastin' away," he said, and the familiar, easy affection between them unfurled.

Those small kindnesses kept the bottom from dropping out. But between the bright spots, something else was growing, an awareness of the times they didn't quite meet in the middle anymore.

More than once, she caught him watching her with an expression she couldn't parse, soft and worried and distant all at once, like he was memorizing her and bracing for impact.

He, in turn, saw her gaze slide away when talk turned too close to the future, saw the flicker of something, hesitation, maybe fear, behind her eyes when town gossip mentioned Abby nearby, and took it as confirmation that she was second-guessing.

He didn't know about Hank's kitchen table conversation, about the way Emma had walked back up the hill that day lighter, more sure. He only knew that since then, the air between them felt more fragile in certain spots, like a piece of glass repaired but not fully cured.

And because he was who he was, a man who'd learned to preempt disasters by retreating first, he slowly, almost unconsciously, started to pull his center of gravity back inside his own ribs.

If she decided to leave at the end of summer, better not to be too entangled. Better to make the eventual goodbye clean, not a tearing.

The omniscient eye, patient and unsentimental, might have pointed out that he was already entangled, that the threads they'd woven weren't going to dissolve just because he stepped a half-step away at dinner. But omniscience is no cure for fear. Knowing something and living as if it's true are different skills entirely.

One afternoon, the misalignment came to a head over something as mundane as a trip to town.

Emma stood by her car, keys in hand, bag over her shoulder. The sun was hot on the gravel; heat shimmered above the hood. Caleb was tightening a strap on a hay load nearby, forearms flexing.

"I'm gonna run into town," she called. "Need more coffee and… paper. My notebook's almost full."

He straightened, wiped his hands on his jeans, and walked closer.

"You good on gas?" he asked automatically.

"Yes, Dad," she teased, the old joke a little too sharp.

He winced slightly. "Just askin'," he said. "Last thing you need is to be stuck on the side of the road in this heat."

"I'll be fine," she said. "I've done this drive like twenty times now."

"I know," he said, and he did. "Still, text me when you get there?"

The request was so habitual he hardly thought before saying it.

It hit her differently this time.

Abby's voice again, superimposed over his. He'd freak out if I didn't text at exactly the right time. It felt like surveillance.

Emma's first impulse was to say, of course. She had for weeks, without feeling weird about it. But now the question snagged on her fresh awareness of how easily these small checks could slide into something else.

She heard Hank's distinction echo, safe versus small, and told herself this was safely in the first category. It was one text. It cost her nothing and it soothed his nerves.

Still, resentment flickered, irrational and petty.

"You know, you don't have to keep tabs on me," she said before she could soften it.

His brows drew together, hurt and confusion surfacing. "I'm not… keepin' tabs," he said. "I just, if somethin' happened on that road and no one knew till morning, I'd never forgive myself. A text takes you ten seconds. It lets me know you didn't hit a deer."

"I'm not made of glass, Caleb," she said. The heat and her own tangled feelings sharpened her tone more than she intended. "I drove in

Denver every day. I've lived in cities that would eat this road for breakfast and ask for seconds."

"This road doesn't care what you've driven before," he said, his own voice flattening into that practical cadence. "Accidents don't ask for résumés."

The air between them crackled, two old patterns glancing off each other.

"I'll text you," she said finally, jaw tight. "Happy?"

"That's not," he started, then cut himself off, shoulders stiffening. He took a step back, putting a little physical space between them. "You know what? Forget it. Do what you want. You always do."

The last part came out harsher than he meant, a defensive swipe at the sudden sting of being cast as the overbearing one again.

She flinched.

"Wow," she said. "Okay."

They stared at each other for a beat, dust motes swirling in the sun between them like something torn up and tossed.

Say something, the tiny rational voices in both their heads urged. Explain. Soften.

Neither of them did.

She got in the car, started the engine. He stepped back further, arms folding across his chest like armor. She reversed too fast, gravel spitting, and headed down the lane, fingers white-knuckled on the steering wheel.

Behind her, in the side mirror, she saw him turn away before she rounded the bend.

In his head, the story spun like this: I pushed. I made her feel monitored. I snapped when she pushed back. Same damn pattern. Back off. Give her no reason to say you're controlling.

In hers, the narrative wrote itself with equal conviction: The minute I push back on one small thing, he sulks. He wants to know where I am at all times. Maybe Abby was right, even if he doesn't mean to be that way, that's where he goes under stress.

Neither version was the whole truth, but both felt real in the moment.

Town didn't help.

Pages & Pours was quieter than usual. Libby slid an iced coffee across the counter with a little frown when Emma asked for something "strong enough to fix my personality."

"You look like you fought a fence post and lost," Libby said.

"More like a conversation," Emma said, attempting a smile.

"Worse," Libby said. "Fence posts can't make you doubt your life choices."

Emma settled into the corner table with her notebook, but the words that came were jagged.

On Main, she spotted Abby through the front window of the florist, hands in motion as she arranged something, laugh visible even if Emma couldn't hear it. Their eyes didn't meet. Emma looked away first, throat tight.

Back at the ranch, Caleb threw himself into work. He fixed a leaky trough that had been on his list for weeks, mowed a strip of pasture Hank had been nagging him about, and reorganized the tool rack in the barn to a degree that made even Hank raise an eyebrow.

"You tryin' to outrun somethin'?" Hank asked eventually, leaning in the doorway as Caleb hammered a hook into place with more force than necessary.

"Just catchin' up," Caleb said.

"On every task we've had since '09?" Hank said. "Impressive."

Caleb said nothing. Hank watched him for another minute, then sighed.

"She went into town," he said casually. "In case you were wonderin'."

"Good," Caleb said, focusing on the hook. "She needed a change of scenery."

"You gonna pretend you don't know that road by heart?" Hank asked.

Caleb drove the nail home and set the hammer down with a sharp clank.

"I asked her to text when she got there," he said finally. "Like I always do. She snapped. Told me she wasn't glass. That I don't need to keep tabs."

Hank's eyebrows rose. "And you said…?"

"I said forget it," Caleb muttered. "And somethin' stupid about how she always does what she wants."

Hank made a low noise. "Ah," he said. "The Walker men's patented foot-in-mouth maneuver."

"She hears her daddy when I talk like that," Caleb said, frustration threading through him. "Or Abby's daddy. Or both. And I… I don't want to be that. So maybe I just… shouldn't say anythin'."

"You're not her daddy," Hank said. "And you're not Abby's either. You're you. That's enough trouble for one man."

Caleb huffed a humorless laugh.

"Look," Hank said. "She's carryin' her own fears. You're carryin' yours. You both got ghosts whisperin' in your ears. But you know what ghosts are terrible at?"

"Subtlety?" Caleb guessed.

"Nuance," Hank said. "They talk in absolutes. Always. Never. If you let 'em drive, you're gonna end up in a ditch."

He crossed his arms.

"You care about her," he said. "She cares about you. That's obvious to everyone with eyes and half a brain. Y'all are gonna bump into each other's bruises. That's part of the deal. But withdrawin' ain't the fix. That's just a slow-motion car crash."

Caleb stared at the rearranged tool rack, lines blurring.

"I don't know how to… not get it wrong," he admitted. The words tasted like failure.

"You start by talkin' instead o' guessin'," Hank said. "Tell her why you worry without makin' it a rule. Ask her what feels like care and what feels like control. And for the love of all that is holy, stop tryin' to pre-grieve somethin' that hasn't happened yet."

Caleb's mouth tightened. "Easy for you to say," he muttered.

"Son," Hank said quietly, "I buried a wife who loved me more than I deserved and still regretted that I held back out o' fear when I could've leaned in. You think I'm talkin' out my hat here?"

The quiet in his voice cut through the haze.

Caleb looked up, meeting his eyes.

"I'm not tellin' you you can outwork your way into a guaranteed happy endin'," Hank said. "Life doesn't offer those. I'm tellin' you that pullin' away now to soften a hypothetical blow later just means you both bleed slow instead of all at once. Might as well fully live while you got the chance."

He straightened, bones creaking.

"Anyway," he added, a little lighter, "if you two keep moonin' around like a pair o' half-broke colts, I'm gonna lose my mind. There's a dance at The Spur Friday. You're both goin'. My sanity depends on it."

Caleb blinked. "We're what?" he asked.

"You heard me," Hank said. "I'm callin' it a… morale event. For ranch staff. Mandatory fun. You can ride together or not, but your boots better hit that floor."

With that, he turned and ambled back toward the house, leaving Caleb staring after him.

In his head, the words slotted into a new shape.

Dance. Emma. Friday. Chance to fix this before the crack widened.

Chapter Eighteen
Dance Night: All Seeing Eyes

By Friday, the air over High Meadow Ranch felt like a held breath.

The storm had come and gone. The heat had settled back in, a little less vicious, like it had gotten the worst of its temper out. The cows grazed. The sky stretched on being sky. From the outside, nothing looked different.

Inside the three people moving through those days, Emma, Caleb, Hank, the week had been anything but ordinary.

"Mandatory fun," Hank had declared Wednesday night at dinner, stabbing the air with a fork as if punctuating each syllable. "Friday. The Spur. You two are goin'."

Emma, halfway through a bite of roasted potatoes, had nearly choked. "Excuse me?" she'd asked.

Caleb had frowned over his plate. "Hank,"

"Don't 'Hank' me," Hank had said. "You think I'm gonna watch you two walk around here like ghosts all damn summer? No. We're implementin' a morale program. Dancing, cheap beer, terrible music. Doctor's orders."

"You are not a doctor," Emma had pointed out.

"Of medicine? No," Hank had said. "Of you two? Absolutely."

Now, as Friday evening stretched its golden fingers across the fields, Hank made good on his threat.

Emma stood in front of the cabin's small mirror, the one propped on top of an old dresser, and tried to remember the last time she'd gotten dressed with the specific intent of being seen.

In Denver, evenings out had been rushed affairs, shower, half-damp hair twisted up, makeup applied in the reflection of her phone screen, one of three "going out" outfits pulled from a crowded closet. It had been about blending in with the crowd, looking like she belonged at rooftop bars and loud restaurants.

This felt different.

Her wardrobe here was… practical. Flannels. Faded tees. Two pairs of jeans that could handle fence splinters. For a second, she considered asking Libby to lend her something that screamed "country bar," then laughed at herself.

You're here. You're enough.

She chose her best jeans, the ones that hugged her hips just right and weren't yet battle-scarred by barbed wire. For a top, she pulled out a sleeveless blue blouse she'd crammed into her suitcase at the last minute, just in case. It draped soft over her shoulders, the color making her eyes look greener than usual in the fading light.

She left her hair mostly down, the waves the humidity coaxed out tamed only by a loose braid at one side. A swipe of mascara, a hint of lip color. Enough that she felt like she'd shown up for herself, not so much that she felt like a stranger.

On the bed, her boots waited, the scuffed pair she'd bought within a week of arriving, dark leather creased to the shape of her ankles. She sat, tugged them on, and exhaled.

The mirror's reflection showed a woman she half recognized, city girl softened at the edges, mountain dust in the lines of her boots, something steadier in her eyes.

Her stomach fluttered, excitement and nerves tangling.

It's just a dance, she told herself. We've done this before.

But the truth hummed under that: It wasn't just a dance. Not now, not with the week they'd had. It was a chance to close the distance, or to widen it.

A knock on the door snapped her out of her thoughts.

"Come in!" she called, turning.

The door opened and Hank stuck his head in, hat already on. He took one look at her and let out a low whistle.

"Well, hell," he said. "The Spur ain't ready."

She rolled her eyes, but the compliment steadied her. "You look very dashing yourself," she said. "Like a man prepared to two-step his way into infamy."

"Only infamy I'm courtin' tonight is in my knees," he said, limping in. "You about ready? Your chariot is sulkin' in the drive."

"My,?" she started, then saw the twinkle in his eye.

He stepped aside, and Caleb appeared in the doorway behind him.

He'd cleaned up, but not in the self-conscious way of someone playing dress-up. Just… Caleb, minus a layer of dust and sweat.

Dark jeans, well-worn but without holes. A button-down shirt the color of the evening sky, sleeves rolled to his forearms, collar open. Clean-shaven, which she hadn't realized she'd now come to prefer stubbled. The absence of rough shadow on his jaw made him look a shade younger, like the boy in the mantel photograph peeking through the man.

His gaze ran over her, slow and unhurried, starting at her boots and traveling up. For a fraction of a second, it snagged at her bare shoulders, throat working.

"You look…" he started, then seemed to realize that whatever word he picked would matter. "Good," he finished lamely.

She laughed, the tension snapping. "You're a poet," she said.

Color rose under his tan. "I was gonna say somethin' else," he muttered.

"I'll take 'good,'" she said. "You clean up okay yourself."

Hank clapped his hands once. "All right, my beautiful idiots," he said. "Let's roll before I change my mind and fall asleep in this chair."

He turned and headed down the steps. Caleb lingered half a beat longer, fingers brushing the doorframe. For a moment, it looked like he might say something, a soft I'm glad we're doing this, maybe, or an apology for the week, but the words stayed lodged.

Instead, he stepped aside in an old-fashioned gesture. "Ladies first," he said.

She moved past him, close enough to catch a hint of soap under the familiar warm scent of him. He resisted the urge to touch her back as she passed, fingers curling into his palm.

One thing at a time, he told himself. Start with showing up.

The drive into Cottonwood Ridge felt both familiar and charged, like a song they'd listened to a hundred times with new lyrics layered over the original.

Hank took the wheel of the old Ford, complaining good-naturedly about traffic that consisted of one slow-moving tractor and a family of deer that had the audacity to cross the road whenever and wherever they liked.

Emma sat in the middle of the bench seat, Caleb by the passenger door. The proximity felt deliberate on Hank's part, accidental on theirs. Every bump in the road brought their shoulders into brief contact, sparks of awareness that neither acknowledged out loud.

"So," Hank said, eyeing the rearview mirror as they rolled down Main. "Ground rules. One: we're here to have fun. That means no starin' at each other like you're at a funeral. Two: I am allowed one dance with each of you, no complaints. Three: if either of you sneaks out the back door before nine, I will tell the entire town you cried durin' the line dance."

"That seems excessive," Emma said.

"Desperate times," Hank replied.

Caleb huffed a small laugh, then glanced sideways at Emma.

"You, okay?" he asked under Hank's chatter.

She thought about answering with a glib "Sure." Instead, she opted for something a shade closer to honest.

"I'm… glad we're doing this," she said. "I've been living mostly inside my own head this week. It's getting… crowded."

"Me too," he said. "On both counts."

Their eyes met briefly, small apology and small acceptance passing between them without a formal handshake.

The Spur squatted at the far end of Main, its neon sign flickering in the twilight, an outline of a boot spur in red and blue. On Fridays, it served as the gravitational center of Cottonwood Ridge. Trucks lined the gravel lot. Music pulsed faintly through the walls, bass and fiddle.

"Remember," Hank said as he parked, "this is not Denver. Folks here know you. Or they know me. Or they know your business. Ignore 'em. Most of 'em mean well. The rest are just bored."

"Comforting," Emma said.

"If anyone says anything that makes you feel small, you tell me, and I'll remind 'em of their mortgage balance," Hank said.

"You know everyone's mortgage balance?" she asked.

He winked. "Perks of listenin' in line at the bank for forty years," he said, pushing his door open.

The heat hit as they stepped out, the evening still holding onto the day's warmth. Crickets chirped. Laughter spilled from the open door of The Spur.

Emma smoothed her blouse out of habit, then caught herself. She didn't need armor here beyond her own skin.

She and Caleb reached the door at the same time and stepped aside for each other, a small moment of awkward chivalry that made them both smile.

"You two are hopeless," Hank muttered fondly, squeezing between them and holding the door open. "Get in there."

Inside, The Spur was a blur of motion and light.

Wood floors scuffed by years of boots, strings of white lights zigzagging overhead, a small stage in the corner where a local band tuned guitars and fiddles. The smell of spilled beer, fried food, and perfume that had been applied too liberally in some cases.

The bar along the back wall was already three-deep in patrons. High-top tables ringed the dance floor, chairs occupied by people who were watching, resting, or pretending not to be watching.

Heads turned as the trio stepped in, a subtle shift in the room's attention. Caleb felt it prickling along his skin, the curious glances, the recognition, the quick up-and-down flicks toward Emma.

There goes Caleb Walker. With someone new.

He resisted the urge to stiffen, to reach for her hand like a territorial marker. That instinct, he knew, belonged to an older version of himself.

Hank's presence at his side helped. There was comfort in the older man's easy way of weaving through the crowd, clapping shoulders, deflecting questions with humor.

"Hey, Hank!" someone called. "You bring chaperones tonight?"

"Brought entertainment," Hank shot back. "Y'all been real dull lately."

At the bar, he ordered three drinks, beer for himself and Caleb, a hard cider for Emma. He slid the bottle toward her with a little flourish.

"Hydration," he said.

"Science," she replied, wrapping her fingers around the cool glass.

For a few minutes, they stood near the edge of the dance floor, getting their bearings. The band launched into an up-tempo number. Couples moved in easy patterns, two-steps, spins, a line dance forming in one corner.

Emma felt the music thrumming in her chest, a steady beat that made her foot tap. She loved the anonymity of city clubs, but this, watching people who'd known each other for decades move together like they'd been practicing since adolescence, had its own kind of magic.

"You two gonna just stand there like decorative fence posts?" Hank asked over the noise. "Or are you gonna use those legs for somethin' other than walkin'?"

Caleb, who had been delaying the inevitable partly out of nerves, drained half his beer and set it on a nearby high-top.

"All right, old man," he said. "You made your point."

He turned to Emma, suddenly aware of how many eyes were on them, not in an aggressive way, but with the avid interest of people watching a story unfold.

"Can I…?" he began, holding out his hand.

She looked at it, then at him, then at the dance floor, heart beating a little faster.

"Yes," she said. "You can."

Her palm met his, warm and calloused. He led her into the throng, weaving between couples until they found a pocket of space.

"Okay," he said, voice dropping to that teasing drawl she'd grown fond of. "Full disclosure. I know what I'm doin', but I am outta practice. If I step on your toes, you're allowed one free insult per offense."

"I'll treasure that power," she said.

He placed his right hand at her waist, light but firm. Her left came to rest on his shoulder. Their clasped hands found a natural height between them.

The band shifted into a slower two-step, the rhythm easy enough for beginners, rich enough for those who knew how to play with it.

"Just follow me," Caleb said. "You're good at that."

She arched an eyebrow. "Sometimes," she said. "Other times I go off-script and make my own trouble."

"That's fair," he conceded.

They moved.

At first, Emma's feet felt awkward, her city-bred body trying to remember the basic two-step Libby had taught her in the bookstore aisle one slow afternoon. Step, close, step, tap. Something like that.

Caleb's lead smoothed the rough edges. He guided with subtle shifts of pressure, a slight tug of their joined hands, a gentle steer at her waist. Within a few measures, her body settled into the pattern, muscle memory forming on the fly.

"Hey," she said, surprised delight bubbling up. "I'm not terrible at this."

"Told you," he said. "You just needed the right teacher."

"Careful," she warned. "I might start expectin' you to be right about things."

"That's a slippery slope," he said.

They laughed, the sound mingling with the music and the hum of other voices.

Around them, the town watched with varying degrees of discretion.

Libby leaned on the bar, chin propped in her hand, grinning as she watched them. Nancy from the florist whispered to a friend, smiling in a way that suggested this development would fuel conversation for weeks. A handful of older women nodded approvingly, seeing the arc of a story they'd been hoping to witness.

At the edge of the floor, Hank claimed a chair, feigning a bad back even as his toes tapped.

"There we go," he murmured to himself. "Look at that. Like they were built for it."

In the swirl of bodies, Emma let herself forget, for whole stretches of song, the niggling doubts and ghost stories. There was only the feel of Caleb's hand warm at her waist, the way his eyes crinkled when she stumbled and he caught her, the steady, unflashy competence of a man who knew this floor and was sharing it with her.

On his side, something eased that had been clenched all week.

Letting himself lead her felt perilously close to old patterns he'd been trying to avoid. But this wasn't about safety briefings or check-in texts. This was about connection. The give and take of momentum, the trust of weight and counterweight.

He found, to his faint astonishment, that he could inhabit the role without sliding into control. He could guide without gripping. He could hold without clutching.

She moved with him, not because he insisted, but because she chose to. Every time she matched his step, every time she followed a turn, it felt like its own small yes.

The song ended. Another began. They stayed on the floor.

"You want a break?" he asked, breath warm near her ear.

"Are you tryin' to get rid of me?" she asked, smiling up at him.

"Not even a little," he said, the truth of it escaping before he could filter it.

Her heart skipped. "Then let's keep going," she said.

They did.

At one point, he spun her, carefully, one hand lifting their joined fingers while the other remained steady at her hip. She laughed, the sound bubbling up from somewhere deep, tipsy on nothing more than motion and proximity.

She came back into his space and their chests brushed, the contact sending a jolt through both of them. For a beat, the world narrowed to the inch between their mouths.

He could have kissed her then. Right there on the dance floor, in front of half of Cottonwood Ridge, under the string lights and the long gaze of the town.

He didn't.

Instead, he smiled, soft, almost shy, and took a half-step back, keeping the frame of the dance but not overwhelming it. It was a choice, and she saw it. Something like gratitude flickered through her.

The omniscient eye, if it had been kind enough to narrate, might have labeled that moment as growth: a man choosing restraint not out of fear, but out of respect.

They danced through two songs, then three, then four. Time blurred, measured in fiddle solos and bass lines instead of minutes.

And then the door opened.

Abby walked into The Spur with three friends and the easy gait of someone who'd grown up crossing that threshold.

She wasn't planning on staying long, just a drink, maybe a couple of dances, a catch-up with people she wouldn't see before heading back to Fort Collins. She'd told herself she was fine. That seeing Caleb in this space, with whoever he chose to be with now, would be… normal. She'd had time. She'd moved on.

The rational pep talk got her as far as the second step inside.

The bar looked the same as it always had in its bones. Different lights, maybe. A new table or two. But the layout was unchanged, the dance floor in the center, the bar along the back, the same jukebox in the corner pretending it wasn't obsolete.

Her eyes moved, almost against her will, to the spot near the stage where she and Caleb had danced their first slow song. Someone else stood there now, laughing at a joke she couldn't hear.

She tracked across the room, scanning.

She saw Hank first, of course, sitting on a chair by the wall, watching the floor with an expression that was equal parts amusement and something softer.

Then she saw Caleb.

He was on the dance floor, moving with a woman Abby recognized from a distance and from town talk, the writer from Denver. Emma.

For a second, Abby's brain offered up the Caleb she'd carried around: twenty-two, all edges and tension, coiled like a spring even when he tried to relax. His eyes always somewhere else, scanning, tallying.

The man in front of her was… the same, and not.

He stood a little taller, somehow, not in height but in how he inhabited his frame. His shoulders, while still broad and capable of hunching defensively, were relaxed. His jaw wasn't clenched. His hand on Emma's waist was firm but gentle, his attention fully, unmistakably on her.

He looked… settled in himself in a way she'd never seen. Softer at the edges, not weaker but anchored.

The sight hit her like a physical blow.

This is the man I thought he could be, she realized, dazed. This is the man I wanted. The one I couldn't bear to wait for.

Regret swelled fast, hot, and sharp. Not self-pitying exactly, but deep and bittersweet.

She wasn't delusional; she knew the breakup had been necessary at the time. They'd been young and scared, trying to build a future on shifting sand. She'd needed to get out to breathe. He'd needed to break to learn how to bend.

But watching him now, easy and present and clearly in love with someone else, she saw, for the first time, the full cost of that choice. Not just what she'd escaped, but what she'd lost, the chance to grow into with him.

Her friends were talking, but their voices blurred.

"Hey, you, okay?" one of them, Jenny, asked, following her gaze.

"Yeah," Abby said automatically. Then, more honestly, "I will be."

She forced herself to unclench her hands, to stand there and face this version of her past without flinching.

From her vantage point, she could see the whole tableau like a stage set. Emma's head tipped back in laughter, her hand resting on Caleb's shoulder. The way he leaned down slightly to hear her over the music. The absentminded way his thumb drew small circles at her waist in time with the beat.

He'd always cared. Intensely. That hadn't changed. What had changed was the way he carried that care. Less like armor, more like an offering.

Abby swallowed hard.

I didn't stay long enough to see him become this, she thought. And that's on me.

She'd told herself, with a stubborn defensiveness, that leaving had freed them both. That he'd find someone better suited to his world, someone who actually wanted to live under that big sky, and that she'd find a life that fit.

It looked like at least half that prophecy had come true.

Emma wasn't an accessory to Caleb in this scene. Abby could see that from here. She moved with her own rhythm, her own light. The laughter was hers, the presence hers. They were two people meeting in the middle, not one orbiting the other.

Abby's chest tightened with a complicated mix of sorrow and relief.

He's okay, she realized. Really okay. And he's not mine to worry about anymore.

Her eyes stung. She blinked hard, refusing to let the tears win.

"Want a drink?" Jenny asked quietly, following her line of sight, understanding dawning.

"Yeah," Abby said. "I really do."

They made their way toward the bar, weaving around the dance floor. As they passed the edge, Caleb's gaze, mid-turn, brushed across their trajectory.

His body reacted first, a tiny hitch in his step, a micro-tightening of his grip on Emma's hand. Years of shared history condensed into a heartbeat's worth of recognition.

Abby saw it happen. Saw the flicker of surprise, the flash of old pain, the instinctive pull of muscle memory.

Then she saw something else.

He didn't break frame.

He didn't let go of Emma's hand to step away. He didn't stare. He didn't pull his attention like a spotlight toward the past.

He glanced, acknowledged, and then deliberately, visibly chose to return his full focus to the woman in his arms.

"You, okay?" Emma asked, feeling the pulse of tension through him, the subtle change in the set of his shoulders.

"Yeah," he said. "Just saw someone I used to know."

His tone was steady, the words flat but not heavy. That told her more than if he'd launched into explanations.

She didn't need to be told who. The room carried gossip like smoke. She'd felt a shift too, the slight hush in the air, the way heads had turned.

The weight of eyes pressed on her skin, curious, speculative, assessing. Some came from strangers. Some, she knew without looking, came from Abby.

Every woman everywhere, at some point, had felt that cold prickle of an ex's gaze. It was its own kind of weather.

Emma swallowed, keeping her breathing even.

"What do you want to do?" she asked. It was an honest question, without accusation.

For a heartbeat, the answer that rose in him unfiltered was: Leave. Avoid. Retreat. Old muscle memory, again.

He looked at her.

Her eyes were clear, steady. Not demanding, not fearful. Just open.

He thought of Hank's words. Stop pre-grieving. Stop running. Choose.

"I want to keep dancin' with you," he said. "If you're okay with that."

Relief and something warmer flowed through her.

"I am," she said. "Very okay."

Behind them, at the bar, Abby saw the exchange. She knew him well enough to catch the micro-expressions, the flash of old instinct, the choice to stay.

It hurt, but in a clean way. Like setting a bone that had been broken for a long time.

She took the drink Jenny handed her, kept her eyes mostly on her friends, let the music wash over her.

She'd told Emma, in her clumsy, self-justifying way, to be careful of him. She saw now that she'd been projecting more of her own ghost onto him than she'd realized.

This man, on this floor, with this woman, wasn't the boy she'd left.

He'd done the work she hadn't stuck around to see.

She took a long sip of her drink, turning her body slightly so she faced the bar instead of the floor. It was a small act of grace, and she knew it. A decision not to haunt.

Back on the dance floor, under the strings of white lights, Emma let the moment filter through her.

She was not immune to jealousy. The idea of one's partner's ex in the same room, watching, was the plot of half the romances she'd ever read. But jealousy wasn't the dominant flavor in her mouth right now.

Mostly, she felt exposed. Seen not just by Caleb, but by the town, by the woman who'd come before. The narrative of "Caleb and Emma" was no longer theirs alone. It had joined the communal storybook.

She also felt… chosen. He'd had an easy out, an excuse to step away, to create distance, to use Abby's presence as a shield. He hadn't taken it.

Later, she would unpack this moment, hold it up against Abby's warnings and Hank's assurances, see in it a small but significant piece of evidence about who Caleb was now.

Right now, she just breathed and moved.

The song shifted into something slower. The couples around them drew a little closer, heads dipping, hands tightening.

"Is this, okay?" Caleb asked quietly, giving her the option, always.

"Yes," she said. "Don't overthink it."

"Overthinkin' is kind of my brand," he admitted.

"I'm familiar," she said.

He slid his hand from her waist to the small of her back, palm warm through the thin fabric of her blouse. The contact sent a different kind of awareness skimming up her spine. She rested her cheek lightly against his chest, feeling the steady thump of his heart.

He breathed in, the scent of her shampoo and whatever it was that was just Emma filling his lungs.

For a few minutes, the room receded. There was only the slow sway, the rise and fall of their breaths, the way her body fit against his, not like a possession, but like a home.

"Emma," he said softly, into her hair.

"Yeah?" she murmured.

"I'm… sorry," he said. "For earlier this week. For bein'… weird. For snappin' about the texts. I'm tryin' so hard not to screw this up that I think I'm… sidewindin' into screwin' it up a different way."

She smiled against his shirt. "You have a talent for that," she said gently.

"I know Abby talked to you," he said. The admission cost him something; she heard it.

"She did," Emma said. "I talked to Hank after. He gave me… context."

A breath he hadn't realized he was holding eased out.

"I don't want to be that man again," he said quietly. "The one who makes someone feel caged tryin' to keep 'em safe. Sometimes I get caught between wantin' to know you're okay and not wantin' to make you feel like I'm… trackin' you. I'm gonna get it wrong sometimes. But I'm tryin'. I swear I'm tryin'."

"I know," she said. She pulled back just enough to look up at him. "You're not him, Caleb. You're you. You get to make new patterns. So do I."

He searched her face. "You believe that?" he asked.

"I do," she said. "Even when my ghosts get loud. And I'm… sorry too. For snapping. For hearing someone else's story louder than my own."

He let out a shaky little laugh. "We're a pair, huh?" he said.

"Terrible communicators, A-plus brooders," she said. "But we dance well."

He smiled, something in him loosening. "We do," he said.

He leaned down, slow enough that she could stop him if she wanted to, and brushed his mouth over hers in the barest of kisses, a soft press, more promise than demand.

No one on the dance floor gasped. The band didn't miss a note. The lights didn't flicker. But there was a subtle shift in the air, an unspoken acknowledgment from the watching room.

Okay, then, the town seemed to say. This is a thing.

At the bar, Abby saw the kiss out of the corner of her eye and made herself keep her gaze on Jenny's story about her kids' 4-H chickens. Her fingers tightened around her glass for a second, then relaxed.

Let it be theirs, she thought.

Hank, by the wall, saw it too and exhaled a long, satisfied breath he hadn't realized he was holding.

"About damn time," he muttered.

He tipped his hat forward to hide the suspicious shine in his eyes.

The song ended. Another began. Feet shuffled. Drinks were refreshed. Life, as always, moved on.

Emma and Caleb stayed on the floor for one more dance, then finally let Hank drag Emma away for his promised turn.

"Don't you dare laugh," Hank warned as they stepped into a basic two-step. "I was smooth as butter in '78."

"I'm not laughing," she said, grinning. "I'm just impressed your knees still bend."

"My knees are offended," he said, but he was smiling too.

Across the floor, Abby let a stranger spin her once, twice, then begged off with a polite smile. She didn't have the heart for new stories tonight.

She slipped out onto the porch for air, the hum of the bar muffled behind her. The sky was deep blue, the first stars pricking through.

The man she'd once loved had become someone even better than she'd dared hope. He'd done it with the help of an old ranch hand, some stubborn cattle, and a woman from the city who looked at him like he was both strong and safe.

It hurt. Of course it did.

Inside, under the lights and the careful eyes of Cottonwood Ridge, Emma and Caleb were finding a way to be fully present with each other while the past watched and then, mercifully, began to look elsewhere.

The all-seeing eyes that had once felt like judgment now bore witness instead, to growth, to choice, to a man and a woman deciding, in small, ordinary acts, to write a different story than the ones they'd been handed.

Under the Colorado sky, on a scuffed wooden floor, the distance between them shrank, not because the town approved or Abby regretted, but because they turned toward each other in spite of all of it.

And for the first time in days, both of them went home with more hope than fear humming under their skin.

Chapter Nineteen
Unwanted Visits

For a little while after the dance, everything felt almost simple.

The drive home from The Spur had been quiet in the best way, Hank humming along with the radio, Emma and Caleb sitting side by side on the bench seat, their shoulders touching more often than not. When Hank had dropped them at the cabin and headed down to the main house with a theatrical groan about his "ancient joints," Caleb had lingered on the porch steps.

"You, okay?" he'd asked softly, thumb brushing her knuckles.

"I am," she'd said, meaning it.

The kiss they'd shared there, under the porch light with moths beating against the bulb, had been soft and sure. No audience, no ex, no town, just them. It had tasted like beer and cinnamon and possibility.

He'd gone back down the hill that night with a weight lifted, some old knot in his chest loosening. She'd gone inside, leaned her back against the door, and smiled into the dark like a teenager.

The next couple of days had that same glow, maybe not constant, but there, under the skin of everything.

They fell back into their rhythms, this time with less second-guessing. Emma helped move a small herd to a greener patch, calves bawling and mothers complaining. Caleb fixed a balky gate with her holding the boards, their banter easy. Hank watched them with the satisfied air of a man who'd finally gotten a stubborn engine to turn over.

They stole small moments where they could. A kiss behind the barn while Lucky tried to chew on Emma's shoelace. A quiet cup of coffee in the early morning, both of them still rumpled from sleep, conversation soft and unhurried.

They weren't officially anything by town standards, no labels, no Facebook announcements, but everyone paying attention could see the direction of travel.

Including, unfortunately, the one person whose gaze made that progress feel less than private.

The first "coincidence" came the following Tuesday.

Emma had driven into Cottonwood Ridge mid-morning with a list in her notebook, coffee, printer paper, sunscreen, maybe something new to cook that didn't involve beef or eggs. She'd promised Hank she'd bring back a second cinnamon roll if Libby had any left and had texted Caleb a simple, be back this afternoon.

At Pages & Pours, the bell over the door chimed as she walked in. The shop was busier than usual for a weekday, tourists in hiking shorts perusing the local trail guides, a couple of teenagers hogging the comfy chairs with textbooks and iced lattes.

"Hey, stranger," Libby called from behind the counter. "Your regular?"

"Please," Emma said. "And a cinnamon roll, if Hank hasn't bribed you to hide them."

"He offered to fix my leaky faucet in exchange for exclusive pastry rights," Libby said. "I turned him down on account of not wantin' my pipes held together with baling wire and prayer."

Emma laughed. The familiarity of it, this little pocket of town where her name was known and her coffee preferences remembered, soothed some deep, city-weary part of her.

She'd just settled at a small table with her iced coffee and notebook when the bell chimed again.

"Abby!" Libby exclaimed, cheerful. "Back so soon?"

Emma's shoulders tensed before her brain caught up. She didn't turn right away, taking a measured sip of her drink instead.

Abby's voice floated over, bright and breezy. "Can't stay away from your cinnamon rolls," she said. "And my mom drank all the good coffee at the house."

Emma could feel her own pulse in her throat. She told herself it would be rude to ignore the other woman, that they lived in a small town and this was inevitable. That she was an adult, not a teenager in a cafeteria.

She looked up as Abby approached the counter. Their eyes met briefly. Abby smiled, more tentative this time than at their first meeting.

"Hey, Emma," she said. "Mind if I...?" She gestured toward the empty chair at Emma's table.

Emma suppressed the instinctive urge to say actually, I was just about to leave, even though she wasn't.

"Sure," she said. "Go ahead."

Abby ordered her drink and a pastry, cinnamon roll, of course, and brought them over, setting them down with the careful economy of someone trying not to intrude but doing it anyway.

"Didn't mean to crash your writing time," she said as she sat. "Just figured it was better than awkwardly pretendin' I didn't see you."

"That would be hard in here," Emma said, forcing a small smile. "It's a bit... cozy."

"That's the diplomatic word," Abby said. "I always said if there was a fire, we'd have to evacuate through the espresso machine."

They both chuckled. The humor broke some of the immediate tension, but an undercurrent still hummed.

"So," Abby said, stirring her iced latte. "How's the writing going?"

"It's... going," Emma said. She looked down at her notebook, where the last line she'd written was something half-formed about sky and fences. "Some days better than others."

"Sounds like life," Abby said.

There was a pause, during which Emma could almost see Abby debating whether to wade into deeper waters.

She chose, this time, to stay nearer the shore.

"I saw you guys at The Spur the other night," she said. "You and Caleb. That was... nice to see."

Emma studied her face. There was genuine softness there, shadowed by something like ache, but no obvious malice.

"It was a good night," Emma said. "Hank… insisted."

"That sounds like Hank," Abby said with a huff of fond exasperation. "He used to drag us down there when we were too moody to talk. Said sulkin' wasn't allowed under his roof. 'If you're gonna be miserable, at least do it where there's a jukebox,'" she mimicked.

Emma laughed. "That tracks."

"I was a little worried," Abby admitted, tracing the rim of her cup with one finger. "After our… talk. That I'd scared you off."

You tried, Emma thought, but bit it back.

"It gave me… things to think about," she said instead. "But Hank filled in some blanks. And Caleb and I have been talking."

"Good," Abby said quietly. Relief flitted across her features. "He deserves someone who'll do that. Talk with him, I mean. Not just… around him."

Emma nodded slowly. "We're… figuring it out," she said. "Like everyone, I guess."

"Yeah," Abby said. She took a bite of her pastry, then added, "For what it's worth, you looked… happy. Both of you."

The compliment landed oddly, warm and uncomfortable at the same time. Being blessed by the ex felt like being handed a bouquet with thorns.

"Thank you," Emma said, because it was the polite response.

They chatted a few more minutes about neutral things, the heat, Libby's latest experiment with flavored syrups, how Emma's city friends reacted to photos of the ranch ("Half of them think I'm on a movie set," Emma said. "The other half want to come 'glamping' and ride a horse once for Instagram.").

Abby laughed at that, something like genuine amusement lighting her face.

"I mean, if you ever need a subject matter expert on how not to do ranch life, I'm your girl," she said. "I once tried to feed a cow a muffin because I thought she looked sad."

"You did not," Emma said, incredulous.

"I absolutely did," Abby said. "Hank still brings it up when he wants to remind me why I left."

They both grinned. For a fleeting, disorienting moment, Emma felt a twinge of something almost like liking the woman in front of her. It made everything more complicated.

"I should let you get back to it," Abby said eventually, nodding at Emma's notebook. "Just… wanted to say hi. And… I don't know, make sure there's no weirdness."

Emma thought, there is weirdness. You can't wish it away with a cinnamon roll. But she also thought, she's trying. In her own flawed way.

"We're… okay," Emma said. It was mostly true. "Small towns, right? We're gonna see each other."

"Yeah," Abby said. "We are." She hesitated, then added, "For what it's worth, I'm… glad he's got someone who sees him the way you seem to. He needed that. Needs that."

Emma's chest tightened. There was something in Abby's tone, a letting go, maybe, that tugged at both her empathy and her irritation.

"Thanks," she said again, because she didn't know what else to say.

Abby offered a faint smile, then retreated to another table, pulling out her phone. The air at Emma's little corner of the café felt less dense without her, but the encounter lingered.

By the time Emma drove back up the ranch road, her thoughts were tangled.

She could acknowledge that Abby was trying not to be the villain here. She could feel for the girl who'd been stuck between a controlling father and an over worried fiancé. But she couldn't ignore the fact that every appearance, every well-meaning comment, kept pulling past and present into collision.

She wanted room to build something with Caleb without constantly being reminded of what came before.

Unwanted visits, even when wrapped in friendliness, were still… unwanted.

The next time, Abby didn't wait for town.

Emma was on the cabin porch two days later, laptop balanced on her knees, the midday sun tempered by the shade of the overhang. She'd written a thousand words already, some of them even good. Caleb and Hank were down by the lower pasture, fixing a section of sagging fence.

She heard the crunch of gravel first. Her brain, attuned now to the sounds of ranch life, catalogued it automatically: not the familiar rumble of Caleb's truck, not Hank's old Ford, not the UPS van. Something lighter. A crossover, maybe.

Sure enough, a moment later, a silver SUV appeared at the bottom of the drive and started up the hill.

Emma's stomach sank even before she recognized the shape of it.

Of course, she thought. Of course.

Gus, lounging in the shade by the steps, lifted his head and gave one half-hearted bark before deciding this visitor didn't warrant the full alarm.

The SUV pulled up beside the cabin. Dust plumed. The engine cut. After a beat, the driver's door opened and Abby stepped out, sunglasses perched on her head, hair pulled into a loose braid, a cardboard box in her arms.

"Hey," she called, bright. "I hope I'm not interrupting."

Emma closed her laptop, marking her place more out of instinct than hope that she'd find the thread again easily.

"Hi," she said. "I wasn't expecting… company."

"Yeah, sorry," Abby said, adjusting her grip on the box. "I probably should've called, but I was already halfway out this way. I needed to drop something off for Hank and Caleb, and it seemed silly not to just… swing by."

She smiled like this was the most natural thing in the world.

"What's that?" Emma asked, eyeing the box.

"Old stuff," Abby said. "My mom was cleaning out the attic and found a bunch of things we still had from Mr. Walker, Caleb's dad. Sheet music Hank lent him, some tools, a couple of photo albums. She wanted them back at the ranch instead of deteriorating in our dust."

Guilt pricked through Emma's frustration. It was hard to argue with returning family belongings.

"Do you want me to get Hank?" she asked. "He's down at the house, I think."

"I can drop it on the porch," Abby said. "He's probably knee-deep in something and I don't want to interrupt."

You interrupted me, Emma thought, then immediately felt petty.

"Unless…" Abby hesitated. "Unless you don't mind me stopping in for a few minutes? It's been a while since I've seen the cabin from the inside."

Emma's spine stiffened almost imperceptibly.

This was her space now. Her retreat. Her writing nest. Her place with Caleb. The idea of the ex wandering through, cataloging the changes, imagining herself in this chair, that bed… made something possessive flare.

"I'm in the middle of a scene," she said, gesturing to the laptop. "I should probably stay in the zone while I've got it. But I can help you carry that down to the house, if you'd like."

Abby's face flickered, a mix of disappointment and understanding.

"Sure," she said. "That'd be great. It's not heavy, just awkward."

Emma stood, smoothing her shorts. She took one side of the box, careful not to let it bump against her legs.

They walked down the hill together, the weight an odd, physical expression of the shared history between Abby and this land. The cardboard edges dug into Emma's palms.

"How's the writing today?" Abby asked as they went.

"It was… okay, until ten minutes ago," Emma said before she could soften it. Then, realizing how that sounded, added, "Not your fault. My attention span's about as reliable as a calf on ice."

Abby huffed a small laugh. "I know that feeling," she said. "I can stare at an open email for twenty minutes and then suddenly decide that organizing my sock drawer is a more important task."

"Creative avoidance," Emma said. "I'm fluent."

They fell silent as they approached the main house. Hank's truck was parked out front, cab door open, radio faintly audible, a talk show host ranting about something or other.

Hank himself appeared on the porch as if summoned, wiping his hands on a rag. His eyes took in the scene, the box, the two women carrying it together, and went fractionally narrower.

"Well, look what the cat dragged in," he said. "Or in this case, what tried to sneak up my driveway unannounced."

Abby smiled, but there was a twitch at the corner of her mouth. "Hi, Hank," she said. "My mom found some of your old stuff in our attic. She wanted it back in the rightful kingdom."

She nodded toward the box.

"Only took her, what, fifteen years?" Hank drawled, but he stepped forward to relieve them of the weight. "Thank her for me. I've been wonderin' where some of this ended up."

He set the box on the porch with a gentle thump, then flipped the lid open. Inside, Emma saw a jumble of objects, an old wrench with tape around the handle, a stack of dog-eared choir music, a framed photo of a much younger Hank and Mr. Walker standing in front of a truck Emma recognized only because it was still rusting away near the north line.

"Well, I'll be," Hank murmured, fingers tracing the edge of the frame. His expression softened. "Thought this was gone."

Abby's smile turned real for a moment. "Mom's attic," she said. "Graveyard of lost treasures."

Caleb's footsteps sounded around the side of the house a second later, boots on gravel. He rounded the corner, hat in hand, sweat darkening the collar of his T-shirt. When he saw who stood on the porch, he stopped just short of visibly flinching.

"Abby," he said. His voice was polite, neutral. If Emma hadn't known him, she might not have caught the tightness around his eyes.

"Hey," she said. "Didn't mean to interrupt fence repairs. Just returning some of your dad's stuff. Mom found it and felt guilty we'd had it this long."

He glanced at the box, then at Hank. "Thanks," he said. "Appreciate it."

He stepped up onto the porch, standing near Emma without quite touching her. She felt the nearness anyway, the line of his arm warming the air between them.

"You could've just called," he added, not unkindly. "We'd have come get it."

Abby shrugged, shifting her weight. "I was headed this way," she said. "Figured it'd be nice to see the place again."

There it was, the part that made it feel less like a favor and more like... hovering.

"Place looks good," she added, gaze flicking briefly to Emma before returning to the yard. "Different. But good."

Hank, sensing currents, clapped his hands with forced briskness.

"Well," he said, "now that the ancient artifacts have been returned from exile, how about some lemonade? I've got a pitcher inside."

Emma opened her mouth to demur, she could feel her patience thinning, but Caleb beat her to it.

"I think we better get back to that fence before the cows decide the grass really is greener on the other side," he said. "Storm the other night did a number on that post."

He looked at Hank as if asking for backup.

Hank read the look, nodded. "He's right," he said. "You know how Daisy gets when she senses an escape route. You stick around long enough, Abby, you'll end up wranglin' her again, and nobody wants that."

Abby laughed, cringing theatrically. "Pass," she said. "I still have nightmares about Daisy and that goat."

She stepped back from the porch, hands up. "I wasn't plannin' on stayin'," she said. "Just wanted to drop the box and run. I've got errands."

Her gaze landed on Emma again, searching for something, approval, maybe. A sign that she wasn't overstepping.

"Thanks for helping me carry it," she said. "And for letting me invade your hill for a second."

"You're welcome," Emma said. It was the correct social script. It felt both true and not, she'd helped, but she hadn't exactly enjoyed the invasion.

Abby nodded at all three of them, then turned and headed back to her SUV. As she drove away, dust rising in her wake, the three people left on the porch exhaled in near-unison.

"That woman has worse timing than a busted alarm clock," Hank muttered.

Emma snorted, tension breaking in a puff of laughter.

Caleb glanced sideways at her, catching the strain beneath the humor.

"I swear I didn't know she was comin'," he said, the words rushing out quicker than usual. "If I had, I'd have… I don't know. Put up a roadblock."

"I know," Emma said. And she did, intellectually. Emotionally, the sight of Abby's SUV cresting the hill had still made something cold flick through her.

"She used to just walk in without knockin'," Hank said, peering into the box again. "So, hey, progress. We've upgraded from house goblin to semi-polite ghost."

Emma shot him a grateful look for lightening the mood.

"I don't want you thinkin' I invited this," Caleb said to her, low. "Any of it. The coffee shop, the driveway, whatever else. I'm not… tryin' to have it both ways."

Something in his tone, the mix of guilt and earnestness, softened her frustration.

"I don't," she said. "Think that. I know you're not… orchestrating surprise visits for fun."

He huffed a small, unhappy laugh. "Good," he said. "Because that sounds like my personal nightmare."

"She's… trying, I think," Emma said reluctantly. "In her own weird way. To be… okay with us."

"And in the process, makin' sure y'all end up in each other's laps at the grocery store," Hank muttered. "Hell of a strategy."

Emma couldn't disagree.

They turned back to the box. Hank pulled out the photo again, thumb running over the faces.

"Anyway," he said. "Look at these fools. Your daddy still thought bell-bottoms were gonna make a comeback."

The conversation shifted to Mr. Walker stories, to the time he'd tried to teach Hank to play harmonica and nearly passed out, to how he'd serenaded the cows one summer out of sheer boredom.

The ghost in the driveway faded for the moment. But she didn't leave.

If the first two encounters could charitably be attributed to coincidence and unfinished business, the third made the pattern harder to ignore.

It happened at the grocery store, three days later.

Emma had gone in for flour and sugar, Hank had announced a craving for biscuits, and she'd volunteered to bake. She steered her cart through the narrow aisles of Cottonwood Ridge Market, humming under her breath to the too-loud classic rock playing over the speakers.

She'd just turned onto the baking aisle when another cart emerged from the opposite end. They both instinctively moved the same way, then the other, nearly colliding before stopping.

"Sorry, oh," Emma said.

Abby, once again. Of course.

For a moment, both women just stood there, gripping cart handles, the absurdity of the situation hanging between them.

"Wow," Emma said finally. "Small town really takes its job seriously, huh?"

Abby huffed a laugh that sounded more tired than amused. "I swear I'm not stalking you," she said quickly. "We ran out of sugar. My mom's making jam for the church sale and I'm her pack mule."

"Biscuits," Emma said, lifting the bag of flour in her hand. "For Hank. He's trying to convert me to the church of Carbs."

"He was baptized in butter," Abby said automatically.

They both chuckled. The repetition of this dynamic, Emma in a space, Abby appearing, explanations, light jokes, was starting to feel like its own script.

"How are things?" Abby asked, reaching for a bag of brown sugar.

"Busy," Emma said. "Words are behaving today, which is… nice. And Caleb and Hank are plotting some kind of epic fence upgrade that I'm pretty sure is just an excuse to buy more tools."

"That sounds right," Abby said.

There was a pause.

"Do you mind if I ask you something?" Abby said, fingers fussing with the sugar bag.

Emma braced. "Depends," she said. "Is it going to make Hank scold us if he hears about it?"

"Probably not," Abby said. "It's just… how's he doin'?"

Emma blinked. "Caleb?"

"Yeah," Abby said. Her eyes were earnest. "I can see he's better. Different. But… you're with him. You see the parts the rest of us don't. Is he… okay?"

It was such a simple question, and such a loaded one.

Emma thought of the nights he still jerked awake at sudden sounds, breathing hard. Of the way he sometimes went quiet mid-story when a memory snagged. Of how careful he'd been with her, sometimes to a fault.

"He's… working on things," she said slowly. "He worries. A lot. But he's… not letting the worry drive anymore. Not all the time. And he's… kind. Deep down. Even when he doesn't know what to do with it."

Abby swallowed, nodding. "Yeah," she said softly. "He always was."

Emma hesitated, then added, "He's… happy, I think. At least… more than he's not."

The answer put a sheen in Abby's eyes. She blinked it away, smiling.

"Good," she said. "I'm glad. I… used to picture him stuck. Alone out there with his ghosts. It's nice to know that's not the story."

Emma's frustration faltered. It was hard to resent someone for wanting reassurance that the person they'd once loved hadn't been left in ruins.

Still, the repeated overlapping of their worlds was starting to feel… crowded.

"We're… trying to write a new one," Emma said. It came out more pointed than she'd planned.

Abby heard the edge. She winced slightly, then nodded.

"Yeah," she said. "And I keep walkin' into shots like it's a cameo in my old show. Sorry. I don't… mean to hang around. I'm… leavin' soon, actually. Back to Fort Collins. Work and all."

Relief and guilt twisted together in Emma's gut.

"That's… good," she said carefully. "I mean, for you. For your life. Not because I,"

"I get it," Abby said, holding up a hand. "You're allowed to be glad my SUV won't keep showin' up in your rearview mirror."

They both laughed, the honesty loosening something.

"I am sorry," Abby added. "If my… presence has been intrusive. I didn't realize how much I was still orbiting all this until… you got here. And it threw everything into sharper relief."

Emma nodded slowly. "I appreciate you saying that," she said. "And I know small towns make clean lines hard. But… yeah. I'd like some room to figure us out without constantly feeling like we're being… compared to what was."

Abby exhaled, shoulders slumping a bit, some defensive posture dropping.

"That's fair," she said. "You deserve that. He does too."

She adjusted her grip on her cart.

"I meant what I said at the café," she added. "You look good together. And he looks… like himself. Not like the version of himself that was tryin' to hold everything in place."

Emma studied her, trying to see past the reflexive wariness.

"Thank you," she said again. "For saying that. And for… returning his dad's things. And not… making this harder than it already is."

Abby snorted. "Girl, if I was really makin' it harder, you'd know," she said. "I've mellowed with age."

They shared a wry smile.

"Okay," Abby said. "I'm gonna go rescue my mom from boiling fruit. Take care of him, okay? And yourself. Both matter."

"I will," Emma said.

"And," Abby added, softer, "don't let him scare you off with his worry. Underneath all that, he'd rather lose a limb than hurt you. It just takes him a minute to trust that."

Emma's eyes stung. "I've… noticed," she said.

They parted then, carts squeaking in opposite directions. It was the most direct, the most honest, their exchanges had been, and somehow that made it both easier and harder.

By the time Emma reached the checkout, her head was buzzing.

It's not her fault, she told herself. She's trying.

Also: I don't owe her reassurance.

Also: I don't owe her hostility either.

Being gracious in the grocery store aisle was one thing. Living with the constant possibility of running into her anywhere, the coffee shop, the feed store, the porch, was another.

The visits, each individually defensible, were starting to feel cumulatively like a crowd at the window of Emma's life. Curious, well-meaning, but watching.

Back at the ranch that evening, Emma found Caleb in the barn, stacking bales of hay with an efficient rhythm. Dust motes floated in the shafts of late-afternoon light. Lucky dozed in a patch of shade, flicking his ears at flies.

"Need a hand?" she asked, stepping inside.

He looked up, face relaxing when he saw her. "Always," he said. "Reckon you can still out-lift Hank."

"His knees are a liability," she said, grabbing one end of a bale.

They worked together in companionable silence for a few minutes, the strain a welcome distraction from the mental noise.

"Ran into Abby at the store," she said eventually, because not saying it would make it bigger than it needed to be.

He stilled for a fraction of a second, then kept stacking. "Yeah?" he asked carefully.

"Sugar emergency," Emma said. "For her mom's jam. We had a… decent conversation."

He set down the bale he was holding and turned to lean against the stack, forearms braced.

"Do you want me to... tell her to stop?" he asked. "Coming by. Talkin' to you. Whatever. I can. I will."

Emma considered. Part of her wanted to say yes, unequivocally. To have him draw a clear line, shut the door, make the ranch a no-fly zone for old ghosts.

Another part of her balked at the idea of dictating his relationships, even former ones. She didn't want to become the barometer by which he measured all future interactions.

"I told her I needed... room," she said. "That we needed room. That her being around all the time made it hard to... focus on us."

He watched her, expression open, the familiar worry there but not panicked.

"And?" he asked.

"She apologized," Emma said, still a bit surprised. "Said she didn't realize how much she was orbiting this place until I showed up. Said she's leaving soon. For work."

Relief crossed his face so clearly, she almost laughed.

"Well," he said. "Good for her. And... good for us."

"She also asked how you were," Emma added. "If you were... okay. Happy. It mattered to her."

He looked away for a second, swallowing. "Yeah," he said. "We didn't end on... an easy note. I guess it's natural to wonder if the other person made it through."

"She seems... glad you did," Emma said softly. "Glad we... did."

He huffed a small, shy laugh. "Then I guess that's that," he said. "Chapter closed."

She stepped closer, hay scratching under her boots. "Mostly," she said. "There's still the part where people in town keep bringing her up every time they see me."

"People in town need new hobbies," he said dryly.

"Maybe we should start a rumor that you secretly moved to Alaska," she suggested.

He smiled.

She laughed, the knot in her chest loosening a little.

He sobered, reaching out to tuck a stray strand of hair behind her ear. His fingers lingered at her jaw, tracing the line lightly.

"For the record," he said, voice low, "if she shows up again and you don't feel like bein' gracious, you can send her my way. You don't have to manage everybody else's feelings about me."

"I know," she said. She turned her face into his palm slightly, pressing a kiss to the heel of his hand.

"I also know you'd try to protect both of us if you could," she added. "Even from awkward run-ins in the baking aisle."

"Occupational hazard," he said. "Once you're wired to scan for threats, 'ex with sugar' reads the same as 'oncoming storm.'"

She snorted. "Those are not the same," she said.

"They both cause trouble if you ignore 'em," he countered.

She smiled, the playfulness easing the last of her defensive edge.

The omniscient narrator, if it had chosen to comment, might have noted that while the unwanted visits hadn't stopped entirely, and the biggest tangle was yet to come, the way Emma and Caleb handled them in this stretch said something important about who they were becoming together.

They didn't hide. They didn't weaponize. They talked through the discomfort, even when the conversations were clumsy and layered with history that wasn't theirs.

Abby, for her part, began to step back, sensing that her attempts at closure were veering toward intrusion. She still showed up once more, uninvited, in a way that would catch them both off guard. But the foundation for that final flare-up was laid here, in the slow accumulation of small, unwanted crossings of paths that made everyone a little more raw.

For now, though, as the sun dipped behind the ridge and the barn filled with the smell of hay and the soft sounds of animals settling, Emma and Caleb stood close in the half-light, hands touching, and chose, again, to face the awkward and the old together.

Unwanted visits might come. Past and present might bump shoulders in coffee shops and on gravel driveways. But under the wide Colorado sky, the story they were writing belonged to them.

Chapter Twenty
Cracks Widen

The day started ordinary, which was probably why the fracture line surprised them both.

Morning dawned clear and bright, the sky scrubbed by a night wind that had rattled the windows but brought no rain. Emma woke to the sound of birds in the cottonwoods and the distant low of cattle, the smells of coffee and dust already familiar anchors.

She pulled on jeans and a T-shirt, braided her hair over one shoulder, and walked down the hill toward the ranch house. Gus trotted at her side, tongue lolling.

In the kitchen, Hank was wrestling with the toaster, muttering dark things about modern appliances. Caleb stood at the counter pouring coffee, his hair still damp from a shower, T-shirt stretched across his shoulders.

"Morning," Emma said.

Caleb looked up. The way his face softened when he saw her did things to her chest she tried not to analyze too closely before caffeine.

"Hey," he said. "There she is."

Hank snorted. "About time," he said. "I was gonna send a search party up that hill."

Emma swiped a piece of toast from the plate and kissed Caleb's cheek in one smooth motion. His hand found the small of her back briefly, a quiet hello.

"You two got big plans?" Hank asked, sliding a plate of scrambled eggs toward Emma.

"Parts run," Caleb said. "Windmill pump's makin' a noise I don't like. Gonna see if Gary's got what we need before it quits on us completely."

"And I," Emma said grandly, "have a hot date with the laundromat and the library's Wi-Fi."

Caleb frowned slightly. "You could've said somethin'," he said. "We could've timed it so you didn't have to sit around waiting for machines by yourself."

"I'll have my riveting pile of dirty clothes for company," she said. "It's fine. We don't have to coordinate every errand."

He opened his mouth, then closed it, catching the hint of teasing challenge in her tone. "All right," he said. "Text me if the dryer eats your quarters."

"You'll come wrestle it into submission?" she asked.

"I'll send Hank," he said. "He's meaner."

"Damn right," Hank said around his coffee.

They ate, the conversation easy, dumb jokes about small-town bulletin boards, a debate about whether the rooster behind the neighbor's place was actively malevolent or just obnoxious. It was the kind of morning that made Emma feel like this life was not just temporary, a season, but something she could actually inhabit.

She and Caleb left within ten minutes of each other, separate trucks kicking up dust on the ranch road. She watched his taillights down the hill, a flicker of satisfaction in the knowledge that even headed to different places, they were moving through the same world.

If the omniscient eye had whispered that by sundown those taillights would feel much farther away, she might not have believed it.

Caleb's errands went as such errands always did: longer and more complicated than he planned.

Gary didn't have the exact pump he needed but thought he could adapt a similar one with a different fitting. That led to twenty minutes in the back corner of the feed store, measuring and debating pipe diameters. Then someone stopped Caleb to ask about a cow for sale. Then another someone wanted to know if he could spare a few bales next week.

By the time he emerged into the parking lot, it was past noon and his patience with small talk was wearing thin.

He loaded the parts into the bed of his truck and was just slamming the tailgate when he heard his name.

"Caleb?"

He turned, squinting against the midday glare.

Abby stood by a dusty blue sedan a couple of spaces over, keys in hand. Her hair was pulled up, sunglasses perched on top of her head, expression uncertain.

"Hey," he said. His stomach did a small, involuntary twist, not of longing but of tired anticipation.

He'd been half-expecting this. Hank had mentioned she was leaving town soon. It made sense she'd want to… say something.

"Got a minute?" she asked, nodding toward the space between their vehicles, away from the main flow of people in and out of the store.

He hesitated. The part of him that wanted clean lines whispered, just say no. You owe her nothing. Another part, the one that hated loose ends, said, five minutes to shut the door is better than leaving it cracked.

"Yeah," he said. "'As long as it really is a minute. Got a pump to install before the cows decide to stage a coup."

She smiled faintly. "I'll be quick," she promised.

They stepped into the shadow between the trucks, the heat radiating up from the asphalt. From the street, it would have looked like any two people catching up, shoulders angled toward each other, heads bent slightly to hear past the noise. From the wrong angle, from a distance, it could have looked like something more intimate.

From the alley that ran behind the row of stores, it looked exactly like that.

Emma had finished at the laundromat faster than expected, the weekday lull meant no wait for machines. She'd swung by the library, sent a couple of emails, then decided to walk to the market for baking powder instead of moving the truck for a distance she could cover in four minutes.

Cutting behind the feed store was habit now, a way to avoid Main's slow parade of trucks and gossip.

She wasn't looking for them. She wasn't looking for anything.

She stepped into the mouth of the alley, adjusting her canvas bag on her shoulder, and there they were.

Caleb by his truck, Abby by hers. The gap between vehicles framed them like a picture.

They stood close enough that she could see the way Abby's hand rested on the open door of her sedan, fingers white where they gripped the metal. Caleb's posture was familiar, weight balanced, shoulders stiff but not aggressive, head tilted down to listen.

Emma couldn't hear words yet over the hum of traffic and the barks from the hardware store dog. But she saw Abby reach out, fingers brushing his forearm in a reflexive gesture.

He didn't step back.

The sight hit Emma in the gut.

She stopped, the bag strap biting into her shoulder.

She knew, in a rational corner of her mind, that people touched when they talked. That a hand on an arm meant nothing on its own. That she'd asked for him to have room to close that chapter without her crawling all over it.

The rational corner got drowned out by something older and sharper.

You always know how to make a girl feel trapped, Caleb.

Abby's voice, from the coffee shop. Her own old fear, from a childhood watching parents' fights turn into cold wars. The sinking sensation of being the last to know when a story had changed.

She could have turned around. Walked back to the truck, taken the long way, confronted him later with the memory cooler.

Instead, she stepped deeper into the alley, drawn in spite of herself.

Voices became audible in snatches.

"…just wanted to say I'm sorry," Abby was saying. "For dumping all my ghosts on Emma. On you. I thought I was warnin' her, but I was mostly just… talkin' to my younger self."

Caleb's jaw worked. "I appreciate you sayin' that," he said. "She and I… we're doin' our best as it is. It doesn't help when folks add commentary from the cheap seats."

Abby winced. "Fair," she said. "I deserved that."

"You didn't deserve to live under your dad's thumb," he said, voice softening. "You didn't deserve to feel like love meant givin' up air. I get that. I just… I'm not that man anymore. If I ever fully was."

His hand moved as he gestured; from Emma's angle, it looked like an almost-touch toward Abby's shoulder that stopped short.

"I know," Abby said. "Seeing you with her… I can tell. You seem… calmer. Less like you're tryin' to hold the sky up by yourself."

He huffed a humorless laugh. "That's mostly Hank," he said. "And her. Pepperin' me till I talk instead o' brood."

Abby smiled briefly, then sobered. "Look," she said. "I'm leavin' tomorrow. For real this time. No more surprise sugar runs, no more drive-bys. You won't have to keep bracin' for my SUV on the hill."

Relief flickered across his face, too quick for him to hide.

"Okay," he said. "Good. For you, I mean. For your life."

"And for you," she said, not unkindly. "And for Emma."

He nodded.

She hesitated, fingers tightening on the door frame.

"I just… needed to tell you," she went on, voice wobbling slightly, "that I did love you. Back then. It wasn't fake. I was just… so tired of feelin' like my life was a series of cages. Home, church, here. I thought if I left you, I'd be free of all of it. I didn't know how to… keep you and lose the rest."

Caleb's throat bobbed. He looked like he'd rather be anywhere else and also knew he owed this moment the dignity of staying.

"I know you loved me," he said quietly. "I never doubted that. I doubted… a lot of other things. But not that."

"I made you the villain in my head to make leavin' easier," she admitted. "That wasn't fair. You were messin' up, yeah. But you were also… survivin' stuff I didn't even begin to understand. I'm sorry I turned you into a cautionary tale instead of just… a boy who was hurtin'."

Silence stretched. The sounds of town filled it, an air brake hiss, a dog bark, someone laughing down the block.

"Thank you," he said finally. "For sayin' that. And… I'm sorry too. For all the ways I made it harder. If I could go back and tell that version of me to get his shit together and a therapist sooner, I would."

Abby huffed a watery laugh. She wiped under one eye with her thumb.

"I just want you to be happy," she said. "Really happy. Not the 'I'll settle for this because it's safe' kind."

He thought of Emma on the porch, laughing at Lucky's attempts to climb into the water trough. Of her in the barn, face smudged with dust, eyes bright. Of her words the other night at The Spur: You get to make new patterns. So do I.

"I am," he said. "Or… I'm gettin' there. With her."

"Good," Abby said. She swallowed hard. "Then do me a favor?"

"What's that?" he asked.

"When you start gettin' in your head, when your worry turns into… that thing where you start tryin' to run scenarios instead of just sit with her… listen to her before you listen to your ghosts. Okay?"

He nodded. "I'll try," he said honestly.

Abby's grip on the door tightened, knuckles whitening.

"You always knew how to make a girl feel trapped, Caleb," she said softly, a sad smile twisting her mouth. "Even when you were tryin' your best to set her free. I hope you learned how to tell the difference now."

Emma froze in the shadow of the alley, the words knifing into her like they'd been aimed at her.

You always knew how to make a girl feel trapped.

Not past tense, not then, but now. It didn't matter that some part of her knew Abby was talking about an old version of him. The present tense stuck.

Caleb flinched, the line clearly landing. "I'm learnin'," he said, and there was enough pain in his voice that Emma had to grip the rough brick wall beside her.

Abby stepped back, opening her car door.

"I should go," she said. "Before I say somethin' even more dramatic and we both end up in tears in front of Gary's feed store."

He huffed a small laugh, but his eyes were tight.

"Take care of yourself, Abby," he said.

"You too," she replied. She slid into the driver's seat, pulled the door shut, and started the engine.

Emma stepped back deeper into the alley shadows as the sedan pulled out of the lot and onto Main. She didn't want to be seen. Not like this, with her heart pounding and her mind replaying a single sentence on loop.

Caleb stood for a moment by his truck, head tipped back, eyes closed. From where she stood, it looked like he was savoring some private ache.

In his chest, guilt and relief wrestled. The chapter was closing. He'd said the things that needed saying, heard the apologies he'd secretly hoped for. It should have felt clean.

Instead, Abby's parting shot echoed.

You always knew how to make a girl feel trapped.

He knew she hadn't meant it as a curse so much as a description of who he'd been. Still, hearing it aloud, now, with Emma's face so present in his mind, stung.

I'm learnin', he'd said. I hope that's true.

He scrubbed a hand over his face, exhaled hard, and climbed into the truck. He didn't see the woman standing in the alley, fingers dug into the crumbling mortar.

Emma waited until he'd driven away before stepping out. The street felt too bright, too open.

She walked to her own truck on shaky legs, dropped the bag of groceries on the passenger seat, and sat there with her hands on the wheel, heart thudding.

Logic tried to assert itself.

He didn't see you. He wasn't hiding anything on purpose. You knew he needed to tie off loose ends. You've talked about this. You asked for this.

Emotion overrode it.

He didn't tell me he was meeting her. He let her touch him. He let her say that and he didn't argue.

A part of her knew she was being unfair, plucking one sentence out of a conversation she'd only heard half of, filling in gaps with her worst fears. Another part, the one that had spent years telling herself she'd never be the woman who ignored warning signs, took the scraps and spun them into a story.

They always say that, she thought bitterly. I'm different now. I've learned. Until they slide right back into old grooves.

She drove back to the ranch without turning on the radio. The silence in the cab felt heavy.

The afternoon passed like a bad rehearsal of normal.

Emma chopped vegetables in the cabin kitchen, knife hitting the board with more force than strictly necessary. She told herself she was just cooking ahead, being practical, when she put together a stew big enough to feed six.

Down at the house, Caleb and Hank wrestled the pump into place, metal clanking, occasional curses floating up the hill. From the cabin porch, she could see them sometimes, two figures bent over the windmill base, working in tandem.

She watched them for a minute, then turned away.

Caleb noticed her absence in small ways. No text about town gossip. No appearance in the pasture that afternoon with a water bottle and a sarcastic remark about him turning into a windmill whisperer.

By the time he washed up and came up the hill, the sun was low and his nerves were frayed.

He knocked lightly on the cabin door despite the fact that it had been open to him for weeks.

"Yeah," Emma called. Her voice sounded off, too bright.

He stepped inside.

The table was set for two. The stew simmered on the stove, filling the space with the smell of tomatoes and herbs. Emma stood by the counter, wiping her hands on a dish towel with a focus that looked a lot like avoidance.

"Something smells good," he said, aiming for normal.

"Thanks," she said. "Stew. Felt like a stew day."

He stepped closer, reaching instinctively to kiss her. She turned her head at the last second so his mouth grazed her cheek instead. It was subtle, but he felt it like a missed step on a dark stair.

"You, okay?" he asked, brows drawing together.

"I'm fine," she said. The word was too crisp.

"Emma," he said quietly.

She set the towel down carefully, lining up its edges on the counter. When she turned, her expression was composed, eyes a little too bright.

"How was town?" she asked, as if the question were casual.

He exhaled slowly. "Busy," he said. "Gary tried to sell me half his inventory. Ran into some folks. Got the pump. You?"

"Laundromat, library, market," she said. "The glamorous life."

He watched her for a beat. Something in the way she held herself, straight-backed, hands folded loosely, reminded him of people he'd seen bracing for bad news.

"You sure you're okay?" he asked again. "You seem… far away."

Her jaw clenched. "Do I?" she asked. "Hard to say. Maybe I'm just… adjusting."

"To what?" he asked, genuinely confused.

"To life in a small town," she said. "Where everyone knows everyone else's business. Or thinks they do."

He frowned. "Did somebody bother you?" he asked. "At the laundromat? Library? Who said somethin'?"

"That's the thing," she said. "They didn't have to. I saw it myself."

Saw. The word pinged his memory like a dropped wrench.

He thought of the parking lot. The alley. The space that had felt private only because they'd chosen a quieter corner. Realization crawled up his spine, chilled and slow.

"You saw me," he said. It wasn't a question.

"Between the feed store and the market," she said. "Hard to miss."

He closed his eyes for half a second, swore under his breath.

"Why didn't you come over?" he asked. "I would've,"

"What?" she cut in. "Introduced me? Juggled us like uncomfortable flaming torches? No, thanks."

Her voice wasn't loud, but the edge on it was sharp.

He took a breath, forcing himself to stay steady.

"It wasn't… like that," he said. "She asked for five minutes. To say goodbye. To apologize. I didn't plan it. I wasn't… keepin' it from you."

"But you didn't tell me either," she said. "You came in here, you said 'busy,' like it was just another trip. Like I hadn't watched you stand between your truck and hers talkin' like," Her voice snagged. She pressed her lips together.

"Like what?" he asked, bristling despite himself. "Like two people who used to be engaged finally havin' the hard conversation they should've had years ago? That's exactly what it was."

"From where I was standing," she said, "it looked like you listening to her pour her heart out without once thinking, 'Hey, maybe the woman I say I'm happy with might want to know about this.'"

"That's not fair," he said. Heat crept into his voice. "You're judgin' a whole conversation off the one angle you saw out of the corner o' your eye."

Her laugh was short and humorless. "Funny thing about angles," she said. "Sometimes they show you exactly what you need to see."

He stared at her. "What did you hear?" he asked. "Besides your own ghosts."

She flinched, the accuracy of that last word landing.

"I heard her," she said. "I heard her say, 'You always know how to make a girl feel trapped, Caleb.' And I heard you... not disagree."

He rocked back as if she'd hit him.

"I told her I was learnin'," he said, voice rough. "I told her I wasn't that man anymore. But she wasn't wrong about who I was back then. I'm not gonna gaslight her into thinkin' she imagined that. I did screw up. I did make her feel caged, even when I thought I was protectin' her. I own that."

"And what about now?" Emma demanded. "What about me?"

He blinked. "What about you?" he asked.

"Am I just... your redemption arc?" she asked, the words tumbling out faster now. "The one you get right after you learned from your mistakes? Because standing there, watching you with her, it didn't feel like a closed chapter. It felt like I was sittin' in the waiting room while you went to revisit the old one."

"That's not what was happenin'," he said, frustration rising to match hers. "I was tellin' her goodbye. I was setting boundaries, for you. For us."

"Then why didn't you tell me?" she shot back. "If it was about 'us,' why was I the last to know? Again?"

He opened his mouth, closed it. He thought of how the day had unfolded, how he'd told himself he'd mention it over dinner, how he'd underestimated the landmines the encounter had dropped.

"I was gonna," he said. "I just… wanted to do it when it wasn't five minutes before you had to stir stew or feed Hank or whatever. I didn't want to walk in here and dump all that on you the second I saw your face."

"That's the problem," she said. "You decide what I can handle. You decide which pieces of your life I get to see, like you're curatin' an exhibit. 'Here's the Caleb who jokes and dances and kisses you on the porch. Don't look behind that door, that's where the messy history lives.'"

"That is not what I'm doin'," he said. His own hurt flared now. "I'm tryin' not to force you to carry weight that isn't yours. I thought by handlin' it, by lettin' her say her piece and move on, I was… protectin' you."

"There it is," she said quietly. "Protecting me. Whether I ask for it or not."

The words, in another context, could have been tender. Here, they were an accusation.

He felt it like a slap.

"So what?" he asked, temper finally slipping a notch. "You'd rather I just ignored her? Left a box of my dad's things sittin' in her attic? Pretended she doesn't exist? That's not protectin' you, Emma, that's bein' a damn coward."

"I'd rather you let me in on it," she said, matching his intensity. "Let me be in the room. Or at least know what room you were in. Instead, I have to literally stumble into the alley to find out my boyfriend is havin' a heart-to-heart with his ex about how he traps women."

"Exaggerate much?" he snapped. "It was five minutes. In a parking lot. You act like I was sneakin' off to some secret rendezvous. Hank knew. Half the town probably guessed. You're the only person I was scared to tell, because I knew you'd hear every word through the filter of what she already told you."

"And maybe I wouldn't if you trusted me enough to show me the whole picture instead of lettin' my imagination fill in the gaps," she shot back.

They stared at each other, both breathing harder now, both aware on some level that this was spiraling and neither sure how to brake.

"Do you trust me?" he asked suddenly.

The question landed between them like a dropped tool.

"I'm here, aren't I?" she said. "I left my job, my city, my entire life to see if this could work. I've been hauling hay and editing chapters on a porch with spotty Wi-Fi. I've been trying to believe you when you say you're different, that we're different. That has to count for something."

"That ain't an answer," he said. "Do you trust me? Me. Not the version of me Abby knew. Not the one you're scared I might turn into. Me, right now."

Her eyes burned. She opened her mouth, closed it. The truth, slippery and painful, would not be forced into a neat yes or no.

"I'm… trying," she said finally. "Most days, yes. Some days… I hear things. I see things. I wonder if I'm bein' naïve. If I'm just the latest girl who's gonna realize too late that what feels like love is actually someone buildin' a cage with really pretty bars."

His face shuttered.

"I have never," he said, voice low and shaking, "wanted to cage you. I have bent myself into knots tryin' not to. You tell me when I'm too much, I back off. You say you need to go hike alone, I swallow my instinct and let you. You want to quit your job, I push you to make sure you're doin' it for you, not for me. What else do you want, Emma? You want me to pretend I don't worry at all? You want me to turn off the part of my brain that counts heads every time we're somewhere crowded?"

"I want you to stop makin' decisions about what's 'too much' without me," she said, tears starting to prick. "I want you to stop shutttin' me out of the parts of your life that scare you, then actin' surprised when those parts scare me too."

"And I want you to stop lookin' at me like you're waitin' for me to turn into your worst-case scenario," he shot back. "Like every mistake I made at twenty-two is a shadow sittin' at our table. I am not him anymore. I'm never gonna be him again. I'm not Abby's father, I'm not your father, I'm not every man who ever used 'protectin' you' as an excuse to control someone. I'm just… me. If that's not enough, tell me now so we don't drag this out."

Silence slammed into the room.

Emma felt like he'd reached into her chest and twisted.

"You think you're not enough?" she whispered. "Is that really what you heard just now?"

"I heard that you don't know if you trust me," he said. "I heard that you're waitin' for the other boot to drop. I heard that when my ex, who I haven't seen in years, says a thing about who I used to be, her words carry more weight in your head than months of what I've shown you."

She pressed her fingers to her eyes, fighting tears.

"Hank told me not to let other people write our story," she said hoarsely. "He said the same thing you just did, that what we have is ours, not the town's, not Abby's. I'm trying, Caleb. I am. But this is… a lot. All at once. A whole life I'm learnin' to live, and all the history that comes with it."

"I know it's a lot," he said. The anger in his voice softened, leaving something raw. "It's a lot for me too. I don't have a map for this. I'm just makin' it up as I go and hopin' I don't screw it up so bad you walk."

She swallowed. The threat in those words wasn't directed at her; it was aimed inward, a fear he'd been holding since the day she arrived.

"I don't want to walk," she said. "I just… don't want to wake up ten years from now and realize I ignored every warning sign because I was in love with some version of you I wanted to believe in."

"I'm right here," he said, gesturing helplessly at himself. "I'm not some version. I'm the man standin' in your kitchen, eatin' stew and listenin' to you and gettin' it wrong half the time but tryin' like hell to get it right the rest. I can't change what she went through with me. I can't change what you watched your folks go through. I can only… show up. Every damn day. If that's not enough, like I said, I need to know."

Her breath hitched.

"Don't make this about 'enough'," she said. "This isn't a test you pass or fail. This is… two people with a lot of baggage tryin' to pack it into the same truck. Sometimes the seams split."

They stared at each other, both blinking too fast.

Hank's voice floated in Emma's memory, you can't protect yourself from heartbreak and still claim you want love, but it sounded distant, like it was coming from the bottom of a well.

"I need some air," Caleb said abruptly. His chest felt too tight. The cabin, once his favorite place to breathe, now felt like it was closing in.

Panic flashed across Emma's face. "So that's it?" she asked. "You're just gonna walk out in the middle of this?"

"I'm gonna walk," he said slowly, working to keep his voice level, "so I don't say somethin' either of us can't take back. I'm not leavin' you. I'm takin' a lap. There's a difference."

She bit down on the inside of her cheek, not trusting herself to speak. Part of her wanted to block the door, to force them to keep talking until it was done. Another part recognized the edge in his voice and, through her own hurt, saw the wisdom in stepping back.

"Fine," she whispered.

He looked like he wanted to touch her, shoulder, cheek, anything. He didn't. His hands stayed at his sides.

"We're not done," he said quietly. "I won't… I'm not lettin' this sit forever. I just,"

"Go," she said, cutting him off, because hearing him try to explain felt like rubbing salt in a raw spot.

He nodded once, jaw tight, and stepped outside.

The door clicked shut behind him, soft but final.

Emma stood in the middle of the cabin kitchen, stew bubbling quietly on the stove as if nothing had happened, her breath loud in the small space.

The fight replayed in flickers, his face when she quoted Abby, her own voice sharper than she'd intended, the moment she hadn't been able to say an unqualified yes to his question about trust.

She hated that. Hated that she'd hesitated. Hated that the honest answer was messier than either of them wanted.

A tear slipped down her cheek. She swiped it away with the heel of her hand, more angry than sad.

"Damn it," she muttered, to no one in particular.

Outside, gravel crunched under Caleb's boots as he walked past the porch and down the hill, hands shoved into his pockets. He didn't head for the truck, that would look too much like leaving. Instead, he cut toward the back acreage, up the faint trail that led to the ridge where the stars felt close enough to touch.

Gus trotted after him for a few steps, then stopped, sensing the tension and choosing to retreat to Hank, who at least might drop crumbs.

Hank, for his part, watched Caleb's silhouette pass the barn from the porch of the main house. He didn't call out. Some lessons, he knew, couldn't be interrupted, only softened later.

He looked up toward the cabin, where the light glowed warm against the gathering dark.

"Lord help 'em," he murmured. "They're in it now."

Up in the cabin, Emma turned the stove down to low and sank into one of the chairs at the table. The steam from the stew fogged the air, making her eyes sting more.

She picked up her notebook, stared at the blank page, and wrote one sentence.

He walked away because it was the only way he knew how not to break something.

She stared at it, then added another line underneath, hand shaking.

She let him because she was afraid if she held on too tight, she'd prove everyone right.

The omniscient eye couldn't fix it for them. It could only see the symmetry: two people, both haunted by being too much and not enough, backing away to avoid hurting each other and in the process hurting anyway.

They both went to bed that night alone, Emma in the cabin, Caleb in his old room at the house, each staring at a dark ceiling, replaying every word, every expression, wondering if this was the crack that would widen into a break.

Neither wanted that. Neither believed they were beyond repair.

But for the first time since Emma had driven up that gravel road, they fell asleep not with a sense of quiet, stubborn hope but with a knot of fear lodged under their ribs.

In the space between their breaths, the question neither had the courage to say out loud hung, heavy and unanswered.

What if love, even the kind you chose with eyes open, wasn't enough to outshout the ghosts?

Chapter Twenty-One
Under the Stars

The morning after the fight came in quiet and pale, like it wasn't sure it wanted to commit to a full day.

Fog clung to the lowest parts of the pasture. The hills were smudged at the edges, shapes waiting to be sharpened. Birds sang anyway, indifferent to human drama.

In the cabin on the hill, Emma woke with a sore throat and the cottonmouth feeling of having slept hard without really resting. Her eyes were gritty. At some point in the night, she'd rolled onto the far side of the bed as if making distance there could solve the distance everywhere else.

She lay still for a long minute, staring at the ceiling beams, listening.

No truck on the gravel outside. No low murmur of Hank's radio drifting up from the house. Just the far-off clank of someone, Caleb, probably, already at work.

Always at work, she thought. Even after he'd walked out of her kitchen with his jaw tight and his shoulders stiff.

She squeezed her eyes shut as last night replayed in jerked, ugly fragments.

You always know how to make a girl feel trapped, Caleb.

Do you trust me?

I'm… trying.

That hesitation was the part that haunted her the most. That and the look on his face when she hadn't been able to give him the neat, reassuring answer they both wanted.

She forced herself to get up anyway. Skipping breakfast and hiding under the covers wasn't going to fix anything. She pulled on jeans and a worn T-shirt, twisted her hair into a messy knot, and walked down the hill with a knot already tight under her sternum.

The main house kitchen smelled like bacon and coffee. Hank sat at the table with the paper unfolded in front of him, glasses low on his nose. He looked up as she stepped in.

"Hey, kid," he said. "You look like you lost a fight with a tumbleweed."

"Feel worse," she said, trying for light and not quite making it.

He took her in, puffy eyes, forced half smile, and something flickered behind his own.

"Coffee's hot," he said, as if nothing were wrong. "Bacon's crisp. Caleb's out checkin' the south fence. Wind blew a branch into it last night near the creek. He'll be back through in a bit."

"Got it," she said, pouring coffee with more focus than the task required.

She could feel Hank's eyes on her as she moved around the kitchen. She braced for questions, for commentary, for the gentle nudging he'd done a dozen times before.

They didn't come.

Instead, he folded the paper, stood with only a soft creak of chair legs, and said, "I'm gonna go scare the eggs outta the hens. You eat somethin'. We'll talk later."

The reprieve felt both kind and suspicious.

She nodded, unable to meet his eyes for long. "Thanks," she murmured.

He hesitated in the doorway, looking back once. "You're both still here," he said simply. "That's somethin'."

Then he left her with the coffee, the bacon, and the hollow ache of unresolved words.

Down by the south fence, Caleb tamped dirt around a freshly replaced post with more force than necessary.

Sweat ran down his back despite the morning chill. His hands ached. Every muscle felt keyed up, as if his body was trying to outwork something his mind wouldn't stop turning over.

God, the look on her face.

She'd been hurt. That part made sense. He could own his half of that, he should have told her about the parking lot, should have invited her into that mess instead of trying to manage it alone. He'd been so busy trying not to scare her off with his ghosts that he'd ended up letting those same ghosts talk to her through somebody else's mouth.

It was the other part, the hesitation when he'd asked if she trusted him, that had him feeling like the ground under his boots was less solid than he'd believed.

"I'm trying," she'd said. Which was honest. Which he respected. Which still, somehow, felt like being told the rope he was hanging onto might snap at any moment.

He jammed the tamping bar into the dirt again. The post thudded, a dull sound in the quiet.

"You plan on beatin' that thing to China?" Hank's voice called.

Caleb glanced up, startled. He hadn't heard the truck pull up.

Hank leaned on the fence a few yards away, hat tipped back, thermos in hand. He'd driven the old Ford along the property line, parking it on the small track that passed for a road out here.

"Thought I'd save us the fuel and dig some irrigation to the Pacific," Caleb said. His attempt at humor fell flat even to his own ears.

Hank grunted. "Well, if you're takin' requests, I wouldn't mind a canal to a donut shop," he said. "But right now, you and that post are havin' a lovers' quarrel and I figured I should check nobody's losin' an eye."

Caleb set the tamping bar aside, wiped his forearm across his forehead. "Fence needed fixin'," he said.

"Fence needed fixin' yesterday," Hank said. "Today you're just usin' it as a prop for your sulk."

"I'm not sulkin'," Caleb said automatically.

Hank took a slow sip from his thermos, eyeing him over the rim. "That right," he said. "Then what do you call stompin' out here at dawn and takin' a post's head off because your feelings are bruised?"

Caleb tensed. "I don't,"

"Son," Hank said, voice gentling but not backing down, "I've known you since you were scarin' the chickens in diapers. You ain't gonna bluff me. Something went sideways last night. Emma came into my kitchen lookin' like the dog told her he was leavin' for college. You trudge out here like the wrath of God. I can do the math."

Caleb's jaw flexed. He leaned both hands on the fence, staring out at the grazing cattle.

"We had a fight," he said finally. The words tasted strange. He and Emma hadn't really fought before, snapped, disagreed, sure. Nothing like last night's jagged edges.

"Healthy couples do that," Hank said. "Unhealthy ones too. The trick is what you do after."

Caleb's fingers curled around the top rail.

"She saw me with Abby," he said. "In town. Thought it was somethin' it wasn't. And… I didn't tell her right away. That's on me."

Hank nodded slowly. "And the rest?" he prompted.

Caleb swallowed. "She heard some of what Abby said. 'You always knew how to make a girl feel trapped.' That line. And I… didn't argue with it. Not about back then."

Hank let out a low whistle. "Ouch," he said. "That's a loaded bullet."

"It was true," Caleb said, staring at the horizon. "I did. I meant well and I still did. I don't get to rewrite that for her."

"But you also told Emma you're not that man anymore," Hank guessed.

"I tried," Caleb said. "We just… kept hittin' the same bruise from different sides. She's scared of bein' caged. I'm scared of losin' her because I'm scared of losin' her." He let out a harsh breath. "Fear is runnin' this whole damn thing and I can't seem to get my hands around it."

"Closest you've come to diagnosin' yourself without a copay," Hank said dryly.

Caleb's mouth twitched despite everything. "That your professional opinion?" he asked.

"From the University of Hard Knocks, yeah," Hank said. He walked closer, boots crunching on the dry ground, and rested his elbows on the fence next to Caleb.

"You're not wrong," Hank went on. "Fear is drivin' the truck right now. Has been for a while. For both of you. Doesn't make either of you bad people. Just makes you bad drivers."

Caleb snorted. "You got a folksy metaphor for everything, don't you," he said.

"Occupational hazard," Hank said. He glanced sideways. "You know, you two remind me of me and Marcie."

Caleb blinked. "You and…?" He caught himself. "You never told me that many stories about her. Just the good ones."

"That was by design," Hank said. "I didn't want you thinkin' love was all sunsets and pie. But maybe I overshot and made it sound too easy. It wasn't."

He took another sip from his thermos, as if steeling himself.

"You know I married late," Hank said. "Didn't get around to it till I was breakin' thirty-five. Before that, it was me, this ranch, and your daddy tryin' to out-stubborn the weather. I'd told myself I didn't have time for all that… heart business. Watched my folks treat each other like barn tools, useful, then put 'em away. Figured I'd spare myself the trouble."

Caleb listened, the familiar ache of curiosity about the woman in the faded photos mixing with surprise at the direction this was going.

"Then Marcie moved to town," Hank continued. "Schoolteacher. Came in with her boxes of books and her laugh and her entirely unreasonable expectation that the world could be a kinder place than it was. She made friends with everybody inside a week. Chickens started layin' better. I swear the tomatoes got sweeter. It was ridiculous."

He smiled faintly at the memory.

"She liked to walk," he said. "Every evenin', around the edges of town. Said it cleared her head after wranglin' kids all day. I started… happenin' to walk my own fence line at the same time. First few times, we just waved. Then we started walkin' together. Next thing I knew, I was tellin' her about the time your daddy got his truck stuck in a ditch tryin' to impress a girl, and she was cryin' laughin'. I hadn't told that story to nobody, not really, in years."

He looked down at his hands, at the creases time had etched there.

"I was gone," he said simply. "Hooked. Scared as hell."

Caleb could picture it, Hank younger, less lined, still with that same stubborn tilt to his chin, falling sideways into love and trying to pretend he wasn't.

"What were you scared of?" he asked, though he could guess.

"Pick one," Hank said. "Scared I'd mess it up. Scared she'd get bored, find some smoother fella with softer hands. Scared I'd turn into my father, who thought bein' a husband meant workin' himself into the grave and never tellin' my mama she was the best thing that ever happened to him." He shrugged. "And under all that, scared of the big one: that if I let her in, really in, losin' her would break somethin' I couldn't fix."

Caleb swallowed. The fear sounded painfully familiar.

"So, what'd you do?" he asked.

"Almost pushed her away," Hank said. "That's what."

He let the words sit there for a beat.

"There was this one night," Hank went on. "We'd been seein' each other a few months. Nothin' big. Church picnics, walks, her comin' out here to pretend she liked watchin' me muck stalls. She was patient. Didn't push for labels. Just… showed up."

He smiled, small and sad and fond all at once.

"One night, she asked if I wanted to go to this teachers' thing with her in the city. Some conference. Stay overnight. Meet her friends. It was a big step for her, introducin' me to that part of her life. And I… panicked."

He shook his head at the memory.

"I told her no," he said. "Said something about the ranch needin' me, about calves and fences and whatever excuse I could think of. But what I meant was, 'If I go, it'll make this real, and if it's real, it can end, and if it ends, I won't know how to breathe.'"

He glanced at Caleb. "Sound familiar?"

It did. Too much. Caleb stared at a cow flicking her tail at flies, throat tight.

"She looked at me for a long minute," Hank continued. "Then she said, very calm-like, 'Hank, I get that this place has your heart. I wouldn't ask you to be someone you're not. But if you keep lettin' fear drive every decision, you're gonna wake up one day on this land surrounded by everything you protected and nothin' you love.'"

He paused, letting the words sink in.

"And then she said the line I'm about to say to you," Hank said. "Because it branded itself into my fool brain."

He turned, leaning more fully on the fence, eyes steady on Caleb.

"You can't protect yourself from heartbreak and still claim you want love," Hank said quietly. "It doesn't work that way."

The words fell between them like a bell note, clear and resonant.

Caleb swallowed hard. "You sayin' I'm tryin' to have it both ways," he said.

"I'm sayin' you're tryin' to pad the corners of this so you don't get cut," Hank said. "You're halfway in, halfway out. You show up. You pour coffee. You fix fences. You kiss her under the porch light. And then the second the Big Scary Past comes knockin', you shut the door in her face 'for her own good' and try to handle it alone. That's fear drivin', not love."

Caleb flinched. The truth of it stung because it was close.

"And Emma?" Hank went on. "She's doin' her own version. Half of her is here, boots on your porch, words on her page. The other half's waitin' for the boom, thinkin' if she anticipates the hurt it'll sting less when it comes. Fear's drivin' her too. You two are lettin' it trade off behind the wheel."

He took off his hat, scrubbed his hand through his thinning hair, then settled the hat back on.

"Marcie told me that line," Hank said, nodding toward the pasture as if his late wife were out there somewhere. "I nearly let my fear talk me out of the best thing that ever happened to me. I almost sent her away because I was more comfortable with bein' alone than I was with the risk of losin' her."

He smiled faintly. "Lucky for me, she was stubborn," he said. "She gave me a week to pull my head outta my rear. Said, 'I'm not gonna chase you, Hank. But I'm not gonna stick around while you build walls, either. You want this, you meet me halfway.'"

He looked back at Caleb.

"I met her halfway," he said simply. "I drove to that city. Sat in a room full of teachers talkin' about curriculum like they were plannin' a moon landing. I shook hands, I smiled, I answered questions about cattle. Then I took her back to the motel and told her I was terrified and that I wanted to marry her anyway."

A softness came over his features that Caleb rarely saw.

"She laughed at me," Hank said. "Said, 'Those two things ain't mutually exclusive, Hank.' We got married six months later. Had ten years before her heart went and did what hearts do sometimes. Ten good, hard, beautiful years. I don't regret one single day I let her in. What I would've regretted, every damn day, is lettin' fear keep me from them."

He tapped his thermos against the fence rail.

"So, you got a choice, kid," he said. "You can keep lettin' fear drive. You can keep tryin' to pre-grieve every possible outcome so you don't get blindsided. But you're gonna end up livin' in a half-life. Or you can say, 'Screw it. I might get my heart broke, but I'm gonna love this woman all the way, not halfway. I'm gonna tell her the ugly stuff and the pretty stuff and let her decide if she wants in.'"

Caleb's throat felt tight. "And if she doesn't?" he asked, voice barely above a whisper. "If I open it all the way and she says no?"

"Then at least you'll know you gave her the truth," Hank said. "Not some curated version. At least you'll know you didn't lose her because you kept her at arm's length and called it protectin' her. That's the thing about love, son. You don't get guarantees. Just the chance to show up honest and see what happens."

He clapped a hand on Caleb's shoulder, the weight steadying.

"You care about her," he said. "More than you want to admit even to yourself. She cares about you. Enough to be scared. That's somethin'. Don't let fear run the show. Not after everything you and I have seen it do."

Caleb stared out at the pasture, Hank's words echoing in his chest alongside Emma's from the night before. The knot inside him tightened, then, slowly, began to loosen.

Can't protect yourself from heartbreak and still claim you want love.

He thought of Emma up on that hill, alone with her coffee and her notebook and whatever story she was telling herself about them right now. He thought of the last time he'd seen fear run him, hands gripping a steering wheel outside a hospital, heart pounding as he weighed whether to walk in and say goodbye to his father or sit outside pretending the inevitable wasn't happening.

He'd gone in. It had broken him. He'd survived.

Maybe this was the same category of thing: too important to keep skirting.

He turned to Hank. "If you were me," he said slowly, "what would you do?"

Hank snorted. "If I were you, I'd be thirty pounds lighter and have less arthritis," he said. "But if I were you in the way you mean? I'd go get that girl. Take her somewhere the town can't watch. Turn my damn phone off. And I'd talk. Really talk. Then I'd shut up and listen. Let her see you bleed a little. See what she does with it."

Caleb huffed a breath that was almost a laugh. "You make it sound so easy," he said.

"Hell no," Hank said. "It'll be hard as sin. But it beats replacin' fence posts all day avoidin' it."

He pushed off the fence. "I'll finish this," he said, nodding toward the half-tamped post. "You go wrangle you a woman and a couple o' bedrolls."

Caleb blinked. "You sure?" he asked.

"I ain't too old to handle some dirt," Hank said. "And if I keel over, at least I'll know it was for a good cause."

He turned away, then glanced back once more. "Caleb," he added, voice softening, "I loved Marcie with all I had and she still died. My heart still broke. But you know what? That heartbreak is proof I lived the way I wanted. If you and Emma crash and burn, it'll hurt. But it'll hurt honest. That's better than livin' safe and lonely, trust me."

Caleb nodded, the decision solidifying like concrete setting.

"All right," he said. "Okay."

He picked up his hat from the fence post, set it on his head, and headed back toward the truck.

Hank watched him go, then turned back to the fence with a sigh.

"Don't screw this up," he muttered to the air, though whether he meant the post or the boy, even he couldn't say.

Emma was on the porch when Caleb's truck came up the hill, notebook open on her lap, pen motionless in her hand. She'd been staring at the same sentence for ten minutes, brain looping the argument instead of the plot.

The sight of his truck made her heart lurch. For a second, panic flared, was he here to say it was too much? That they were too different? That it was easier to pull the plug now than later?

She tamped it down, forcing herself to breathe.

He parked slightly crooked, like he'd been in a hurry and hadn't bothered to straighten out. That alone told her something.

He stepped out, boots hitting the gravel with more purpose than she'd seen that morning. He walked toward the porch, hat in his hand instead of on his head, a sign of seriousness she recognized.

She stayed seated, partly out of stubbornness, partly because her knees felt unreliable.

"Hey," he said, stopping at the bottom of the steps.

"Hey," she replied, trying to keep her voice neutral.

They looked at each other for a long moment, the weight of last night hanging between them like fog.

"Can I sit?" he asked finally, nodding toward the porch.

She gestured to the empty chair. "It is your cabin," she said, then winced at how that sounded. "I mean, your ranch."

He half-smiled, acknowledging the awkwardness, and climbed the steps. The boards creaked under his weight. He sat on the edge of the chair, forearms resting on his thighs, hat turning slowly in his hands.

"I talked to Hank," he said.

Emma snorted softly. "Of course you did," she said. "He's your… relationship chaplain."

"Guess he is," Caleb said. "He told me somethin' I needed to hear. A few somethings."

She waited, not quite ready to help him out of the silence.

"I don't want fear drivin' this," he said finally, looking at his hands. "Mine or yours."

Her throat tightened. "Me either," she said quietly.

He took a breath, then another, as if steadying himself before a jump.

"Come with me tonight," he said.

She blinked. "Come with you… where?"

"Up back," he said, nodding toward the rear of the property. "High meadow, behind the ridge. Where the cell service gives up and the only thing watchin' you is the sky."

She stared. "You want to… camp?" she asked, thrown by the sudden left turn.

"Sort of," he said. "More… sit by a fire till too many stars come out and we can't ignore what we've been avoidin'. Sleep under 'em if we have to. I don't care if we freeze our butts off or get eaten alive by mosquitoes. I just… need to get us away from the house, from Hank, from town, from… everything. Just for a night."

She searched his face. There was determination there, and fear, and something like hope.

"You want to talk," she said.

"Yeah," he said. "Really talk. Not in a kitchen where one of us is worried about burnin' stew or Hank walkin' in. Not with the town two-steppin' its opinions around us. Just… you and me and whatever's left when we put it all on the table."

A part of her, the hurt and defensive one, wanted to say, you could have done that last night. Another part, the one that had lain awake wishing she'd handled things differently too, saw the offering for what it was: a risk. A reach.

"What if we just… fight again?" she asked softly. "Somewhere colder."

"We might," he said, not flinching. "We might say hard things. But I'd rather say 'em up there where we can't storm out the door and go hide in separate houses. Up there we'll at least have to sit in it till the coyotes get bored of our whining."

She almost laughed at that. Almost.

"Hank told me a story," he added. "About him and Marcie. About how he almost lost her 'cause he let fear keep him halfway in. I don't… want that to be us. Halfway anything. If this ends, I want it to be because we tried and it didn't work, not 'cause we were too scared to try all the way."

Her chest ached.

"He said something else," Caleb said, eyes meeting hers now. "Said you can't protect yourself from heartbreak and still claim you want love. Doesn't work that way."

The line hit her like a bell. She could hear Hank in it, but she could also feel the truth underneath.

"I know you're scared," he went on. "So am I. For different reasons, maybe, but… same game. I'm not askin' you to stop bein' scared. I'm askin' you to come up that hill with me anyway. To sit under the sky and tell me the real stuff. I promise I'll do the same. No more curatin'."

Silence stretched.

She thought of that alley, of Abby's voice, of her own voice saying things edged with old pain. She thought of her parents' marriage, years of quiet resentment that hadn't ever blown up, just… eroded. She thought of the Scrivener file she'd left on her laptop, blinking cursor waiting where she'd written and erased the same paragraph half a dozen times.

Fear had been driving her too, if she was honest. Fear of being foolish. Fear of being wrong. Fear of waking up one day and realizing she'd traded one version of trapped for another.

"If we do this," she said slowly, "you have to let me be messy."

He huffed a small breath. "Have you met me?" he asked. "Messy is the only thing I'm consistent at. I'm not expectin' polished. I'm expectin'… you."

"And you'll give me you?" she asked. "Not the you that's tryin' not to scare me. The whole one?"

"That's the deal," he said. "Whole me, whole you. Under the Colorado sky, no witnesses but whatever birds decide to judge us."

A smile tugged at her mouth despite everything. "That's a bad title," she said. "For a romance novel, I mean."

"We can workshop it later," he said. "So… will you come?"

She looked past him, at the hills rolling out behind the ranch, at the line of trees that hid the high meadow from view. The idea of being out there, just the two of them and the stars, scared her as much as it tugged at her.

But it felt right, too. Like a pivot point.

"Yes," she said, the word landing between them with quiet finality. "I'll come."

Relief washed across his face so plainly she had to look down for a second.

"Okay," he said, standing. "I'll get the horses saddled. Couple bedrolls, some blankets, coffee, somethin' to burn that won't start a forest fire. Meet me at the barn in an hour?"

"Make it forty-five," she said. "I need time to panic and pack snacks."

He chuckled, some of the tension easing from his shoulders. "We'll need the snacks," he said. "I fight better when I'm fed."

"You'd better not be planning on fightin'," she said, but there was a thread of humor in it now.

"Talkin'," he corrected. "Then maybe other things if we survive the talkin'."

Color rose in her cheeks. "Go saddle your horse, Walker," she said.

"Yes, ma'am," he replied, and for the first time since last night, the endearment felt warm again instead of heavy.

The ride up to the high meadow was longer than Emma remembered. The last time she'd gone that far back, Hank had been driving and she'd been too busy trying not to throw up in the ruts to pay attention.

On horseback, the landscape unfolded slower and more deliberately.

They left the barn in late afternoon, sun slanting golden across the pasture. Caleb rode Raven, his dark gelding, with easy familiarity. Emma rode Bella, who seemed glad to have a job that didn't involve nosy calves for once.

Bedrolls and a small tent were tied to the back of Caleb's saddle. Emma carried a pack with food, water, and a battered thermos Hank had pressed into her hands with a stern "Don't come back without emptyin' it."

The first part of the trail wound along the creek, its water low this late in the summer but still laughing over stones. The air smelled like sun-warmed pine and dust.

For a while, they rode in comfortable silence, the creak of saddle leather and the clop of hooves filling in the spaces where words could have gone.

Emma focused on the rhythm of Bella's gait; on the way the mare's ears flicked toward birds and rustling branches. It gave her somewhere to put her nervous energy.

"You remember the first time you came up here?" Caleb asked eventually, breaking the quiet.

Emma thought. "The overlook?" she said. "Where you took me after I got lost near the creek and you scolded me for hiking alone?"

"Guilty," he said. "Same way. Just keep goin' a couple miles past that."

She smiled faintly. "That was the first time I think I really... saw this place," she said. "Not just the ranch, but... all of it. The way the hills fold over each other. The way the sky doesn't stop."

"First time I saw you see it," he said. "That's when I started thinkin'... maybe this ain't just a temporary stop for you."

Something warm moved in her chest at that.

"I didn't come out here thinkin' I'd stay," she admitted. "It was... a break. An escape. Now I can't picture going back to... what I had."

"That scares you too," he said. It wasn't a question.

She exhaled. "Yeah," she said. "It does."

They rode on, the trail narrowing as it climbed. Scrub oak gave way to taller pines. The air cooled. Emma felt sweat gather under her shirt and didn't mind; it meant she was doing something real, not just sitting in front of a screen.

When they reached the overlook, he slowed, letting Bella catch up with Raven. They stopped side by side, looking out.

The valley below spread out like a painting, patchwork fields, the thin thread of the creek, Cottonwood Ridge's few clustered buildings a smudge in the distance. The sky arched wide, already tinged with the first hints of sunset pink.

"Still hits me every time," she murmured.

"Me too," he said. "Keeps me from forgettin' why I bother fixin' fences."

They didn't linger long. He nudged Raven onward along a narrower path that hugged the ridge. Eventually, the trail opened into a high, hidden meadow, ringed by trees on three sides and dropping off into a view of distant peaks on the fourth.

Wildflowers, stubborn and late-blooming, dotted the grass. A small fire ring of stones showed where someone, Hank, most likely, had camped here before.

"This is it," Caleb said, swinging down from the saddle.

Emma dismounted less gracefully, legs protesting. She stood for a moment, stretching, taking it in.

"It's… beautiful," she said. The word felt insufficient.

"Not bad for the back forty," he said, trying for casual and failing to hide his pride.

They moved into an easy choreography, unsaddling the horses, picketing them where the grass was thickest, unloading bedrolls and packs. Caleb gathered fallen branches and twigs while Emma laid out a blanket near the fire ring.

By the time the sun dropped behind the ridge, casting long shadows, a small fire crackled, sending sparks up toward the darkening sky. The air cooled quickly, mountain nights indifferent to daytime heat.

They sat side by side on the blanket, shoulders almost touching, the firelight painting their faces in flickers.

"Okay," Emma said, wrapping her arms around her knees. "We're here. No cell service. No Hank. No Abby. No town. Just us and whatever mountain lions you forgot to warn me about."

"They're on vacation," Caleb said. "Sent a postcard."

She huffed a breath, half-laugh, half-question.

"Who goes first?" she asked.

He stared into the fire for a long moment, then lifted his gaze to the strip of sky visible between the tree tops.

"I will," he said.

He shifted, turning to face her more fully.

"I told you bits," he said. "Little pieces. About my deployments. About my dad. About... all of it. But I never put it in a straight line. Maybe 'cause I didn't want to see it that way myself. Maybe 'cause I didn't think you'd want to hold the whole string. That wasn't fair."

She said nothing, giving him space.

"I joined up because I didn't know what else to do," he began. "You probably guessed that. High school, I was... okay. Decent grades, decent at sports, decent at not gettin' in trouble. But I didn't have a... thing. The ranch was my dad's. I thought if I stayed, I'd just... sink into bein' 'Tom Walker's boy' for the rest o' my life."

He picked up a small twig, rolling it between his fingers.

"Recruiter came around junior year," he said. "Showed us pictures of mountains and uniforms and talked about brotherhood and purpose. Sounded a lot like the movies. I wanted... somethin' bigger than this little town. Somethin' I could point at and say, 'I did that.' So, I signed up."

He half-smiled. "My dad was proud and pissed at the same time," he said. "Said, 'You know there's enough work here to keep you busy till you're ninety.' I said, 'That's the problem.' We yelled. Then we hugged. That was kind of our thing."

Emma could almost see it, the younger versions of them, stubbornness in identical lines of their jaws.

"I deployed at twenty," he went on. "Sand, heat, noise. Nights where the stars looked close enough to grab, days where I thought my skull was gonna melt. Saw some things I still don't have words for. Lost some good men. Carried that with me. Came home once between deployments, kissed Abby under this same sky like the world wasn't on fire somewhere else. Told her I'd marry her when I got out. Promised her safe and steady."

He shook his head, gaze distant.

"Second deployment… broke somethin'," he said. "We had a bad one. Convoy went sideways. We lost a guy who'd been coverin' my ass for months. I came back with all my limbs and this feelin' like I shouldn't have. Survivor's guilt, they call it. Felt more like I'd swallowed a bomb that might go off anytime."

He tossed the twig into the fire, watching it catch.

"I came home and tried to fit right back into the life I'd planned," he said. "Ranch, Abby, ring on a finger, white picket fence if we could afford the lumber. But I was… different. Jumpy. Overprotective. I needed control 'cause I'd spent two years learnin' that when you don't have it, bad things happen."

His mouth tightened.

"So yeah," he said. "I got intense. If she was late comin' home from visitin' her mama, I paced. If she wanted to drive to the city by herself, I made a checklist of routes and times and what to do if she got a flat. Thought I was helpin'. She just felt watched. Cornered. Like I'd traded her daddy's rules for mine."

He glanced at Emma, eyes shadowed. "She wasn't wrong," he said. "I loved her, but I was lovin' her through a fog of fear. I was tryin' to keep her safe and, in the process, I made her feel small. I own that. I hate it, but I own it."

He drew in a breath of cold, pine-scented air.

"Then my dad got sick," he said quietly. "Real sick. Fast. One minute he was givin' me hell about fixin' the tractor wrong, the next he was sittin' in a doctor's office hearin' words neither of us were ready for. I moved back full-time to run the ranch, thinkin' we'd beat it. We didn't."

He swallowed. The firelight glinted in his eyes.

"I watched him go from the strongest man I knew to… bones and a stubborn spark," he said. "Held his hand at the end. Promised him I'd keep this place alive. That I wouldn't let it go to some developer who'd put condos where his barn stood. He nodded and said, 'Don't be an idiot. If it kills you, sell it.' Then he died anyway."

Emma's hand moved of its own accord, finding his on the blanket. He didn't pull away.

"I was grievin' him, grievin' the guys I lost, tryin' to hold the ranch together with duct tape and prayer," he went on. "Abby was there. She tried. But every time she walked out the door, I saw every worst-case scenario. I made that her problem. She wanted… air. A chance to travel, to see somethin' besides these hills. I wanted her here where I could see her breathin'."

He gave a humorless huff. "That's how you trap someone," he said. "With your fear. Not with locks, but with expectations."

He looked at her, letting her see the shame and the regret, not hiding behind jokes.

"When she left," he said, "it damn near broke me. Not 'cause she was wrong to go, but 'cause it proved my worst fear right, that I was too much. Too intense. Too… everything. So, I shut it down. Decided I'd pour all that into the ranch instead. Cows can't get mad at you for worryin' too much about 'em. Land doesn't roll its eyes when you walk the fence twice."

He gave her hand a small squeeze.

"Then you showed up," he said softly. "With your notebook and your city shoes and that look on your face like you were tryin' to outrun somethin' too."

Her throat tightened. "I was," she said.

"I liked you right away," he admitted. "Tried not to. Told myself you were temporary, a guest, a line item in the budget. But then you sat on that porch and watched the sunset like it was the first one you'd seen in months, and I thought, 'Ah, hell.'"

A reluctant smile tugged at her mouth.

"You made me laugh again," he said. "At stupid stuff. At myself. You helped with calves without complainin', even when you were knee-deep in mud you didn't sign up for. You asked questions nobody'd ever asked me, not about the ranch, but about me. You listened."

His voice went softer.

"When you said you were thinkin' about stayin' longer," he said, "I felt this… surge of joy and terror. Joy because… selfishly, I wanted you here. Terror because I thought, 'If she stays, I could lose her too. And if I do, I don't know if I've got it in me to build myself back again.'"

He looked down at their joined hands.

"That's when fear started drivin' again," he said. "Not as loud as before, but still there. Every time I told you to text when you got to town, every time I made a suggestion 'for your safety,' part of me was tryin' to love you well. Another part was tryin' to keep you inside a radius where bad things couldn't get to you, or where, if they did, I could throw myself in front first."

He took a breath, slow and shaky.

"I'm tellin' you all this 'cause you deserve to know what you're walkin' into," he said. "Not some cleaned-up version. The real thing. My instinct is always gonna be to protect. It's baked in. But I don't want to protect you into a box. I don't want to love you like a cage. I want to learn how to love you like a… like a wide-open gate. Safe, but not shut."

He swallowed, throat working.

"And Emma," he said quietly, "you mean… more to me than I know how to say. That's part of what scares me. If you walk away, it's gonna hurt. A lot. I'm not gonna pretend otherwise. But I'd rather risk that than keep standin' here half in, half out, pretendin' that's safer. If you stay, if we figure this out, I want it to be because you know exactly who you're takin' on. Ghosts and all."

She blinked hard, tears standing in her eyes, not from pity but from the weight of being trusted with this unvarnished version of him.

For a long moment, the only sounds were the crackle of the fire and the soft rustle of the wind in the trees.

"Your turn," he said finally, voice gentle. "If you want."

She stared into the flames, heart pounding. It would be easy to say something surface-level, something that acknowledged his vulnerability without matching it. Easy and unworthy.

She let herself tip forward instead.

"My parents fought quietly," she said. "No big blowouts. No plates thrown. Just… little cuts. Snipes over bills and whose turn it was to take out the trash. My mom wanted more, she always said that. More travel, more art, more… life. My dad wanted… peace. A job that paid the mortgage, a couch, a TV, a beer. Somewhere between those wants, love… just thinned out."

She picked up a small stone, turned it over in her fingers.

"They never divorced," she said. "Never even separated. They just… turned into roommates who shared a last name. They smiled in photos and died a little every day in between. I watched my mom shrink herself to make peace. Watched my dad dig in to keep everything the same. I promised myself I'd never be either of them."

She tossed the stone into the fire ring, where it landed with a harmless thunk.

"So, I went the other way," she said. "I moved to the city. Took the first job that let me write and ran with it. I wrote about other people's lives, murders and scandals and city council meetings that turned into shouting matches. I told myself that was safer. That if I watched from the outside, took notes, I'd never get stuck on the inside of something that hurt."

She laughed once, bitter and soft.

"Turns out, watching everything and living none of it is its own kind of trap," she said. "I'd go home after covering a car crash or a budget vote and sit in my apartment, half-dead from adrenaline, and think, 'Is this it? Is this what I came here for? To chase other people's heartbreak and call it a career?'"

She drew her knees up, hugging them.

"When I decided to come here, it felt… reckless," she admitted. "My editor thought I was having a breakdown. My friends joked about Eat Pray Love. I told everyone it was temporary, a summer thing, a little sabbatical. But deep down, I knew I was… running. Not just from the job, but from the fear that if I stopped moving long enough to look at my life, I'd realize I'd built my own cage. One that looked like success from the outside."

She looked at him, eyes shiny.

"Then I got here," she said. "And the quiet… scared me. So did the way you looked at me like I wasn't just… visiting. Like you could imagine me in this picture long-term when I couldn't yet. It felt… dangerous. Like one wrong step and I'd wake up twenty years from now, my world as small as my parents' had been, wondering where the time went."

He winced, but didn't interrupt.

"I like this life," she said, voice thick. "I like waking up to cows instead of sirens. I like the way the work makes my body ache and my brain… ease. I like having dinner with you and Hank at that table. I like the way you… see me. Not just as 'the writer,' but as… me. That scares me, because it means I have something real to lose."

She blew out a breath.

"When Abby warned me about you," she said, "she poked right where those fears live. The fear of bein' small, of bein' watched, of being some man's fragile thing instead of my own person. I heard her and I thought, 'What if she's right? What if I'm about to repeat my mother's life, just in prettier scenery?'"

She swallowed.

"So, when I saw you with her, and heard that line, it… hit all that." Her voice wobbled. "I didn't see you settin' boundaries. I saw every warning light I'd ever told myself not to ignore lighting up. It wasn't fair. To you. To who you are now. But it felt… real in that moment."

She looked down at their still-joined hands, thumb stroking over his knuckles unconsciously.

"I do trust you," she said slowly. "Maybe not in the neat, no-questions-asked way you were hopin' for last night. I trust your intentions. I trust your heart. I trust that you don't want to hurt me. I don't always trust… your fear. Or mine. I don't trust that we won't both, sometimes, listen to those voices more than we should."

She looked up at him again.

"But I want to," she said. "God, I want to. I'm here, aren't I? On a mountain, in the cold, with way too few bathrooms, because I want this. I want… us. Not the idea of us, but the real, messy version. Even if it scares me."

His eyes searched hers, the firelight flaring amber there.

"I'm sorry," she added, voice breaking a little. "For not givin' you the benefit of the doubt when I should have. For throwin' that line at you like it's who you are now instead of who you were then. For… making you feel like you had to pass some test to earn my trust when I haven't exactly been acing it myself."

He exhaled, something loosening in his shoulders.

"I'm sorry too," he said. "For keepin' you out of that parking lot conversation. For thinkin' I was sparin' you when I was really just sparin' myself from havin' to see disappointment on your face. For lettin' fear decide when I share things instead of lettin' you decide what you can handle."

They sat there in the flickering half-light, apologies and confessions hanging between them like fragile glass.

"So, what do we do?" she asked after a moment, voice soft. "With all this?"

He looked up at the sky, where the first stars had begun to push through the deepening blue.

"We choose," he said. "Not once, but... over and over. To talk instead of guessin'. To tell each other when fear's drivin' instead o' lettin' it take the wheel. To let each other be messy without boltin'."

He looked back at her, eyes steady.

"I can't promise I won't screw up," he said. "I probably will. I can't promise you'll never feel cramped by my worry. Cannot promise I'll never flinch when you talk about leavin' the ranch for a couple weeks to see your folks. But I can promise I'll keep talkin' to you about it. That I'll let you in, even when it scares me. That I won't decide what's best for you without you in the room."

Her eyes brimmed, a tear slipping free. He reached up gently, thumb brushing it away.

"And I can promise," she said, "that I'll... check myself before I let other people's stories drown out ours. That when I hear a ghost whispering, I'll tell you, instead of just assum, " Her voice broke.

"Assumin' I'm the ghost," he finished for her, soft.

She nodded, laughing a little through the tears.

A cool breeze stirred the grasses around them. Overhead, the sky had deepened to indigo, stars sharpening by the minute. The fire burned lower, heat radiating in a smaller circle.

Without really deciding to, they leaned toward each other, drawn by something that had been tugging at them since that first fence line at sunset.

His hand cupped her jaw, rough palm warm against her cheek. She slid closer, knees brushing his.

"You cold?" he asked.

"A little," she admitted. "Mountain nights are rude."

He smiled, that half-crooked smile she'd grown fond of.

"We got a remedy for that," he said, nodding toward the bedroll laid out behind them. "At least the PG-13 one. Hank'd have my hide if I let you freeze up here."

She laughed, breath catching. "You sure Hank's not hiding in a bush watching?" she asked.

"He'd better not be," Caleb said. "Or I'm changin' the locks."

He shifted, moving back onto the bedroll, and held out a hand. She hesitated a fraction of a second, then took it, letting him draw her down with him.

They lay side by side at first, on top of the sleeping bag, staring up at the sky. It was full now, constellations she half-recognized, the faint smudge of the Milky Way like someone had brushed a thumb across the dark.

"It's a little terrifying," she murmured.

"What is?" he asked.

"All of it," she said. "How big it is. How small we are. How… much I feel right now."

He turned his head, studying her profile in the starlight.

"Yeah," he said. "Me too."

He lifted a hand, tucking a strand of hair behind her ear. She turned toward him, the space between them shrinking.

"Emma," he said, voice low.

"Yeah," she whispered.

"I'm in this," he said simply. "With you. Not halfway. I don't have all the words yet, but… I am. If you are too… we'll figure the rest out."

Her heart thudded, heavy and sure.

"I am," she said. "With you."

The words weren't a formal declaration, no trumpets, no grand speeches. But they were a choice. Clear.

He closed the last inches between them, his mouth finding hers in a kiss that was nothing like the almost-angry ones that had followed their fight, nothing like the tentative brushes of their early days.

This kiss was… full.

Slow. Certain. He kissed her like he had nowhere else to be, nothing else to do. Like the only thing that mattered was reassuring her, and himself, that they were still here, together, under this impossible sky.

She answered with equal softness, fingers curling in the fabric of his shirt. The static of the last twenty-four hours crackled between them and then, slowly, began to dissolve, replaced by something warmer and steadier.

He pulled back just enough to search her face.

"You, okay?" he asked, needing the answer.

She nodded, breath warm against his skin. "Yeah," she said. "Better than."

He smiled, relief visible even in the dim.

"Good," he murmured.

He kissed her again, deeper this time. She melted into it, letting herself stop thinking for once, no analyzing angles, no cataloging reasons why this could go wrong. Just him, and her, and the press of his chest against hers, the way his hand splayed warm over her back.

When the air grew colder, they eased into the sleeping bag, awkward laughter and whispered curses about zippers cutting through the tenderness without breaking it.

They shed layers, not in some frenzied rush, but in the unhurried, almost reverent way of people who knew exactly what they were stepping into and had decided, together, to go anyway.

He checked in more than once, even when she rolled her eyes and told him he didn't have to.

"I want to," he said. "You say stop, we stop. No questions."

"I know," she said. "That's part of why I'm not gonna."

He laughed, a soft, disbelieving sound, and kissed her forehead.

Their bodies came together with the same care they'd just put into their words. It wasn't about erasing what had hurt or distracting from the hard conversations. It was about sealing something they'd just opened, choosing, with skin and breath and heartbeat, what they'd already chosen with voices around the fire.

Under the wide Colorado sky, wrapped in canvas and blankets and each other, they let themselves be seen.

The details belonged to them, the whispered names, the way his hand trembled once against her hip and she covered it with her own, the tears that slipped from the corner of her eye and he kissed away without asking if they were from joy or fear or both.

When it was done, they lay tangled, breathing slowing, the fire now only a faint glow of embers.

"Still cold?" he asked eventually, voice rough.

"Not even a little," she said, half-laughing, half-sighing. "I might actually be a furnace."

He tightened his arm around her, pressing a kiss to her hairline.

"Good," he murmured. "Means I get to sleep."

She rested her head on his chest, listening to the steady thump of his heart, the slow in and out of his breath. Above them, the stars watched, indifferent and eternal.

They didn't say the word that hovered on the edges of everything, they weren't quite ready to give it voice. But they'd said enough, in other ways, that it didn't feel like a lack.

Tonight, under the stars, they'd chosen each other.

Tomorrow, the world, Hank, the town, their fears, would still be there. Missteps would still happen. Ghosts would still whisper.

But for the first time since she'd driven up that gravel road, Emma fell asleep not worrying about whether she was building a cage or stepping into one.

She fell asleep feeling… held.

And for the first time since he'd watched Abby drive away all those years ago, Caleb closed his eyes beside someone and didn't flinch at the thought that they might one day not be there.

He knew it was possible. Hearts broke. People left. Life did what it did.

But tonight, he wasn't trying to pre-grieve anything. He was just… here. With her. Under the Colorado sky.

Letting love, not fear, drive.

Chapter Twenty-Two
Daylight Decisions

Morning came gentler than either of them deserved.

Emma woke to warmth at her back and the sound of birds trilling in the treeline. For a moment she didn't know where she was, the air too cold for her apartment, the mattress too lumpy for the cabin bed. Then the smell of smoke and pine threaded through the fuzz of sleep and she realized she was lying half-twisted in a sleeping bag, pressed against Caleb's side, under a sky that was already paling from deep indigo to soft gray-blue.

She blinked up.

The stars were gone, washed out by a shy dawn. In their place, a few high strands of cloud glowed faintly. The fire pit held only a scatter of glowing embers, occasional sparks winking like tired fireflies.

Caleb's chest rose and fell under her cheek, his heartbeat a slow, steady drum. His arm was slung around her waist, heavy and absent-minded in sleep. She could feel the rasp of his shirt against her bare shoulder where the sleeping bag had slipped down.

She lay still, feeling everything.

Her body ached pleasantly in places she refused to categorize too closely yet. Her muscles complained about horseback riding and cold ground. Her heart felt... oddly quiet. Not empty, full, but not racing with the old, familiar anxiety.

She rolled the last twelve hours back through her mind like a film reel. The fire. His voice when he'd talked about his deployments. Her own words, halting and messy, about her parents and her job and the cages she'd built. The way they'd chosen each other, plainly, before the sleeping bag had ever unzipped.

No one had said love. The word hovered, still, like something they were circling around. But whatever they'd done under that sky, it had been more than comfort, more than rebound from a fight.

It felt... like a line crossed that you didn't cross back.

Caleb stirred beneath her, breath catching for a half-second. His arm tightened reflexively.

"You awake?" he mumbled, voice rough with sleep.

"Mm-hmm," she said against his chest. "Have been for a bit."

He made a small, displeased noise. "Should've woken me," he said. "Could've watched the sunrise together."

"We still can," she said. "I think it's waiting for you to get your act together."

He huffed a sleep-heavy laugh. "Bossy," he murmured.

"Only when I'm right," she said.

He shifted, craning his head to look past her at the horizon. The first real streaks of gold were just beginning to edge the distant peaks, like someone had taken a highlighter to the mountains.

"Damn," he said quietly. "That's somethin'."

"Yeah," she whispered.

They watched without speaking for a while, the sky brightening from gray to pink to blue. The world slowly sharpened, individual blades of grass at the edge of the blanket, the dark shapes of the horses dozing a little farther off, a hawk gliding lazy circles above the far slope.

She could feel his hand absently tracing circles on her hip through the sleeping bag. It was a small, unconscious gesture, but it felt like an entire statement: you're here, I'm here, I'm not pulling away.

"You, okay?" he asked after a bit, tilting his head enough to see her face.

She turned her cheek against his chest to look up at him. His hair was a disaster, flattened on one side, sticking up on the other. She smiled.

"You've got… this whole rooster thing goin' on," she said, touching the wilder side of his hair.

He squinted at her. "You sayin' my morning look isn't irresistible?" he asked.

"Oh, it's irresistible," she said solemnly. "Just… in a barnyard kinda way."

He grinned, and something in her unclenched further. That he could make jokes, that she could tease, after everything they'd dredged up, that felt like its own quiet miracle.

"Seriously," he said more softly. "How's your head? Your heart?"

She thought about it.

"Raw," she said honestly. "But in a… good way? Like when you finally clean out a cut instead of keepin' it under a Band-Aid too long."

He nodded, understanding flickering in his eyes. "Yeah," he said. "Feels kind of like debriding."

She blinked. "That's a horrifying word," she said. "Let's not use that for our relationship maintenance."

He chuckled. "Fair," he said. "But you know what I mean."

"I do," she said. "What about you?"

He looked up at the sky for a moment before answering.

"I feel… lighter," he said. "Like I've been carryin' a rucksack so long I forgot it was on. Then I took it off last night and now my shoulders don't quite know what to do."

"Probably still expectin' to be dragged into another deployment at any minute," she said softly.

He nodded once, accepting that without comment.

He looked back at her, expression turning more serious.

"Emma," he said, "about last night… everything I told you… that doesn't go back in the box."

"I know," she said immediately. "Same here. We can't… pretend we didn't say what we said."

He searched her face. "You still feel like… this is somethin' you want to be in?" he asked. "Given all of it?"

The old Emma, the one who lived in city apartments and kept her feelings triple-wrapped, might have deflected with a joke, might have bought time with a light answer.

The Emma lying here, under this sky, with this man who'd told her his worst and best, found she didn't want to hedge.

"Yes," she said simply. "I do."

The word didn't feel naïve. It felt chosen.

Relief flickered across his features again, edging into something like quiet happiness.

"Good," he murmured. "'Cause I do too."

He dipped his head to kiss her, soft, morning-slow, no urgency, just affirmation.

When they broke apart, the world had shifted up another notch on the brightness scale. The sun had cleared the peaks, casting their little clearing in a wash of gold.

She squinted at it, then at him.

"We should… probably get up," she said reluctantly. "Before Bella decides to join us in the sleeping bag."

"Horse cuddles are extra," he said. "Not included in the Airbnb listing."

She laughed.

They disentangled themselves with the kind of awkwardness that came from being both newly intimate and very aware that the sleeping bag zipper had teeth. There was a lot of muttered "sorry" and half-stifled laughter as knees bumped and elbows caught.

They dressed in layers, fingers numb in the morning chill, then poured coffee from the thermos Hank had insisted on. It was lukewarm but strong. It tasted like sanity.

They ate granola bars and apples. Caleb checked the horses while Emma doused the embers with water from a canteen, watching the last little curls of smoke disappear into the cold air.

As they packed up the bedrolls, her gaze snagged on the flattened patch of grass where they'd lain.

It hit her then; in a way it hadn't fully the night before: this wasn't just a nice memory to file away. It was a hinge.

The choices they'd made up here were going to follow them back down the hill, into Hank's kitchen and town and the conversation they'd been avoiding for weeks.

What happens when summer ends?

The thought slid into her mind like a pebble down a slope.

She glanced at Caleb. He must have seen something shift in her expression, because he paused mid-roll, eyebrow lifting.

"Penny for your thoughts," he said.

She chewed the inside of her cheek. "You can't afford 'em," she said lightly.

He didn't bite. "Try me," he said.

She hesitated. Some stubborn part of her wanted to keep the magic of the morning intact a little longer before dropping real-world logistics on it.

But that was what had gotten them tangled before, saving the hard conversations for some mythical better time.

She blew out a breath.

"I was just… thinkin' about August," she said. "About… the fact that technically, at the end of this summer, I'm supposed to… go back."

The words felt heavy, like she was naming a storm they could both see on the horizon.

He stilled completely, hands tightening on the bedroll. For a second, something flashed across his face, fear, reflex, the old instinct to tense against impending loss.

Then he inhaled, slow and deliberate, as if remembering someone else's words ringing in his ears.

You can't protect yourself from heartbreak and still claim you want love.

He set the bedroll down, took a small step closer, and leaned back against the nearest tree as if he was bracing himself on purpose.

"Okay," he said. "Let's… talk about that."

She looked at him, surprised by the steady tone.

"You could've just said, 'We'll cross that bridge when we come to it,'" she said. "Pretend we don't see it."

"Yeah," he said. "I've been tryin' that. Doesn't seem to work." He cracked a half-smile. "Besides, if I'm gonna screw somethin' up, I'd rather do it on purpose than by accident."

She huffed a laugh despite herself.

He tipped his head. "So," he said. "When exactly are you supposed to be back in Denver?"

"Officially?" she said. "My sabbatical runs through the end of August. I told my editor I'd check in around the middle of the month to talk about... what's next."

"And what did you intend to do when you made that plan?" he asked. "Before all... this."

She thought back to that day in her tiny kitchen, the email thread, the way her hands had shaken as she'd typed.

"Honestly?" she said. "I figured I'd come back... rested. Maybe with a few chapters. And then slide back into the job. Tell myself the break had scratched the itch and that I should be grateful to have a steady paycheck and a byline. Maybe start lookin' for positions at a magazine instead of the paper. Nothing too drastic. Just... enough to keep from losin' my mind."

"And now?" he asked softly.

She looked out at the view, the sweep of forested slopes, the thin silver line of a distant creek, the way the light caught on the backs of the horses grazing nearby. She thought of mornings at the cabin, coffee and cows and that odd sense of safety she'd never felt in the city. She thought of her notebook, thicker now with pages that didn't make her skin crawl when she reread them.

"Now..." she said slowly, "it feels... wrong. The idea of goin' back to... that exact life. That apartment, that commute, that version of me who lives on caffeine and headlines. I keep thinkin' about it and my chest feels tight."

"Wrong like dangerous?" he asked. "Or wrong like… doesn't fit anymore?"

The question caught her. He was trying not to put his thumb on the scale; she could hear it.

She took stock.

"Doesn't fit," she said at last. "Like tryin' to put on jeans that shrunk in the wash. You can force it, but you can't breathe."

He nodded slowly. Relief flickered again, but he kept it tamped down.

"What about the work itself?" he asked. "The writing. The parts of the job that aren't about the office or the city. Do you love that part?"

"I love storytelling," she said. "I love words. I love piecing things together and makin' people feel something. But… chasing breaking news, writin' about car wrecks and scandals and school board fights… it's like eating junk food. Feels exciting in the moment, leaves you sick after. The stuff I've written here…" She looked down at her hands. "That feels like actual food."

"My happiest days in Denver were days I was on assignment out somewhere with a notebook, talking to people, not days I was in the newsroom," she admitted. "My happiest days here are… most of them. Even the ones where I end up covered in mud."

He took that in, quiet.

"So maybe," he said slowly, "it's not a choice between writin' and this place. Maybe it's a choice between… what kind of writin'. Who you write for. Where you do it from."

She looked at him, that simple reframing shifting something in her.

"I always thought… if I left the paper, I was givin' up the dream," she said. "All the professors who told me gettin' a staff job was the golden ticket. All the classmates who didn't make it. It felt… ungrateful to walk away."

"I get that," he said. "But maybe that was the dream for that version of you. The one who needed out of her parents' house and into somethin' big and loud. Maybe it's okay if your dreams change when you do."

He shrugged, eyes flicking away briefly.

"Comin' back here from the Army felt like failure at first," he admitted. "Like I couldn't hack the rest of the world so I crawled back to what I knew. Took me a long time to realize… this is where I do my best work. Where I can actually do some good. Didn't make me less of a man because my battlefield turned out to be fences and calves instead of… whatever the recruiters show in their brochures."

She absorbed that. It rang true in a way that made her chest ache.

"It's weird," she said. "If you told my twenty-two-year-old self that thirty-two-year-old me would be considerin' stayin' on a ranch with a quiet man and a nosy old mentor, she would've thought we'd been… body-snatched."

"She'd probably think you were sellin' out," he said.

"Yeah," she agreed. "But that girl… didn't know what she didn't know. She didn't know how tiring it is to be 'on' all the time, to live in the middle of a story instead of just writin' one. She didn't know… this existed. The way my brain feels when it's not clogged with sirens and city noise. The way… this feels. With you."

His fingers twitched where they hung at his sides, like he wasn't sure yet if he had the right to reach for her.

"You talkin' about stayin'," he said carefully, "because of me? Because of the ranch? Or because… when you picture your life, this is the backdrop you see now?"

She forced herself to answer honestly.

"Both," she said. "I'd be lyin' if I said you weren't a giant part of the equation. If we were a disaster, if this was all wrong, I'd probably be packin' my car already. But even if…" She swallowed. "Even if we didn't work out, I think I'd still… want this kind of life. Somewhere like this. I don't… want to go back to the way I was livin'."

He exhaled; some deep knot loosening.

"That… helps," he said.

A beat later, he added, almost abruptly, "I don't want you to give up your career for me."

There it was, the instinct surfacing, the push away disguised as nobility. She could hear the edges of it, the way he'd probably rehearsed that line in his head as the Good, Selfless Boyfriend thing to say.

He heard it too.

He caught his own words, frowned, and shook his head like he was clearing it.

"That's not quite right," he corrected. "What I mean is… I don't want you to… shrink yourself for me. Or wake up resentin' me 'cause you didn't chase somethin' you really wanted. If you stay, I want it to be because this is what you want, not because you think I'll fall apart if you leave."

"Caleb," she said gently, "you wouldn't fall apart. You'd hurt. But you'd be okay. You've survived worse."

"I know that," he said. "Now. But there's still a piece of me that wants to make your choices for you to keep you from makin' ones that might hurt. That's the part I'm tryin' not to listen to. So, I'm tellin' you straight: I want you to stay. I really, really do. I can't imagine this place without you now. But if you look at your life and think, 'I need to go back to Denver for a while. I need to do this job longer,' I'll let you. I won't guilt you. I won't… turn into your dad or mine. I'll… learn to live with it."

He looked at her, eyes bare.

"I'd rather hurt honest than keep you here on a lie," he said quietly.

The simplicity of it, wanting her to stay and still refusing to hold her there, hit her harder than any declaration could have.

She stepped closer, closing the gap between them. The bedroll lay forgotten at their feet.

"Thank you," she said. "For sayin' both parts. For not pretendin' you don't care what I choose."

He huffed a shaky laugh. "I care," he said. "Way too much."

"I know," she said.

She looked past him, toward the way home, the trail winding back down, the cabin perched on its hill, the little town beyond. Then she looked back up, toward the peaks and the wild sky that had seen last night and now this.

"When I think about goin' back to Denver," she said slowly, "I picture fluorescent lights and stale coffee and waking up already dreadin' the day. When I think about stayin'... I picture my laptop on that cabin table, pages stackin' up. I picture Hank complainin' about his knees and secretly lovin' it when I make biscuits. I picture you comin' up that hill with dust on your boots and somethin' in your eyes you want to tell me about."

She swallowed.

"Maybe that's romanticizin'," she said. "Maybe ranch life will get old. Maybe there'll be winters where I'll be cursin' frozen water lines and wonderin' what on earth I was thinkin'. But even that..." She smiled wryly. "Feels more like the kind of hard I want. Hard tied to somethin' real."

His throat worked. "So... what are you sayin'?" he asked, voice rough.

She took a breath, deep and clear and a little terrifying.

"I'm sayin' I don't want to go back to Denver the way I left it," she said. "I'm sayin' when I call my editor in a couple weeks, I'm not gonna be askin' about my old desk. I'm gonna be tellin' her... thank you for everything, but I'm not comin' back full-time. I'll freelance if she wants my stuff. I'll pitch stories I actually care about. But my... base? My life? I want that to be... here. Or somewhere like here. Which, honestly, at this point mostly means 'where you are.'"

It was out. Not a spur-of-the-moment pledge whispered in the dark, not a half-joke. A daylight decision, named and owned.

He stared at her as if he was afraid any sudden movement might make the words scatter.

"You're… sure?" he asked finally.

She thought about the blinking cursor back in Denver, about the nights she'd lain awake listening to sirens and her neighbors' arguments through thin walls. She thought about the way her notebook had filled here without her even trying some days.

She thought about his hand on her back this morning, the way it had felt like something that belonged.

"Yes," she said. "I am."

He laughed then, not a loud, boisterous sound, but a disbelieving, relieved exhale that turned into something like joy.

"Okay," he said, voice a little shaky. "Okay."

He stepped forward, closing the space between them entirely now. He framed her face with his hands, searching it as if trying to memorize every line.

"I want you here," he said, no qualifiers this time. "I want to wake up knowin' you're up on that hill or down in that kitchen or cussin' at Hank's toaster. I want you to write your books on this land. I want to be in the margins of them, even if nobody else ever knows."

Her eyes burned. "You already are," she said. "You and Hank both."

He smiled, thumb brushing away a tear that had slipped free.

"We'll figure the work part out," he said. "Money, schedule, all that. I'm not sayin' it'll be easy. This place is… a lot. But we'll… make room. For you. For your words. I won't let the ranch swallow you."

"I'll hold you to that," she said.

"Good," he said. "I want you to."

She rested her forehead against his chest, breathing him in.

In the distance, a hawk cried, a sharp sound that somehow didn't break the moment. The wind shifted through the trees, carrying the faintest smell of home, hay and dust and the promise of coffee in Hank's battered thermos.

After a long moment, she pulled back, wiping her cheeks with the heel of her hand.

"We should head down," she said, voice steadier. "Before Hank decides we froze to death and comes up here with a rescue party."

"Hank would give us forty-eight hours and then claim he got distracted by a crossword," Caleb said. "But yeah. Let's go."

They finished packing in a new kind of silence, not the brittle, waiting-for-the-other-shoe kind, but a thoughtful, full one. The kind that comes after decisions that will take time to ripple out.

On the ride down, Emma noticed everything more sharply.

The way the trail dipped and rose, the way the trees changed from tall pines to scrub oak to open pasture. The way the cabin came into view like a small punctuation mark on the hill, their hill now in a way that had more weight than ever.

As they crested the last rise before the barn, she felt a strange mix of emotions, anticipation, nervousness, a quiet excitement that sat low and warm in her belly.

This was where the decision would start to turn into actions. Calls. Emails. Talks with Hank. Maybe long-distance deals with her editor.

Daylight had a way of stripping away the romance of choices made under stars. She knew that. She'd seen enough mornings after to understand the difference between last night's vows and today's realities.

But as she rode behind Caleb, watching the easy way he sat the saddle, feeling the sun on her shoulders and the ache in her thighs, she realized she didn't feel like she was sobering up from some misguided impulse.

She felt… woke up. In a way she hadn't been when she'd driven up that gravel road months ago with her trunk full of city clothes and an overstuffed laptop bag.

Hank was on the porch when they rode into the yard, a mug in his hand, Gus at his feet. He shaded his eyes with one palm, taking in the sight of them, rumpled, tired, undeniably different in some way that went beyond the physical.

"Well," he called as they swung down from their horses, "the good news is you ain't dead. The bad news is I lost the bet with myself about whether you'd come back mad or happy."

"Which one did you bet on?" Emma asked, patting Bella's neck.

"Mad," Hank said cheerfully. "Experience told me that was safer odds. Glad to be wrong."

She laughed, glancing at Caleb. Their eyes met, a flicker of shared conspiracy. They didn't need to tell Hank everything. He'd read most of it anyway.

"How'd the fence post hold up?" Caleb asked, leading Raven toward the barn.

"Better than you," Hank retorted. "Post is standin'. You look like you got rolled down a hill by an enthusiastic elk."

"Sleepin' on the ground will do that," Caleb said.

Emma led Bella past them, pausing at the porch steps. Hank's gaze flicked between her and Caleb, settling briefly on the way she and the ranch looked together, as if measuring.

"Y'all talk?" he asked her quietly, sotto voce as Caleb disappeared around the corner of the barn.

"We did," she said. "A lot."

"And?" he prompted.

"And…" she took a breath, feeling the truth settle in her bones. "I think… I'm stayin'."

His eyebrows rose, but he didn't look surprised so much as… satisfied, like a man whose prediction had finally panned out.

"Yeah," he said. "Figured that was comin' down the line."

She huffed a laugh. "Did you," she said.

"Girl, like you doesn't learn how to muck stalls and bake biscuits that fast if she's plannin' on leavin'," he said. "Plus, you been lookin' at this place like somebody eyein' a house they want to buy. Not just rent."

Emotion tugged at her. "What if I'm… makin' a mistake?" she asked before she could stop herself. "What if I wake up one day and realize I shouldn't have left that job, that life, that… version?"

Hank looked out at the pasture for a moment, then back at her.

"You might," he said. "Can't lie to you and say you won't. You might have days where you miss the noise, miss seein' your name in print every morning. Might have days where the snow's six feet deep and you think, 'Lord, I was an idiot.' That's life. But let me ask you this: you got more days in Denver where you thought, 'I'm makin' it,' or more days where you thought, 'I'm barely survivin' this'?"

She didn't have to think long.

"Barely survivin'," she said.

"And here?" he asked.

More days where I'm happy, she thought. More days where the words come.

"More days where I feel… like myself," she said. "Whoever that is."

He nodded. "Trust that," he said. "Jobs can be replaced. Apartments can be swapped. You only get one you. If she feels more at home here, that's worth payin' attention to."

He took a sip of his coffee, then added, "Besides, if it all goes to hell, you can always write one hell of a book about the time you ran off to a ranch and fell for a stubborn fool."

She smiled, the knot of fear easing again.

"I might," she said. "Change the names, though. To protect the guilty."

"Good luck," he snorted. "Ain't nobody gonna believe there's more than one me."

Behind them, Caleb emerged from the barn, wiping his hands on a rag. He looked up at the porch, at Emma standing there with Hank, and something in his expression softened further, like seeing them together cemented something he'd let himself hope for on the hill.

He walked over, touching the brim of his hat in a mock salute.

"You two plottin' against me?" he asked.

"Always," Emma said. "Consider yourself outnumbered."

"Story of my life," he replied, but there was no complaint in it.

The sun climbed higher, burning off the last of the morning chill. Chores waited, water troughs to check, eggs to collect, dishes to wash. Calls would need to be made soon, to editors, to friends, to the versions of themselves that needed to be told the plan had changed.

None of it felt simple. None of it would be without bumps.

But as they moved into the day, Emma helping Hank in the kitchen, Caleb checking the herd, all three eventually ending up around the table with plates of eggs and toast, the choices made under the stars began to feel less like fragile ideas and more like the first steps of a life.

Daylight had a way of testing midnight promises. Emma, watching Caleb laugh at something Hank said, feeling the weight of her decision settle in, realized that for the first time in a long time, she wasn't waiting for waking reality to disappoint her dreams.

Instead, she had the quiet sense that she'd finally aligned the two.

Her happiest days had been here. Her most creative ones too. And now, with the sun high over High Meadow Ranch and the Colorado sky stretching wide above it all, she'd decided to give herself more of them.

Not as a vacation.

As a life.

Chapter Twenty-Three
Emma Stands Up

The decision to stay didn't change Emma's to-do list overnight, but it changed the way she moved through her tasks.

The next morning, she drove into Cottonwood Ridge with a mental checklist: mail a letter to her parents, pick up a few groceries, swing by the coffee shop for Wi-Fi and the latest email from her editor. Even the familiar creak of the truck door sounded different now, less like the borrowed vehicle of a temporary guest, more like the beat-up chariot of someone building a life.

She parked on Main, the August sun already bright on the hood, and stepped out into the lazy hum of a weekday in a small town. A couple of kids on bikes cruised past, one hand on the handlebars, the other clutching a Popsicle. Across the street, the florist was arranging a bucket of sunflowers in the window. Inside the hardware store, she could hear Gary telling someone, loudly, that the new shipment of fence staples was late and it was a conspiracy.

Normal, Emma thought, shutting the truck door with her hip. Hers, now, in a way that made her chest feel… good. Big.

She hit the post office first, sliding her letter through the slot, a handwritten note to her parents that said most of what her email would later, about staying, about the ranch, about the man who'd somehow become the center of her orbit. She wanted them to see her handwriting on something other than a Christmas card for once.

Then she walked down to the coffee shop.

The bell over the door chimed as she pushed it open. The familiar smell, espresso, pastry, and a hint of whatever scented candle the barista had burning, wrapped around her.

"Hey, Emma," called Lily from behind the counter. "Same as usual?"

"Yeah, thanks," Emma said, pulling a crumpled five from her pocket.

She took her drink, an iced coffee with too much milk and not enough sugar, just the way she liked it now, and claimed a small table near the back. The Wi-Fi connected on the second try. Her inbox greeted her with the usual mix: one email from her editor with the subject line "Checking in?", a couple of newsletters she never read, and a spammy note insisting she'd won a gift card to a store that didn't exist in Colorado.

She opened her editor's email.

Hope the summer's treating you well. Things are ramping up here, we've got a major corruption story breaking next month and we'd love to have you on the team if you're ready to come back. Can we hop on a call later this week to talk next steps?

Emma smiled, not with glee but with a calm she wouldn't have recognized a month ago. Before last night, this would have twisted her stomach into knots. Now, it felt... like an offer from a past life. An important one, deserving of respect, but not a command.

She thumbed out a quick reply on her phone to buy time:

Hey! Summer's been... eye-opening. I can do a call Friday afternoon? Want to talk about some changes on my end.

There. A small step. The big one, actually telling her editor she was quitting full-time, would come soon enough.

She put the phone facedown on the table, opened her notebook, and scribbled at the top of a clean page:

What does it mean to choose a smaller life on purpose?

The words felt heavy and right. Her hand moved almost of its own accord, filling the lines with questions, images: Hank on the porch. Caleb at the fence line. The way the sky here made her feel both tiny and held. The way spreadsheets and story budgets suddenly seemed, in comparison, like the wrong kind of important.

She was so lost in the flow that she didn't register the bell over the door again, didn't feel the subtle change in the room's temperature until a shadow fell across her table.

"Emma."

She looked up, pen still poised midway through a sentence.

Abby stood there, coffee cup in hand, heat already frizzing her hair at the edges. There was a tightness around her mouth, but her eyes were clear, not the pinched, defensive look Emma had seen the last few times.

For a second, something inside Emma tensed, that ready-for-impact reflex that came from years of bracing in newsroom conferences and at family dinners.

Then she remembered last night. Caleb's voice under the stars. Her own. The decision they'd made together, the one she'd just written down the edges of in her notebook.

Fear doesn't get to drive.

She exhaled slowly and sat back.

"Hey," she said. "Want to sit?"

Abby hesitated, caught off guard by the lack of visible flinch, then pulled out the chair across from her and sat down. She set her coffee on the table; fingers wrapped around it a little too tightly.

"I was hopin' I'd run into you," she said.

Emma's brows lifted. "Really?" she said. "Most people hope not to run into me before I've finished my second coffee."

Abby huffed a laugh, quick and thin. "You're funny," she said.

A flicker crossed Abby's face, something like regret or nostalgia, hard to parse. She took a sip of coffee, then set the cup down again with a small clink.

"Look," she said, leaning forward slightly. "I know… you and I didn't start off on the best foot. I was… goin' through some stuff. Seeing him again, seeing you… stirred it up."

"That's one way to put it," Emma said. She didn't add: you tried to scare me off. She didn't have to.

Abby pressed her lips together. "Right," she said. "Anyway. I just… I wanted to talk to you. Woman to woman. Before I leave."

"You're leaving," Emma repeated.

"Tomorrow," Abby said. "Headin' back to Denver for a bit, then maybe Arizona. My sister's got a place there. I don't… think I'll be back here for a while."

Something in Emma eased. The town would exhale too, she suspected.

"I hope it's good for you," Emma said, and meant it.

"Thanks," Abby said softly. Then her gaze sharpened, the old urgency surging back. "That's kinda why I wanted to talk. To make sure you… know what you're doin'."

Ah, Emma thought. There it is.

She closed her notebook slowly, sliding the pen into the spiral, and folded her hands on the table.

"What do you think I'm doin'?" she asked.

Abby studied her, as if trying to read something in the lines of her face. "Throwin' yourself into somethin' you don't fully understand," she said. "With someone you don't fully understand."

Emma arched an eyebrow. "You mean Caleb," she said. "The man I share a kitchen table with most nights. The one I spent last night camped under the stars with, talkin' about our trauma like it was a book club assignment."

Abby blinked, thrown for a second by the frankness.

"How… how serious is this?" she asked. "With you two?"

Emma could have deflected. Could have protected the fragile, new-solid thing between her and Caleb by wrapping it in privacy.

Instead, she found herself saying, calmly, "Serious enough that I'm talkin' about leavin' my job to stay on the ranch. Serious enough that we're layin' out our worst fears in front of each other instead of pretendin' they're not there. Serious enough that I don't really appreciate someone from his past tryin' to write our story for us."

Abby flinched, color rising in her cheeks.

"I'm not tryin' to write your story," she said quickly. "I just… don't want you to get blindsided like I did. He's… he's intense, Emma. He always has been. When he loves, it's…" She searched for a word. "Big. All-encompassin'."

She leaned forward, voice dropping.

"He'll smother you eventually," she said. "Ask me how I know."

There it was, the line she'd used before, polished by repetition. It hit the table between them like a gauntlet.

A week ago, it would have lodged in Emma's chest like a thorn, nagging at every quiet moment. It had. It had crawled into bed with her and whispered in her ear every time Caleb reminded her to text when she got into town or reached for her hand in a room full of people.

Now, though, it ran into something else first.

The conversation on the hill. His honesty. Her own.

Fear doesn't get to run the show.

Emma felt the old automatic response begin, doubt, the urge to scan her memory for evidence, the mental calculus of risk, and gently set it aside.

She took a sip of her coffee, buying herself one extra heartbeat.

"Okay," she said. "So, ask you how you know."

Abby frowned, clearly not expecting that. "I… just told you," she said, flustered. "We were engaged. He was overprotective, bossy, jealous. It got worse after his second deployment. I felt like I couldn't breathe. That's why I left."

"Right," Emma said. "You've told me your side. A few times now. But here's the thing, Abby: your experience is valid. It is. I'm not sayin' you didn't feel trapped. I'm not sayin' he didn't mess up. He did. He'll be the first to tell you that."

Abby huffed. "So, he's got you believin' he's the villain," she said, sarcasm edging in. "Great."

"No," Emma said evenly. "He's got me believin' he's human. That's different."

Abby opened her mouth, then shut it as Emma went on.

"He told me about how he was back then," Emma said. "Protective to the point of smothering, yeah. Tryin' to control every variable 'cause he'd seen what happens when you don't. Expectin' you to stay put because his world had shrunk to this town and this ranch and he couldn't imagine wantin' anything else. He knows now that wasn't fair. He doesn't excuse it. But he also doesn't pretend it means he's a monster."

"I never said monster," Abby muttered, but the word hung there anyway, implied.

"You've painted him as one, though," Emma said. Her tone stayed calm, but there was steel underneath. "To me. To yourself. Maybe to half this town. Every time you tell the story, you're the girl who escaped the controlling rancher. He's the guy with the hands around your throat. That might've been true for you then. I'm not here to argue how you felt."

She leaned in too, closing the distance, eyes steady on Abby's.

"But here's what I know from my side," she said. "I know Caleb now. Not the twenty-two-year-old who came home from war with his brain on fire and no tools. The man sitting at that kitchen table askin' Hank how not to screw this up. The one who checks himself every time he feels that old panic rise. The one who invited me up to that meadow last night not to… convince me to stay with some big romantic gesture, but to lay his fear out in front of me and let me decide if I still wanted in."

Abby swallowed, throat working.

Emma didn't stop.

"I know a man who worries, yeah," she said. "Who asks me to text when I get to town. Who reminds me about rattlesnakes and storms and not takin' the old logging road after dark. But I also know a man who, when I told him I might stay here and leave my job, didn't say 'good, you belong here with me.' He said, 'Only if it's what you want. Only if you won't resent me later.' He told me he'd rather hurt honest than keep me here on a lie. That's not control. That's love tryin' its damnedest not to tip into fear."

The coffee shop had gone quiet around them, or maybe that was just how it felt. For all Emma knew, Lily was still steaming milk and someone was still typing furiously on a laptop in the corner. But in the bubble of their table, it was just the two of them and the histories they'd been using as weapons.

Abby looked away first, jaw tight.

"He's good at soundin' noble," she said. "Always was."

Emma's laugh was soft but without much humor. "He is possibly the least polished person I've ever met," she said. "Half the time he puts his foot so far in his mouth I'm amazed he can still walk. Noble, sure. But that doesn't mean he's manipulative. It means he cares."

She laced her fingers together on the table to keep from jabbing them at the air.

"You left because you wanted something else," she said plainly. "Because this town and this ranch and this man weren't what you wanted then. You wanted cities and travel and… not being tied down. That's okay. Honestly. You had the right to want that and go get it."

Abby's eyes flashed, defensive. "And he had no right to be hurt, I guess," she said.

"That's not what I'm sayin'," Emma replied. "Of course, he had that right. But you keep tellin' the story like he was the only problem. Like if he'd just been less… him, you'd have stayed. Maybe. Maybe not. But you didn't leave just because of him. You left because this life wasn't your dream. You don't have to turn him into the villain to justify that."

Abby flinched as if the words had landed somewhere she didn't expect anyone to see.

"I," she started, then stopped. Her fingers tightened around her coffee cup until the cardboard crinkled.

Emma softened her tone, just slightly.

"I get it," she said quietly. "It's easier, sometimes, to frame ourselves as the one who escaped somethin' bad than as the one who just… chose somethin' different and hurt someone in the process. I've done it. With jobs, with people. 'They were toxic' is easier to say than 'we wanted different things and I didn't know how to own my part.'"

Abby's eyes shimmered briefly, then cleared, the tears retreating out of sheer stubbornness.

"I didn't come here to get psychoanalyzed," she said, but there was less bite in it than Emma expected.

"No," Emma agreed. "You came here to warn me. Again. To plant that seed that he's gonna smother me eventually. And I'm tellin' you… I'm not takin' it. Not this time."

She straightened, shoulders squaring.

"I'm not a placeholder," she said. "I'm not the next girl in some cautionary tale you tell over coffee. I know who I'm choosing. I know what he's been through. I know the worst and the best of him that he's willing to show so far. And I'm makin' my decision based on that, not on the shadow version you carry around."

Abby stared at her, something like incredulity in her expression.

"He ever lose his temper with you?" she asked suddenly. "Ever slam a door, raise his voice, tell you he knows what's best?"

Emma thought about their fight in the cabin kitchen. The way his voice had sharpened, the way he'd walked out instead of staying and making it uglier. The way he'd come back.

"He's gotten mad," she said. "We've fought. But he's never… scared me. Not once. Even when we were both hurtin'. He walks away when he's close to sayin' somethin' he can't un-say. He comes back when he's ready to listen. And when I told him his fear was makin' choices for us, he actually… heard me. And did somethin' about it."

She held Abby's gaze.

"He is not perfect," she said. "But he's not your father either. And he's not the man you were with. He's the man he is now. And I am not you at twenty-two. I am me, now. With my eyes open."

Silence stretched. Emma could hear the hiss of the espresso machine again, the gentle clink of a spoon against a mug somewhere behind her. The world came humming back, threading around them.

Abby swallowed, looking down at the swirl of foam in her cup.

"You sound… sure," she said finally.

"I am," Emma said. The surprise was that it was true. Saying it out loud made it settle even more.

Abby sat back, shoulders sagging a little. Some of the sharpness drained out of her face, leaving something more vulnerable.

"I wasn't," she said quietly. "Back then. I wasn't sure of anything except that I was… suffocatin'. Maybe you're right. Maybe it wasn't just him. Maybe my own fear was… shovin' his into boxes it didn't always fit."

She gave a short, humorless laugh.

"I told myself leaving would fix everything," she said. "That I'd go find myself in big cities and small apartments. That I'd get to be the person I couldn't be here. Turns out you can drag your cages with you."

She picked at the edge of the cardboard sleeve around her cup.

"I drank a lot," she admitted. "Got into some situations… worse than anything Caleb ever did to me. Dated men who were actually controlling, not just overprotective. Men who didn't listen, didn't apologize, didn't walk away instead of slamming doors. I still managed to tell myself it was all better than 'bein' stuck' with him." She shook her head. "Fear does weird things to your sense of scale."

Emma stayed quiet, letting her talk. It was the first time she'd heard Abby's story without the bitter coating, the first time the younger woman underneath the defenses peeked through.

"When I saw him with you," Abby went on, voice thin, "I thought, 'She doesn't know. She doesn't see what he can turn into.' It didn't occur to me that… maybe he'd changed. That maybe I had too, and not all for the better."

She looked up again, eyes bright.

"It's hard," she said, "to look at someone and realize they became the version you always hoped they'd be… just not with you."

The ache in the admission was so naked that Emma's anger softened another notch. It didn't disappear, she couldn't pretend the woman sitting across from her hadn't tried, repeatedly, to wedge herself into their business, but it evolved, making room for a strange sort of compassion.

"I get that," Emma said quietly. "I do. That… sucks. No other word for it."

Abby's mouth twitched. "You cuss prettier than I do," she said.

"But here's the line," Emma continued. "You don't get to punish him, or me, for bein' that person now. You don't get to keep walking into our lives like you're the ghost of girlfriends past, droppin' warnings and waitin' for us to fall into the same script."

She leaned in one more time, voice steady.

"You left," she said. "You had your reasons. You own them or you don't, that's between you and your mirror. But you don't get to keep standin' in the doorway. You're either in or you're out, and from everything you've said, you're out. So stop inserting yourself into our story like you're an inevitable chapter. You're not."

The words landed with a quiet thud. Not shouted, not public, but firm.

Abby's eyes filled properly now, a couple of tears actually escaping before she could stop them. She wiped them away with the back of her hand, annoyed at herself.

"I didn't mean to…" She trailed off, then barked a laugh at her own attempted excuse. "Who am I kiddin'? I did mean to. I wanted to shake you. Make you… scared enough to run before you got hurt."

"And in the process, you were hurtin' both of us," Emma said. "Me with your stories. Him by keepin' him in this box you put him in years ago."

Abby winced. "I know," she said. "I... know. I think a part of me wanted to prove I was right. That leavin' was the only smart move. If you stayed and it worked... what did that say about my decision?"

"That you made the best choice you could with who you were then," Emma said. "And that I'm makin' a different choice because I'm someone else now. That's all. It doesn't erase what you went through. It doesn't rewrite your past. It just... adds another chapter that doesn't belong to you."

Abby let out a shaky breath.

"You sound like a writer," she said.

"I am one," Emma replied. "It's my job to know whose story is whose."

They sat in silence for a beat, the weight of the conversation settling.

"So... what now?" Abby asked quietly. "You want me to... never come back? Never say his name again?"

"I'm not in charge of your itinerary," Emma said dryly. "Go wherever you want. Say whatever you want when my back's turned. It's a free country. But if you come back here, if you see us in town, I'd appreciate it if you'd treat us like... people livin' our lives, not characters in your past. Nod, say hi, talk about the weather. Not about who you think Caleb is or will be. He gets to show me that himself."

She held Abby's gaze a moment longer.

"And if you can't do that," she added calmly, "then yeah. Please stay out of our way. Let us be."

The quiet that followed wasn't empty. It was full of all the things that might be said and weren't.

Finally, Abby nodded, a small, jerky motion.

"Okay," she said. "I can... do that. Or I can try, anyway."

She took a breath, then reached for her coffee.

"For what it's worth," she said, fingers twisting the sleeve again, "I do think he's lucky. That you're the one here with him now."

Emma's throat tightened, unexpected emotion catching.

"I'm lucky too," she said softly. "He's… a lot. And he's good. Both."

Abby smiled, the expression lopsided and a little watery.

"Yeah," she said. "He always was."

She stood, chair scraping gently against the floor.

"I should go," she said. "Finish packin'. Say goodbye to my folks. Try not to burn any more bridges than I already have."

She hesitated, then extended her hand across the table.

"Thank you," she said, voice rough. "For bein' straight with me. For… not sugarcoatin' it to spare my feelin's."

Emma looked at the offered hand for half a second, then took it. Abby's grip was firmer than she expected.

"Take care of yourself, Abby," she said. "Really. Go find the life that fits you. And let us have ours."

Abby nodded once, eyes shining again.

"Yeah," she said. "I think it's about time."

She let go and walked toward the door. Emma watched her go, watched the way the coffee shop's light fell across her as she stepped outside into the bright street. For a second, Abby paused on the sidewalk, shoulders rising and falling on a deep breath, then turned left toward the part of town where her parents' house sat.

Emma stared at the closed door for a long moment, aware of her own heartbeat, of the slight tremble in her hands. It wasn't the shaking of fear, though. It was adrenaline's aftertaste, the body's way of saying, that mattered.

"Everything okay over here?" Lily's voice drifted from behind the counter, casual, but Emma could see the way the barista's eyes flicked with interest. Small towns didn't need CCTV; they had curiosity.

"Yeah," Emma said, managing a smile. "Just… resolvin' some… ongoing character arcs."

"Cool," Lily said, as if that made complete sense. "Need a refill?"

"I'm good," Emma said. "I think I've got enough fuel to write three chapters and confront my editor."

She reopened her notebook, staring at the sentence she'd written before Abby walked in.

What does it mean to choose a smaller life on purpose?

She added, beneath it, in firm handwriting:

It means choosin' your own story, not lettin' someone else's fear write it for you.

By the time she drove back to High Meadow Ranch, the initial rush of the encounter had mellowed into something steadier. She could already hear how the story would trickle through town, in altered forms, coffee shop talk had a way of mutating.

She half expected Hank to be on the porch with popcorn.

Instead, when she pulled up, he was at the woodpile, splitting logs with a rhythm that suggested he was either working off some energy or had gotten into a fight with the weather forecast.

She climbed out of the truck, dust puffing around her boots, and walked over.

"Hey," she called. "Need a hand?"

"Always," he said, not pausing the swing of the axe. "How was town? Anybody get arrested for loiterin' outside the bakery again?"

"Not that I saw," she said. "But I did have coffee with Abby."

The axe thunked into the block harder than necessary. Hank straightened slowly, wiping sweat from his brow with the back of his wrist.

"That so," he said. "Voluntary coffee, or the kind where you run into somebody and they trap you in a booth?"

"A little bit of both," Emma said. "She… wanted to talk. One last time, I think."

Hank grunted. "And?" he asked, voice carefully neutral.

"And I told her to stop insertin' herself into our business," Emma said, letting the satisfaction of that sentence sit on her tongue for a second. "Told her Caleb's not the monster her fear turned him into. That she left because she wanted somethin' else, and that doesn't make him bad. Or me stupid."

Hank's eyebrows climbed.

"You did, huh," he said.

"Yeah," she said. "In slightly more… polite words. But I… pushed back. For real this time. Didn't just absorb it and go ask you to translate."

A slow, genuine smile spread across Hank's face. It made him look ten years younger.

"Well I'll be damned," he said. "You went and got your spine outta storage."

Emma laughed. "I've always had a spine," she protested.

"Oh, I know," Hank said. "But there's a difference between havin' one and usin' it when folks try to poke holes in your life. A lot of people just… duck. You didn't duck."

He set the axe aside, leaning on the handle like a cane.

"How'd she take it?" he asked.

"Not great at first," Emma said. "Then… better. I think she heard more than she wanted to. Might actually leave town with a little more… self-awareness than she came in with."

Hank snorted. "Miracles do happen," he said. "I'll listen for thunder."

He sobered a hair, studying her.

"You, okay?" he asked. "I know that kind o' thing can shake loose more than you expect."

Emma considered the question, scanning herself.

"I'm… better than okay," she said slowly. "It was… cathartic. I said what I needed to say. For me. For him. Felt like… closing a door that's been bangin' on its hinges for weeks."

Hank nodded, satisfaction deepening.

"Good," he said. "About damn time somebody told that girl her story ain't the only one in circulation."

He bent to pick up another piece of wood, then paused.

"Caleb know yet?" he asked.

"Not yet," Emma said. "He's still out checkin' the north pasture, I think. I wanted to… tell you first, for some reason."

He smiled, a little softer.

"I'm honored," he said. "And I'll do my level best not to embellish when the coffee shop version of the tale gets to me. Though from what I can tell, you handled it fine without any Greek chorus."

Emma rolled her eyes. "Please don't turn it into a ballad," she said.

"No promises," he said. "But I'll keep the rhymes tasteful."

She shook her head, but her heart felt… full. Seen. Supported.

"Thanks, Hank," she said quietly.

"For what?" he asked.

"For… backin' me," she said. "For not makin' this about you and Caleb being right or Abby being wrong. For lettin' me… figure out how to stand up for him and for myself."

He waved a hand, as if swatting away a fly. "I just made coffee and told stories," he said. "You did the rest. You're the one stayin'. You two are the ones buildin' this thing. Hell, I'm just happy I get a front-row seat. And pies, if you're takin' requests."

She laughed. "We'll see," she said. "You're still on probation after that comment about my biscuits last week."

"They were more weapon than pastry," he countered.

"That's because you overbaked them when I turned my back," she shot back.

He grinned, unoffended. "Details," he said, picking up the axe again.

Caleb came back late that afternoon, dust on his jeans and a smear of grease on his forearm from coaxing a reluctant gate hinge back into cooperation. He spotted Emma on the cabin porch, laptop closed beside her, notebook open in her lap.

Just the sight of her there, at the place where hill met sky, sent a rush of something warm through him.

You're sure?

Yes. I am.

Those words had been emerging from the background of his thoughts all day, like a song that kept looping. He still didn't quite know what he'd done to deserve them. Hank would say "not a damn thing" and tell him to just be grateful.

He scrubbed his hands on a rag as he walked up, trying to get rid of the worst of the grease. She looked up at the sound of his boots on the steps and smiled in a way that hit him somewhere under the ribs.

"Hey," she said.

"Hey yourself," he replied. "How's the small-town Internet circus today?"

"Full of lions and clowns in equal measure," she said. "I emailed my editor. Told her we needed to talk. That Friday would be good."

He whistled low. "Big step," he said.

"Yeah," she said. "Felt… big. But… right."

He sat on the chair opposite her, stretching his legs out, feeling the ache of the day settle in.

"Hank said you had coffee with Abby," he said after a moment.

"Of course he did," Emma said. "Gossip travels faster than Wi-Fi around here."

"Depends on the wind," he said. "You, okay?"

She nodded, more certain than he'd ever seen her on that question. "I am," she said. "Do you… want to know what happened?"

"Yes," he said simply. "If you want to tell me."

She took a breath, then told him, about Abby approaching her at the coffee shop, about the same old warning words and how this time, they'd hit something different and bounced off. She told him how she'd laid out her perspective: that he wasn't the monster of someone else's memory; that Abby had left in part because she wanted a different life; that it was time for her to stop standing in the doorway of something she'd chosen to walk out of.

She didn't quote herself verbatim, some things belonged only to those two women at that table, but she gave him the heart of it.

As she spoke, his expression moved through a whole storm front of emotions: shame when she told him what Abby had said again, anger on Emma's behalf, then stunned awe as she described calmly, point by point, how she'd defended him.

"And then I told her," Emma finished, "that she doesn't get to keep insertin' herself into our story like she's an inevitable chapter. That it's ours now. Not hers. And that if she can't treat us like two people livin' our lives instead of… props in her narrative, she needs to stay out of the way."

She shrugged. "It was… a lot," she said. "But it needed sayin'."

For a long moment, Caleb didn't speak.

He looked at her like he was seeing her again for the first time, the woman who'd arrived with city shoes and a cautious smile, and the one sitting here now, boots dusty, eyes steady.

"You… said all that," he said quietly.

"Yeah," she said. "I mean, probably with more 'ums' and hand-wavin' than I'm ownin' up to, but… yeah."

He blew out a breath, looking away for a second as if he needed to recalibrate.

"Damn," he said.

She tilted her head. "Is that a good 'damn' or a 'what have you done' 'damn'?" she asked.

He laughed, a little raw. "Good," he said. "Very good. Just… wow."

He leaned forward, elbows on his knees, hands dangling.

"She… hurt me," he said finally. "Back then. I let her. I hurt her too. We left a lot o' broken glass behind. But I never… asked anybody to pick up a broom for me. I made my bed. I just figured I'd… lie in it alone, I guess."

He looked up at her again, eyes bright in the late afternoon light.

"And then you," he said, "walked into that coffee shop and told her to stop draggin' my name through the mud on her way outta town. Told her the man I am now is… worth stayin' for. That's…" He shook his head, searching for words and coming up empty for a moment. "I don't think… anyone's ever done that for me. Not like that. Not… all in."

Her chest tightened, something like indignation on his behalf flaring.

"Well, someone should have," she said. "You deserved it."

He swallowed, visibly moved.

"Thank you," he said quietly. "For standin' up for me. For us. You didn't… have to."

"Yes, I did," she said. "That's what… this is. Being in something together. We stand up for each other when the other person's not there to do it themselves."

He considered that, then nodded, as if tucking it away as a working definition.

"I know it wasn't just about me," he added. "It was about you claimin' your space. Your choice. I'm… proud of you. If that doesn't sound too condescendin'."

She smiled, warmth spreading through her.

"From you, I'll allow it," she said. "You're at least qualified to know how hard it is to tell someone to back off."

He chuckled. "Yeah," he said. "Hank's been tellin' me that for years. 'Say what you mean, boy. People ain't mind readers.'"

He sat back, gaze drifting out across the pasture for a moment, then back to her.

"Does this mean," he asked cautiously, "that if someone else in town starts runnin' their mouth about me, I can send my fierce writer girlfriend to handle it?"

She snorted. "No," she said. "It means if someone in town starts runnin' their mouth about us, we handle it together. But I reserve the right to… take point occasionally."

He grinned, the expression softening all the sharp edges of his face.

"Deal," he said.

They sat in companionable quiet for a bit, watching the light change on the hills. The day was slipping toward evening; the sky was already tinting toward gold.

"So," Emma said eventually, half-teasing. "You wanna know the best part?"

"There's more?" he asked. "Lay it on me."

"She admitted," Emma said, savoring it, "that you've changed. That you're calmer now. Steadier. That… seeing you with me made her realize you became the man she always wanted, but she didn't stick around long enough to see it."

His face flickered with conflicting emotions, gratification, sadness, something like pity.

"That's…" He blew out a breath. "That's tough. For her."

"Yeah," Emma said. "It is. And… I actually feel bad about that. A little. But I'm not gonna… apologize for the fact that I get the version of you who went through all that and came out the other side. Just like you don't apologize that you get the version of me who's finally ready to stop runnin'."

He looked at her, something open and almost reverent in his expression.

"Good," he said. "I don't want apologies for that. I just… want to make sure I use what I learned. That I don't waste the pain. Yours or mine. Or hers."

Emma nodded. "Me too," she said.

He reached across the small gap between their chairs, palm up. She placed her hand in his without thinking, their fingers lacing together easily now.

"Feels like we closed somethin' today," he said quietly.

"Yeah," she agreed. "We did."

The door Abby had been standing in had finally swung shut. Not slammed, not locked, but closed. What lay beyond it for her was her business now. What lay on this side, for Emma, for Caleb, was theirs.

As the sun dipped lower and the sky over High Meadow Ranch turned the color of ripe peaches, Emma felt the day settle into her like a new page closing over old ink.

Fear hadn't disappeared. Doubt hadn't gone extinct. But they weren't at the mic anymore.

Her voice was. His was. Hank's, sometimes, chiming in from the wings.

For the first time in a long time, Emma felt not just like a character in someone else's chaos, but like a woman who had stepped fully into her own story, and decided, out loud and in public, who got to share the page.

Caleb's hand tightened around hers, warm and solid.

She squeezed back, eyes on the wide, clear Colorado sky above them, and thought, with a steadiness that surprised her:

This is mine. This is ours. And no one gets to narrate it for us.

Chapter Twenty-Four
Career Crossroads

The call came on a Thursday afternoon, when the sky over High Meadow Ranch had settled into that washed-out blue that meant the real heat was still on its way.

Emma was at the cabin table, laptop open, cursor blinking at a paragraph about a fictional rancher who sounded suspiciously like the real one mending a gate down the hill. A half-empty mug of coffee sat within reach. Two flies performed an irritating duet against the screen.

Her phone buzzed beside the notebook. Denver area code.

Her stomach did that old familiar flip.

She stared at the name, MARTINEZ, J., for one beat, then another. For just long enough to notice that the girl she'd been three months ago would have snatched it up by the second ring, apology ready for not answering on the first.

The woman she was now let it vibrate once more, then exhaled and swiped.

"Hey, Julia," she said, aiming for steady.

"Emma," her editor's voice came, brisk and warm and layered with newsroom background noise, phones ringing, someone calling for a copy editor, the faint clatter of a dropped stapler. "You got a minute?"

"Yeah," Emma said, closing the laptop slowly. "What's up?"

"I know you said Friday," Julia went on, "but something landed today and I didn't want to sit on it. How's your mountain retreat treating you, first of all? You coming back enlightened and tan?"

Emma glanced toward the window. Dust motes hung in shafts of bright light; a hawk wheeled beyond the hill.

"Enlightened, maybe," she said. "Tan, not so much. I think that requires actual beach time."

"Fair," Julia said. "Listen, I'll cut to it. We've been keeping your chair warm, metaphorically speaking, but the paper's… evolving. Budget tightening, reshuffling. You know the song. But we just got a lead on something big. A corruption story that could be a career-maker. Front page, weeks of coverage, maybe a podcast spin-off if the audio people don't eat each other alive." She gave a short laugh. "It's… exactly the kind of thing you're stupidly good at."

Emma felt her pulse pick up, the old instinctive thrill flickering like static.

"Give me the broad strokes," she said, because the reporter in her wasn't dead; she'd just been napping.

"City contracts, shady shell companies, a councilman who's a little too good at funneling taxpayer money into pet projects," Julia said. "There's an anonymous source with documents, but they'll only talk to someone off the record at first. Someone they feel they can trust. I… thought of you. They read your series on the housing authority last year. They specifically asked if you were still at the paper."

Emma's grip on the phone tightened. The housing series had almost broken her in half, hours of interviews, endless spreadsheets, late nights trying to turn bureaucratic rot into something readers could care about. It had also been one of the pieces of work she was proudest of.

"A source asked for me," she repeated, feeling that old mix of responsibility and ego.

"Yeah," Julia said. "Look, I'm going to be straight with you. We want you back, Emma. Not just as a body in a chair, but… on this. If you come back at the end of the summer, we slot you onto this story as lead. You'd have support, data people, an extra reporter for grunt work. I'm pretty sure we could also justify moving you up to senior staff when reviews roll around. Title bump, pay bump, more say in what you cover. It's… the thing we always talked about. Remember? 'Give me a big story with teeth and the runway to do it right.' This is that."

Prestige. Front page. Promotion. Words that had once felt like stars on a map she'd been plotting toward since college.

A part of her, deep down, straightened like a soldier at attention.

"What's the timeline?" she asked, voice carefully neutral.

"We'd need you back by the first week of September," Julia said. "Your unpaid leave runs through the end of August, right? You'd have the first couple of weeks ramping up, meeting with the source, digging into records. We'd aim to start rolling out stories in October. The series would be… I don't know. Six parts at least. Maybe more if the rabbit hole goes as deep as I think."

"And if I don't come back?" Emma asked, keeping her tone light, as if the answer didn't have the power to rearrange her life.

There was a tiny pause on the line. In the background, someone laughed too loudly, a sound cut off as a door closed.

"Then we'll find someone else," Julia said, and Emma heard the very real regret under the professionalism. "We'll make it work. The story doesn't hinge on any one reporter. You know how it is."

"But?" Emma prompted.

"But it'll be… different," Julia admitted. "There are maybe three people in this building I'd trust to handle something this sticky without either getting us sued into oblivion or boring readers to death. You're at the top of that list. Selfishly, I want you. The paper needs someone like you. And…" Her voice softened a notch. "I think you would eat this story alive in the best possible way. It's the kind of thing you'd look back on in ten years and say, 'That mattered.'"

The words landed in a place that still remembered what it felt like to walk into the newsroom with a fresh scoop and see heads turn, to have readers send emails saying, Thank you for telling this.

"I need to think about it," Emma said, the only honest response possible.

"Of course," Julia said quickly. "I'm not expecting you to decide on a dime. I just… needed to put it on your radar. The offer stands: front page series, lead byline, serious consideration for a promotion if you perform like you always have. Plus, selfishly, I miss having you here to complain about the coffee with."

Emma smiled despite the weight in her chest.

"I miss parts of it too," she said.

"So… take a day," Julia said. "Walk around your mountain or whatever zen writer thing you're doing. Call me tomorrow, we'll talk it through. No pressure. Well, some pressure. But the good kind."

"Is there a good kind?" Emma asked, half joking.

"Only when it comes with a pay raise," Julia said.

They said goodbye with the easy familiarity of women who'd been through breaking news and budget meetings together. When the call ended, the cabin felt unnaturally quiet. The clock on the wall ticked too loudly. Outside, the wind moved through the grass with a sound like someone shushing.

Emma set the phone on the table, screen down, and just sat.

Her heart was thumping too hard for how still she was.

Front page. Senior staff. Lead on a corruption scandal that could actually do something, change policy, oust crooked officials, make life better for people who didn't have the time or energy to dig through records themselves.

She could see it: her byline in bold above the fold. Her parents buying multiple copies. Professors in the journalism department back at her university pointing to it in lectures about investigative work. Younger reporters watching her stride through the newsroom with equal parts admiration and envy.

She could also see herself in that dingy office, under yellowing fluorescent lights, nursing a stress headache and her third cup of burnt coffee at midnight while she combed through campaign finance reports for the fifth time.

She stood abruptly, the chair scraping. The cabin walls felt too close.

The dog, napping in a patch of shade under the porch, looked up as she stepped outside. Daisy flicked her tail once, then decided the situation was not biscuit-related and put her head back down.

Emma shoved her hands into her pockets and started walking.

From his spot near the hay barn, Caleb glanced up as Emma passed below the cabin path, stride quick, jaw set. She didn't see him; she was looking straight ahead, in that way she did when the words in her head were louder than anything outside.

He knew that walk by now. The one that said something had gotten under her skin, and she needed distance and motion to shake it out.

His first instinct twitched, follow, ask, fix.

He tightened his grip on the pitchfork instead, hearing Hank's voice in the back of his mind.

Let her tell you in her time, boy. Not every storm needs you chasin' it with a bucket.

He watched her for another moment, making sure there was no immediate danger in her path. Just the familiar trail curling toward the creek and the fence line.

Then he bent back over the hay, muscles working on autopilot, heart tuned to the knowledge that when she looped back, she'd either seek him out or sit on that porch with a notebook. Either way, he'd be here.

Emma walked.

Down the hill, across the yard, through the gate Hank had fixed last week. Past the paddock where a couple of curious heifers lifted their heads to watch her go, chewing in unhurried rhythm.

By the time she reached the fence line that bordered the grazing pasture from the scrubby hillside beyond, her thoughts had settled into a frantic shuffle, tripping over each other.

Front page series.

Promotion.

What about the book?

What about Caleb?

What about this?

She slipped between two fence posts at a spot where the wire dipped, feet already knowing the path to the creek. The air cooled a few degrees as the trees closed over her, the light shifting green-gold.

The creek was low this time of year, more rocks than water, trickling over stones with the stubborn persistence of something that refused to stop even when reduced to a thread.

She dropped down onto her usual flat rock, the one that fit the curve of her backside as if shaped for her, and pulled out her notebook.

For a minute she just stared at the blank page, hand not yet ready to move. Her mind churned.

She thought of the newsroom, the battered desks, the perpetual buzz of scanners and phones, the television mounted in the corner tuned to some cable news station with the sound off, a crawl of headlines whispering non-stop at the bottom. She thought of walking into that space early, staying late, feeding herself on adrenaline and deadline pressure.

She thought of the feeling of a story clicking into place, that moment when disparate threads wove into a narrative that could make sense to readers. She remembered the rush of seeing her name at the top of page A1, her article squinting up from newsstands across the city.

She owed a lot to that world. To Julia. To the older reporters who'd taken her under their wing and taught her tricks they'd learned the hard way.

She also remembered the nights she'd fallen into bed too wired to sleep, brain buzzing with details of tragedies that weren't hers and yet clung as if they were.

She remembered the couple who'd shown her their flooded apartment, waterlines like bruises on the walls, and how she'd gone home afterward and stared at her own landlord-color-beige paint, feeling guilty for every comfort.

She remembered the woman who'd thanked her, tears in her eyes, for the housing series, and how Emma had cried in the bathroom at work afterward, exhausted, empty, and completely unsure of how to hold the weight of having mattered.

She flipped to a fresh page and wrote, at the top:

WHAT DO I ACTUALLY WANT?

Then below it, she made two columns and labeled them in block letters:

DENVER / PAPER

and

RANCH / HERE

In the first column, her hand flew.

CITY APARTMENT

PAYCHECK (REGULAR)

HEALTH INSURANCE (NOT NOTHING)

FRONT-PAGE SERIES

PROMOTION (TITLE, MONEY, RESPECT)

"REAL" JOURNALIST CRED

COLLEAGUES I LIKE (MOST DAYS)

STORIES THAT MATTER

STORIES THAT HURT

LATE NIGHTS

BURNOUT

SIRENS

COMMUTE

FANCY COFFEE (SOMETIMES)

HAPPY HOURS (SMALL TALK, NETWORKING)

LONELY IN A CROWD

BEING "ON" ALL THE TIME

In the second column:

SUNRISES

STARS (ALL OF THEM)

QUIET

COWS (LOUD, BUT STILL)

PHYSICAL WORK

MY BODY TIRED, NOT JUST MY BRAIN

DINNERS WITH CALEB & HANK

REAL CONVERSATIONS
MY OWN BOOK(S)
FREELANCE? (???)
LESS MONEY (PROBABLY)
UNPREDICTABLE, BUT… MINE
WRITING ABOUT WHAT I CARE ABOUT
NO BYLINE ABOVE THE FOLD (MAYBE)
LOCAL PAPER? BLOG?
POSSIBLE ISOLATION (WINTERS!)
COMMUNITY (DIFFERENT KIND)
BEING SEEN, NOT JUST READ

She sat back, looking at the uneven lists. It wasn't a perfect pros-and-cons chart. Some things belonged in both columns. Some were unknowable.

She tapped the pen against the paper.

It would be easy to frame this as noble sacrifice: look at me, giving up my big-city career to live a simple life on a ranch with my man. The story wrote itself if she let it: rustic selflessness, romantic, possibly irritating to anyone who knew the actual intersection of manure and frostbite.

But that wasn't what this was. Not if she was honest.

She wasn't running away from the paper because it was hard. Hard work hadn't scared her since she'd been twelve and watching her mother come home from double shifts.

She was running toward something. The way her brain felt here. The way her words felt when they weren't wrapped around car crashes and scandals.

And yet… the idea of walking away from the paper entirely still made something in her recoil. Journalism wasn't just a job; it was a way she'd learned to see the world. She didn't want to turn that off like a light.

Do I really have to choose between being a "real journalist" and being… this version of myself?

She thought of Julia's voice on the phone. Of the anonymous source who'd specifically asked for her byline.

It meant something that her work had reached someone that way. That they'd trusted her enough to tie their risky story to her competence.

Did staying here mean abandoning them? Abandoning everyone who might benefit from that series? Or could she… still contribute, just differently? As a freelancer? As an occasional investigator instead of a full-time storm chaser?

She scribbled near the bottom of the page:

WHAT IF IT'S NOT ALL OR NOTHING?

The idea felt… radical. Her industry didn't like nuance; you were either in the trenches or you'd sold out. That was the narrative she'd swallowed for years.

But sitting here, with a grass stain on her jeans and creek water seeping slowly into her boot where she'd misjudged a rock, she found herself questioning it.

Who decided that writing had to look one way? That being serious meant living tired and half-broken because you were Doing Important Things?

She thought of the novel she'd been pecking away at. Of the paragraphs that had flowed in the last few days, almost without effort, as she poured her own questions and this land into fictional veins.

The joy in that felt different from the grim satisfaction of pinning down a crooked bureaucrat. Not better, not worse, just… different. Softer. Kind. But no less necessary, maybe, for a world that needed both accountability and hope.

She wrote, in larger letters now:

I DON'T HAVE TO STOP WRITING. I JUST HAVE TO STOP LETTING THE JOB OWN ME.

The truth of that nearly knocked the breath from her.

The job had become her identity so quietly. Somewhere between the first byline and the first front-page story, "Emma Taylor, human" had become "Emma Taylor, reporter." The latter had swallowed the former whole on some days.

Here, she'd felt parts of herself uncurl that had nothing to do with deadlines: the girl who liked baking, even if Hank roasted her for her first attempts; the woman who could spend an hour watching light move across a field and not feel guilty for "wasting" time

Could she carry any of that back into the paper? Or would that environment demand the old Emma, all sharp edges and perpetual motion?

She pictured herself saying no to Julia's offer. Hanging up. Staying here. Freelancing articles on her own terms, maybe writing for smaller outlets that cared less about clicks and more about depth. Working on her book in the mornings, helping with ranch chores in the afternoons. Building a life with Caleb that wasn't measured in promotions but in seasons.

Fear flared, about money, about credibility, about how her peers would perceive her. She forced herself to sit with it.

Then she pictured saying yes. Going back. Putting on her City Emma armor, stepping into that newsroom and letting it swallow her time, her attention, her bandwidth. Trying to be the partner she wanted to be to Caleb while also chasing a corrupt councilman across months of grueling work.

What would give? The ranch? The relationship? Her health?

She wrote two simple sentences on the page:

If I say yes to Julia, what am I saying no to?

If I say no to Julia, what am I saying yes to?

Answers spilled out beneath each, messier now, less list and more confession.

YES TO JULIA = NO to slow mornings with Caleb & Hank, to having energy for my own stories, to learning the rhythms of this land not as a guest but as a co-steward. Possibly NO to a version of myself who isn't always "on."

NO TO JULIA = YES to uncertainty. YES to building my own structure instead of inheriting one. YES to trusting that my work matters even if it doesn't come with a header attached. YES to this man, this place, this quieter, deeper life.

Tears pricked unexpectedly at the corners of her eyes. Not from sadness exactly, but from the enormity of the choice, and from the relief of realizing there was, in fact, a choice.

No one was forcing her back to Denver. No one was chaining her to this ranch. She was an adult woman with agency. That was the terrifying, freeing part.

She wiped her cheek with the back of her wrist, sniffed once, and leaned back on her hands, letting her gaze go soft over the water.

In her mind, the omniscient narrator she sometimes imagined, neutral, amused, watching her from some vantage point above the cottonwoods, did its own comparing.

In one possible future, Emma walked into the Denver newsroom wearing a blazer she'd dug out of her closet, hair pulled back, press badge swinging. She shook hands, took the file from Julia, and plunged in. Her days filled with calls, document requests, interviews in coffee shops and parking garages. She stayed late, ate at her desk, felt that white-hot purpose sing in her veins when the first story ran and the comment section burned with outrage and gratitude.

She rode that wave to a promotion, a bigger expense account, more clout in editorial meetings. Her byline became known in certain circles. Journalism awards committees learned how to spell her last name on the first try.

Back at the ranch, if she even still had time to come back, everything had to be scheduled within an inch of its life. Weekends carved out months in advance. Phone calls with Caleb squeezed between stakeouts. Hank's birthday missed because a source had finally agreed to talk.

She might manage it. People did. Women did. They juggled careers and relationships and families and hobbies like circus performers. But the image of herself in that version of life looked… thinner. Sharper. A little haunted around the eyes.

In the other future, Emma stayed.

She called Julia and said no to the series, explained that she'd be happy to contribute as a freelancer, offer investigative work on a slower timeline, maybe collaborate with staffers on pieces when she had bandwidth, but that she wasn't coming back to full-time under fluorescent lights.

Her days here would be simpler in some ways, harder in others. Money would be tighter. Health insurance would be an irritating puzzle. Winters would bite. She'd fight with Caleb about ridiculous things like whether it was worth fixing the old tractor or finally scrapping it.

She'd also wake up most mornings knowing she'd write something that mattered to her, whether anyone else ever saw it. She'd walk the fence lines as a woman who lived here, not just one who rented a cabin for a summer. She'd sit at this creek and not feel like she was stealing time from "real work," because this would be part of the work now, filling the well.

She'd still be a journalist, in a way. Once a reporter, always looking at the world with that tilt. She could pitch stories about rural life, about water rights, about the realities of small-town economies. She could write essays, op-eds, longform pieces for magazines that didn't care where she sat while she filed, only that she met deadlines and told the truth.

And she'd write fiction that took all of it, the big-city chaos, the quiet ranch mornings, the messy, brave love she'd found, and turned it into stories that might land in the hearts of women like her, sitting in apartments or on porches, trying to figure their lives out.

Both paths mattered. Both could do good.

Which one made her feel more like herself?

She closed her eyes, took a deep breath of creekside air, wet stone, damp earth, a hint of cow from somewhere upwind.

When she opened them, the answer felt… less murky.

She didn't want to stop being a journalist.

She just didn't want being a journalist to be the only thing she was.

She didn't want every story she told to be about what was broken. She wanted some to be about what people built anyway.

She didn't want her worth to hinge on whether the front page had her name on it this week.

She wanted a life where her book and her relationship and her morning coffee all mattered as much as her byline.

The job had owned her for so long because she'd let it. She'd fed it every spare ounce of energy, every weekend, every bit of her identity. It wasn't a monster; it was just a hungry thing. If she went back, it would happily devour her again if she let it.

She had to decide, if she returned to that world at all, what the terms would be.

Probably not full-time, then. Not right away. Not when everything in her softened at the thought of staying here and stiffened at the thought of moving back into that apartment.

She flipped to the back of the notebook and wrote, in big letters that took up almost the whole page:

I AM NOT "JUST" MY JOB. I AM A WRITER. I AM A PARTNER. I AM A WOMAN WHO GETS TO CHOOSE.

The words looked messy and too earnest, but they were hers.

The sun had shifted by the time she pushed herself up from the rock, knees creaking in protest. Her stomach growled, reminding her that she hadn't eaten since breakfast.

She tucked the notebook under her arm and started back toward the ranch, feeling like she'd walked a much longer distance than the loop to the creek and back.

On the way, she traced the fence with her fingers, the rough wood grounding. A part of her thought about what Hank would say, probably something about not bein' a mule for someone else's wagon. Another part thought about Julia, the lines at the corners of her eyes deepening after each crisis, and felt a pang of guilt at the idea of saying no.

She'd call tomorrow, just like she'd promised. She'd tell Julia the truth, not the polished version, but the real one. That she was grateful. That the offer meant more than the editor might know. That if they wanted her brain and her pen, they could have them… just not full-time, not at the cost of this life.

The decision wasn't going to make everyone happy. It might not always make her happy. There would be days she'd miss the rush. Days she'd wonder what that front-page series might have been under her name.

But sitting here, now, with dust on her boots and the smell of the ranch drifting on the breeze, she realized that no choice came without some grief. Saying yes to one thing meant saying no to something else. There was no clean, consequence-free path.

She just had to pick the one whose tradeoffs she could live with.

The one that, when she imagined herself five, ten years down the line, didn't make her shoulders tense in advance.

By the time she saw the cabin again, perched on its little hill like a punctuation mark, the knot in her chest had loosened.

She spotted Caleb near the barn, talking with Hank beside a stack of feed bags. They both looked up as she approached.

"How's the creek?" Caleb called, shading his eyes.

"Still babblin'," she said. "Unlike me, hopefully."

Hank eyed her notebook. "You do your homework?" he asked.

"Yeah," she said, patting it. "Got an essay and a half in here."

"You gonna share with the class?" he asked.

"Soon," she said. "I need to… call my editor first. Tell her I won't be takin' the big shiny thing she dangled."

Caleb's brows rose, but he didn't rush in with questions. He just nodded, a quiet acceptance that she'd fill him in when she was ready.

"That sounds like a conversation that requires at least one biscuit," Hank said. "Conveniently, I made some that are only half suitable as building materials."

"Progress," Emma said, smiling.

As she followed them toward the house, notebook under her arm, she felt the two paths she'd been weighing all day settle into place behind her not as ghosts but as roads not taken.

The path she was on now might not lead to awards or panel invitations. It might never land her name in some hall of fame for investigative journalists.

But it would lead to other things: pages filled under this sky, dinners at that table, love that grew in the spaces between chores and chapters.

She didn't know yet exactly what her writing career would look like from here. Freelance, fiction, the occasional big story that let her use those old muscles, it was all still fluid.

What she did know, as she stepped into the cool of the kitchen and the smell of Hank's biscuits hit her, was this:

She was done letting a job, any job, define her.

She was done measuring her worth in headlines.

From now on, she'd write because it was who she was, not because someone in a corner office had circled a topic on a whiteboard.

And she'd build this life, messy, beautiful, undesigned by any HR department, with the man who'd once thought his only option was to carry everything alone and the old friend who told stories like they were scripture.

Career crossroads, she thought, as she set her notebook on the table and reached for a biscuit. Today, she'd taken a step down the unpaved road.

The paper would go on without her full-time. The story in Denver would find another byline.

But the story here, the one under the Colorado sky, on this ranch, with these people, could only be written by her.

And she was finally ready to give it the pages it deserved.

Chapter Twenty-Five
The Choice

Emma made the call in the late afternoon, when the heat had finally broken and the light spilling through the cabin windows had gone soft and honey-colored.

She stood by the counter instead of sitting, cell phone pressed to her ear, notebook open beside the sink. The page with her scribbled lists stared up at her like witnesses.

Julia picked up on the second ring.

"Tell me the mountains haven't swallowed you whole," she said by way of greeting.

Emma smiled, nerves tightening in her chest. "Not yet," she said. "But they're makin' a good case."

"Good," Julia replied. "So. You've done your walking meditation or whatever it was. What's the verdict? Ready to come back and save this place from mediocrity?"

Emma glanced out the window. From here she could see the barn roof, a corner of the corral, and beyond that the smear of distant hills. Caleb's truck was a small dark shape near the equipment shed. Somewhere out of sight, Hank's laugh carried faintly on the breeze.

She took a breath.

"I'm not coming back full-time," she said.

Silence hummed down the line. The kind that said more than any exclamation could.

"Okay," Julia said after a beat. Her voice was level, but the disappointment threaded through was unmistakable. "Can I ask why, or is this one of those 'it's not you, it's me' situations?"

"It is me," Emma said, because she owed her that. "It's… my life. This place. I thought a lot about the series, about the promotion, about what it would mean to say yes. And it would be… huge. I know that. But I also realized that if I step back into that newsroom the way I was, it's gonna own me again. I don't know how to do that job halfway. And I'm not willing to lose… what I've built here to it."

"You've built something in three months," Julia said. It wasn't contemptuous, just incredulous.

"Yeah," Emma said. "Apparently you can lay a lot of foundation in that time if you take a hard look at yourself. I've started a book that feels more like me than anything I've written in years. I've… found a community. A… person." Her throat tightened, but she pushed through. "And more than that, I just… don't want to live the way I was livin' before. It was burning me out, and I kept tellin' myself it was noble. That if I wasn't exhausted and half broken, I wasn't doing it right."

Julia let out a slow breath.

"I didn't know it was that bad," she said quietly.

"I didn't either," Emma admitted. "I thought it was just… what the job required. But living out here, working differently, made me realize how much of myself I'd handed over without noticing."

On the other end of the line, paper rustled, as if Julia was rearranging something on her desk just to have something to do with her hands.

"So, this is you… what?" she asked. "Retiring to a ranch to write novels?"

Emma huffed a small laugh. "You make it sound like I'm eighty with a trust fund," she said. "No. I'm still gonna work. I'd like to freelance. For you, if you'll have me. Longer pieces, maybe some investigative stuff, just… on a timeline that doesn't eat my whole life. I can pitch stories from out here, water rights, rural politics, all the stuff city readers pretend doesn't exist until it hits their tap."

Silence again, but different this time. Thoughtful.

"Remote investigative work is… a nightmare," Julia said. "You know that."

"I do," Emma said. "But maybe it doesn't have to be full-blown six-part series. Maybe it's one big story a year, with me embedded in it from here. Or maybe it's essays. Profiles. I don't know yet. I just know I can't keep doing the grind. Not and be… the person I want to be."

There it was, the naked truth. Not the speech she would have written for herself, but the one that felt honest in her mouth.

Julia was quiet for a long beat.

"You're really not coming back," she said, as if tasting the sentence.

"Not to the old job," Emma said. "Not full-time. I'm… stayin' out here. On the ranch. Working on my book. Figuring out how to make the freelance thing viable so I can afford to keep my coffee addiction."

"You know the gig economy is a vulture," Julia said. "It loves young idealists with bylines."

"I know," Emma said, smiling faintly. "But if I'm gonna get picked at, I want it to be on my terms."

A soft snort. "God, you're stubborn," Julia said. "You always were."

"Coming from you, I'm takin' that as a compliment," Emma replied.

"It is," Julia said. The resignation in her tone shifted, warmed by something like reluctant respect. "Look, I'm not going to lie to you. Professionally, this kinda sucks for me. For the paper. You're good, Emma. Losing you as staff is a hit."

"I know," Emma whispered.

"But personally…" Julia continued, and Emma heard the chair creak as if she'd leaned back, "I get it. More than you think. I never had the guts to step off the treadmill. My life is… fine. Good, even. But there are days I wonder what it would've looked like if I'd left when everything in me wanted to. I don't think you'll regret… listening to that voice. Not long-term."

Emotion tightened Emma's throat unexpectedly. "Thank you," she said, the words unsteady.

"So," Julia said briskly, clearing her throat. "Let's talk logistics. I'm not letting you disappear entirely. You want to freelance? Great. I'll fight for you as a stringer. We can put together a contract. Pitch me your best ideas from cow country. If you ever get the itch to chase a big fish and can commit to the timeline, call me. We'll build something around it. No promises on budget, but I'll try."

Relief washed over Emma, warm and dizzying. She hadn't realized how much she'd braced for a door to slam.

"That sounds… fair," she said. "More than fair."

"And for the record," Julia added, "if you ever change your mind and want to come back full-time… the door's not locked. It might not be the same desk, the same beat, but I'd rather have you with us than against us."

Against us. The old framing: in the trenches or out in the civilian world, never quite both.

Maybe she'd be something in between now.

"I appreciate that," Emma said. "Really. And if you need someone to write a scathing op-ed about city council members misusing town funds, you know where to find me."

"Yeah, on a horse with spotty reception," Julia said dryly. "All right, cowgirl. Go live your rustic dreams. I'll email you some paperwork and a list of stories I'd love pitches on if you're bored between branding sessions or whatever."

"Branding season's over," Emma said automatically, then laughed at herself. "Look at me, bein' all agriculturally timely."

"God help us all," Julia replied. Her voice softened once more. "I'm proud of you, you know. Not for leaving us, that part I'm still mad about, but for… choosing something that feels right for you. It's… not easy. Especially when you're good at the thing you're walking away from."

Tears stung again, but they were easier this time. "Thank you," Emma said.

"Now hang up before I start getting sentimental and the interns think I've gone soft," Julia said. "Email's coming. Don't ghost me."

"Wouldn't dream of it," Emma replied.

They ended the call.

Emma stood in the quiet cabin, phone still in hand, and felt like someone had just cut a heavy tether she hadn't realized was wrapped around her ribs. For a second, she wobbled, weightless.

Then her feet found the floor again. The cabin walls, the table, the mug ring on the counter, all anchored her to this new reality.

She had done it.

She had just quit her job.

Not with a slammed door or a dramatic speech in the newsroom, but with a calm, honest conversation and an agreement to find a new way to work.

It felt less like burning a bridge and more like… choosing a different road that still occasionally crossed the old one.

Her pulse began to slow. In the distance, she heard the faint rumble of the tractor shutting off. The day was tipping toward evening.

Time to tell the men whose lives this choice would intersect with most.

Dinner that night was simple: leftover roast chicken reimagined as sandwiches, a big bowl of Hank's potato salad, slices of watermelon sweating on a plate.

The kitchen of the ranch house was warm and lived-in, the overhead light casting a cozy glow over the scuffed table. The dog sprawled underfoot, occasionally thumping his tail when a scrap fell "by accident."

Caleb sat at his usual spot, chair tipped back just enough to make Hank grumble about broken legs. He'd showered the day's dust off; his dark hair still held the faint dampness of having been pushed back with wet hands. A bruise was blooming on his forearm where a gate latch had gotten the better of him.

Emma took the seat across from him, notebook conspicuously present beside her plate.

Hank hovered by the counter for a moment, watching the two of them with the practiced eye of a man who could smell a moment coming before the participants admitted to it.

"You two look like you're either about to get married or break up," he said. "Should I eat in the other room or sit down with popcorn?"

Emma laughed, a little too loudly. "Neither," she said. "Well. Definitely not break up. And marriage is… not on tonight's agenda."

Caleb's eyes flicked to hers at the word, then back down to his sandwich. If his pulse jumped, he didn't show it.

Hank plopped into his chair, grumbling theatrically as his knees bent. "All right then," he said. "Mystery option number three. Hit me."

They ate for a few minutes in relative quiet, the clink of forks and murmur of small talk filling the edges. How the north pasture was drying faster than expected. How Lily at the coffee shop had switched to a new pastry supplier and everyone was in an uproar. How the forecast threatened an early storm next week.

Emma chewed mechanically, the words she needed to say bouncing around her mouth with the food. Her appetite was there, but her focus wasn't; she had to catch herself before she took a bite of sandwich without swallowing the last.

Halfway through her plate, she set her fork down. Her heart thudded once, hard, then settled into a fast drum.

"Okay," she said. "I have news."

Both heads turned toward her. Caleb's brows drew together, alert. Hank's gaze sharpened but stayed relaxed, like a man watching a rodeo rider sit deep in the saddle.

"Did the coffee shop finally get rid of that blueberry scone abomination?" Hank asked.

"No," Emma said. "Though we should start a petition. This is… bigger."

She glanced at Caleb, took in the way his hand tightened slightly around his glass, the way his jaw worked as if bracing.

"I talked to my editor today," she said. "About… the offer she mentioned. The big series. The promotion."

Caleb's throat bobbed. "Yeah?" he asked. "What'd she say?"

"It was legit," Emma said. "Front-page series. Lead byline. Solid shot at a senior staff title. The whole… dream package my twenty-two-year-old self would've tattooed on her forehead."

"And?" Hank prompted, eyes twinkling.

Emma slid her notebook toward the center of the table like an exhibit.

"And I told her no," she said.

Silence fell. Not shocked, more like the small, stunned pause after a loud noise.

Caleb blinked. "No," he repeated.

"No," Emma said. "To the full-time job. To going back in September and climbing that ladder. I told her I'm stayin' here. That I want to freelance instead. That I want to… write my book and build a life that isn't… tethered to that newsroom."

She kept her gaze steady, though her heart was racing hard enough she could feel it in her fingertips.

Caleb looked at her as if he'd misheard. Or as if his ears were trying to reconcile her words with the file, he'd kept on her in his head: ambitious, driven, city-girl who measured success in column inches.

"You… quit," he said slowly. "Your job. That job."

"Yes," she said. There was a moment's wobble on the word, then it settled. "I did."

His chair thumped back onto all four legs. He leaned forward, forearms braced on his thighs, like a man grounding himself.

"What did she say?" he asked.

"That she was disappointed. That it sucks for the paper," Emma said. "And that she gets it. That she'll bring me on as a freelancer if I want. That if I ever decide to go back full-time, the door's not locked, even if it won't be the exact same role."

The information seemed to land in stages. Relief flickered across both men's faces at the notion that she hadn't blown the bridge entirely.

"And… you're… okay with that?" Caleb asked. "With… stepping away? With not… being there for this big story?"

He was treading carefully, Emma could tell. Wanting to be supportive without putting his thumb on the scale.

"I'm more than okay," she said. "I'm… at peace with it. Which is not a thing I say lightly. I spent all day walking and writing and thinking it through. I'm not… reacting. I'm choosing."

Hank swallowed his bite, setting his fork down with exaggerated ceremony.

"Well," he said. "That's one hell of a thing."

Emma laughed, tension easing a notch.

"So," Hank went on, folding his hands on the table like a judge. "Walk us through it, counselor. What does this look like, practically? You stayin' up in that cabin for the next fifty years?"

She smiled. "I mean, eventually I'd like to have consistent hot water and a closet that's not a single pole," she said. "So… probably not. But for now, yeah. I want to stay in the cabin long-term. At least through the year. Give myself space to finish the first draft of the novel, get the freelance stuff sorted."

She glanced around the kitchen, the worn cabinets, the dented fridge covered in ancient magnets, the table with its constellation of knife nicks.

"And then…" she added, feeling her face heat slightly, "if y'all can stand me, maybe… move into the house. Or build a small place nearby. Somethin' that says 'I live here' instead of 'I'm a long-term guest.'"

Caleb's hand, resting on the table, curled into a fist. She saw his knuckles go white; saw the effort he made to unclench them again.

"You… want to live here," he said. "Really live here. Not just… summer in, winter out."

"Yes," she said. The simplicity of the answer surprised even her. "I thought I wanted… a break. Turns out I wanted… a different life. And this is the one I want to try building."

He studied her, eyes searching for any crack that might hint at a hidden "but."

"You're sure," he said quietly. Not a demand; a safeguard.

"I'm sure," she replied just as quietly. "I know what I'm saying no to. I know what I'm saying yes to. I'm not… givin' up my writing. I'm not giving up the chance to do work that matters. I'm just… changing the terms. Letting my work serve my life instead of the other way around."

Caleb's gaze dropped to the table, then back up. There was a jumble of things in his eyes: shock, relief, fear, gratitude so intense it almost looked like pain.

"You don't… owe me this," he said. "You know that, right? You don't owe this ranch. Or Hank." He flicked a look at the older man. "You could've said yes to that job, lived that life, and I would've… figured out how to be okay with it. Hurting, but okay. I don't want you to… wake up in five years and look at me like I'm the reason you're not where you're supposed to be."

Emma reached across the table and laid her hand over his. His skin was warm, calloused, familiar.

"You're not the reason I'm not goin' back, Caleb," she said. "You're one of the reasons I want to stay. That's different. Even if… whatever this is between us went sideways tomorrow, which I really hope it doesn't, this would still be a life I'd want. Maybe not on this exact ranch, not in this exact kitchen. But this kind of life. This pace. This… balance."

She squeezed his fingers once.

"I'm not making this choice for you," she said. "I'm makin' it for me. You just… happen to be one of the very best parts of the life I'm choosing."

Hank made a small, approving noise, like a man tasting a well-seasoned stew.

"That right there," he said, "oughta be printed on wedding invitations. 'I'm not here out of obligation, I'm here 'cause I damn well want to be.'"

Caleb's mouth quirked despite the emotion tight in his throat.

"Never thought I'd be the kind of man someone chose over a front page," he said slowly. "Feels like I oughta send that newspaper a thank you note for bein' such a pain in the ass they made you question your life choices."

Emma laughed. "They did plenty of good too," she said. "I'm not leavin' mad. I'm leavin'… grateful for what they gave me and clear-eyed about what they cost."

He shook his head slightly, as if still adjusting to the shape of this reality.

"I'm… scared for you," he admitted. "A little. Freelancin' is… unstable. The ranch is… a money pit half the time. You're leavin' a steady paycheck in a world where… steady is hard to come by."

"I know," she said. "I'm scared too. I'd be an idiot if I wasn't. But… I'd also be miserable if I went back just because it was safe. It's not the kind of safe that… makes me feel whole. It's the kind that keeps you busy enough you don't notice you're shrinking."

She sat back, letting her hand slide from his but keeping her gaze locked to his.

"Fear's gonna be there either way," she said. "If I stay, I'm scared about money, about whether I'm actually a good enough writer to make this work on my own. If I go, I'm scared about losin' myself again. I just… picked the fear I can live with."

Hank leaned back, chair creaking.

"Well," he said. "That's about the clearest explanation I've heard in a decade."

He pushed his plate back, wiped his mouth with the back of his hand, and nodded to himself as if concluding a private calculation.

"Hold on," he said, and hauled himself to his feet.

He shuffled to the cabinet above the stove and pulled down an old bottle of whiskey, the glass amber with age and dust. He blew off the top, squinting at the label as if to make sure it hadn't turned into vinegar while his back was turned.

"This," he said, carrying it back to the table, "was supposed to stay sealed till Caleb did somethin' truly stupid or truly brave. I figured it'd be the former. Glad to be proven wrong."

He fetched three mismatched glasses from the cupboard, set them down with ceremony, and poured a finger into each. The smell of oak and time drifted up.

"I'm not much of a speechmaker," Hank said, picking up his glass. "Talk plenty, sure, but most of it's about weather and cows. Tonight, though…" He looked between them, the amused lines on his face deepened by something softer. "Tonight, calls for a few words."

Emma and Caleb each took their glasses. The dog watched hopefully, as if whiskey might magically become meat if he stared hard enough.

Hank lifted his drink.

"To brave choices and stubborn hearts," he said. "To a girl smart enough to walk away from what was killin' her soft, and a boy dumb enough to think he was safer alone. To the fact that somehow, the Good Lord and pure dumb luck landed you both at this table at the same time. May you keep choosin' each other even when it's hard. May you keep choosin' yourselves in the process. And may this ranch not fall to pieces while you're busy figurin' it out."

Emma laughed through the sting in her eyes. Caleb's mouth twitched into a grin.

"Cheers," Hank finished, clinking his glass against theirs.

Emma lifted hers, the liquid catching the kitchen light.

"To brave choices and stubborn hearts," she echoed.

Caleb's voice was low but clear. "To… not runnin'," he added. "Not anymore."

They drank.

The whiskey burned its way down her throat, hot and sharp, then spread out in her chest like a small, controlled fire. It felt like how this moment deserved to feel: a little painful, a little exhilarating, undeniably alive.

Caleb winced at the burn, then let out a small, surprised hum. "That's... not bad," he said.

"Only took thirty years to mellow," Hank replied. "Hope the same's true for you."

They laughed, the tension that had strung the room tight loosening into something warmer.

Conversation drifted back to practicalities then, as it always did.

"How's the freelance thing actually work?" Caleb asked. "They just send you money every time you write somethin' nasty about some politician?"

"More or less," Emma said. "I pitch ideas. They either say, 'Yes, please, expose this terrible thing,' or 'No one wants to read three thousand words about rural zoning laws.' Then we argue, compromise, negotiate rates. It's like... herding cats with bank accounts."

"And the book?" Hank asked. "You got a plan for that, or you just tappin' away till your fingers fall off?"

"Finish the draft by winter," Emma said. "Let it rest while we survive the first snow. Revise in the spring. Start querying agents after that. Best case, someone falls in love with it and wants to help me get it out into the world. Worst case, I put it out myself. Either way, it'll exist. And I'll move on to the next."

Caleb absorbed this, nodding slowly.

"And in the meantime," he said, "there's fences to fix, calves to check, water lines to monitor. Plenty of work if you find yourself missin' deadlines."

"I plan to split my time," she said. "Morning's writing, afternoons helpin' on the ranch. Or vice versa, dependin' on the season. We can experiment. See what works. I'm not… expectin' you to carry me. I'll pull my weight."

"I know you will," he said. Pride warmed the words. "You already do."

Hank made a face. "If you two start complimentin' each other any harder, I'm gonna have to go sit on the porch till I stop feelin' single," he said.

Emma grinned. "You know you love it," she said.

"Maybe," he admitted. "Reminds me I didn't screw up raisin' that one too bad." He jerked his chin toward Caleb.

Caleb rolled his eyes, but the tips of his ears went pink.

They finished eating with more ease after that. Emma told them about Julia's reaction in more detail. Hank shared an exaggerated story about the time he'd almost left the ranch for a "real job" in town and lasted three weeks before the walls closed in. Caleb listened, occasionally slicing in with his own dry commentary that made Emma's stomach flip in that now-familiar way.

After dishes were done, Emma washing, Caleb drying, Hank supervising from his chair like a foreman, they drifted toward the front porch, drawn by the cooling air.

The sky was clear, the first stars already pricking through the deepening blue. Crickets sang in the tall grass. Somewhere off to the east, a coyote sounded a lonely bark.

They sat, Hank in his regular chair, Caleb on the top step, Emma beside him. Their shoulders touched, casual and intentional all at once.

For a long moment they just watched the sky.

"Feels different," Caleb said eventually, breaking the quiet.

"What does?" Emma asked.

"Tonight," he said. "Us. This." He gestured vaguely at the yard, the house, the stretch of dark land beyond. "Like… it's more solid. Less… fragile. Like if I reach for it, it's not gonna vanish."

Emma glanced at him, taking in the profile she'd come to know so well: the strong nose, the scar that nicked his eyebrow, the way his mouth bent when he was thinking hard.

"That's 'cause it is more solid," she said. "We made decisions today. Not just… feelin's. That matters."

He nodded, the simple affirmation of someone who'd built fences and knew the difference between wire just laid out and wire stapled tight.

Hank shifted, the old porch board under his chair groaning sympathetically.

"You know," he said, "when your daddy was dyin', Caleb, he made me promise I'd keep an eye on you. Make sure you didn't disappear into yourself out here. I told him I'd try. Didn't do such a hot job at first. You got real good at hidin' in plain sight."

Caleb's jaw flexed, but he didn't look away.

"Then this one shows up," Hank went on, pointing his chin toward Emma. "City girl with worn-out eyes and a notebook she treated like a shield. And I thought, 'Well now. Maybe the good Lord's decidin' to multitask. Answer two prayers with one rental agreement.'"

Emma huffed a laugh. "You prayed for me?" she asked skeptically.

"I prayed for somethin' to crack both your skulls open," Hank said. "I ain't picky about the method."

He leaned back, the chair creaking again.

"You quit your job, girl," he said, a note of wonder still in his voice. "That's no small thing. Takes courage to walk away from somethin' everyone else thinks you should want. Takes even more to do it for a life most folks don't understand the appeal of."

"I understand it," Emma said softly. "That's enough."

"Damn right it is," Hank said.

Caleb reached for her hand then, in the open, in front of Hank, under the emerging stars. He didn't make a show of it; he just laced their fingers together and rested them on his knee.

His palm was rough, his grip sure.

"You know I'm gonna spend the next year lookin' for ways to make this easier on you," he said. "Tryin' to fix things before they can go wrong, tryin' to keep you from regrettin' this choice. That's just… who I am."

"I know," she said. "And I'm gonna spend the next year reminding you I'm not made of glass. That I signed up for the hard parts too. That you don't have to… manage my happiness like another head of cattle."

He snorted. "Romantic," he said.

"You love it," she replied.

He squeezed her hand. "I do," he said quietly. "I love… a lot."

The word hung there, heavy and light all at once.

He hadn't said I love you. Not yet. Neither had she. The L-word hovered around them like a bird waiting for the right wind.

Tonight, didn't need it, Emma realized. They'd done something that, in some ways, was even harder. They'd chosen.

Chairs, jobs, cabins, futures.

Hank yawned theatrically. "All right, you two love-struck squirrels," he said, slapping his knees as he stood. "Old man needs his beauty sleep. Y'all can sit out here and count constellations or whatever it is young folks do these days, but keep it PG on my porch."

Emma laughed. "We'll try," she said.

Hank shuffled inside, the screen door creaking shut behind him.

The night seemed to expand in his absence. Crickets grew louder. Stars multiplied.

Caleb turned his head, looking at her fully now.

"You, okay?" he asked, for what felt like the hundredth time that day, but each time had landed a little differently.

She thought about the job she'd left, the book she was writing, the man holding her hand. The risk. The fear. The quiet, steady rightness of sitting here with all of it.

"Yeah," she said. "I am."

He studied her for a moment, then nodded, as if filing that away in some internal log he kept.

"Ask me again tomorrow, though," she added wryly. "I'll probably still be okay, just… more aware of how much my bank account hates me."

"We'll figure it out," he said. "Between the three of us, we've survived war, drought, and Hank's cookin'. We can survive freelancin' and ranch budgets."

"Hey," she said. "Hank's cookin' is solid these days."

"That's 'cause you keep rescuing his recipes," he replied.

They fell into an easy quiet again, shoulders touching, fingers entwined.

Above them, the Colorado sky spread wide and indifferent, full of stars that had watched countless people make choices on nights not so different from this one. Some had chosen safety. Some had chosen adventure. Some had chosen love. Some had chosen themselves, for the first time.

Emma tilted her head back, letting the view fill her.

"You know," she said softly, "if somebody'd told me a year ago that I'd be sittin' on a porch in a town called Cottonwood Ridge, holdin' hands with a rancher and feelin' at peace about quittin' my job, I'd have assumed they'd mixed up my future with somebody else's."

"Yeah," Caleb said. "If somebody'd told me I'd be sittin' on this porch not alone, I'd have assumed they'd had too much of Hank's whiskey."

"And yet," she said.

"And yet," he echoed.

He turned his hand under hers, so their palms aligned completely, fingers interlaced like they'd been made to fit.

"Thank you," he said quietly.

"For what?" she asked.

"For choosin' this," he said. "For choosin' me. For choosin' you. For not lettin' fear or obligation write your story."

Emotion swelled again, but it felt less like a wave threatening to drown her and more like a tide lifting her up.

"You're welcome," she said. "Now you just have to keep bein' worth it."

He smiled, small and sure. "I plan to," he said.

The porch creaked beneath them, the night hummed, the ranch breathed.

Inside, in the kitchen they'd just left, three glasses sat on the table, a smear of whiskey clinging to each, catching the faint light from the stove like tiny, abandoned suns.

Brave choices and stubborn hearts, Hank had said.

Emma thought of the notebook on her bedside table up in the cabin, the one filled with scribbles about paths and lives and that sentence in big, messy letters:

I am not "just" my job.

Tonight, in this house, with these people, under this sky, she'd proved it.

Tomorrow, and the day after, and all the days to come, she'd live it.

Chapter Twenty-Six
Building a Shared Life

The days after the choice didn't arrive with trumpets or confetti. They came the way days always did on High Meadow Ranch: with the sun nudging over the ridge, the dogs stretching on the porch, and the to-do list already half-written by weather and livestock.

The difference now was that Emma moved through them as someone rooted, not visiting.

She started with the mornings.

For the first week, she experimented, waking before dawn one day to write before chores, sleeping a little later the next and trying to compose sentences with hay bits still stuck in her hair. By the end of that week, she found her rhythm.

She set an alarm for five-thirty. The sky at that hour was a soft, uncertain gray, as if the world hadn't quite decided to commit to day yet. She'd shuffle to the kitchen of the cabin, start coffee, and stand at the window watching the barn emerge from the dark like some old animal lifting its head.

She gave herself one cup of coffee and ten minutes to scroll aimlessly on her phone, check emails, glance at headlines, remind herself the rest of the world still existed. Then the phone went face-down on the counter, and she sat at her makeshift desk with the second cup and her laptop.

From six to eight, she wrote.

Sometimes it was easy, the words unspooling, scenes from her novel dropping into place as if they'd just been waiting for her to show up. Other mornings it was like pulling teeth. On those days, she gave herself permission to write badly, to pour out awkward dialogue and half-baked descriptions. The rule was simple: fingers moving, no self-loathing until after eight.

By the time the sun broke fully over the hill and the cabin filled with light, she'd usually have 1,000 words. Sometimes more, sometimes less.

She kept a tally in the back of her notebook: date, word count, small notes about what she'd worked on.

After that came the physical shift: trade writer's brain for ranch hands.

She'd close the laptop, stretch until her spine popped, then pull on jeans, boots, and whatever shirt she didn't mind reeking of manure by noon. On the mornings she knew they'd be working near the east pasture; she'd braid her hair tight so it wouldn't snag on low branches.

At eight-thirty, right on cue, Caleb's truck would rumble into view below the cabin. He pretended he just happened to be driving by on his way to whatever the day demanded. They both knew better.

Some mornings he'd honk once, lazy. Others, if he needed an extra set of hands right away, he'd text:

Bring gloves. And that stubborn streak.

She'd grab both.

Caleb adjusted slowly, quietly, the way he did everything. There was no grand speech about integrating her into the operation. He just... started making room.

He no longer rattled off the day's tasks as if they were his alone. Instead, he'd lean against the truck, arms folded, and say, "Thinkin' we move the heifers to the southern pasture after we check the water line. You up for helpin' with the gate?" Or, "We gotta check the back fence for weak spots. I'd like your eyes on it too, two people see more than one."

He taught her more advanced tasks in small increments.

One day, he handed her the keys to the battered ATV and said, "You drive this section. Just don't outrun my horse. Brakes are... more a suggestion than a guarantee."

She'd laughed, heart thudding, and eased the machine along the ridge road while he rode parallel, calling out points where the fence dipped or posts leaned. The wind had whipped her hair free of its braid, dust painting her cheeks, but she'd felt more alive than she had behind any steering wheel in Denver.

Another day, he showed her how to read the irrigation ditches, how to tell, by color and speed, whether they were flowing right or needed clearing.

"See how that one's kind of sluggish?" he said, squatting by a muddy bank. "Means somethin's cloggin' upstream. Branch, rock, somebody's lost boot."

"You're kidding," she said. "People lose boots in irrigation ditches?"

"People lose everything in irrigation ditches," he said solemnly. "If we ever get bored, we'll start a museum."

He handed her the shovel, stepped back, and let her dig for the obstruction. By the time she'd freed the branch wedged under the culvert, her arms ached and her jeans were streaked brown up to mid-thigh, but the water ran clearer, faster.

"Good eye," he said, and something in his tone told her it wasn't just about the ditch.

He asked her opinion more, too, not just on pretty things like where to plant the wildflowers she'd bought in town, but on actual operations.

"You've got a better sense of story than I do," he said once, frowning at a flyer on the table for the county fair. "If we sponsor a thing, you think folks around here would care more about a ranch logo on the 4-H stall or on the rodeo program?"

She studied the flyer, then the calendar.

"Where's your heart?" she asked.

"With the kids," he said without hesitation. "They work hard. And the fair's about them, really."

"Then do the stall," she said. "It'll mean more to the families. People'll see your name when they're takin' pictures, not glancin' at the program for two seconds."

He nodded, trusting that without question. "Stall it is," he said, jotting a note.

Sometimes the adjustments were even smaller, almost invisible gestures that said more than words.

He moved an extra hook onto the back porch for her jacket. Cleared a shelf in the mudroom for her boots. Installed a second hook in the tack room so her borrowed saddle and bridle didn't have to share space with whatever spare gear had been there before.

He started saying "we" more than "I" when talking about the ranch.

"We need to get hay ordered before prices spike," he'd say. "We should think about reseeding that patch by the west fence come spring."

The first time she heard it, the word snagged in her chest like a pleasantly hooked fish.

We.

Her writing and ranch work found a sort of seesaw balance.

There were days when she honored her two-hour writing block and then lost herself so completely in moving cattle or repairing fencing that she didn't think about fictional people again until her head hit the pillow.

There were other days when a scene dug its claws into her so deeply, she'd scribble notes on the back of feed invoices while Caleb and Hank argued good-naturedly about whether the new vet was too soft on them.

"You're listenin'?" Caleb would say, catching her faraway look as they bounced in the truck over a rut.

"Yeah," she'd reply, a little guilty. "Just also eavesdroppin' on my imaginary people."

"As long as you can still count to ten when we're movin' cows, I won't be offended," he'd say.

"You love my imaginary people," she'd shoot back. "Keeps you from havin' to listen to your own thoughts."

He'd grin, acknowledging the hit.

In the evenings, she carved out time for freelance pitches. On nights when her brain wasn't fried, she'd sit at the kitchen table with Hank's old laptop (her own in constant danger of being drafted into Netflix duty) and craft emails to Julia: an essay idea about small-town rumor mills, a potential feature on water rights battles in rural Colorado, a profile of the retired teacher who'd single-handedly run the library for thirty years.

Sometimes Julia replied with a quick, enthusiastic yes. Sometimes with a regretful no. But every acceptance that came later, with a check attached, felt like another brick in the foundation she was building.

"I got paid today," Emma would say, flashing a grin across the table, and Hank would announce instructions for how she should invest it. Caleb would roll his eyes and remind Hank that keeping the lights on was also a valid financial plan.

They were small wins. They were hers.

The town, for its part, watched and adapted in its own way.

Cottonwood Ridge was a place where people noticed things. They noticed the city license plates on Emma's car that first week. They noticed when she started showing up at the feed store in boots instead of sneakers. They noticed when she stood next to Caleb at the farmer's market, laughing at something Hank said, one hand resting on the back pocket of his jeans like it had a right to be there.

There were glances and whispers, sure. A few raised eyebrows from older women who remembered Abby's ring and its sudden disappearance. A few knowing nods from men who'd watched Caleb's years of solitude and silently hoped they didn't calcify into permanent loneliness.

As the weeks stretched, as Emma's presence shifted from novelty to part of the scenery, the murmurs softened into acceptance.

It helped that she didn't stand off in a corner staring at her phone during community events. She listened. She asked questions that weren't for articles. She remembered people's names.

When she heard that the local library's summer reading program was short on volunteers, she signed up and found herself reading picture books about farm animals to a cluster of children who interrupted every page to say, "We got one of those!" about every illustrated cow or chicken.

"You figure they'd be bored, hearin' about barns," Hank whispered from the back of the room.

"Everybody loves seein' their own life in a story," Emma whispered back. "Even if they're six."

One Saturday, the town held its annual late-summer fair and rodeo, a mash-up of 4-H competitions, craft booths, an amateur bronc riding event, and enough fried food to endanger the county's collective cholesterol.

They made a day of it.

Emma rode into town with Caleb and Hank in the truck, all three squeezed into the cab, the dashboard rattling to a radio station that alternated between George Strait and static. She wore jeans and a chambray shirt, her hair in a loose braid. Caleb wore his usual uniform, faded denim, t-shirt, hat, but the way his hand rested on her knee during red lights was new.

At the fairgrounds, the air was thick with dust, livestock, and the smell of funnel cake. Sun glared off the metal bleachers. Kids shrieked near the bouncy house set up by the volunteer fire department.

They walked through it together, not making a show of themselves, but not hiding either.

When Mrs. Kellerman from the diner waved and called, "Caleb! You bringin' that pretty girl around to show her what real fun looks like?" he simply slipped his arm around Emma's shoulders and replied, "Figured it was time."

Mrs. Kellerman's eyes widened a fraction, then her face broke into a genuine grin. "'Bout time, boy," she said. To Emma she added, "Don't let him talk you into tryin' the chili cook-off samples unless you got a strong constitution."

"I survived his coffee," Emma said. "I think I can handle small-town chili."

"Watch it," Caleb muttered.

They wandered among the stalls. Emma bought a jar of honey from a teenager proudly explaining how his bees were "happy, ethically treated pollinators." Caleb picked up a bag of kettle corn so large Emma suspected it had its own gravitational pull.

At the 4-H pavilion, they paused by a stall with a hand-painted sign that read:

HIGH MEADOW RANCH – SPONSORED HEIFER

The calf inside was a deep russet color, with eyes too big for its head and a new halter that glinted against her coat.

"Hey there, Daisy 2.0," Emma murmured, reaching out to scratch gently between its ears.

A girl of about twelve stepped forward, nervously adjusting her belt. "Her name's Clover," she said. "My dad said we should call her that 'cause she got stuck in the clover patch when she was born."

"Clover's a lot more dignified than Daisy 2.0," Emma conceded.

The girl's gaze flicked between Emma and Caleb. "You're Emma, right?" she asked. "From the big city?"

"Guilty," Emma said.

"My dad said you used to write in the newspaper," the girl said. "Now you're… here?"

There was curiosity there, not judgment.

"Yep," Emma said. "Turns out country stories are pretty good too."

The girl considered that, then nodded as if accepting a perfectly reasonable career trajectory.

"Thanks for sponsorin' her," she said to Caleb, cheeks pink. "The halter and feed help a lot."

Caleb shrugged, uncomfortable with praise. "She's a good calf," he said. "You're doin' right by her. Keep it up."

As they walked away, Emma nudged him with her elbow.

"Softie," she said.

"Don't tell anyone," he replied.

They watched the barrel racing from the bleachers, Emma half-covering her eyes every time a rider leaned dangerously close to the saddle horn around a tight turn. Caleb narrated in a low voice, pointing out good lines, unnecessary risks, moments where you could see a horse and rider truly trust each other.

Hank, sitting on the other side of Emma, dropped dry commentary about the announcer's fondness for obvious clichés.

"'She's givin' it all she's got!'" Hank mimicked after one run. "No kidding, that's kind of the point when you're competing, son."

Emma laughed, leaning lightly into Caleb's shoulder. He didn't pull away.

Instead, he threaded his fingers through hers where their hands rested on his thigh. The contact was casual and complete, the kind that said clearly to anyone watching: Yes, this is us. No, we're not taking a survey about it.

They drifted toward the rodeo arena when the bronco riding started, Hank declaring that if he had to watch one more goat-tying run, he would defect to the rival town's fair.

Dust rose in clouds as horses bucked and men tried to prove their bones were as stubborn as their pride. Emma watched the first rider get tossed onto the dirt, scramble up with his hat somehow still on, and shake it off like he hadn't almost been impaled on his own courage.

"You ever do that?" she murmured to Caleb, not taking her eyes off the arena.

"Once," he said. "When I was stupid and sixteen."

"How'd it go?"

"Let's just say my daddy said, 'If you want to get your head knocked in, Uncle Sam will pay you for it,'" he replied. "Two years later, I was in basic training."

She looked at him then, understanding hitting in a new way, that thread from restless teenager on a bronco to soldier on a deployment, then back here, older and quieter. Decisions that felt small at the time but bent entire lives.

Out of the corner of her eye, movement caught her attention, a figure standing near the edge of the fairgrounds, by the parking lot.

Abby.

She was dressed for travel, jeans, sneakers, a duffel bag at her feet, a backpack slung over one shoulder. Her hair was pulled back in a messy bun, sunglasses perched on top of her head like an afterthought.

She wasn't walking toward them. She wasn't pacing or posturing. She was just… standing, watching the arena, watching the crowd.

Emma's first instinct was to stiffen. Old habits. Old hurt.

But then she remembered their conversation in the coffee shop. The way Abby's voice had broken when she'd admitted some hard truths. The way she'd said she was leaving. That this chapter, for her, needed to end.

Abby's gaze landed on Emma and Caleb where they sat, hands linked, bodies angled comfortably toward each other. Emma saw the flinch, the quick tightening around the mouth.

Then Abby's expression shifted. The tension eased. Her shoulders dropped a fraction of an inch. Her face took on a look that was part sadness, and part acceptance.

She lifted one hand in a small, almost shy wave. Not a summons. Not a beckon. Just… acknowledgment.

Emma squeezed Caleb's hand.

He followed her line of sight. When he saw Abby, his back stiffened briefly, then relaxed as well. He blinked once, like a man seeing someone in a picture that had finally been put back in the right album.

He lifted his free hand, returning the wave. It was small, contained. A good-bye without fanfare.

Abby nodded once. She picked up her duffel, slung it over her free shoulder, and turned away. A few seconds later, a car door opened and closed at the far edge of the lot. An engine started. The vehicle pulled out and merged onto the road, heading toward the highway that would take her away from Cottonwood Ridge.

From this distance, she was just another car leaving a fairground.

Emma watched until the dust settled back on the gravel and the gap in the parked cars closed in her vision.

"You, okay?" she asked quietly.

Caleb's jaw moved side to side once, then stilled.

"Yeah," he said. "I think… we both are, finally."

She leaned her shoulder against his, wordless comfort.

The bronco in the arena exploded out of the chute. The crowd roared. The moment faded into the larger noise of the day, into the smell of dust and sweat and fried dough, into the rhythm of hoofbeats and laughter.

For Abby, this had been an end.

For Emma and Caleb, it was a point on a longer line.

The days that followed settled into a pattern that felt, to Emma, like a braid, strands of work and love and friendship weaving together, overlapping, sometimes tangling, always holding.

There were mornings when she overslept, groggy from staying up too late revising a scene, and tumbled out of bed to find Caleb already at the cabin door, hat in hand, smirk firmly in place.

"You're behind schedule, Taylor," he'd say. "The cows don't care about your creative process."

"Cows are philistines," she'd yawn, pulling on boots.

There were afternoons when Caleb lingered near the cabin porch as she wrote outside, pretending to adjust a fence post just to be near the sound of her typing.

"Don't you have real work to do?" she'd call.

"This is real work," he'd say, leaning on the post driver. "Supportin' the arts."

There were evenings when Hank would wander up to the cabin with a deck of cards and a six-pack, plunking himself down with a sigh.

"Can't let you young folks hog all the wisdom time," he'd say. "I got stories that'll go stale if I don't tell 'em."

He'd talk while Emma shuffled and Caleb dealt, stories of his late wife, of blizzards survived, of neighbors who'd come and gone. Emma would file details away in that mental drawer labeled "for later," knowing some of them would eventually feed her pages.

They weren't perfect, these days. There were spats about silly things, Emma leaving boots in the hallway for someone to trip over, Caleb forgetting to tell her he'd be out late checking the distant water tanks, Hank's tendency to volunteer her for town committees without asking.

There were bigger tensions, too.

A freelance payment would be late, and Emma's financial anxiety would flare. They'd sit at the table with spreadsheets and sigh over the realities of ranch economics and artist incomes. Caleb would offer to "cover things" for a while, and Emma would bristle, insisting she was a partner, not a dependent.

They'd have to talk it out: pride and practicality, independence and interdependence.

"Maybe the point isn't that we split everything fifty-fifty," Hank said once, listening to them go around the same circle. "Maybe it's that we both put in what we got, when we got it, and stop keepin' score like this is a basketball game."

It wasn't a magic solution, but it shifted something. They started measuring contributions not just in dollars but in hours worked, meals cooked, emotional labor done. It didn't make the money stretch further, but it made the load feel more shared.

On particularly hard days, when a calf died despite their best efforts, or when Emma got an email from a friend in Denver posting pictures from a swanky press event, one of them would catch the other staring out at the horizon with a tight expression.

"Regrets?" one would ask.

"Doubts," the other would correct. "Regrets are for things you can't change. Doubts are just… questions you haven't answered yet."

They got better, over time, at answering them together.

Some nights, exhausted, they'd tumble into bed at the cabin and fall asleep tangled around each other, too tired to do anything more than murmur a few words about the day. Other nights, they'd drive back up to that same high meadow where they'd first laid everything out, spreading a blanket to watch meteor showers or just the slow spin of constellations.

The sky stayed big. Their lives, somehow, felt big within it, even though the radius of their daily travel had shrunk compared to city days.

Emma wrote more pages. Caleb built more fence. Hank told more stories. The dog chased more rabbits than he ever caught.

Little by little, High Meadow Ranch stopped being the place Emma had come for a summer and became the place she lived.

People in town stopped introducing her as "Emma from Denver" and started saying "Emma from up at Caleb's place." Kids at the library asked her when her book would be out like it was a foregone conclusion.

One morning, in the general store, Mrs. Kellerman's husband, Harold, held the door open for her and said, "Mornin', Emma. How's things up at your place?"

Not Caleb's. Not the ranch.

Your place.

It was a tiny shift in language, tossed out casually, but it lodged in her like honey on toast.

Her place.

Their place.

The life they were building wasn't flashy. It wouldn't make for a glossy magazine spread. But it was, in its quiet, stubborn way, exactly what she'd chosen: a shared life, built day by day, fence post by fence post, page by page, under a sky that'd seen more stories than any city skyline ever would.

And for the first time in a very long time, when she thought about the future, she didn't just see deadlines or vague "somedays."

She saw mornings at this table, nights on that porch, seasons turning, words accumulating, love deepening.

She saw, simply and profoundly, a life.

Chapter Twenty-Seven
The First Novel

By the time the cottonwoods along the creek started to yellow at the edges, the pages on Emma's laptop had begun to feel like a living thing.

The days were shorter now. Mornings arrived with a chill that made her breath ghost when she stepped onto the porch. At night, she swapped her lightweight blanket for an extra quilt, one Hank had pulled from a cedar chest with a mumbled, "My mama made that. Don't spill coffee on it."

Somewhere in that slow tilt from late summer to early autumn, the scattered scenes she'd been writing coalesced into something with a spine.

She noticed it one morning when she scrolled to the top of the document and saw chapter numbers marching down the left margin like fence posts in a straight line. No more loose, untitled blocks of text. No more "fix later" notes wedged between paragraphs like caution tape. Just… a story.

The last two weeks, her writing hours had turned sharp, purposeful.

She still woke at five-thirty, still made coffee and watched the barn appear out of the gray. But there was less meandering in her notebook and more quiet, focused typing. Whole mornings disappeared into the screen; she'd jerk back into her body to find the coffee gone cold and the sun already high.

Caleb and Hank gave her space without making a production of it.

"You're in the home stretch," Hank said once, leaning on the doorframe of the cabin, hat in hand. "Like calving season in reverse. Everything hurts, but there's a good reason."

Caleb just pressed a thermos into her hands before heading out and said, "Eat somethin' on the breaks, okay? Words don't count as calories."

On a Thursday morning in early September, she wrote the last sentence of the last chapter and stared at the blinking cursor as if it were an animal she'd finally cornered.

Emma's fingers hovered, then added two more words.

The End.

The moment didn't come with a choir of angels. It came with the creak of the cabin settling, the ticking of the wall clock, and Emma's own ragged breath.

She leaned back in her chair, heart pounding, and stared at the words until they blurred. Then she laughed, a short, disbelieving puff.

"I finished," she whispered to the empty room. Saying it made it real.

She stood on shaky legs, paced the small space once, then twice, then sank back into the chair and laid her forehead briefly on the cool surface of the table.

It wasn't perfect. God, it was nowhere near perfect. Whole chapters sagged. A side character disappeared for fifty pages and then reappeared as if she'd just gone to the grocery store. Some metaphors made her cringe even now. The love scenes were probably too tender for some readers and too spicy for others.

But it existed. Beginning, middle, and end. A story that hadn't existed in the world three months ago now sat on her hard drive and in the faint ache of muscles that had typed it into being.

When she could trust her voice again, she whispered to the cabin, "First draft done," just to hear it out loud.

The cabin, nonplussed, continued being a cabin.

Printing it felt necessary. She needed to feel the weight of it in her hands, not just see it as a scroll of digital text that could evaporate with a spilled mug or glitch.

The ranch printer was older than some of the fence posts, prone to chewing on paper and streaking ink like modern art, so she took the manuscript into town.

Lily at the coffee shop waved her toward the corner where the communal printer purred in a small alcove.

"Using the big gun today," Lily said, eyeing the stack of paper in Emma's arms. "That a manifesto, a novel, or the collected secrets of Cottonwood Ridge?"

Emma swallowed. The paper already felt like something she wanted to hide and show at the same time.

"Novel," she said. "First draft. I think. Unless it's secretly trash."

Lily's eyes lit up. "Shut up," she said. "That's amazing. You finishing a whole book and my basil plant survivin' August are the only good things that have happened this month."

Emma smiled, throat tight. "We'll see how good it is when I try to read it without wanting to light it on fire," she said.

"Author self-loathing, step three of the process," Lily said cheerfully. "Go hit print. I'll look the other way if you cry."

The printer churned for what felt like an hour. Page after page slid into the tray, black words on white paper. Emma stood there watching them accumulate, chest tightening in tandem.

By the time the last sheet emerged, the stack was thick, three hundred and some pages, single-sided, twelve-point font, line spacing generous enough for future edits.

She gathered them carefully, squared the edges on the counter until they aligned, and clipped them with a binder clip she'd bought specifically for this purpose and kept in her bag for weeks like a talisman.

As she walked out of the coffee shop, pages heavy against her chest, she had the brief, irrational fear that she'd trip and the manuscript would explode into the street, scattering her innermost thoughts across Main for everyone to read. The idea was mortifying and somehow fitting.

In the truck, she set the stack on the passenger seat and put her hand on top of it for a second, as if to reassure both of them.

"That's you," she murmured. "You exist."

The pages, being pages, offered no commentary.

She didn't give the manuscript to Caleb that day.

She brought it back to the cabin, set it on the table, and stared at it from various angles. She circled it like a wary animal. She picked it up, sniffed the paper (it smelled like toner and coffee shop air), flipped through to random pages and read sentences she barely remembered writing.

And yet, lying there on the table, it felt like a mirror tilted slightly. Enough that the reflection wasn't exact, but not so much that anyone close wouldn't recognize the shapes.

She wasn't sure if that was brave or foolish.

She agonized for two days about giving it to him.

On the one hand, he'd been there for the entire process. He knew what it meant to her. He'd asked, gently but repeatedly, "How's the book?" in the same tone he used to ask how a stubborn calf was doing.

On the other hand, he wasn't a reader. Not in the way her city friends were. He didn't curl up with novels for fun. He read weather reports, seed catalogs, grazing leases. When he did pick up a book, it was most likely a dog-eared paperback left behind by a previous generation, read in snatches over breakfast or in the cab of the truck while waiting at the vet.

What if he didn't like it? What if he did but didn't know how to say it?

Hank, of course, read her anxiety like a bulletin board.

"You look constipated," he said on the second evening, peering at her over his glasses as she shuffled dishes at the sink.

"Thanks," she said. "That's the look I was goin' for."

He jerked his chin toward the cabin, visible from the ranch house window. "Manuscript still sittin' on the table like the elephant in the room?" he asked.

"Yes," she said.

"You plannin' to let it gather dust till the mice start usin' it for nests?" he asked mildly.

She sighed. "I want Caleb to read it," she said. "But also, I want to hide it under the bed and never speak of it again."

Hank snorted. "Welcome to bein' an artist," he said. "You want folks to see your heart and also, you'd like to keep your ribcage intact. Sadly, those two things don't go together."

The way you make sense of what happened. Art ain't a mirror, Emma. It's more like one of those funhouse things, bends the light. Shows you somethin' true, even if it ain't exact."

"You and your metaphors," she muttered.

He grinned. "You ain't the only one who knows how to spin a yarn." He sobered a notch.

"Give it to him," he said gently. "Don't make him ask. Let him be part of this for you. He's sturdier than you think."

She knew that. Of course she did. Fear just had a way of making her forget.

The next evening, she finally picked up the stack, took a breath, and walked down the path to the ranch house.

The porch light was on, casting a warm circle on the steps. Crickets sang in the tall grass. Inside, she could hear the murmur of the television, some old Western Hank liked to fall asleep in front of.

Caleb sat on the porch, boots propped on the railing, chair tipped back just enough to make her nervous on his behalf. He was shirt-sleeved, forearms tan against the worn wood of the armrests, breath fogging faintly in the cooling air.

He looked up as she approached, the automatic smile he gave her slipping into something softer when he saw what she was holding.

"That it?" he asked.

She clutched the pages closer, suddenly aware of how ridiculous she must look, hugging paper like an infant.

"That it," she echoed. "First draft, anyway. It'll need… a lot of work. Probably some surgery. Maybe an exorcism."

He chuckled, setting his chair down on all fours. "Can I see it?" he asked.

She stepped up onto the porch, heart thudding.

"If you want to," she said. "No pressure. I know you don't… read a ton of this kind of thing. Or at all. It's long. Also, maybe terrible. Also, possibly the best thing I've ever done. I don't know. My brain keeps flipping between those opinions every ten minutes."

He took the manuscript from her hands carefully, as if it were something fragile, he wasn't sure the weight of yet.

His thumb rubbed along the edge of the pages, feeling the thickness.

"This is… a lot of you," he said quietly.

She swallowed. "Yeah," she said. "It is."

He looked up. "Then I want to read it," he said simply. "Even if it takes me till Christmas."

She exhaled, some of the tension leaving her shoulders. "Okay," she said. "Just… remember it's fiction. I changed things. On purpose. It's not… a diary. It's an omniscient narrator, third-person, all-seeing, all that jazz. It's… a story, not a transcript."

He smiled faintly at the cascade of terms he only half understood.

"Got it," he said. "Third person, omnipresent,"

"Omniscient," she corrected, laughing.

"Right," he said. "All-knowing. Like Hank, but without the coffee breath."

From inside, Hank called, "I heard that!"

They both laughed.

Caleb sobered again, holding the manuscript between them.

"Thank you," he said. "For trusting me with this."

Something in his tone made her throat go tight.

"Thank you for wanting it," she managed.

He tapped the top page with one finger.

"What's it called?" he asked. "You tell me yet?"

She hesitated. The title felt almost as vulnerable as the contents.

"Under the Colorado Sky," she said. "Working title, anyway. I might change it. I liked the idea of… this big sky hangin' over everything, watching, but,"

He started that night.

After dinner and dishes, after Hank had declared he was too old to stay awake for anything more complicated than the weather, the older man went to bed, leaving the house quiet except for the ticking of the kitchen clock and the occasional creak of the settling frame.

Caleb carried the manuscript out to the porch, a mug of coffee in one hand and a blanket thrown over his shoulder. The air had a bite to it now in the evenings; he'd already had to fetch one space heater from the barn for the mudroom.

He settled into his usual chair, the book, because that's what it felt like, even unbound, on his lap.

He wasn't a fast reader. He knew that. He'd always preferred people and land and animals over pages. But he also knew that this mattered, so he gave it the same attention he offered to a newborn calf or a balky tractor: patient, methodical, present.

He peeled the binder clip off, set it on the armrest, and turned to the first page.

The opening line surprised him.

The narrator didn't start in the city, like he'd half expected. Not in a newsroom like Emma's old life. It started with the land.

Before the girl came with her city shoes and her tired eyes, the ranch existed as it always had: a patch of stubborn green under a wide, indifferent sky.

The language was simple but... sure. Not fancy, but not plain either. It sounded a little like Emma and a little not, as if some other voice had stepped in between her and the page and shaped the words.

She introduced the place first, then the town she called Cotton Creek, with its single stoplight and gossip concentration. Only after a few paragraphs did the city woman arrive, tired from deadlines and late-night bars, driving a car packed with books and uncertainty.

Her name, on the page, was Lily.

He smiled at that and understood why Emma refused to set more than coffee shop scenes in town; she stole names like a magpie.

Lily wasn't Emma exactly. She was… sharper in some ways, more brittle at the start. Her burnout was more dramatic, her thoughts harsher toward herself and the world. But the bones were there: the sleepless nights, the blinking cursor, the hollow feeling of writing about fires instead of putting any out.

Jack, her rancher, showed up in chapter two.

He rode in on horseback, of course, like some cliché of a Western hero, but the way Emma wrote him, he wasn't a fantasy. He was tired, a little bruised around the edges, carrying ghosts from a war she never named outright but sketched in just enough for anyone who'd lived through it to fill in the blanks.

Jack was taller than Caleb, if the descriptions were to be believed. Broader. His scars were visible, marked on his skin in ways Emma's real-life rancher would never let stranger's catalogue. His temper was shorter in the early chapters. His grief sharper. He made more mistakes, said the wrong thing more often, pulled away harder than even Caleb thought he had in those first weeks.

Walt, the older hand, lurked around both of them like a benevolent ghost, delivering one-liners and wisdom with equal ease.

"I like that old guy," Caleb muttered under his breath by page twenty.

Inside, in the cabin up the hill, Emma paced.

She tried to pretend she wasn't listening. The night air carried sound strangely; sometimes, if she sat on her own porch and the wind was right, she could catch the low murmur of voices from the ranch house porch. Not the words, just the cadence. Tonight, she heard a rumble that might have been Caleb's laugh and decided to take it as a good sign.

She made tea she didn't drink. Opened her laptop and stared at the "The End" until it felt melodramatic and changed it to a more modest line break. Then changed it back. Closed the laptop, opened it again.

At one point, she texted Lily a single line:

He's reading.

Lily replied with a string of emojis, books, hearts, a sweating smiley.

Emma set the phone down and tried to breathe.

Inside his chair, Caleb turned pages slowly.

He didn't devour the manuscript in one sitting. After an hour, his eyes started to blur, and the words slipped into a hum. He set the stack on a side table, carefully marking his place with a torn envelope, and sat back to stare at the stars.

He thought about Jack and Lily and Walt. About the way the narration slid in and out of their heads, sometimes describing what they felt, other times zooming out to talk about the land or the town as if those were characters too.

He liked that. The omniscient… whatever Emma had called it. It made sense to him that no one person could hold the whole story.

He thought about the way Emma had changed things. The first meeting between Lily and Jack in the book didn't happen at an Airbnb cabin. It happened when Lily's rental car got stuck in a rutted road, she'd been too stubborn to turn back on. Jack arrived in a cloud of dust, cursing the weather and tourists in equal measure.

"That never happened," Caleb murmured, amused. "But it could've."

The next night, he picked the pages up again. And the next.

Some scenes knocked the breath out of him.

In one, Jack wakes from a nightmare, the taste of dust and cordite still in his mouth, and stumbles onto the porch to find Walt already there, pretending not to notice the tremor in Jack's hands.

"You can't outrun what's in your head, boy," Walt says. "But you can give it somethin' new to chew on."

It wasn't word-for-word something Hank had said. But it was… the same frequency.

In another, Lily stands alone at the edge of a pasture at sunset, notebook in hand, trying to capture the way the light turns the grass to fire and the sky to something beyond words.

She writes, then crosses out, writes, crosses out. Finally, she gives up and just looks.

The narrator dips in:

For the first time in years, she let herself stand in front of something beautiful and not try to turn it into content.

Caleb felt his throat tighten at that. He'd watched Emma do that in real life, watched her put the notebook down, watched the way her shoulders dropped when she wasn't performing for an invisible audience.

He wondered, not for the first time, what it had cost her to live in a world where everything was material.

He reached for his mug and realized the coffee was cold. He drank it anyway.

By the third night, he'd reached the sections that mirrored their own turning points more closely.

The "under the stars" scene, for example.

In Emma's book, Lily and Jack's off-grid night didn't happen exactly the way his and Emma's had. There was no shared sleeping bag, Emma had replaced it with two blankets and a tent flap that wouldn't stay zipped. The conversation was shifted around, some lines combined, others invented out of whole cloth.

But the heart of it was there: two people under a ridiculous number of stars, finally telling the whole truth. The way fear and love sat next to each other like uneasy siblings. The way choosing felt less like fireworks and more like a quiet, steady thing.

As he read Jack saying, I can't promise I won't be scared, but I can promise I won't run, Caleb felt a jolt of recognition.

He hadn't used those exact words. Not out loud. But he'd thought them. Felt them. Emma had translated his clumsy internal vows into something cleaner.

"Show-off," he muttered under his breath, half proud, half stunned.

He didn't dwell on the love scene that followed. Emma had faded to the edge of the tent flap anyway, pulling the narrator back to the sky and the sound of their voices, leaving the details to the imagination.

He was grateful for that. Some things, even fictionalized, were better left in shadow.

He closed the manuscript around midnight that third night, rubbing stiffness out of his neck, and realized he was three-quarters of the way through.

He hadn't meant to read that much. He'd planned to take it slow, piece by piece. But the story had its own gravity. Not just because it was theirs, but because Emma had made it… compelling. The characters breathed on the page. The land felt real, almost like another person in the room.

He wasn't thinking in terms of pacing or structure. He was thinking, simply, I want to know what happens next, even though he already did.

Hank pretended not to care, but he hovered.

"How's the smut?" he asked on the fourth morning over coffee.

Caleb choked. "It is not smut," he said.

Hank's eyes crinkled. "So, what is it?" he asked. "Good? Bad? Ugly?"

"Good," Caleb said. The word came out before he could qualify it. "Really good."

Hank raised his brows. "Big praise from a man whose favorite book is the tractor manual," he said.

Caleb ignored that, staring into his mug.

"It's… us," he said slowly. "But… not. She changed things, but the… feelin's are the same. The parts that hurt. The parts that… don't." He searched for words, frustrated by their slipperiness. "She wrote stuff I never said. Stuff I… didn't know I felt till I read it."

Hank nodded, unsurprised. "That's what a writer does," he said. "Digs out what's under the floorboards. Sometimes it's treasure. Sometimes it's somethin' you forgot you buried."

"You okay with your… fictional self?" Caleb asked, half teasing now. "Walt's a charmer."

Hank smirked. "He handsome?" he asked.

"Too handsome," Caleb said. "Suspiciously so."

Hank lifted his chin. "Sounds accurate."

They both laughed.

"Finish it tonight," Hank said. "Then tell her. Don't wait till she chews her nails down to nubs."

Caleb glanced toward the hill where the cabin sat, a single rectangle of light still glowing in the early morning.

"I will," he said. "I just… wanna do it right."

He finished the book on the fifth night.

The air had turned crisp enough that he wore a jacket on the porch, breath visible in faint puffs. The dogs curled at his feet, occasionally lifting their heads when a night sound caught their attention.

He read the last fifty pages in a rush he didn't try to slow. The climax wasn't a gunfight or a dramatic rescue; it was Lily sitting at a table with a phone in her hand, turning down a promotion from a big-city magazine and choosing to stay, to freelance, to write her own stories on her own terms.

He knew that scene. He'd watched its real-world version play out in this very kitchen. Still, seeing it on the page, filtered through Emma's voice, hit hard.

In the book, the conversation with the editor was sharper, more dramatic. The stakes spelled out more clearly. Fiction liked its lines drawn thicker.

But the core was the same: a woman choosing the smaller, truer life on purpose.

By the time he reached the porch scene, the fictional one, where Lily and Jack sat under a "vast, attentive sky" and talked about the future, his throat ached.

The book ended not with a proposal or a wedding, but with a sense of ongoingness. Two people who had chosen each other, still facing messy days ahead, but facing them together.

The final line made him smile.

The sky above them wasn't promising anything. It had seen too much of people's plans to pretend. But it witnessed them anyway: two stubborn hearts, choosing and choosing again, under its patient, endless watch.

He sat for a long moment after reading that, pages resting on his knees, staring at the real sky above, a smattering of stars like faint nails pinning the darkness in place.

He thought of Emma at her desk, typing that line. Of the way she must have felt, adding those last words to the draft.

He thought of the book they'd actually lived this summer, messier, less neat, with more missteps and more jokes about biscuits that could double as self-defense weapons.

He thought about how, if you laid Emma's manuscript over their months like a piece of tracing paper, some lines would line up perfectly, the cabin, the ranch, an old man with a sharp tongue and a soft center. Others would be shifted, exaggerated for effect, smoothed for narrative.

The story we've been living, he thought, is one version. Hers is another. Both true. In different ways.

He clipped the manuscript back together, his place now somewhere beyond the last page, and stood, feeling his joints pop.

Time to tell her.

She'd been pretending not to listen again, up at the cabin, when the night suddenly went quiet of page-turn rustle. Her heart leaped.

She met him halfway down the path, unable to keep herself from doing so. The grass brushed her ankles; the air bit at her cheeks.

He was carrying the manuscript, bundled back into its thick stack. From his expression, serious, thoughtful, not shell-shocked, she couldn't immediately tell which way this was going to swing.

"Hey," she said, stopping in front of him. Her voice sounded small in the open space.

"Hey," he said.

Silence stretched.

"If you say, 'It was fine,' I'm movin' back to Denver," she blurted.

He barked a laugh, the tension cracking.

"I'd never," he said. "Even my limited social training knows 'fine' is a death word."

"Smart man," she said, though her stomach still felt like it had dropped onto the path.

He looked down at the pages, then back up at her.

"It's good, Emma," he said quietly. "It's really, really good."

Her lungs forgot how to work for a second. "You're not just sayin' that 'cause you're in it?" she asked.

He shook his head. "Half the time I forgot I was in it," he said. "I mean, yeah, there were parts where I went, 'Hey, that's me,' or, 'That's Hank with a different hat,' but... mostly, I was just... in it. Like, wantin' to know what happened. Hurting when they hurt. Wantin' to shake Jack when he said something stupid. Which was often."

"Rude," she said weakly. "I made him nicer than you."

He gave her a look. "You did not," he said. "He's worse at talkin' than I am. Which I didn't think was possible."

Despite everything, she grinned. "Artistic license," she said. "I needed some conflict."

He sobered again, stepping a little closer, the manuscript a solid weight between them.

"You did this," he said, as if the fact still amazed him. "You took... this summer, and your years before it, and stuff from my life and Hank's, and... turned it into... that. A story that... feels like it matters. Even if nobody ever reads it but us."

Emotion rose in her, thick and hot.

"Do you… see yourself?" she asked, almost afraid of the answer. "I mean, in Jack. Or… do you feel like I turned you into some… stereotype of a broody cowboy?"

He considered.

"I see… parts of myself," he said slowly. "The protectiveness. The fear. The way he… wants to do right and doesn't always know how. Some of the dumb things he says." He paused. "But I also see… things you added. Places where you made him… rougher, or braver, or more of a… story version."

He tilted his head.

"I don't mind," he said. "It's like… when you tell someone about your day. You don't include every stubbed toe. You hit the highlights. That's what you did. You made a version o' me that… makes sense in a book. Even if he's not exactly me."

She exhaled, some deeply held tension easing.

"That was the goal," she said. "I didn't want to… put you on display. I wanted to… build a character that felt true enough but still… somebody you could just… be a reader about."

He nodded.

"You did," he said. "I got mad at him sometimes. Sympathetic mad. The same way I get mad at myself when I replay things in my head. That means you did somethin' right."

She swallowed hard.

"What about… Lily?" she asked. "Did you… feel like I stole myself and dropped her in there, or…?"

He smiled softly.

"She's braver than you think you are," he said. "And more reckless. But half the things she says… yeah, that's you. The good and the ugly."

He tapped the top page with his fingers.

"And the way you wrote her… not always nice," he added. "You showed when she was selfish. When she judged people. When she almost ran. That took guts."

"I didn't want to write a saint," Emma said. "Saints are boring. And I wanted to be fair to the version of you in there. You can't have a hero and a flawless heroine. That's... not how humans work."

He chuckled. "Hero, huh?" he said.

"Well, in the book," she said, rolling her eyes. "Don't let it go to your head."

He looked down at the manuscript again, thumb rubbing slowly along the edge.

"You know what my favorite part was?" he asked.

She shook her head, bracing herself. "Please don't say 'the dedication,'" she said. "'To everyone who's ever chosen the small life' is not exactly a tearjerker."

He smiled, then shook his head.

"No," he said. "It was the... voice. The way you had the narrator... float around. One minute we're in Lily's head, next we're in Jack's, then we're over with Walt, then we're... up somewhere above them all, talkin' about the land like it's watchin'."

He glanced up at the sky, then back at her.

"It felt... right," he said. "'Cause that's how life is. It ain't just me and you. It's Hank. The cows. The town. The weather. All of it. Nobody's the main character all the time. Your book... gets that."

She blinked, surprised and touched by his articulation.

"That's why I picked omniscient," she said quietly. "Third person, all-seeing. I... never felt like I could stick in one head and be honest. Not with... this place. There's too many stories. Too many angles. I wanted to... be able to step back sometimes and say, 'Look. This isn't just about their love story. It's about the town. The land. The... sky, even.'"

He nodded, as if this confirmed something he'd intuitively felt.

"Sounds familiar," he said.

It took her a second to realize what he meant.

The story we're in now. The one with its own omniscient narrator, who occasionally steps back to show the land, the town, even Hank's thoughts.

She looked around, at the hill, the cabin behind her, the porch behind him, the sweep of dark under the stars.

"Guess I've got a type," she said, half to him, half to whatever was listening.

He stepped closer, closing the small gap between them. The manuscript was still in his hands, pressing lightly against her chest now.

"This is good, Emma," he said again, with quiet conviction. "And I don't mean 'good like the pie was good' when Hank burns the crust. I mean… it made me feel things. It made me think. It made me… see us and not us. And I think… if people who've never set foot on a ranch read it, they'd still understand somethin' about… why this life matters. Why choices like yours matter."

Her eyes burned.

"Do you… think people will read it?" she whispered.

He shrugged, that practical shrug that always grounded her.

"I don't know how the book world works," he said. "Seems like a crapshoot, like plantin' in a drought. But I know you've got somethin' worth plantin'. And I know you've got more stubbornness than half the publishers in New York put together." His mouth twitched. "And you've got me and Hank and half this town to annoy people online for you when the time comes."

She laughed, a wet, shaky sound.

"That's the modern marketing plan," she said. "Weaponize the locals."

He smiled.

"You gonna revise it?" he asked, practical now. "Make it even better?"

"Yeah," she said. "I'll let it sit for a few weeks. Then I'll print it again, bleed red ink all over it, cry, drink too much coffee, cut whole chapters, add new ones. Then… start sending it out into the world. See who, if anyone, bites."

He nodded, as if she'd described the most normal process in the world.

"If they don't see it," he said, "it'll be their loss. Not yours."

She reached up then, letting her fingers curl around the edge of the manuscript, and gently tugged until his grip loosened enough for her to set it aside on the porch railing.

With their hands freed, she stepped closer, slid her arms around his waist, and pressed her forehead to his chest.

"So," she said, voice muffled, "you're not breakin' up with me because of my literary portrayals?"

He huffed a laugh, arms wrapping around her in return.

"Not unless you write a sequel where I get stupider," he said. "Then we'll have words."

"Noted," she said, smile curving against him.

He kissed the top of her head.

"You're a writer," he said simply, like a fact. "Not just 'cause of this," he nodded toward the pages, "but… 'cause it's who you are. I'm proud of you."

The words landed deep, in a place that had always tied her identity to mastheads and job titles.

She pulled back just enough to look up at him.

"Thank you," she said. "For readin' it. For… seein' it. For seein' me."

"Always," he said.

Above them, the sky stretched, vast and indifferent and, in some strange way, bearing witness.

If someone had laid Emma's printed pages over the months they'd lived on High Meadow Ranch, the match wouldn't have been perfect. Scenes would be moved, words changed, rough edges sanded for narrative cohesion. The fights might be sharper, the reconciliations neater. The town's quirks would be slightly exaggerated, Hank's wisdom condensed into clichés, Caleb's silences filled with interior monologue.

But the shape, the arc of two people finding each other, choosing the small life on purpose under an endless western sky, would be the same.

The book she'd written was not this story.

It was a story born from it, bent through her voice, carrying its own truth.

And as Caleb held her on the path between the cabin and the ranch house, the first draft of Under the Colorado Sky resting heavy and real on the railing behind him, the narrator who watched all of this knew one more thing Emma didn't yet:

This would not be her last book.

It was the first.

The proof that she could take a summer, a man, a place, a choice, and build from them something that would outlast the season.

In the weeks to come, she'd revise, curse, query. She'd get polite rejections and painful silences. Eventually, she'd get interest, then notes, then a contract that would make her hands shake when she signed.

But for now, in the cool breath of early autumn, Emma Taylor stood in the dark with the man she loved, the story she'd written, and the life she'd chosen, and felt, perhaps for the first time, like all three belonged together.

Chapter Twenty-Eight
Epilogue: Under the Same Sky

A year later, the ranch still woke up before the sun.

Some things hadn't changed and probably never would. The cows still bawled when the feed truck came late. Fences still leaned at the exact moment everyone was too busy to fix them. The water lines still chose the hottest week of August to clog with mysterious debris, as if offended by predictability.

Money still came in like a trickle and went out like a flash flood.

And yet, there was a difference in the way High Meadow Ranch held itself against the sky now. It showed in subtle things: the new steel gate at the south entrance, bought after six months of Emma's freelance paychecks. The reseeded patch by the west fence, grass in its first determined year of growth. The fact that the old tractor, which had once sounded like a death rattle on wheels, now coughed to life with something bordering on enthusiasm after Caleb and an optimistic mechanic from town rebuilt half its insides.

Stable wasn't the same as easy. But it was a step up from hanging on by fingernails.

In the mornings, Emma still wrote from five-thirty to eight, the cabin now less a temporary refuge and more her official "overly drafty writing studio." A new bookshelf lined one wall, holding everything from battered Westerns Hank claimed he hated to reread (he didn't) to journalism anthologies and, near the center, a small, neat row of copies of her own book.

Under the Colorado Sky had not set the world on fire. It had not shot to the top of any bestseller list, nor had it been optioned for a movie where actors with perfectly white teeth pretended to understand dirt.

It had, however, done something quieter and, to Emma, just as miraculous.

It had sold steadily.

After months of revision and querying and enough polite rejections to wallpaper the cabin, a mid-sized press with a lean literary list and a fondness for "place-driven stories" had taken a chance. The advance had been modest but real. The edit letters had been brutal and bracing. The day she held the first finished copy in her hands, trade paperback, matte cover, her name printed in a font that made her eyes sting, she'd sat on the porch and cried so hard Caleb had assumed someone had died.

Now, a year later, there were reviews online from strangers who had no reason to be kind and yet were. There were dog-eared copies at the Cottonwood Ridge library, with waitlist slips tucked in the back. There was a stack on a little display table near the register at the coffee shop, propped up with a hand-lettered sign Lily had made that read:

LOCAL AUTHOR!

UNDER THE COLORADO SKY

READ IT OR SHE'LL WRITE YOU INTO THE NEXT ONE

People in town had taken to teasing her about "the book," but they'd also shown up, in surprising numbers, to the signing that Lily insisted on hosting. They'd stood in line holding copies, some purchased, some borrowed, some clearly read in one sitting. Old men from the feed store, teenage girls in rodeo jackets, moms with toddlers on hips, all stepping up to say, "I liked the part where…" or "My grandma used to say that exact thing…" or simply, "I saw myself in there."

Emma had gone home that night exhausted and glowing, the kind of tired that felt earned.

Now, she was working on book two. This one took place mostly in town and featured, among other things, a retired mailman who refused to stop delivering wisdom even after his route ended. The land was still there, the sky still watching, but the story's center of gravity had shifted slightly. She was learning she could write more than one kind of small life.

Freelance work trickled in around it. Essays about rural internet access and the stubbornness of small-town rumor mills. Profiles of women running family farms. A longer piece on drought that had taken her and Caleb on a three-day road trip to interview a rancher further west, where the land was even less forgiving.

The city paper in Denver ran her byline a few times a year now, often accompanied by a note: "Special to The Herald." Julia emailed her occasionally with curse-filled praise and the occasional plea to "come in for one hell of a corruption story." Emma always answered with gratitude and, so far, a no. Not never, but not now.

On the ranch side of things, Caleb still moved through his days with the steady, list-oriented focus of a man whose brain had been trained by both the Army and the land. But there were visible shifts if you knew where to look.

He laughed more. Out loud, not just in those small air puffs he'd used to let slip when something amused him. He reached for Emma's hand instinctively in public. He spoke in "we" almost exclusively when talking about the ranch's future.

He also, to Hank's endless delight, kept a dog-eared copy of Under the Colorado Sky on a shelf near his bed. He claimed it was just in case he ever needed to check whether Walt said something wiser than he did on a given subject. No one believed him, but no one argued.

Hank, for his part, had added another year's worth of creaks and aches to his collection but shrugged them off like old coats.

"Gettin' old is just God's way of sayin' He thinks you're still interesting enough to keep around," he told Emma once, when she fussed over his knee.

He watched the two of them, this boy he'd watched grow into a man, this woman who'd arrived with city shoes and a restless soul and somehow stayed, with a satisfaction that settled deep in his bones.

He'd been wrong many times in his life. About crops, about people, about which colt would turn out steady and which would always spook at shadows.

On this, he thought, sitting at the kitchen table one late September evening as he listened to their voices drift in from the porch, he'd been right. Pushing Caleb, nudging Emma, telling them the truth even when it hurt, they'd needed it. And they'd done the hard work themselves.

He felt a little like a man who'd watched a sapling take root on land everyone said was too rocky to grow anything. Now, the tree was young and still vulnerable to storms, but its roots were widening, reaching for water he suspected they'd find.

He sipped his coffee, grimaced at the taste, and made a mental note to teach Emma how to brew it right before his time ran out.

The night they went back up to the hilltop, the sky was as clear as fresh-washed glass.

It was late September again, almost exactly a year since Emma had signed her contract, almost two since she'd driven her overstuffed car into Cottonwood Ridge with more questions than answers.

The air held that specific bite that spoke of summer's departure and winter's impatient approach. Crickets still sang, but softer now, as if conserving energy.

Caleb had suggested it casually two days before.

"Forecast says clear Friday night," he'd said, eyes on the feed ledger. "No storms, no moon worth mentionin'. Be a good night for star-watchin', if you're into that kinda thing."

Emma, washing dishes, had arched a brow. "You makin' a date with me or yourself?" she asked.

He'd shrugged, too nonchalant by half. "I can't talk to myself about constellations," he said. "I barely remember the Big Dipper."

"Sold," she replied.

Now, as the truck bumped along the back road toward the highest meadow, a blanket and a small cooler rattling in the bed, she watched the world shrink behind them.

The ranch house lights faded first, then the cabin's single window winked out as Hank turned it off from below. The sounds of the main yard, the clank of a gate, the low murmur of Hank's radio from the kitchen, diminished until all she could hear was the rattle of the truck and, beneath it, the steady thrum of her own heart.

He parked near the same copse of scrubby pines they'd tied the horses to that first night. The truck's headlights washed the meadow in pale beams for a moment before he killed the engine, plunging them into a softer, star-pricked dark.

They climbed out, breath ghosting in the chill. The elevation made the air thinner; the sky felt closer, the stars brighter, as if someone had tilted the planet a little closer to the rest of the universe.

Caleb reached into the truck bed, grabbed the blanket, and shook it out onto the ground with the practiced motion of a man who'd done this before. Which, of course, he had.

Emma stood for a moment, just looking.

The hilltop hadn't changed. Grass still rolled away in gentle swells. The town lights in the distance still glowed like a scattered handful of coins. The mountains beyond still sat in their usual place, shadowy and solid against the horizon.

She had changed.

She lowered herself onto the blanket, crossing her legs, arms wrapped around her knees. Caleb settled beside her, close enough that their shoulders brushed.

"Deja vu," she murmured.

"Less fear this time," he said.

"Speak for yourself," she replied. "I'm always at least a little scared."

He glanced at her, smiling. "Of what?"

She considered.

"Of… wasting time," she said slowly. "Of writing bad books. Of hurtin' people without meaning to. Of… waking up one day and realizing I accidentally turned my life back into something that owns me instead of somethin' I own."

He nodded. "Same as last year, then," he said. "More or less."

She bumped his shoulder with hers. "You?" she asked.

He looked out over the dark shapes of his land.

"Of losin' you or Hank," he said simply. "Of the ranch goin' under and takin' years of my family with it. Of… gettin' so comfortable I stop payin' attention."

"Guess we're both cowards," she said lightly, though there was no mocking in it.

"Nah," he said. "Cowards don't say their fears out loud."

They fell quiet, letting the sky fill the space.

After a while, Emma lay back, folding her hands under her head. Caleb stretched out beside her, one hand resting on his chest, the other loosely between them, close but not quite touching.

The stars were ridiculous. There were too many. They cluttered the blackness in every direction, some faint, some sharp. The Milky Way smeared across the sky like someone had swiped a thumb through a dusting of sugar.

Emma exhaled slowly.

"This is my favorite ceiling," she said.

"Expensive to heat," he replied.

She laughed, the sound carrying out over the grass.

They lay there for a while, pointing out shapes.

"That one looks like a busted fence," Caleb said.

"That's because you have trauma," she said. "That's Cassiopeia."

He snorted. "You makin' that up?" he asked.

"Would I lie to you about Greek mythology?" she replied.

"Yes," he said promptly.

"Fair," she conceded.

He turned his head, studying her profile in the starlight. The faint lines at the corners of her eyes were new, carved by laughter and squinting into sun. The way she breathed deeper now when she looked at the sky was new too, less like she was bracing for impact and more like she was filling her lungs with something she intended to keep.

"You happy?" he asked, the question simple and enormous.

She considered that, really considered it, instead of reaching for the automatic "yes, of course" politeness had trained into her.

"I am," she said finally. "Not every second. Not every hour. Some days are hard. Some days I want to throw the whole book in the creek and the laptop with it. Some days the cows scare me more than they should. Some days money stress makes me snap at you or Hank. But… overall?" She shifted, turning her face fully toward him. "Yeah. I'm happy. This is… the life I wanted and didn't know how to ask for."

Relief and something like awe flickered across his face.

"Good," he said.

She nudged him. "You?" she countered. "Mister 'I don't need much, just a ranch and a purpose and not too many people talkin' to me.'"

He huffed a soft laugh.

"I got more people talkin' to me than I bargained for," he said. "But I… wouldn't change it. Not a bit." He looked back up at the sky. "I used to think… this was it. Me, the land, Hank, the work. And that if I wanted anything else, I'd have to give this up. I thought… love and… peace like this couldn't exist in the same space. That was before you showed up and rearranged all my math."

Her throat tightened.

"That's… a lot nicer than callin' me a complication," she said.

"You are a complication," he said. "Just a good one."

They lapsed into silence again, the comfortable kind that came from countless shared evenings.

Crickets. A distant owl. The faint rustle of something small in the grass.

Caleb's fingers inched toward hers, found them, and curled around. She let her hand be held.

After a while, he cleared his throat.

"There's somethin' I've been meanin' to tell you," he said.

She turned her head, studying his profile.

"If you say 'I never finished your book,' I'm pushin' you down the hill," she said.

He smiled, but didn't take the out.

"Since you stayed," he said slowly, "since that night at the table when you told your editor no… I've been waitin' for the day you'd wake up and regret it. Even just a little. I told myself I'd see it." He tapped his own chest with his free hand. "That it'd show up here first. In my gut."

He swallowed.

"It hasn't," he said. "Not once. Not even on the days that were bad. And there've been some. Drought, busted water lines, that mess with the stray bull from next door. Even on those days… when I look at you here… this life… there's not one piece of me that thinks you should've chosen different."

Emma's eyes blurred.

"That's good," she said thickly. "'Cause if you'd been secretly wishin' me gone all this time, that would've been a rough twist."

He laughed softly.

He shifted then, rolling onto his side to face her fully. The movement made the blanket rustle, the night feel more intimate.

She mirrored him without thinking, turning to meet his gaze.

His eyes were dark in the starlight, but she could read them anyway. She'd had a year's practice.

He reached into his jacket pocket with his free hand, fingers fumbling for a second before finding what he'd hidden there.

Her breath hitched when she saw the small box.

"Oh," she said, eloquently.

He cleared his throat again, suddenly more nervous than she'd seen him in months. His hand wasn't quite steady as he flipped the lid open.

"It ain't much," he said quickly, as if he wanted to apologize before she even saw it. "It was my mama's. Hank had it tucked away with the rest of the things he thought I wasn't ready for. It's not… fancy. Not like somethin' you'd see in those city jewelry stores. But it's… got history. And it's… from here."

Inside, nestled in worn velvet, was a ring.

The band was simple gold, worn soft at the edges by years of wear. The stone in the center was small, not some ostentatious diamond, but a pale blue sapphire, almost the color of the sky on a washed-out afternoon.

It was lovely in a quiet way, like everything else about this life.

Emma's vision swam.

"Caleb," she whispered.

He took a breath, steadied himself, and reached for her hand again, his rough fingers holding it gently.

"I've thought about doin' this a dozen different ways," he said. "At the fair, at the kitchen table, with Hank makin' some speech. In town, maybe, so Lily could take a picture for that wall o' hers. But every time I tried to plan it, it felt… wrong. Like I was tryin' to make it into something it ain't. This…" He nodded toward the sky. "This is where things turned for me. Where I stopped just… survivin' and started thinkin' about… somethin' bigger. So, it felt right to… ask you here."

He swallowed, thumb brushing the inside of her wrist.

"You stayed," he said. "When every part of your old life said you were crazy. You built somethin' with me here. You wrote our summers into pages. You… made this place feel… full in a way it never did when it was just me and my ghosts."

He paused, exhaled.

"I ain't perfect," he said. "You know that better than anyone. I'm gonna say the wrong thing, forget important dates, get too wrapped up in cattle prices. I'll probably be down in the yard muckin' out a stall the day you win some big book prize. I can promise you… one thing, and only one thing with my whole chest: I'll keep choosin' you. Every boring, hard, beautiful day. I'll keep showin' up. I'll keep doin' the work. I'll keep… not regrettin' you bein' here."

He lifted the ring slightly.

"So," he said, voice steady now, simple as sunrise. "Emma Taylor… will you marry me?"

The night held its breath.

Emma didn't cry at first, which surprised her. She felt everything tighten inside, heart, throat, lungs, as if her body was trying to make more room for the moment.

In some other life, she'd pictured proposals with elaborate setups: restaurants with candles, crowds applauding, speeches rehearsed. In some part of her twenty-year-old brain, she'd thought that level of spectacle was proof.

Here, on a blanket on a hilltop under a sky that didn't give a damn about human rituals, listening to the distant lowing of cattle and the faint hum of town, she realized proof looked different.

Proof was this: a man who had once thought he was safer alone, laying himself bare with seven or eight halting sentences and a ring that had belonged to his mother.

Proof was the fact that she wasn't thinking about what anyone else would think. Only what she felt.

She laughed then; a sound tangled with tears.

"Yes," she said, because there was never really another answer in her. "Of course yes. Are you insane? You think I quit my job, moved to a ranch, and wrote you into a book just to say no now?"

Relief and joy crashed across his face like a wave.

"Just makin' sure," he said hoarsely.

He slid the ring onto her finger. It fit. Not perfectly, her knuckles were a little bigger than his mother's had been, years of typing and hauling buckets giving her hands their own history, but it went on with only a little resistance, settling naturally at the base.

The sapphire caught some stray starlight and flashed, a tiny piece of sky trapped in metal.

Tears finally spilled over. She let them, laughing as she wiped at her cheeks with the back of her free hand.

"You, okay?" he asked, thumb brushing her wet skin.

"I'm cryin' in a good way," she said. "I didn't know the good way could feel this… big."

He leaned in, kissing her once, softly. Then again, deeper, sealing the yes between them.

When they broke apart, breathless, she rested her forehead against his.

"You know this doesn't get you out of the mandatory wedding planning," she said.

He groaned. "Can't we just have Hank say some words over us by the creek and call it good?" he asked.

"We might," she said. "But my mama's gonna want a cake. And your town's gonna want a party. We can negotiate the trimmings. The core is… this." She lifted their joined hands, ring glinting.

He nodded. "Long as we don't have to do any of those choreographed dances," he said. "I draw the line there."

"Deal," she said.

They lay back again, side by side now in a new way.

Her hand rested on his chest, ring cooling against warm skin. His arm curved under her shoulders, pulling her in close.

The sky above them watched, as indifferent and attentive as ever.

From the town's perspective, this would barely register. Tomorrow, word would get out in its usual ways, someone would see the ring at the diner, someone else would spot them at the feed store looking suspiciously glowy, and the ripple would spread.

Hank, when they told him, would pretend to be shocked.

"Well, I'll be," he'd say, eyes shining. "Took you long enough. I was about to start interviewin' new ranch hands with better decision-makin' skills."

He'd hug Emma so hard she'd wheeze, clap Caleb on the back hard enough to stagger him, and then pour whiskey into three glasses without waiting for anyone's permission.

Over at the coffee shop, Lily would rearrange her "Local Author" display to include a hand-drawn sign that read:

SHE SAID YES!

BOOKS & COWBOYS: BOTH AVAILABLE HERE

People would gossip, speculate about dates, venue, dress, weather. There would be talk of potluck dishes and whether the community hall needed new string lights.

The land would absorb it all with its usual calm. Seasons would keep turning. Calves would keep being born. Rain would come late some years, early others.

Underneath the noise, the core would remain what it had been this whole time:

Two stubborn hearts, choosing and choosing again.

The omniscient narrator, who had been with them from the beginning, watching Emma pack her car in Denver, watching Caleb mend fences alone, watching Hank pour coffee and wisdom in equal measure, could see further than they could tonight.

The narrator could see arguments they hadn't had yet, over money or timing or who forgot to close which gate.

Could see them holding onto each other at kitchen tables and on porches not yet built, through losses and additions and droughts and floods.

Could see Emma hunched over a laptop, years from now, hair streaked with silver, writing yet another story about small lives and big skies. Could see Caleb teaching some small, stubborn child how to read the herd, how to patch a fence, how to tell the difference between fear that keeps you alive and fear that keeps you from living.

Could see Hank's chair eventually standing empty on the porch one quiet morning, the echo of his laughter still hanging in the beams. Could see how the hole he left would never fully close, and how the stories he poured into them would keep ringing in their choices.

Could see, in short, that this yes under the stars was not an ending.

It was another beginning. One of many.

Tonight, though, the narrator did what good narrators sometimes do: stepped back, softened focus, let the moment be what it was without crowding it with prophecy.

On a hill above High Meadow Ranch, under a Colorado sky strewn with more stars than anyone could reasonably need, Emma and Caleb lay on a blanket.

Her hand, ring sparkling faintly, rested over his heart. His arm held her like something he knew the value of and did not intend to drop.

They had chosen a small life. Not as consolation, not as settling, but as a deliberate, brave act.

It wasn't flashy.

It was stubborn. Steady. Quiet as fence posts driven deep into rocky ground.

And as the night wrapped around them, thick and familiar, they did what they had been doing, in one way or another, since the day she'd pulled into town with a packed car and tired eyes.

They chose each other, under the same wide sky.